poles
apart
Kirsty Moseley

ISBN-10: 1502763605
ISBN-13: 978-1502763600

Interior Formatting by Cassy Roop of Pink Ink Designs
https://www.facebook.com/PinkInkDesignsbyCassy

Pink Ink Designs

Acknowledgements

I have a lot of people to say thank you to so please bear with me!

First off, to Sarah at Okay Creations. Thanks so much for the beautiful cover. I absolutely love it!

Secondly, to the ladies at Hot Tree Editing. Thank you so much for taking my baby in your hands and making it all shiny and mistake-free!

Thirdly, huge thanks to the beautiful Cassy Roop at Pink Ink Designs for making the interior of the book just as amazeballs as the exterior! You all rock, so thank you a million times over.

Lastly, I want to thank my 'PA Lady', Keelie Chatfield, for taking me under her wing and making my life so much easier with her freaky organisation skills and spectacular talent for making forms! Woman, you're amazing. Mwah xx

Dedication

For my mum, Sandra.
You're the best mum a girl could ask for, and I love you to bits. xx

Chapter One

Tired did not begin to explain how I felt as I stood at the bar waiting for my order to be filled. My feet were hurting in the stupid 'uniform' they provided for me – the cheap, white plastic shoes with the four-inch heels. The tiny, black booty-shorts, which barely covered to the bottom of my butt cheeks, were slowly creeping higher and higher, making me shift on my feet uncomfortably. I glanced at my watch. 10:24p.m.

Great, only another three and a half hours to go!

The only good thing about today: tomorrow was Sunday, and I had the night off for a change.

The door opened and a cool breeze blew through from the foyer, moving around some of the stuffy air in the club. A group of lads stepped in, and I felt the smile creep onto my lips.

Scratch that, there were two good things about today now. Carson Matthews was here.

Without my permission, my eyes dragged down his body as he laughed with one of his friends. He looked so incredibly hot tonight in nicely fitted blue jeans and a white short-sleeve shirt, undone teasingly low. It exposed his throat and part of the incredible chest I knew was hidden under the material. Forcing my gaze back to his face, I swallowed the desire rising in my throat. His light-brown hair was styled to perfection, as usual. His face was flawless, his deliciously full lips made my finger long to reach out and trace them. The air left my body in one long, breathy, needy sigh.

When his head turned in the direction of the bar where I was standing, a sexy little smile tugged at the corners of his mouth.

"Lover boy's here," the bar manager, Jason, teased, pushing the tray of drinks toward me. "Table five."

I nodded but didn't say anything. What was there to say? He knew how I felt about Carson so there was no point in denying it; it was clear on my face, I'd bet. I picked up the tray of drinks and turned to deliver them to the waiting clients, attempting to look sexy as I strutted across the room in my four-inch plastic stilettos. The music started up, the lights went down and the next 'performer' stuck her leg out of the curtain. She began teasingly running her hand up the bare skin as the men all started howling and crowding around the stage, waiting for the big reveal.

That's right. I work in a strip club. Of course, probably like everyone who did this job, I didn't *want* to do it. It was more like I *had* to. There are things people have to do to avoid sleeping on the streets. Waiting tables in cheap shoes, booty shorts and a figure-hugging vest top is one of those things for me. My job included nightly lap dances to clients and the occasional pole dance on stage, but thankfully, that didn't happen particularly often. We had proper performers for stage shows. Not many people would request me over someone who looked like a glamour model. Not that I had a horrible figure. In fact, I was happy with my body, but I was *real*, and most guys didn't like real. They also didn't like average size. Instead, the men who came to this club usually abide by the rule 'the bigger the better' – hence me waiting tables and barely bringing in enough money to pay the rent, pay for my university fees, and feed the two other people I was responsible for.

The group of middle-aged, desperate men all rushed toward the stage as 'Precious' stepped into the spotlight in her little black, corseted burlesque outfit. She started to shake her booty to the beat of the music, hypnotising the dirty men with ease.

Hoisting the heavy tray above my head with both hands, I wove through the crowd, trying not to spill the five beers and two whisky shots. I couldn't afford to spill anything; I had a lot to pay out for this month. Whatever I dropped, spilt, smashed, or even had stolen from my tray was docked from my wages, and let me tell you, drinks were freaking expensive in this place. The order I was carrying probably came close to fifty quid.

'Precious' dropped to her knees, arse in the air, and started whipping her head around, flicking her hair. In his excitement, one guy surged forward and crashed into me, sending me sprawling to the floor, drinks smashing all over the place. I closed my eyes and yelped as the cheap carpet burnt my hands where I'd put them out to protect myself.

People jeered around me, laughing and clapping at my stupidity.

Cringing, I pushed myself up onto my hands and knees, my cheeks flaming with embarrassment. This was a typical moment for me: a sexy girl on stage shaking her thing, and what do I do? I fall and make a complete idiot of myself. I had a sudden urge to pat myself on the back and award myself the medal for being the biggest loser.

Oh, you are so awesome, Emma!

Not one person offered to help me up. The balding, beady-eyed man who'd bumped me had skulked off into the crowd – probably so he didn't have to pay for damages – leaving *me* to clear up the mess. I sniffed, swallowing my sob as I grabbed the tray and started picking up the bigger bits of broken glass from the floor. Crestfallen, I silently wondered how I was going to pay for the drinks. I needed to pay for my little brother's school trip this month, £365 to go to freaking Scotland for some weeklong field trip.

Stupid, stupid Emma!

Sometimes, I hated my life. I was almost nineteen and had been responsible for my fifteen-year-old brother, Rory, for the past year. As if my life wasn't already hard enough without having to look after him, too, but in truth, I wouldn't be able to get through the day without his help, so I couldn't exactly complain. Rory was a godsend, just a freaking expensive godsend.

I reached out for a smashed bottle, tossing the glass onto the tray angrily. Just as my hand closed around another piece, someone grabbed my waist, hoisting me up. I squeaked in surprise, panic rising in my chest as I frantically looked around for a bouncer to come and help me; they usually milled around to take care of the girls. The warm hands lifted me to my feet, and a hard chest pressed against my back. Sweet, hot breath blew down my neck, brushing across my almost-exposed chest in my stupid uniform.

"Tut tut, Em. You should be more careful," the voice whispered in my ear, sending a little shiver through my body.

Carson Matthews.

My face grew hotter as his hand brushed across my stomach, straightening my top for me before he rested his hands on my hips, still standing dangerously close to my back. I could barely breathe. He always caused this reaction in me; he had since the first time I laid eyes on him when I was sixteen. That was on my first shift here at the club, a night which changed my life forever, yet it was just another Saturday night for him.

I gulped, willing my voice not to betray me. Turning to look at him over my shoulder, I attempted to look seductive even though I had just fallen to the floor like a moron. His pale-blue eyes locked on mine. The sexy little smirk on his lips made my heart flutter erratically.

So. Damn. Handsome.

"Thanks for the concern, Mr Matthews. I'm fine, by the way; thanks for asking," I teased.

"That you are, Emma. That you are." He slapped my bum and laughed as I gasped at the slight stinging pain. "Come on, you're waiting on us tonight." Grabbing my hand, he lifted it up high, guiding me to do a graceful little turn to face him. His smell filled my lungs – the unmistakeable scent of orange blossom and chocolate, mixed with dirt and car grease.

So hot! Why does he have to be so hot?

Wait a second, what did he say? Waiting on him?

I flicked my eyes over to his six friends; they weren't sitting in my section tonight. Their waitress was Charlotte, not me. Resisting the urge to pout, I shook my head. "You're not in my section tonight, baby."

He frowned, looking over at the table, clearly bewildered. "I thought you worked tables eighteen to twenty-four?"

I smiled because he would recall something like that. That was when I noticed he and his friends had sat themselves firmly on twenty, a table which, up until two weeks ago, would have been mine. "We had a little move around. I'm one to six now." I bit my lip, looking at him apologetically, but he'd probably prefer Charlotte anyway; she was much prettier and flirtier than me.

"Shit," he muttered, frowning. Then he gave me a mischievous grin. "Well, just for the night, you can swap back." He bent down quickly, gripped hold of my waist tightly and threw me over his muscular shoulder, making me whimper in surprise. Laughing, he slapped my bum again, a little lower this time so his hand actually made contact with the skin rather than the material of the ridiculously short shorts. There was a loud smacking sound and a couple of guys near us cheered again, causing me to blush harder and press my face into Carson's toned back.

"Put me down!" I ordered breathlessly as he carried me effortlessly across the room toward his table. Catching sight of the tray of broken glass I had just left lying in the middle of the floor, I groaned. "Carson, I need to sort out that mess!"

Gently shifting me on his shoulder, he altered his course and strutted to the bar instead. "Emma had an accident. Get someone to clear that up, would ya?" he said to Jason, tossing two crisp fifty-pound notes down before turning away, not waiting for an answer. Behind me, Jason laughed as I struggled to get down. Well, *struggled* wasn't exactly the right word. Of course, I really didn't try very hard because this was Carson Matthews, the guy I had been totally and utterly in love with for almost three years. Carson Matthews, the world famous Grand Prix Motorcycle driver and most eligible bachelor in England. No girl in her right mind would seriously want this experience to end.

As we got to his table, he tugged on my legs, making me slide down his hard body. His arms tightened around my waist, crushing my body against his, our faces were level so my feet dangled a little way off the floor. He smiled his nice smile, the one which made him get the adorable little dimples in his cheeks, and I couldn't help but smile back at him.

"Now then, champagne, I think..." he trailed off, setting me gently onto my feet, straightening my top again because it had risen up from being thrown around so much.

I rolled my eyes and did a little curtsy, forcing a sweet smile. "Anything your heart desires, Mr Matthews," I replied sarcastically.

He laughed and reached out, brushing the hair away from my face, pushing it behind my ear. "You've had your hair cut since I last saw you," he mused, playing with my dirty-blonde hair, which now hung in natural, loose curls down to my bra strap instead of my bum. I winced, thinking it probably looked like I'd been dragged through a hedge backwards because of being upside-down.

I smiled and nodded in confirmation. "Yeah." My heart sped because he'd noticed even though I hadn't seen him for close to three weeks. He'd been off being the big-shot celebrity, doing a modelling shoot in LA before kicking butt in all of his races in a bid to get to number one on the leader board. Carson was the hottest driver around at the moment, winning everything. At only twenty-one, he had the whole world watching, captivated, just waiting for the 'young rookie English driver' to become this year's MotoGP champion.

"It looks good, Em. *You* look good." He smiled softly.

I needed to go; I couldn't keep standing here having this conversation with him. It was hard when I hadn't seen him for a while. My resistance to his charm faded the longer I was away from him, and then when I did see him, I could barely control my emotions as everything threatened to burst out of me.

"Thanks. You do, too." *Wow, that's the understatement of the century right there!* "I'd better go get you some drinks then." My skin was blazing under the layers of make-up I was wearing as I turned back to the table of his friends. "Right then, boys, what can I get you?" I asked, forcing my work-smile onto my face.

Carson traced his hand across the small of my back as he slid into an empty seat.

The boys wanted three bottles of champagne – easy enough to remember. I just prayed I didn't drop this order, especially not at two hundred quid a bottle.

I walked to the bar quickly and looked at Jason apologetically. "Sorry. Did someone clear it up, or do you want me to do it?"

He waved a hand dismissively. "Don't worry about it, it's done. Lover boy even covered the cost, so don't stress about Rory's trip, okay?" He smiled kindly and I sighed in relief. Jason was a nice guy; he was the son of the owner and someone who I could talk to. We'd always got along well.

Charlotte trotted over, scowling at me as I went to pick up the tray containing the expensive fizz. "What are you doing? That's my table!" she growled possessively, grabbing my wrist to stop me from picking up the tray.

I sighed and instantly released my grip. It *was* her table and, to be honest, I didn't really want to see Carson too much tonight. The damn boy literally drove me crazy, and I knew I would be crying myself to sleep tonight because of him.

She huffed and threw her long, silky brown hair over her shoulder, tugging her top down more than necessary as she plumped up her cleavage. I tried not to roll my eyes. Weren't girls supposed to have a slight air of mystery about them? She obviously didn't understand that you didn't need to show everything to get attention. Wordlessly, she grabbed the tray and slinked her way over to Carson's table.

I tried not to watch. I tried *really* hard not to watch... but I just couldn't help myself.

Carson frowned as she put the tray down on his table and threw him a seductive smile. His eyes flicked to me and one eyebrow rose, silently asking why I wasn't working his table tonight. I shrugged, chewing on my lip. It really wasn't my call, so he'd just have to do without me for one night.

I turned back to Jason thinking maybe I could ask to leave early tonight, pretend I was sick or something. I loved seeing Carson, I really did, but it was pure agony most of the time.

Suddenly, two muscular arms rested on either side of my body, trapping me against the bar as his smell surrounded me, making my scalp prickle. I didn't move, didn't speak, just stood there like a statue as he pressed against my back almost possessively.

"Jason, I want Emma to work my table. Tell the other girl to take a break or something," Carson insisted, as if he just got to make demands like this. Well, in total honesty, he did. He was one of the most prestigious members of the club, and they did a lot to keep him

7

happy. We had different rules for high-paying celebrities, and they got special treatment.

Jason shrugged, his eyes darting to me for a split-second. "That's Charlotte's section, Mr Matthews. I can't take a table away from her, she'll be losing out..." he trailed off, clearly uncomfortable.

One of Carson's arms moved off the bar; there was a fumbling near my hip and then he threw a wad of cash. I gulped as I looked at it; it was more money than I earned in a couple weeks. Crisp fifty-pound notes, easily about three hundred pounds' worth, dismissed, just like that, as if it were nothing. Well, in all honesty, it probably *was* nothing to him. It must be a great feeling to never have to worry about money. I silently wondered what it was like to never go hungry because you could only afford to buy enough food for two people instead of three or to not have to scrape pennies from the back of the sofa because you were thirty-seven pence short for the electricity bill. I just couldn't imagine having enough money to throw it away like that. My eyes prickled with tears because it just reminded me how hard my life was. I looked away, willing the tears not to fall. I couldn't cry here; instead, I'd cry when I was in bed tonight.

"Now she won't be losing out," Carson stated, taking my hand and pulling me toward his table. "I want Emma exclusively tonight. I don't want to share her with other tables, so take her off the floor, too, okay?" he called to Jason over his shoulder.

TWO HOURS LATER, they were getting pretty rowdy. They didn't watch the show at all; only a couple of them even glanced in the direction of the stage. They came here for the privacy, the selective clientele, the expensive champagne, and the ambiance of being in a high-class establishment. Angels Gentlemen's Club was the best of its type in London.

After nine bottles of champagne between six of them, they were more than a little tipsy. The more they drank, the flirtier they became. I had always liked waiting on them, though, because none of them ever touched me – unlike some of the drunken clients I had to deal with.

I'd had two glasses of champagne, so I was a little merry myself. Carson had insisted I sit and have a drink with him. The whole time I had sat there blushing like crazy while he played with my hair, telling me time and time again he liked the cut, that it suited me, how good I looked, and how it felt like he hadn't seen me in forever. It had felt like forever for me, too. Especially when he was plastered all over the papers, celebrating his victories with beautiful celebrities in LA, sunning himself on a beach with swimwear models, or the worst one, him on a billboard right outside my crappy little flat. Oh, and did I mention it was for Calvin Klein and he was only wearing a pair of white boxers in the photo? Every day, I opened my curtains and was greeted by a ten-foot picture of the guy I was in love with – not good for the soul, that one.

Carson came to the club once a week at the very least, more if he could. He came every Saturday night for almost three years, missing only when he was out of town. These last three weeks had been like torture.

He leant in closer to me, his breath blowing down my neck, and I knew what he was going to say before he even opened his mouth. My body was already on high alert waiting for it. As soon as he'd walked through the door tonight I knew this would happen.

"How about a dance, Em?" he purred.

I gulped, swallowing my nervousness; I should have been used to doing this by now. In all honesty, I *was* used to it. Clients weren't allowed to touch me. I'd done this hundreds of times, to hundreds of guys, and it had never bothered me. It was just business, a job, something I *had* to do for money. But for some reason, when I did it for Carson, my whole body vibrated with excitement. It wasn't a job for me because I liked it way too much.

I nodded and stood, looking down at his handsome face as my heart started to thump wildly in my chest. He smiled and sat back on the black-velvet seat, spreading his arms along the top of the little

9

sofa. He tipped his head back slightly, just watching me with his full lips parted fractionally.

I did my usual routine, doing everything he liked, grinding against him, making his breathing accelerate. I traced my hands up my body as I danced in front of him, swaying my hips seductively to the beat of the song, looking at him through my eyelashes. He was clearly enjoying it. His eyes were raking down my body, his hands in tight fists, his hips moving in time with mine, grinding back against me. I could feel how much he was enjoying it – maybe even as much as I was.

When the song finished I smiled and stopped, but he shook his head. "No, I have three weeks to make up for. Don't stop. Keep 'em coming," he instructed, his voice so husky and thick with lust I could barely breathe.

Smiling, I went in for another song, this time actually straddling him and gripping the front of his shirt as I pressed my forehead to his. My hair fell around our faces like a thick, silky curtain. His head tipped back and his lips brushed mine softly. The familiar feeling of lust sparked inside me at the gentle touch of his mouth on mine.

I wasn't allowed to kiss him; it was against the rules for the main room. There were backrooms for that, for girls who wanted to take it that bit further with a client. I'd been in those rooms out the back numerous times over the last three years, at least once a week – well, when he was in town, that is. Only one man got behind my defences. Only one man was allowed to touch me. Only one man was allowed to make me feel like I was in Heaven.

Carson Matthews.

His lips found mine again, this time kissing me almost desperately. I kissed him back for a split-second before pulling away. I needed my job and this was against the rules; I couldn't afford to get the sack. Wordlessly, I motioned my head toward the backrooms, keeping my eyes locked on his. With his breathing ragged, he nodded in agreement. His expression was pure want, pure need, and it made my mouth water.

Pushing myself off him, I took his hand, tugging him to his feet before leading him through the crowd to the back of the club and the private rooms which awaited us. As soon as the door was closed, his arms wrapped tightly around me, pushing me against the wall as his lips pressed against mine. The kiss was so sweet, so passionate, so tender it made me want to cry.

His lips travelled down my neck, making me gasp and tip my head back. I hadn't had sex in three weeks and my goodness, the feelings had been building up inside me. Until that moment, I hadn't realised how much I needed this to happen.

"I missed you, Em," he whispered against my skin.

I tightened my hand in his light-brown hair. "I missed you, too, Carson."

"How have you been? You need anything?" he asked, gently nibbling on my collarbone.

I gulped, not really knowing how to answer that question. I never wanted anything from him; I never expected anything from him. He had already given me the best thing he could have ever given me... but he didn't know anything about that.

"I'm good," I lied, gasping as his hands slowly roamed my body. He made a muffled reply as he kissed up my neck again, his fingers winding into my hair. "I saw you on TV," I breathed.

Oh, God, why am I talking right now? Why can't I just be quiet and enjoy it?

He pulled back a little and smiled his cute, dimpled smile. "You did?"

I nodded and pulled him closer to me again, not wanting any space between us. His hands slipped down to my bum, lifting me gently. Instinctively, my legs wrapped around his waist, clamping myself to him as tightly as I could, locking my ankles behind his back.

"You won your race in Spain. I saw you on the podium, spraying champagne," I mumbled, unsure as to why I was still talking to him when all I wanted to do was throw him on the chair and ravage him to within an inch of his life.

He nodded and brushed my hair off my flushed face, his thumb tracing over my burning cheek. "Yeah. Did you watch the race?"

I gulped and shook my head. In total honesty, I *couldn't* watch it. I hated to see him race; just the thought of him going 200mph and leaning so close to the ground made my blood turn to ice in my

I hid my smile and nodded. "Yeah, they're getting to be a little off-putting," I lied.

He laughed. "Then no, I won't get anymore. Just for you, Em." Letting out a deep sigh, he kissed my forehead before pushing himself off the floor. He reached down a hand to me and I slipped mine in his, letting him help me to my feet. His eyes wandered my body and suddenly his forehead crinkled with a frown. "Did you lose weight?"

I gulped. *Crap, what am I supposed to say to that?* I had lost a little in the last couple weeks. The club had been slow; I couldn't afford to eat properly for the last few weeks what with my rent going up and now Rory's trip. I didn't think anyone would notice four or five pounds, but obviously I was wrong.

I shrugged, trying to play it cool. "Maybe. I don't know."

His frown deepened as he gripped my hips, turning me to the side as he looked me over, making me cringe under his intense scrutiny. "You did," he confirmed. "You know, you shouldn't lose too much. There's barely anything to you as it is."

I smiled at his concern. "Okay, baby, whatever you say."

Rolling his eyes, he pulled away from me, gathering up my almost non-existent uniform and passing it to me. I smiled gratefully and shrugged it on, watching as he did the same, pulling on his designer clothes, which probably cost enough to pay my rent for a month.

Once dressed, he grabbed my shoes and inspected them, wincing. "Don't these hurt you? They don't look very comfortable."

I laughed and rolled my eyes, taking them from his hands and sitting on the table to put them on. "They're okay. It's only a couple of nights a week," I answered, trying not to show him that, yes, they did in fact feel like they were lined with razorblades as I pushed my feet in.

"How many days do you work now?"

I shrugged; I worked as many shifts as I needed to. I didn't want to do more than just the weekends, but sometimes, if I was having a tough month, then I worked more than that. This week I had worked every night. "Just weekends still," I lied.

"How's uni going?" he asked, crouching down at my feet so he could look at my face as I buckled my shoes.

"All right, I guess. I've got a lot of work at the moment. It's coming up to end of term, so I get a couple of weeks off which will be good."

He nodded, smiling. "Cool."

When I was done with my shoes, he pulled me to my feet, grabbing his wallet and counting out a load of notes. I looked away; this was the bit I hated. The payment. When it was happening, I fooled myself into thinking Carson was actually making love to me. I didn't want payment for it; I wanted him to want me, for me, not just for my body. I would happily give my body to him for free, but if he wanted to give me money then I wasn't in a position to turn it down. The money I got from Carson went on something else – the most important thing in the world.

He held out a handful of cash, and I didn't bother to count it; he knew the prices. He'd had two lap dances and a backroom – for a normal girl they would be charging £200 for that, £50 for each lap dance and then £100 for backroom action. I slid the money into my pocket without looking at him. This was the part which made me feel dirty and a little used. This was the part which broke my heart every time.

He stepped closer to me, wrapping his arms around my waist, bending his head so I would meet his eyes. "I won't see you next week; I'm going away again tomorrow. But I'll see you in two weeks, okay?" he said softly. I nodded, not knowing what else to say. "I'm racing again next Saturday; maybe you could watch me on TV. I'll wave to you in my leather jumpsuit if you want," he teased, grinning.

I giggled despite the pain I was feeling inside. "I might flick the TV on as it finishes, just to see you in the outfit."

He smiled and nodded. "Okay, here's what I'm gonna do. When I win my race they're gonna interview me after. You tell me a word or phrase and I'll work it into the interview, just so you know I'm thinking about you."

We'd done this once before and I had made it too easy for him last time – he was *so* in for it now. "How about you have to say two things?" I bartered.

He rolled his eyes. "You're getting so demanding, Emma!" he scolded playfully. "What are the two things? It had better not be something like 'I sleep with little boys'…" He trailed off, clearly worried.

"No, I'll make it easier than that. Although, the 'sleeping with little boys' one is pretty awesome," I joked, pretending to consider it. He dug me in the ribs with one finger, making me giggle and pull away from him. "Okay, okay, fine. You have to say Zip-a-dee-do-da, and fried chicken." I shrugged. That was the best I could come up with at short notice. I was pretty sure I would come up with way better things than that while I was crying in bed tonight.

He laughed and nodded. "Done and done." Dipping his head he kissed me softly, pulling me closer to him with one hand gripping the back of my neck, his fingers tangling into my hair as the kiss deepened. He pulled away when I was a little breathless and our eyes locked. Everything seemed to disappear when he looked at me like this; all I could see was him.

"I'd better get going; it's almost closing time," he murmured.

I nodded, feeling my heart sink because my night with him was over. He turned, opening the door before taking my hand and pulling me close to his back as we walked back to his friends. The club was starting to empty, and I was definitely more than ready to go home now.

Bradley, one of Carson's friends, smirked at us as we reached them. "Wow, you two took your sweet time. Making up for three weeks' worth of pent-up sexual frustration, Carson?"

Carson frowned, throwing him a death glare before slapping him on the back of the head. "Shut it, dipshit!"

Pent-up sexual frustration? What was that about? How could he be frustrated? I'd seen him in the newspapers lying on a yacht with a Playboy Bunny and two other girls who were wearing bikinis so small there was barely enough material for you to be able to name the colour of them. There was no way Carson Matthews had been frustrated about anything! I hated to see those pictures of him like that: coming out of a club with a girl draped all over him, him fooling around with girls on a beach, the stupid 'MotoGP cheer squad' strutting their little outfits in front of him while he smiles. Those pictures broke my heart a little, but he wasn't mine to be jealous of. I had no right to feel like this about him. To him, I was just a lap dancer at a club who he liked to screw when he was in town. However, I'd never let myself think about him like that. He would always be my first love.

"No fighting, boys. You take it outside, or I'll be forced to kick all your arses," I joked, collecting their empty glasses and bottles.

"Em, I'm gonna take off. I'll see you in a couple of weeks and I'll make sure to sit in your section next time. Tables one to six, right?" Carson called as I headed to the bar with the empties.

"Yep. See you then, Mr Matthews," I confirmed.

He winked at me and then turned to leave with his friends. Sighing, I watched his back until he was out of sight. *Just 2 weeks. 14 days. 336 hours, and then I'll see him again.* It felt like an eternity.

When the last client left, I pulled on jeans and a hoodie over the top of my uniform, slipped on a pair of worn-out trainers, and then headed out of the club. It was almost two-thirty in the morning now; I had just a fifteen-minute walk to make and then I could crawl into bed and sleep.

As I walked toward the block of flats I called home, I gripped my pepper spray in my hand, keeping it hidden in my pocket. I was always careful. This wasn't the nicest part of London, after all. It was stupid for me to be walking the streets at this time of night, but I didn't have the money for a taxi, so I had no choice.

Thankfully, the journey was uneventful. By the time I made it up the seven flights of stairs and stopped outside my front door, I was exhausted.

I sighed and headed inside, making sure to secure the three locks we had on our door. When we were safely locked in, I sighed and immediately headed to the fridge to see if there was anything in there for me to eat. I hadn't eaten since breakfast and my stomach hurt. I knew I hadn't bought anything, but I was hoping something would magically appear in there to make my hunger pains subside.

Just like I thought, though, the fridge was almost empty. There was a little milk, which would be enough for two bowls of cereal in the morning, a little cheese and about four eggs, which would do for lunch. I spotted half a loaf of bread on the side, and I swore under my breath when I noticed Rory had left the bag open so it would have gone a little stale. I shoved my hand in, squeezing it to see if it could be saved. It was a little firmer than I would have liked, but it was still edible. Sighing, I wrapped it back up before quietly heading into Rory's room. He was sprawled out on his bed, fully clothed, one arm hanging off onto the floor, snoring, TV still on. I smiled and threw the quilt over him to keep him warm and turned his TV off. Rory was a good kid, a little troubled what with our parents' strict and mostly-harsh upbringing, but he was still a good kid. As little brothers went, he was the best.

I snuck out, closing the door silently, heading to my room next. After slipping out of my clothes and pulling on a worn old nightshirt, I shoved my hand into the pocket of my work shorts and pulled out the wad of cash from Carson. It was thick; he'd overpaid.

I counted it out onto the bedside cabinet. £400. I smiled and closed my eyes, a tear falling down my cheek as relief washed over my body. That would pay for Rory's trip and would leave some left over, too. Now I could stop worrying so much.

After taking out forty pounds, I shoved the rest down the back of my chest of drawers, pushing it into the little envelope I'd taped there for cash. I pushed the forty back into my jeans pocket. I could eat tomorrow now, too, thanks to Carson.

I smiled and headed over to the little cot at the foot of my bed. Leaning my arms on the rails, I looked over the side to see my little girl sleeping peacefully, exactly where I left her before going to work tonight. I smiled when I saw her perfect, angelic face. She was so beautiful, just like her daddy. Her mess of curly, light-brown hair was all strewn out on the pillow; she was hugging her teddy bear tightly in her sleep. Her features were so perfect, just like Carson's. She had his cute little nose and the same shape to her pretty face. If she opened her eyes it would be like looking into the eyes I had stared into tonight.

I reached out a hand and, being careful not to wake her, stroked the side of her face. "I love you, Sasha," I whispered.

She was my reason for living, my motivation for getting up in the morning, my incentive for going on with each day when all I wanted to do was break down and sob. Sasha and Rory were my reasons for working in that horrible place, for wearing that nasty uniform, for almost crippling myself in those cheap shoes. Both of them were so totally worth it, though.

I sighed and decided to go to bed. Sadness started to build inside me, and I knew it wouldn't be long before I broke down. Grabbing the pillow from the empty side, I hugged it tightly as the tears I knew would come started flowing silently down my face. Climbing into the bed, I pulled the quilt over my head to muffle the sound, and then I did what I did every night after seeing Carson: I sobbed until I fell asleep.

Chapter Two

In the morning, I woke to the sound of cooing and the covers being gently pulled near my feet. When I opened my eyes, they stung so much I actually hissed through my teeth. My gaze settled on the clock, seeing it was just after six-thirty. This was the downside of working nights in a club: the getting up in the morning with your almost two-year-old after having around four hours sleep.

Pushing myself up, I crawled to the foot of my bed, looking at the best thing I'd ever done. She was sitting up in her cot, her big blue eyes just looking at me, a beautiful smile around her dummy she had in her mouth.

"Hey, Sasha," I whispered, sticking my hand through the bars.

She smiled and took the dummy out of her mouth, placing it in my hand, still smiling. "Mummy, up, up!"

I smiled at her latest attempts to speak. It was so cute and every word melted my heart. "Want to get up, Sash?" I asked, sitting up and rubbing a hand over my face. She pushed herself to her feet, standing at the bars, her arms outstretched. I smiled and plucked her out of the cot, sitting her on the bed next to me. "Hungry?"

She didn't answer, just pushed herself up, climbing over me and plopping down onto the floor, looking at me expectantly. "No," she stated confidently.

"Drink?"

"No." She shook her head, turning to walk out of my bedroom. We shared my bedroom because this was only a two-bed flat and Rory (being a fifteen-year-old doing his GCSEs soon) needed his own space, so she'd moved in here with me when he came to live with us.

"Can't you say something else?" I teased, grinning.

"No."

I laughed and followed her out of the room, grabbing a nappy and baby wipes on the way past. Sasha was just learning how to speak. She was a little under two years old; her birthday was in two months. She knew about fifteen words which were understandable to a stranger, but her favourite, by far, was 'no'.

I scooped her into my arms as we approached Rory's bedroom door, heading past quickly so she didn't bang and wake him up. There was no point in both of us being awake at stupid o'clock on a Sunday morning. After changing her nappy, we settled onto the floor to play dolls for a little while before I made breakfast. I had money to go shopping today so there was no need to just eat cereal this morning. I boiled two of the four eggs, leaving two for Rory.

While Sasha and I were sitting at the table, Rory graced us with his presence, stretching like a cat and yawning as he walked up the hallway. "Morning," I greeted, smiling at his dishevelled appearance. He was still in yesterday's clothes he'd fallen asleep in.

He grunted in response. Rory wasn't a morning person.

"Raw-ee!" Sasha cried, holding out her arms for him. She adored him. He was more like a dad than a teenage uncle. I was lucky to have him.

Three years ago, when my parents kicked me out of the house, Rory was the only one who stuck up for me. Then, when I got pregnant a few months later, my parents disowned me even more, if that were possible. From what Rory had told me, when they found out I was pregnant at sixteen, they took down every single picture of me and literally pretended they didn't ever have a daughter. It didn't surprise me, though; I had always been a disappointment to them, even before everything that happened. I was a disappointment to them from the day I was born, it seemed.

They were very strict, very religious, and I guess once I hit my teens, my natural rebellious instincts kicked in, and I started to go a little wild. Well, that wasn't strictly true. I was never *wild*, but I'd snuck out to parties, I'd tried my hand at smoking, I'd gotten myself a boyfriend – and all the other normal things a teenage girl did.

The last straw for them was when I gave my virginity to the boy I was dating whilst drunk at a party. When they found out about it, they went crazy. Screaming about how I had brought shame on the whole family, how *they* were going to be punished because of *my* disgusting and disgraceful actions. Having sex outside of wedlock was strictly prohibited in their eyes. They gave me two options: either I join a convent – which is not something a sixteen-year-old girl wants to do – or I move out on my own and lead my life of shame without them.

Obviously, I chose the second option. They gave me access to my savings account which they had been paying into since my birth, signing over to me just under £3,000. With that money I moved out to more central London and registered for school. I was fine for a little while, but then very quickly I started to run out of money. I'd looked for a job for weeks but nowhere would employ a sixteen-year-old schoolgirl who could only work weekends. Thankfully, the last-resort place took a risk on me. Angels Gentlemen's Club. The place saved my life because without it I would have lost my flat, and I would have either been sleeping on the streets or in that convent my parents wanted me to go to.

Technically, I was too young to work at the club at the time, but Jason took pity on me and gave me a shot. Up until I was eighteen, I had to be careful because I was underage, but I never got into any trouble for it. Angels was a respectable 'members only' club, so the police didn't come round very often to check staff IDs.

When I first started working there, I was a shy, naïve, little sixteen-year-old girl who blushed when the girls started taking their clothes off. On my first night working, I met a handsome boy who was out celebrating his eighteenth birthday with some friends. I'd been attracted to him immediately.

As time passed, I fooled myself into thinking he liked me, too. He kept coming back every week, sitting in my section, asking me for dances all the time. Rather naively, I let myself fall in love with him, forgetting it was just a job and he was just a client. I gave him my heart – but it never went anywhere. Sure, he continued to come to the club every week, but it was just a night out for him, a bit of fun and a laugh.

After a couple of months, his racing career took off; he was signed by a good team as a second driver. He, of course, came to the club to celebrate with his friends that night. We'd been messing around, flirting back and forth as usual; that was when his friend suggested he pay for Carson to go to the backroom with me as a congratulations gift. I'd had a little to drink that night, so I'd agreed to it because I was already crazy about him by then – even if he wasn't crazy about me.

That night was the most incredible night of my life; it was beautiful and tender and was better than anything I had ever experienced. Every kiss and every touch was perfect and special with him, not like the one time I had been with a guy before. From that night on, every week would be the same. He'd flirt and behave like an adorable guy, and we'd go to the backroom after. We never had anything other than those nights, I never got his phone number, and I never saw him outside work. We were just two separate people who had sex in the backroom of a club for money once or twice a week.

Three months later, I missed a period.

I never told him about it. His dreams were just starting to take flight. The team he was driving for were becoming more impressed with him, and he was climbing higher and higher up the leader board, travelling here, there and everywhere. The press were starting to pay him attention, people started asking for his autograph, and he started wearing designer shoes. Everything was rosy for Carson; his future was bright and shiny.

I couldn't take those things away from him, so I said nothing. I loved him too much to trap him with a stupid sixteen-year-old girl he didn't care about. So I let him go. I told Jason about being pregnant, and as soon as I'd started to show, at around four months, he moved me to another club they owned, promising not to tell Carson anything about it.

Because it was totally obvious I was pregnant, I couldn't wait tables and dance anymore, so I'd cleaned the clubs instead, doing their paperwork just to earn money. It was hard, *really* hard. I was alone and depressed. It was the darkest time of my life.

The only thing that pulled me out of my slump was seeing Carson do so well, reading the articles about him being the new protégé of MotoGP, and seeing pictures of him in the paper holding up his trophies. No matter how hard my life was, I genuinely believed I was doing the right thing by letting him live his dream.

When Sasha was born, I immediately climbed out of my slump and started to rebuild my life. With the help of a good friend I had met at the club, another single mother, I was able to carry on studying. About a month after giving birth, my body was near enough back to normal, so I went back to work at the club, waiting tables and dancing. I needed the money because cleaning just wasn't enough to support a child.

To this day, my parents have never once seen Sasha; they maintain the act that she doesn't exist, just like they do to me. Rory, on the other hand, would skip school once a week and would travel two hours on the bus just to spend the day with us.

When Sasha was a year old, Rory asked if he could move in with us. So, just like that, I was seventeen, a single mother, a student, a part-time waitress/lap dancer, and sole guardian of a fourteen-year-old boy. How we managed I really don't know, but we did. We got through it, and it made me a stronger person. I was incredibly lucky to have such an amazing brother and an incredible friend because without them I surely wouldn't have made it through.

While I was gone for those six months, apparently Carson had asked about me a lot. Jason told him I had family issues and I didn't work there anymore. According to Jason, Carson came in once a month and asked about me, but he stopped visiting the club weekly like he used to.

Exactly seven weeks after giving birth, I was working at the club on a Saturday night when the door opened and the love of my life walked in. His eyes had scanned the room, a hopeful, almost-pleading expression on his face I can still see when I close my eyes. His gaze had settled on me and a beautiful, dimpled smile had spread across his face – and just like that, we were back to normal. Except now, we were parents… but he didn't need to know about that. As long as he, my baby girl, and my little brother were happy, then that made me happy.

I looked up at Sasha who had her arms wrapped around Rory's neck, probably choking him, while he just laughed and tickled her like crazy. I smiled happily and got up, grabbing the cheese and eggs from the fridge and looking at Rory expectantly. "Omelette or fried eggs?" I asked.

His mouth dropped open. "Really? I thought we were on a strict 'cereal for breakfast' diet."

I shrugged. "Not anymore, kiddo, not anymore." I smiled at the thought of having it easy for a couple of weeks. Carson's money would pay for Rory's trip, so that meant the wages I had slaved for last week would pay the rent and the bills for the next month. I would even have money left over for nice food for a change. Usually, toward the end of the month, Rory and Sasha were eating cheaper things like jacket potatoes and beans or egg on toast. That was about the time of the month I would start to go hungry. I couldn't afford to feed three of us for the month on my wages alone, so as long as they both ate three times a day, I was fine with once.

Rory set Sasha down in the highchair again and kissed the side of my head. "Emma, how did you get the money then? Did you get paid early?" he asked, eyeing me worriedly. He knew we were tight on money. I didn't tell him how bad it got sometimes, but he knew we had a budget we stuck to rigidly. I smiled at the concern on his face; he was so old in some ways, yet so young in others. He was my little brother, but there was actually nothing *little* about him. He was just under six-foot tall and had a muscular build.

I shrugged, not really wanting to lie to him, but I didn't want him to know what his big sister had to do to look after him and keep him in trainers. He thought I was a waitress at the club and nothing more. "Yep, got paid early for all the extra shifts I did last week. And there was a big party last night so I got a big tip."

A grin split his face. "Well, in that case, I'll have the omelette!" he replied, flicking on the kettle to make a cup of tea.

THE WEEK PASSED QUICKLY. I went to university during the day, and Sasha went into the nursery funded by the university, so I got it at a discounted rate. In the evenings, once I had done the whole 'running a house' thing, I did my motherly duties before putting Sasha to bed and then either studied or went to work at the club. I never got time to just chill like a normal eighteen-year-old, but I wasn't sorry about it. As hard as my life was, I wouldn't change a single thing. Well, apart from maybe making Carson fall madly in love with me, but that was nothing more than a fairy-tale pipe dream.

The following Saturday, I was practically bouncing in my seat waiting for the time to come when Carson's race would be finished so I could turn on the TV. Rory was just watching me curiously. He knew I knew Carson. I'd told him I met him through the club and we were friends, but I didn't tell him anything else. The only people who knew the truth were Jason, my friend Lucie, Mr Wilkinson, my boss and me.

"So, how's this guy gonna work fried chicken into a conversation?" Rory asked, glancing at his watch. "By the way, you *so* should have gone for something cruel like 'I wanna kick a puppy' or something. That would have been so funny." He laughed and shook his head.

I wrung my hands together nervously. What if he forgot to do it? I would have made myself look like a complete and utter twit sitting here waiting and he was too busy getting it on with one of his little fan girls to remember something he'd said to me a week ago.

"It would've finished by now," I said, ignoring how my voice shook a little as I spoke. What if I turned the TV on and he'd crashed? What if he was seriously hurt and I never got a chance to tell him I loved him? These thoughts went through my head every race day. I couldn't bring myself to watch, but that didn't stop me from imagining horrible things though.

Rory flicked the TV on and we both sat there watching.

"Here they come now. They're just pulling in to the pits and then we'll be able to have a quick word with them," a grey-haired guy said as he practically ran toward the pit lane. The huge bikes roared past, making the microphone feedback for a second because of the vibrations from the engine. "There's Stuart McCoulis," the guy shouted over the noise as a driver dismounted his bike. He waved him over. "Stuart, can we have a word?"

The guy called Stuart nodded and answered a few questions as he walked to the pits, his Scottish accent making it hard to understand over the roar of the bikes. The camera flicked to a light blue bike going around the track on its own, a guy in a blue jumpsuit and helmet was pumping his fist in the air as the crowd cheered for him.

"There's Carson Matthews. Another victory lap for the youngster. Can no one knock his winning streak? That's a record-breaking eleven wins in a row. He just seems unstoppable at the moment. They really have their work cut out to catch him up!" the voiceover guy announced.

As if he knew he was on camera, Carson raised both arms in celebration, seeming to completely forget he was driving. My heart took off in overdrive as my eyes widened. "Hold the bloody handlebars, you idiot!" I screamed at the TV, jumping out of my seat and gripping fistfuls of my hair. Sasha jumped, dropped the toy she was playing with and stared at me in shock, and Rory burst into hysterical laughter. My eyes were glued on the screen until both of Carson's hands were firmly on the handlebars again, but I knew what was coming next. This was his thing lately, the damn show-off. He gunned the engine loudly and sped off, his front wheel lifting from the tarmac, doing a wheelie along the straight track, while the crowd just screamed and clapped louder and louder for him.

Stupid flipping idiot!

The camera angle changed and he was now driving toward the screen, into the pit lanes. The same interviewer was standing there with a smile on his face, waiting to talk to him for a couple of minutes before he went to be presented with his trophy and champagne. The bike pulled up and Carson climbed off, letting a couple members of his team push it off to where it needed to be.

My breath caught in my throat. That really was one hot little jumpsuit.

"Carson, got a couple of minutes?" the interviewer asked.

Carson gave him the thumbs-up and fiddled with the strap under his chin, pulling off the helmet to reveal a sort of white balaclava he was wearing underneath. He pulled it off as well as he walked toward the camera, seeming to breathe a sigh of relief as he ruffled a hand in his sweaty hair, making it stick out everywhere.

So. Damn. Hot!

I mentally swooned, as did probably half the female population.

"Win number eleven, Carson. How does it feel?" the guy asked him, shoving the microphone in his direction.

Carson smiled his sexy little smile. "It feels great. You know like in that Disney movie with the guy who has the bluebird on his shoulder… yeah, that's pretty much how I feel right now. Zip-a-dee-do-dah, what a wonderful day," Carson answered, laughing quietly to himself as he looked down the camera lens. My cheeks flamed because it felt like he was looking directly at me.

The interviewer laughed and regarded him as if he'd lost his mind. "Okay, that's a weird analogy," he jibed. "We're over halfway through the season now, and you're firmly at the top of the leader board. Your win today takes you twenty-one points clear of second place."

The guy shoved the microphone back to Carson, who smiled and nodded. "Yeah, that's awesome, but I can't let it drop now. There's still plenty of time for someone to come in and steal the championship. I can't get complacent."

"So, what are you doing tonight then? Plans for celebrating? Going out on the town?"

Carson shrugged. "Not sure what I'm doing yet. We'll probably go for a couple of celebration drinks. The only thing I want to do is get some fried chicken. You know anywhere that does good fried chicken?" Carson asked, grinning his secret little smile.

I giggled in my seat, chewing on the knuckle of my index finger, trying to contain my excitement that Carson Matthews just gave me a little shout-out on TV like he promised he would do. I felt so special it actually made me want to cry.

The interviewer laughed and shook his head, looking at him like he'd inhaled too many bike fumes. "Er, no, I don't. Hopefully you'll find somewhere."

Carson nodded. "Yeah, they don't have fried chicken over here like they do back home. English fried chicken is the best; I miss it when I'm away..." He trailed off, laughing as one of his team grabbed him into a headlock, rubbing their knuckles in his sweaty hair. He dragged him away, Carson shouting bye at the camera as he play-fought with the guy who was holding him.

The interviewer turned back to the camera, a bemused smile on his lips. "Well, there you have it. Carson Matthews' eleventh straight win. I think he's now going to get some lunch. Back to you, Steve," he said laughing, and then they cut back to the studio.

I miss it when I'm away... oh, God, that was so freaking sweet! Was he really missing me? I sure as hell knew I was missing him, and he always told me that he missed me, but did he really?

I bit my lip as the happiness built even more. That was so incredible. He'd remembered to say those things, just for me. I sighed contentedly and sat back in my seat, ignoring the way Rory looked at me – one eyebrow raised, a quizzical-yet-knowing smile pulling at his lips.

"Well, he either just said hi to you on TV, or the guy's hungry," Rory teased, shaking his head.

I didn't say anything, just watched the TV as Carson climbed the stairs, heading to the number one podium, standing there smiling proudly while they played the English national anthem. I couldn't keep the smile from my face because of just how adorable he looked standing there. I was so proud of him that happy tears prickled in my eyes.

After, Carson shook up a big bottle of champagne, spraying it over the two guys who had come second and third. In return, they both seemed to dump the entire contents of theirs right in his face. When the spray died down, Carson took a big swig out of his bottle. Champagne dribbled down his chin, dripping from his clothes and the brim of the team hat he was wearing.

I let out a breath I didn't realise I was holding and felt myself relax. Another race over and he was fine. I didn't need to worry about him again for at least another week.

Suddenly, Sasha threw her juice cup into my lap, making me jump because I was in my own little Carson-land. "Drink!" she demanded. Her big blue eyes were so like her father's that seeing them made my heart stutter.

"Drink, *please*," I corrected, smiling as I pushed myself off the

MY HAPPY MOOD lasted all through the rest of the day; I couldn't keep the smile at bay even when I was at work that night. My feet were hurting, my eyes were stinging with tiredness, my whole body felt like it weighed a thousand pounds, but I still smiled happily. All because the adorable boy had given me a little attention on TV in front of millions of people. Sure, no one knew he was talking to me, but *he* did and so did I.

In fact, my happy mood lasted well into the next day, too, right up until the point when Rory came back from the shop and tossed the newspaper down onto the table in front of me. That was when the happy smile finally slid from my face as my heart sank.

On the front of the paper was a picture of Carson, obviously out celebrating his win from the night before. The big picture on the front was him with an extremely pretty, exotic-looking, olive-skinned goddess in his arms. *Literally.* He was carrying her bridal-style out of a club. She had one shoe on, her arms tight around his neck, her other shoe hung from one of her fingers, resting against his chest with the heel broken. He was looking down at her with a sexy little smirk, which promised she was in for a good night. There were a couple of smaller pictures from earlier in the night, too, taken inside the club. The two of them dancing, her hand on his arm as he laughed with a guy standing next to him.

I couldn't bring myself to read the article. When my eyes started to prickle with tears, I knew I needed to go before I broke down in front of Rory and Sasha. "Rory, can you watch Sash while I go for a shower?" My voice broke as I spoke but, thankfully, he didn't seem to notice.

"Sure, no worries." He sat himself on the floor next to her, picking up the coloured shape sorter toy Sasha liked, gaining her attention immediately.

I gulped and headed to the bathroom. Sitting on the edge of the bath as I turned on the shower, I let the water heat because it always took a few minutes for the hot water to come through. As I sat there, I looked down at the beautiful girl in the picture on the paper. She was wearing a gorgeous yellow dress, which looked extremely expensive. My eyes flicked up from the paper to the mirror on the wall. I stared at myself in my cheap, supermarket-brand tracksuit bottoms and vest top. I looked an absolute mess compared to the girl in Carson's arms in the paper.

As I looked at myself in the mirror, a wave of hatred washed over me. I hated everything about myself in that moment because I would never be that girl in Carson's arms he smiled down at so unashamedly. I would always be a lap dancer. That stigma would follow me around long after I graduated university and finally had enough money to leave there. I would always be that dirty little girl who danced for money in a seedy club. I would never, ever be good enough. That knowledge made my hand tighten on the newspaper, screwing it up into a ball before tossing it across the room and into the bin, which stood in the corner. I barely had enough time to strip out of my clothes and step into the shower before the tears hit me. I cried in the spray until I felt sick.

Times like this just forced me to face the fact that Carson wasn't mine. He never had been.

Chapter Three

On top of the sadness which was eating me up because of the newspaper article and the stunner in the yellow dress, on Tuesday I started getting ill. My throat was killing me and I could barely swallow. After a couple of days of suffering in silence, I finally gave in and went to the doctor. I hated to make a fuss out of things about myself or admit I was sick. I was the person who took care of others, not the other way around.

As it turned out, I had tonsillitis. I was given a course of antibiotics and sat munching on throat lozenges like they were going out of fashion, but my life couldn't stop just because I was feeling poorly. The flat didn't clean itself, Sasha didn't magically raise herself, and my university classes didn't suddenly disappear. So I struggled on, the same as normal. Except, instead of my life just feeling like hard work, everything felt almost impossible at the moment.

By the time Saturday came around, I was feeling a little better, but everything was taking its toll on me. I looked a mess. I was extremely tired because my sore throat stopped me from sleeping very well for the last few days, and I was just generally more exhausted than normal.

Once Sasha had settled to sleep, I grabbed my uniform for work and went for a quick shower. When I was dry, I pulled on warmer clothes over the top of my uniform. I was going to be freezing at work tonight. I'd been so cold for the last couple of days that I'd had to sleep in tracksuit bottoms and a hoodie.

As I dried my hair in the kitchen, I tried not to look in the mirror at the dark circles residing under my eyes; I'd sort them out with some concealer at work. I didn't own much make-up, mainly because I couldn't afford to buy it, so I always just used the stuff they had at the club.

I plopped down next to Rory, resting my head back on the sofa. I really could just do with going to sleep right now instead of going to work until after two in the morning. "Sasha's asleep. Don't stay up too late tonight, okay?" I croaked, my voice sounding husky and sore.

He smiled sympathetically. "Are you sure you can't just call in sick?"

I shook my head. "Can't afford it. I'll be fine; it won't be too busy tonight." At least I *hoped* it wasn't too busy. If it was too much I could pull in a favour and have Lucie do one of my tables if I got too tired. She owed me because I worked three of her tables a couple of weeks ago when she was sick. Lucie Cooper was my good friend at the club; she was the person who made it possible for me to go back to school when I got pregnant. She was a single mother, too. Her man had walked out on her about three years ago, leaving her with three kids on her own. We helped each other out with babysitting and sleepovers when we needed to. It was nice; she was my best friend even though she was ten years older than me.

Rory sighed. "I wish I could go to work instead of you. As soon as I've done my exams, I'll get a job and take care of you and Sash for a change." He patted my leg, smiling sadly.

I looked at my little brother. He really was my rock and I loved him so much. "When you finish your exams you'll be doing your A-levels, buster," I rebutted sternly, but it sounded a little weak because of me barely being able to talk. "Besides, you take care of us all the time."

He smiled and shook his head, frowning. This was an old argument. I wanted him to stay in school, and he wanted to leave and get a job. Rory was a smart kid; I couldn't let him waste his brain because I needed money. That wouldn't be good for anyone in the long run.

"I'm going now," I said before he could protest. I couldn't argue with him tonight, my throat was too sore. "Lock the door and I'll see you in the morning." I pushed myself off the sofa and grabbed my keys, mobile phone and purse from the sideboard.

"Emma," Rory called as I had my hand on the door about to open it. I turned back to face him, just as something came flying towards me. I instinctively caught it and looked down to see a packet of throat sweets. "Don't forget those."

I smiled gratefully. "Thanks. See ya."

The walk to work was uneventful. Well, as uneventful as Central London after dark can be. I ignored a couple of comments from guys drinking and hanging out in the streets. I crossed the road when the door of a pub burst open and two men fell out, fighting and shouting at each other.

By the time I got to work, I was shivering so hard my back was aching. I headed to the shared dressing rooms, saying my hellos to the performers and waitresses as I flopped down into an empty chair. Looking into the mirror, I silently wondered what I could do to salvage the mess that was my face. I really should have called in sick tonight, but I just needed the money too badly. Carson's money from two weeks ago was already gone, and my wages from the previous week were dwindling down too fast for comfort. I liked to have spare money; I didn't like to literally live off my wages and then have nothing when it was gone. If I had called in sick tonight then I would be short next week instead, and I couldn't have that.

Lucie plopped down in the seat next to mine and looked at me worriedly. "Wow, you still look like shit."

I laughed humourlessly. *Way to make a girl feel better about herself, Lucie!* "Thanks for that. You look totally bangin' as usual."

She laughed and grabbed the make-up bag from the counter, gripping the arm of my swivel chair and turning me to face her. "You obviously don't feel much better." She sighed, smiling sympathetically as she started plastering make-up on my face. I closed my eyes and just let her do it, grateful I didn't have to lift my arms and do it myself.

"I'm okay. I just hope tonight goes quickly. You think if I get in trouble I could push a table or two your way tonight?" I asked hopefully.

"Of course you can, sweetie! Hey, is Carson coming tonight?" she asked, dabbing a thick layer of concealer under my eyes.

I shrugged, not really wanting to think about him. I was still hurting over the beauty in the paper last week. What with being sick, everything just seemed to pile up and I couldn't stop myself wallowing in self-pity about him. "I hope not," I admitted. I didn't want to see him while I was sick. There were two reasons, really. One, I didn't want him to get sick, as well. And two, I looked a mess, and I didn't want him taking one look at me and requesting a different waitress. That would kill me, seeing him get dances and flirting with other waitresses right in front of me.

At exactly ten o'clock, there was a bang on the dressing room door. "Doors are now opening, ladies. Waitresses need to come out and take their places to welcome the customers," Jason called through the door.

I groaned, not wanting to get up. "Let's get this over with," I mumbled to Lucie as the six waitresses all stood up, along with the six reserve girls who floated around doing lap dances or covering sections if a girl went to the backroom. Lucie was floating tonight so that was great for me; I knew she'd help me out. I pulled off my tracksuit bottoms and hoodie, slipped on my heels, and then followed them into the club.

I headed straight over to the bar, leaning against it, praying as the customers walked in that that they would choose a table which wasn't mine so I wouldn't have to start working yet. Luckily for me, no one sat in my section until just after ten-thirty. I just hung out at the bar with Jason and bitched about being sick and tired, while he laughed at me and rolled his eyes.

So far, I only had one table. It was occupied by three middle-aged men who didn't seem to be interested in me in the slightest and were watching the empty stage eagerly.

The door opened and I heard a lot of commotion. I flicked my eyes to the door, seeing about twelve guys all walking in, laughing, and pushing each other around teasingly. Raising one eyebrow, I looked at Jason in question. He usually knew if there was to be a big party like this booked in.

He shrugged. "Stag night, apparently," he answered my unspoken question.

Stag night? Oh, no! Not my section! Please, not my section!

I watched them walk in, looking through the photos of the waitresses on the board by the door. They got to choose a waitress if they wanted to, and the photos showed which sections to sit in if you liked the look of a particular girl.

Please, please, please not me!

I held my breath as they sauntered across the room, bypassing Charlotte's and Andie's tables. I watched with wide eyes as they checked table numbers as they walked past.

Please, no!

Lucie walked up to them and flashed her killer smile, making them stop and talk to her. She pointed to Kaitlin and then waved at Kaitlin's section. I felt like doing a little happy dance – until the guy at the front shook his head and said something to Lucie. Her eyes flicked to me and I groaned. They wanted me. The guy turned around and looked at me before nodding. I plastered on a fake smile. The only upside to this was, with it being a stag-do I would get a lot of dances tonight, and the money would definitely come in handy. Lucie smiled and nodded, showing them over to table three.

I looked back at Jason and sighed in defeat. He shrugged in response. "Sorry. Maybe they like blondes?" he suggested.

"Awesome," I grunted, grabbing the tray of drinks from the bar and going to deliver them to the three older guys in my section. After bringing their drinks, I put on my brightest smile and headed to the stag party. They were all sitting, talking animatedly and looking around excitedly, obviously waiting for the show to start. I leant on the back of one of the chairs, sticking my hip out sexily as I balanced the tray on one hand.

"Well, hi there, boys. Who's the lucky guy getting married?" I asked, scanning them quickly. I put them all in their mid-twenties. A couple of them were raking their eyes down my body already, and I knew those were the ones I needed to stay away from. Those would be the ones who get a little touchy-feely after a few drinks.

A guy with brown hair and a black shirt put his hand up, grinning. "That would be me."

I smiled seductively. "Name?"

"Tyson."

I bit my lip and nodded, trying to look sexy, even though I felt anything but at that moment. "Well then, Tyson, I hope you have a great night. I'm Emma, and I'll be your waitress. We also have some dancers who walk around. Dances are fifty pounds cash to the girl before it starts. The show starts in about ten minutes," I reeled off my spiel, nodding toward the stage.

"Perfect," one guy purred. He was one of the touchy ones I had sussed out earlier. His eyes were watching me like they were glued to me, clearly mentally undressing me as I stood there.

I shifted uncomfortably. "The menus are on the table. I'll be back in a couple of minutes to take your orders." I turned and went to walk off just as I felt someone slap my bum. Gritting my teeth, I carried on walking; I didn't have the energy or the patience to explain the rules to them right now. Hopefully they'd behave. If not, then I would have to ask one of the bouncers to come, have a polite word, and explain the rules to them.

AFTER HALF AN HOUR, I had already done two dances and they were only just finishing their first drinks. This was going to be a long night. I already felt dead on my feet. Obviously, the germs and bags under my eyes didn't put some people off.

As I was scribbling down their next drink order, an arm wrapped around my waist and a hand clamped over my mouth, effortlessly lifting me off my feet. I yelped against the hand and tried to struggle free. I couldn't move. I flicked my eyes to the guys at the table, but they were staring over my shoulder with wide eyes and their mouths hanging open. Panicked, I jerked my elbow into my attacker's stomach, making him grunt and release me. As soon as I was free, I jumped away and turned to see who it was. Carson was clutching at his stomach, laughing.

The first thing that entered my head was he looked beautiful; his smile was dazzling as he chuckled, rubbing his stomach where I'd elbowed him. My chest tightened as happiness consumed me. All thoughts of him and the girl from the paper were completely gone because, for tonight, he was here with me.

The second thought which entered my head was that he had just frightened the shit out of me on purpose.

I slapped his arm with my order pad, which just made him laugh harder. "That wasn't funny, dickhead. That scared me!" I cried angrily, making my throat hurt even more. He smirked at me so I slapped his arm again with my pad, pushing on his chest. "You idiot! Seriously, you could've given me a heart attack!"

He grabbed my wrist as I went to hit him again. "Hey, I could get you fired for hitting a customer," he teased cockily.

I rolled my eyes and pulled my hand away from him before slapping him again with my pad for emphasis. "If you did that, then who'd bring your champagne, Mr Matthews?"

He tapped his chin, pretending to think. "You're right there. I doubt anyone can carry the tray with the finesse you have. And I'd miss that hot little behind of yours in those shorts if you weren't here."

I stuck my tongue out at him and he just laughed. "Go find a table, Mr Matthews, I'm busy," I instructed, waving my hand dismissively, trying hard to keep the excited smile from my face.

"You're so rude nowadays. You used to be so polite," he joked, winking at me teasingly.

"That was before you started scaring the crap out of me by grabbing me when I'm at work," I protested.

He smiled, stepping closer to me, taking hold of my chin with his thumb and forefinger. He tipped my head back slightly, just looking into my eyes. "Did you see me on TV?" he asked, smiling his little dimpled smile. I nodded, unable to speak. He was so close, so teasingly close. "People thought I was going mad with my little rant about fried chicken. I got a lot of stick for it from my mates and the press. I hope you appreciated it."

I bit my lip and laughed. "You did look a little crazy. Maybe you should eat before you race next time?"

He leant in closer to me, brushing his nose against mine in a little Eskimo kiss. "Maybe I should. Or I could just find a less-demanding waitress."

I opened my mouth to answer but nothing came out, so I cleared my throat and tried again. "Maybe you should," I croaked, my voice barely above a whisper. I desperately needed another throat lozenge.

He frowned and pulled back. "You okay?"

I shrugged and nodded. "I've got tonsillitis. Don't worry though, it's not catching. Well, unless we share saliva," I joked. I just wouldn't be able to kiss him tonight and then he'd be fine. It wasn't an airborne infection so he couldn't catch it.

He frowned and reached out, stroking the side of my face with one finger. "You're sick? Why are you here then?" He looked at me like I was crazy; he actually seemed a little annoyed about it.

Oh, crap, is he angry with me because I could make him sick? "You won't catch it. You don't need to worry."

His frown grew more pronounced. "Emma, what are you talking about? I'm not worried because of me. I'm asking why you're here if you should be in bed!" he scoffed.

I shrugged. "Needed the money. I'm okay," I croaked, swallowing painfully.

He shook his head and looked back at the table containing the stag party. "I'm stealing your waitress for the night, boys." His hand slid down my arm, gripping my hand.

I sighed and tugged my hand from his. "Carson, just go find a table. I'll be there in a couple of minutes," I protested. I could work his table too; he didn't need to worry about that.

He shook his head. "I want backroom... all night." He took my hand again, pulling me a little closer to him, making the hair on the back of my neck stand up.

Backroom, all night? He couldn't do that, it wasn't allowed like that. It wasn't like you rented it by the hour or anything, but I wouldn't be allowed to go out there all night with him. It was only just after eleven and I was supposed to be working.

"I can't, baby. That's not allowed." Besides the fact it wasn't allowed, I couldn't really do that with him tonight anyway. I wouldn't be able to kiss him, and I definitely wouldn't have the energy to ravage him all night.

"I'll swing it with Jason. Finish your order and I'll go sort it out." He squeezed my hand and turned on his heel, stalking off without another word. I opened my mouth to call him back, but all that came out was a whisper of his name before I cleared my throat again. I shrugged. *Let Jason explain it to him. That will save me the job of speaking too much.*

I turned back to the table, smiling apologetically because I'd ignored them for the last few minutes. "So, who was I up to?" I asked, glancing down at my order pad to see what I had already written down.

"That was Carson Matthews!" Tyson said with wide eyes as he stared over my shoulder, obviously watching Carson speak to Jason.

I nodded. "Yep, he's a member here. So, who else wants a drink?"

"Do you know him? Oh, man, that dude is so awesome, and he's shit-hot at driving. I can't believe I'm in the same room as him!" Tyson gushed excitedly. "Do you think you could get me his autograph? Oh, my God, do you think he'd take a photo with me?"

I laughed. It amused me when people went a little gaga over Carson; it was almost as if they forgot he was a real person. This guy looked like he would ditch his upcoming wedding if he had a shot with Carson.

"I'll ask him if you want," I offered. Tyson nodded, practically bouncing in his seat, and I could tell that Carson just made this guy's stag night. The most memorable thing of the night for him would be meeting a celebrity.

It took a while to finish taking the order, considering most of the time Tyson kept butting in and asking me questions about Carson. What he was like, if he was a nice guy, who he came in here with, did any other MotoGP drivers come in here, etc. The questioning was relentless, and I was more than a little glad to take the last order so I could stop speaking.

I headed to the bar, pushing the order slip across the counter to Jason. Carson was off talking to his friends. When he spotted me, he walked over, snaking his arm around my waist and pulling me close to his side as he smiled. I couldn't help but smile back.

Jason cleared his throat so I looked back at him curiously, leaning over the bar and grabbing my lozenges I'd tucked down there. "Mr Matthews wants backroom, Emma. How do you feel about that?" Jason asked, as I popped a sweet into my mouth.

I shrugged knowing he wouldn't go for it anyway, so it didn't really matter what my answer was. "It's not allowed."

He cocked his head to the side. "Mr Matthews wants to hire the room for the night. He'll pay you separately for your services. I've agreed that if it's something you want to do, then you can do it. I'll just pull one of the floating dancers off and they can work your section tonight."

I looked at him, shocked. I really wasn't expecting that at all. Turning to Carson, I frowned worriedly. As much as I would love to do that and spend the night just with him, I really couldn't in case he *did* end up getting sick. "I can't, really. I'm ill. That's not a good idea," I protested, biting my lip, fighting with myself because I would get to touch his body until closing time, and have him touch me. The thought of that was just too inviting, and I really wanted to accept.

"Em, you already said I couldn't catch it. And anyway, I don't care if I get ill; I just really want to spend some private time with you." He gave me his puppy dog face, and I could feel my will to say no crumbling with each passing second I looked into his baby-blues. "Please?" he whispered.

Unable to resist, I gulped and nodded in agreement. I really couldn't say no to the stupid guy; that wasn't fair at all.

He smiled happily and turned back to Jason. "Great. Just charge the rental fee we discussed to my tab and I'll settle up at the end of the night. If you could add Emma's fee onto my card, too, and then you pay her the money, like we agreed, so she doesn't have to have cash?" He looked at Jason hopefully.

I looked at Jason for confirmation and he nodded. "You're okay with that, Emma?"

I nodded and shrugged. I never wanted the money from Carson, but Sasha's birthday was coming up at the end of next month and mine was in two weeks. I knew Lucie wanted to go out for my birthday; it would be nice to have the money to do that this year. I never got to go out.

Carson smiled and took my hand, interlacing our fingers as he started to pull me away from the bar. I gave him a little tug to tell him to stop. "Jason, can I get a couple of bottles of water to take?"

He nodded and threw me two. Carson took them from my hands and smiled his cute little dimpled smile as he pulled me in the direction of the back of the club again.

That was when I remembered Tyson. "Baby, wait a second. There's a guy on his stag night. He's a big fan of yours, and I told him I'd ask if you'd do an autograph or photo or something for him…" I trailed off uncomfortably. Had I overstepped my boundaries by asking him for a favour? After all, he was *just* a client of mine.

He smiled and laughed before rolling his eyes. "Sure. Which one is he?"

I led him over to the table and stood back as he chatted to the guys for a couple of minutes, signing napkins, posing for photos on mobile phones. When he was finally done, he wound his arm around my waist and pulled me quickly toward the backrooms. I laughed at his eagerness; he seemed almost as desperate as me. Two weeks was definitely a long time.

Once we were in, he pushed the door closed and put the drinks on the table. Usually, he would have attacked me by now; I would have been off my feet with him kissing me passionately. Instead, he led me over to the little couch, sitting down and pulling me onto his lap. His hands went straight for the buckles of my shoes as mine went to the buttons of his shirt. He smiled and pushed my hands off him as I kissed the exposed skin of his chest, running my tongue there, tasting his skin. I moaned breathlessly. He tasted so incredible. His smell was all around me, making me feel safe, wanted and needed, just like he always made me feel.

I kissed his neck again, sucking on the skin lightly, but he gripped my shoulders, pushing me back a little. "No kissing. Just stop," he whispered, tapping his finger on the tip of my nose.

He slipped my shoes off one at a time. His other arm wrapped around me, laying me back on the sofa as he settled down next to me. He gripped my chin and tipped my head back as he kissed the side of my neck. "I'm going to kiss your sore throat better," he breathed.

I gasped at the feel of it; it felt so nice that my whole body broke out in goose bumps. I gripped my hand into the back of his hair as he planted gentle little kisses around my throat and jawline, and I must admit, it *was* making it feel a little better.

Moving my legs, I tried to shift to the side so I could pull him on top of me and wrap my legs around him, but he just pushed my legs away effortlessly. He moved closer to my side, bending his knees and pushing them under my bum so I had to drape my legs over the top of his. One of his hands traced down my thigh, over my shin and down to my foot, which he started to massage gently. My whole body relaxed as I melted against him, tangling my hand in his hair as he nibbled on my neck gently. He rubbed my foot at the same time, rubbing the tension and pain away caused by my shoes.

"I missed you, Emma." His hot breath blew down across my collarbone, teasing my overheated skin. His smell was surrounding me – that unmistakeable Carson Matthews scent of beautiful, mixed with a little biker. *Jeez, that smell!* "I hate that you're sick. I wish you would just stay at home and take it easy," he whispered, his words vibrating against my throat. "Close your eyes for a couple of minutes and just let me rub your feet," he instructed, moving slightly higher and kissing each of my eyelids before heading back to my sore throat.

"EMMA?"

Huh? What time is it? Oh, man, please don't be morning yet because I need more sleep!

"Sasha?" I croaked, wincing as my throat rasped and scratched. I blinked rapidly, trying to focus.

"Do I sound like a girl?" a husky voice asked, laughing quietly.

I turned my head in the direction of the voice and saw Carson. His head was level with mine, and his breath blew across my cheeks as he laughed. One of his arms was wrapped around me tightly and I was cuddled into his chest. He was playing with my hair.

What the hell?

"Who's Sasha?" he asked, looking at me curiously as his finger traced across my cheekbone.

I couldn't make sense of this situation at all. Was I still asleep and this was another dream I'd had about him or something? Flicking my eyes around the room, I tried to work out why he would be in my flat. But I quickly realised this wasn't my flat – it was the backroom of the club.

I gasped. "Oh, my God, did I fall asleep on you?" I asked, horrified. The last thing I remembered was him telling me to close my eyes and then he'd carried on massaging my feet and kissing my neck.

He smiled and kissed my forehead. "Yeah. Did I bore you?" he teased, tracing his thumb across my now burning cheek.

How bloody embarrassing! I hated that this happened, and to him of all people. As if Carson would ever bore me! This happened because I felt too comfortable with him, and because he made me feel so relaxed and safe.

"I'm so sorry. I didn't mean to fall asleep; you didn't bore me, I swear!"

He grinned and shook his head. "I was kidding, Em. That was the whole point of us coming back here, so you could relax and take it easy. I thought you'd fall asleep. You looked really tired." Shrugging, he pulled me a little closer to him, tangling his legs with mine. It was so comfortable that I didn't ever want to move.

That was when I realised what he'd said. He'd paid for the backroom all night so I could relax. I smiled and couldn't stop the little "aww" which crept out of my lips.

"You feeling any better?" he inquired, looking into my eyes, making me feel slightly weightless as butterflies started to swoop around in my stomach.

I nodded and yawned. I actually *was* feeling a little better; I really needed that little nap. "Yeah, thanks."

I had no idea what the time was, but I was definitely up for a little backroom action now. His body was so teasingly close; every inch of him was pressed against me. Running my hand down his chest slowly, I slipped it under his shirt, tracing my fingers across the muscles I could feel on his stomach. He shivered and his lips parted fractionally as he sucked in a breath through his teeth. I watched as his pupils dilated before he leant down, heading to kiss me.

Just as his lips were about to press against mine, I remembered I couldn't kiss him. I whimpered and pulled back quickly, shaking my head. "No. It's catching that way," I protested breathlessly.

He frowned and inched closer again, his gaze firmly fixed on my lips, as if they were his next meal. "I don't care."

I wanted to kiss him so much but I couldn't; I would feel terribly guilty if he got sick, too. I shook my head and turned my face to the side, putting my hand on his chest and pushing him away from me gently.

"Please don't, Carson. I don't want you to get sick. We can still have some fun without kissing," I suggested, my fingers starting on the buttons of his shirt.

He smiled his dimpled little smile before shaking his head and pressing his face into the crook of my neck. "We can't, Em. It's closing time, that's why I woke you up."

I gasped and jerked up. I had wasted the whole three hours? My whole night with him and I was asleep through it? Disappointment bubbled inside me. I'd waited three two weeks to get my hands on him again, and I ruined it by falling asleep!

"It's closing time? Damn it. I'm so sorry!" I bit my lip and tried not to cry about it. "I wasted the whole night by being asleep! Oh,

God, you paid for the room and everything! Shit. I'm so sorry, Carson. I'll speak to Jason. You won't have to pay for it," I promised, looking at him apologetically. I had no clue how I was going to smooth this over with Jason; my guess would be that *I* would be paying for the room out of my own pocket, paying the fee Carson had agreed on. I tried desperately not to panic about it.

Carson rolled his eyes and gripped my waist, lying back down on the little sofa and pulling me on top of him. "Emma, will you stop? I paid for the room so you could chill. I wasn't expecting anything else. I just didn't want you to work if you're not well. I got exactly what I paid for." He cupped my face in his hands and tipped my head back, kissing around my throat again.

He actually paid for the whole night so I could sleep? My love for him made my eyes prickle, so I closed them and just savoured the feel of his soft lips against my skin. I savoured the heat from his hands warming my face. I savoured the way he seemed to make my whole body feel so hot, yet so cold at the same time.

I dug my fingers in his sides as my whole body screamed for more. Carson was the only one who ever made me feel like this, and I loved him so much it was almost painful. He guided my head down onto his shoulder, wrapping his arms around me and rolling to the side, trapping me against the back of the sofa and throwing his leg over the top of mine. He just smiled at me as he looked into my eyes, playing with my hair.

"How do you get home, usually?" he questioned, running his nose along the edge of my jaw.

I whimpered because that little movement made my body ache for his. I silently wished he'd stop teasing me. If this wasn't going to end with sex then this was going to be keeping me awake tonight like some sort of frustrated horny monster.

"Walk." I shrugged and played with the collar of his shirt, wishing I could take it off and feel his skin on mine.

He grinned at my answer. "I'm driving you tonight."

He'd never taken me home before. The night always finished when the club closed; I'd never once seen him outside work. "It's fine. I'll walk. It's only fifteen minutes away." I wanted to accept so badly but another part of me didn't really want to tell him where I lived. The block of flats I lived in wasn't exactly known for its luxury and glamour. He was a millionaire for goodness' sake; he would probably take one look at it and think I was some sort of damaged goods because of where I came from.

"I'm driving you, Emma. Come on, let's go." He pushed himself up, taking my hand and helping me to my feet. I bent to grab my shoes but he scooped them up before I did, smirking at me. "You don't really want to put those back on; they hurt your feet."

How did he know that? I nodded. It was true, there no point in denying it. I reached for the water from the table, taking a big swig of it and wincing as it burnt my throat. I greedily shoved in a lozenge, sucking on it, trying to numb my throat a little.

He smiled sympathetically and pulled open the door to the room. "It's just after two; the club will be closing any minute. You have something to change into so you don't get cold?" Carson asked, slowly dragging his eyes down my body. A little smile tugged at the corner of his mouth as his gaze lingered on my cleavage.

I playfully slapped his chest lightly as I followed him out of the room. "Pervert," I scolded.

Suddenly, I realised what he said and I winced. I came here in tracksuit bottoms and a hoodie, and not nice ones either! I couldn't let him see me in that, but then again, I couldn't exactly go outside in my uniform; I'd freeze to death or catch pneumonia or something.

"I'm going to go settle my tab. You go get changed and meet me by the bar, okay?" he instructed, holding out my shoes to me.

I bit my lip and reluctantly nodded before heading to the dressing rooms at the back. Once there, I took off my uniform, leaving it in my locker, and pulled on the crappy clothes I'd come in tonight. I looked at myself in the mirror and grimaced at my reflection. I looked awful. My hair was frizzy and sticking out everywhere because of being asleep, and my mascara had smudged under my eyes, giving me a panda look. I was in baggy, grey tracksuit bottoms, dirty trainers, and one of Rory's black hoodies.

Finding a pack of baby wipes on the side, I dragged one under my eyes to wipe the smudges away, and then ran my fingers through my hair, attempting to tame it a little. When I looked a little less like a homeless person, I grabbed my phone, purse and keys, and headed out to find Carson.

Chapter Four

As I entered the main room of the club, my eyes settled on Carson immediately. He was sitting on a stool at the bar, chatting to Jason about racing. I touched his back as I got level with him, holding my breath, waiting for him to laugh at the way I looked and withdraw his offer of a lift.

He smiled down at me, his face not dropping like I was expecting. "Hey, all ready?" he asked, slipping his arm around my shoulder as he stood up.

I nodded and looked at Jason. "See you tomorrow night."

"Yep. G'night, Emma. Good night, Mr Matthews," Jason replied, smirking at me knowingly.

I blushed because of his accusing look. Did he think I was taking Carson home with me tonight? He knew how I felt about him, and he knew we had Sasha. I guess it *did* look a little like I was taking him back to continue the night.

Carson frowned, looking at me with hard eyes before his hand closed over mine and he gave me a little tug toward the exit. I smiled and followed him out, both of us stopping at the coat desk in the foyer. He handed Jasmine, the desk clerk, a little orange ticket before turning to me. "No jacket?" he asked. I shook my head in answer, watching a disapproving frown line his forehead. He didn't say anything else, just took hold of my hips, lifting me effortlessly to sit on the desk.

Jasmine came back a few seconds later, holding out a black leather jacket and black helmet.

I looked at the items curiously. *Helmet? Wait, oh, God no! He came here by motorbike? Is he seriously expecting me to ride on a freaking motorbike with him?* My eyes widened as he pushed the helmet onto my head, his hands instantly going to the straps at the bottom of my chin.

"No. No way! Not happening, baby!" I cried, trying to pull it back off, but he held fast, pinning it on my head.

"It's happening, Emma," he said sternly. "I'm not letting you walk home in the dark on your own while you're sick."

I gulped as I heard the ominous click of the chinstrap. The helmet was a lot heavier than it looked. "I always walk home; it's not a problem," I countered, my voice slightly muffled because of the helmet going around my face. He smiled and grabbed the leather jacket, holding it out for me to put my arms through. I pushed it back toward him; he was only wearing a shirt so he needed that, not me. "I've got a jumper. You wear that."

"Stop being so bloody stubborn. Put the jacket on and let's get you home. I've wanted to drive you home for a long time, but usually I drink so I can't. Well, tonight I can." He smiled and grabbed my hand, forcing it into the sleeve of the jacket.

I sighed and nodded but felt my head sway forward a little too far. *Note to self, don't move head too much while wearing a helmet!* Once I had the jacket on he helped me down to the floor, guiding me out of the building and into the car park located at the side. He stopped next to a terrifyingly large, black motorbike. I looked at it with wide, horrified eyes. The thing was huge and the seat came up to my waist; it was shiny and expensive-looking. I felt sick just thinking about riding on it.

When he smiled and swung a leg over the bike, starting it up, I jumped at the roar of the engine. *Oh, shit, I'm going to die! Should I tell him I love him, just in case we don't make it to my flat?* He turned and patted the seat behind him. Even though I was terrified, I couldn't help but notice how sexy he looked sitting on that bike. His hair was all messy, a smirk resided on his full lips – he looked like the perfect bad boy. He gripped my hand and helped me onto the seat behind him.

"Oh, God. Please don't kill me!" I begged, wrapping my arms around his waist, probably squeezing the life out of him as I pressed my helmeted head into his back. He laughed and gripped one of my ankles, putting my foot on the little footrest, then did the same to the other.

"So, where am I going?" he asked. He gripped my hands and pulled them off him, guiding me to grip my own wrists instead. "Maybe you could find something else to hold onto, instead of my skin?" He laughed.

I gripped my wrist tightly and gave him my address, telling him which streets to take. He nodded and turned back to the road, twisting the throttle, and we took off. Fast. Whimpering, I squeezed him tighter as the wind whipped the bottom of my hair around. I looked at the street as we were driving, seeing the buildings whip past in a blur. Everything felt so fast, close and dangerous. My heart was hammering. I felt sick. I needed to stop. All I could think about was that if I died, Rory and Sasha would be on their own.

"Carson, stop!" I screamed. My throat cracked and hurt but I didn't care. "Stop! I want to get off!" I cried, digging my fingers into his stomach. Almost immediately, he pulled over and looked over his shoulder at me. I gasped for breath and pushed myself off the bike. My legs felt like they'd turned to jelly. I fumbled with the helmet, needing fresh air. I pushed it off and shoved it into his chest. "I can't. I…I…I'll walk," I stuttered breathlessly.

He frowned. "Emma, seriously, I promise it's safe. I won't let you get hurt." He gripped my hand and pulled me closer to him, looking into my eyes. "I promise. Cross my heart." He crossed one finger over his chest. "Trust me?"

The streetlight cast a yellowish hue over his face, highlighting some of his features, yet covering others. The shadows somehow made him look even more attractive. I gulped. I didn't want to get back on the bike but his eyes were pleading, begging me to trust him. He gripped my waist and pulled me onto his lap. Moving one of my legs so I was now straddling him, he scooted back on the seat slightly and stroked my face lightly.

"I wouldn't let you get hurt. I promise it's safe," he whispered, kissing my forehead. He gripped the helmet and positioned it above my head, pulling it down a little but giving me a chance to stop him. I didn't move. I wanted to trust him. He did this for a living for goodness' sake, and I *knew* he was a good driver, so I was being a total wimp right now. When I didn't protest, he smiled and pulled the helmet down over my head again, clipping it back on. He took my arms and wrapped them around him before starting the bike up. "You just keep your eyes on me, okay?" he instructed, smirking at me cockily.

Wait, I'm not moving back behind him? He's going to drive with me on his lap like this? I did as I was told, keeping my eyes locked on his face and watching the small smile, which didn't seem to leave his mouth the whole time. It felt like as soon as we started driving, we stopped again, but I knew that was just because I was sitting on his lap with my body wrapped around his, staring at his face.

He cut the engine and looked down at me while he ran a hand through his windswept hair, obviously trying to fix it. He didn't really need to, though; he looked as inhumanly beautiful as ever. I gulped and laid back against the handlebars, pulling the helmet off and breathing a sigh of relief that I would get to kiss my little girl goodnight. Closing my eyes and gulping in lungfuls of fresh air, I let my heart slow down to normal. Carson groaned quietly, and then his hand cupped the side of my neck. His palm trailed slowly down my body, brushing against my breasts before pushing against my stomach lightly, guiding the material of my jumper up and exposing the skin of my belly. I moaned at the exquisite feel of it. His fingers traced across my stomach, one finger dipping into my bellybutton before he bent forward and pressed his body to mine, making my legs instinctively tighten around his waist.

He kissed the side of my neck gently, his finger still playing with my bellybutton. "Thank you for trusting me," he whispered in my ear, nibbling on my earlobe.

I smiled and stroked the back of his head. "Thanks for the lift home, even though you almost gave me a heart attack doing it."

He laughed and pulled back, his face inches from mine, making my whole body hot despite the cold temperature. "You'll get used to

it. It's all about practice; it'll just get easier and easier each time."
He kissed my cheek and straightened up and I looked at him a little
shocked. What was that supposed to mean? Was he planning to give
me a lift home again another time? I wasn't really sure how to feel
about that. On the one hand, it was terrifying, but on the other hand,
I liked seeing him outside the club; it felt different, more intimate,
more real.

"I don't think I will," I admitted.

I pushed up and forced myself to get off his lap and onto the
curb. I opened my mouth to thank him for the lift and say goodnight,
but he swung his leg off the bike, too. My heart leapt into my throat.
Was he assuming he was going to spend the night? I couldn't let him
do that. He'd see Sasha, and although he wouldn't know she was his,
he would still know I had a daughter.

"I'll walk you up," he said, shrugging and slipping an arm
around my waist, bringing my body closer to his.

I glanced back at his bike and chewed on my lip. He really
shouldn't leave that there; the shininess to it practically screamed
'steal me'. By the time he got back to it after walking me up the
seven flights of stairs, all that would be left would be the tyre marks
on the road.

"Carson, don't walk me up. Seriously, I'm fine from here.
Thanks for the lift, but you really can't leave your bike outside my
flat." I winced as I admitted how bad this area was.

He laughed and shrugged dismissively. "It's insured. Come on."
He guided me to start walking again, and I felt my heart sink. My
block of flats was awful, and the shame of bringing him here made
my face burn.

When we got up to my door, I smiled apologetically. *He must
think I'm such a dirty hoe right now – a dirty scrubber who works in
a strip club and lives in a hell-hole.*

"Want to come in for coffee?" I asked, praying he would say no.

He smiled and nodded, looking a little eager about it. I guess,
deep down, I was a little eager, too. If I got him in my flat then
maybe he'd ease a little of this sexual frustration I was feeling
inside. We'd just have to be really quiet and either do it in the lounge
or bathroom so we didn't wake Rory and Sasha.

"I'd love a coffee, actually, unless you don't want me to. You must want to get more sleep," he replied, his tone sympathetic.

I waved my hand dismissively and opened the door. Heading inside and motioning for him to come in, I silently hoped Rory hadn't made too much mess while I was at work.

Carson followed me into the kitchen and I tried not to pay attention to the look on his face, which plainly said he thought my place was small and crappy. I admit that, yes, it was basic, but it was all I could afford, and I kept it immaculately clean, so that was all that mattered.

He sat at my kitchen table while I made coffee. I couldn't help but make a direct contrast to him sitting there all beautiful and handsome, but yet his arms were folded on top of my cheap second-hand table, while he sat on a chair that creaked when he moved. He looked slightly odd being in my decrepit old kitchen wearing a Gucci shirt.

Just as the kettle boiled, Rory walked in, wearing only boxer shorts. "Hey. You're a little early," he mused sheepishly. The table was behind him so he probably hadn't noticed Carson sitting there; if he did then he hadn't reacted to him in any way.

I raised one eyebrow at Rory. I *was* a little earlier than usual. I'd left about five minutes earlier and the trip was only five minutes instead of fifteen. He probably thought he would have time to sneak to bed and pretend like he'd been there for hours before I got home. "Thought you'd get away with staying up, did ya? I bet you thought that as long as you were in bed by half-two I wouldn't know any different, right?" I teased with mock anger as I slapped the back of his head.

He winced and rubbed the back of his head. "Ouch! I was watching a film!" he whined.

"What part of 'don't wait up for me' don't you understand, Rory?" I asked, rolling my eyes.

He shrugged dismissively. Most of the time, he waited up to make sure I got home safe from work, even though I always told him not to. "Why are you making two coffees? I don't want one," he stated, frowning at the two mugs on the side.

I smiled and looked back to Carson who, at this point, just looked a little confused as he took in a half-naked Rory standing in my kitchen. "A friend gave me a lift home." I shrugged. Rory turned and jumped as he noticed another person sitting in our kitchen. "Rory, this is Carson Matthews. Carson, my little brother, Rory." I waved a hand between the two of them.

Carson smiled and actually looked a little relieved as he nodded in greeting. "Hey. Nice to meet you."

Rory smiled, his eyes flicking back to me knowingly. He probably knew I liked Carson; no doubt it was obvious when I watched him on TV or talked about him. I shot my brother a little glare, warning him not to say anything. He chuckled quietly and grinned at Carson. "Yeah, it's good to meet you, too. I've seen you on TV and stuff." He smirked at me and I tried to kill him with my eyes. "Well, I'm going to bed. See you in the morning, Emma."

I let out a relieved breath because he hadn't made anything awkward between me and Carson. "Was everything okay tonight?" I asked curiously.

Rory knew what I meant; I was talking about Sasha. "Yep, just like usual." He kissed the side of my head and practically ran out of the room.

When we were on our own again, Carson laughed. "He's a little bigger than I thought he would be. When you told me you lived with your little brother, I was actually expecting something little," he teased, grinning as I pushed the coffee mug toward him.

"Yeah, he took off in the last year. He used to be small for his age." I sipped my hot coffee, scalding my tongue, but I just needed to drink something because my throat was starting to hurt again. "Want to take these into the other room?"

He nodded and picked up his mug, standing. I led him into the lounge and breathed a sigh of relief that Rory hadn't trashed the place. As I sat down on the sofa, Carson sat next to me and hooked his arm under my knees, pulling my legs onto his lap casually, as if this happened every day.

"These clothes are sexy," he joked, pulling playfully at the leg of my trousers.

I laughed and rolled my eyes. "They're warm and comfortable. Usually no one sees me when I finish work." I pouted at him, feeling like a dirty tramp again.

He smiled and ran his hand up my leg, his fingers curling around the back of my knee. "I wasn't joking, Em. These clothes are sexy on you. Though, maybe one of my hoodies would suit you better. I'll bring you one, a team one. Then you can really show an interest in what I do, instead of the fake *'I'll turn the TV on when you're done racing'* interest you normally show," he teased, grinning.

We chatted easily about random things for well over an hour. He was incredibly easy to talk to. He seemed genuinely interested in what I had to say, which confused me a little. We usually talked and stuff, but this just felt different for some reason, nicer, more intimate. The whole time we were talking, he rubbed my feet again gently. I sighed contentedly and rested my head against the back of the sofa. This would be a perfect life, sitting and chilling with Carson, our little girl asleep peacefully in the other room. I couldn't ask for more than that.

"So, about what you said to Jason about going to work tomorrow night…" he trailed off, frowning.

"Yeah, are you coming to the club?" I asked, trying not to sound too hopeful.

"Emma, if you're ill you shouldn't be going to work. Take the night off," he insisted sternly.

I shrugged, making a scoffing noise, which hurt my throat again. "Carson, I'd love to, really I would, but I can't. This flat doesn't pay for itself, my student fees are already building up, and Rory eats like a horse. I need the money."

He sighed. "How much do you earn a night?"

I bit my lip. Did I really want to be having this conversation with him? "That's not really any of your business. I don't ask you how much you earn."

"I'd tell you if you did. Want me to tell you?" he asked, smirking at me cockily. I shook my head quickly. I didn't really want to know, because I didn't really like to think of him as having money. To me, he would always just be Carson, the guy I met on the first night of my job, the one I fell in love with, the father of my angel. "Seriously, though. How much do you earn, on an average night?"

"I don't know really. I get paid about fifty quid for working a shift and then maybe a dance or two on top, but that's not all the time." I shrugged. That was why my life was so hard; sometimes I lived off the bare minimum and that wasn't even enough to pay my rent.

"How about the backroom?" he asked, frowning.

I laughed and rolled my eyes. "You know how much I get for that; you're the one who gives me the money."

He swallowed, still frowning and looking a little angry for some reason. "Other than me, Emma."

I shook my head. "It's only you," I replied, shifting in my seat uncomfortably. Did he think I slept with a load of guys at the club?

His eyes widened and his mouth popped open in evident shock. "Just me? You don't… not with anyone else?"

I grabbed another throat sweet, popping it in my mouth and sucking on it as I shrugged. "No one else. Not ever."

Before I could protest, his lips crashed against mine. I went to pull back because of my throat, but one of his hands went to the back of my head, holding me still, his fingers tangling into my hair. He made a little moan, which seemed to set my skin alight with passion. My fingers curled, gripping his shirt as I pulled him toward me roughly, making him practically fall down on top of me, crushing me for a split-second before he gained his balance and pushed himself up to hover above me. He sucked on my bottom lip, asking for entrance and I couldn't refuse him, not again. I opened my mouth, kissing him eagerly as his other hand cupped the side of my neck. I dug my fingers into his back as he kissed me deeply. The kiss was so good it made me go weak at the knees, and I was suddenly glad we were lying down because if I had been standing, I would have fallen for sure.

He pulled back just as I was getting slightly breathless. His beautiful, dimpled smile stretched across his face. "You lost something," he chuckled, opening his mouth and showing me the little red throat lozenge sitting on his tongue.

I snickered awkwardly, feeling heat creep over my cheeks. "I'm gonna need that back." I gripped my hand around the back of his head, pulling his mouth back to mine. I giggled against his lips as he pushed the sweet back into my mouth, his tongue tracing across mine slowly before he pulled back.

"Mmm, cherry flavour. Nice. I guess I'm gonna need to buy some of those when I get your germs," he teased, digging me in the ribs with one finger. I giggled and squirmed under him while he just laughed. He stopped tickling me and brushed my hair back from my forehead before he just stared into my eyes with a hopeful expression on his face. "You really don't go into the backroom with anyone else but me?" he asked quietly.

I shook my head. "It's only ever been you there." That was the truth. He was the second person I had ever been with intimately, my first time being the one and only time I had ever been with anyone other than him. I couldn't see that changing anytime soon, either. I would never sleep with someone else while I was in love with Carson, and I just couldn't see myself falling out of love with the stupid guy.

His face broke into a beautiful grin before he bent his head and traced his nose up the side of my face, kissing my cheek lightly. "Okay, good. So, getting back to what we were talking about before I stole your germs." He pulled back, hovering above me as he continued. "With a dance on top of your wages, you earn, on average, about £100 a night. That's what you would have probably earned tonight and the same again tomorrow, right?" he asked, looking at me seriously.

I nodded, unsure as to where he was going with this. "Mmm hmm."

"Right. Well, then you've already earned enough to take the night off tomorrow," he replied, rolling off me and lying against my side. I looked at him, confused. How could I have done that? That didn't make sense at all. He smiled. "I paid you more than that for the backroom tonight. You earned more tonight than you would normally earn over two nights. So, that means you can afford to call in sick tomorrow."

I frowned at that. He'd overpaid me again; the stupid boy really did like to throw his money at me sometimes! "Carson, you didn't overpay me again, did you?" I closed my eyes and shook my head; he really needed to stop doing that.

He laughed. "Just a little. But on the plus side, you can now take the night off tomorrow and you'll still be up on what you would have earned." He kissed my cheek, his hand tracing down my arm, cupping my elbow before sliding down my wrist and interlacing our fingers. "Please, take the night off and just get yourself better."

I thought it through. I would love to have an early night for a change, to wake up on a Monday morning for university and have had more than four hours sleep the night before. That would be a totally new experience for me. I smiled at the thought of just chilling out, sitting around in a pair of thick socks and a hoodie, watching bad movies with Rory. "Okay, I will. Thank you, baby."

He smiled and kissed me again, stealing my breath and making my heart rate increase. This time, I managed to keep hold of my sweet. He pulled out of the kiss and put his forehead to mine.

"I guess I'd better go see what's left of my bike," he said, chuckling to himself.

I groaned as he mentioned his bike. "If you're expecting it to still be there then I think you're gonna be really disappointed." I looked at him apologetically.

He just laughed and shrugged. "The coffee was worth it, don't worry." He kissed my forehead again before pushing himself off me. "I won't bother coming to the club tomorrow then, seeing as you're not going to be there." He looked at me sternly and I did a mock salute, giggling. "So, I guess I'll see you the weekend after next. I'm racing next weekend in Italy so I won't see you then. Wanna do the interview thing again?" he asked, raising one eyebrow, pulling me to my feet.

I grinned. "Sure. How about you get the word 'fluffy' in there somewhere?" I offered, laughing at his horrified expression.

"That's not a very macho word. Fluffy. Really?" he scoffed.

I rolled my eyes and pushed on his chest. "Get out of my place so I can go to sleep!" I ordered playfully.

His hand closed over mine as he tugged me to the door with him. He pulled it open and then turned back to me, pressing his lips against mine again for a couple of seconds before walking off without another word. I sighed dreamily and traced my finger over my lips, watching until I couldn't see him anymore. Then I practically ran back to the lounge, looking out the window down toward the square where he'd parked his bike. He came out of the building moments later and walked over to his bike, which, surprisingly, was still there *and* still had both wheels. I watched him roar out of the car park, and I couldn't keep the smile off my face as I skipped to my bedroom, tucking the covers around Sasha and falling asleep with a smile on my face for a change.

Chapter Five

As it turns out, Carson *did* get sick. It was splashed all over the papers – how he was sick and his team was worried if he was going to be well enough to race on Saturday. I felt incredibly guilty, but it wasn't entirely my fault. He was the one who kissed me, after all, not the other way around.

Despite the illness, he still did well in his race, coming in first and breaking his own record, upping it to twelve straight wins. When he did his interview after, he barely spoke, and when he did he sounded so husky and raspy it made me wince. He, of course, managed to work the word 'fluffy' into the conversation, which made me smile even though he looked a little worse for wear.

I was seriously on easy street moneywise. It turns out Carson had paid me £1,000 to go to the backroom with him all night, so I almost had enough money to completely pay off my overdrafts with the bank, which I had never done in my life.

Everything was going great. I was feeling completely better; I was almost breaking even with money - if you ignored my £3,600 credit card bill - and tomorrow was my nineteenth birthday. Tonight, I was working, but tomorrow I had arranged to go out with Lucie to celebrate. We were going to dinner and then meeting a few of my friends from Uni in a bar. It was going to be fun, and I hadn't been out in what felt like forever. I didn't usually have the money to waste on things for myself, but Rory and Lucie had convinced me I needed to treat myself for a change.

I was even looking forward to working tonight because Carson said he'd be here. Because I'd been ill last time I saw him, it had been over a month since I had any physical attention. Just the thought of him was sending little sparks of electricity flowing around my body. I could barely keep still as I watched the door, waiting for him to arrive.

Just after half past eleven he walked in, on his own for a change. He grinned at me and headed over to the bar where I was standing. "So, what's a nice girl like you doing in a place like this?" he teased.

"I'm not a nice girl," I replied, raising my eyebrows suggestively.

He narrowed his eyes playfully. "No, you're not. You're a disease-ridden little temptress. I had antibiotics for a week because of your germs, you know!"

I laughed and patted his chest, leaving my hand there, feeling his heart beating under my palm. "Aww, poor baby. Did you catch a little sore throat?" I teased, running my fingertip over his Adam's apple.

He nodded, pouting. "And I had no one to kiss mine better and rub my feet for me. I had to suffer all alone." His hands gripped my hips, pulling me closer to him. His smell surrounded me, making my mouth water. *Is it too early to ask him if he wants to go to the backroom?* I could barely breathe through my excitement.

I flicked my eyes behind him, waiting for his friends to walk in; he never came here on his own. "Where's your entourage?" I joked, rubbing myself against him teasingly, making his fingers dig into my skin.

"I'm on my own. They don't know I'm here. I only came for an hour then I need to drive back to Dorset. I have a meeting tomorrow morning with my sponsors, so I have to leave soon. I just need to wait until after midnight." He shrugged and traced his hand up and down my back, making goosebumps erupt on my skin.

"You have to drive to Dorset for a meeting tomorrow? What time does it start?" I questioned. Dorset was where his team were based so he usually spent a lot of time there, probably about half of the week, at least from what he'd told me.

"Nine."

I frowned. "Isn't it like a two-and-a-half-hour drive from here to Dorset?"

He nodded. "Just under," he confirmed, taking my hand and pulling me toward the last empty table in my section. "That's why I'm late. I wanted to get here for ten so I could see you, but my time trials ran late and then I had a meeting with the engineers. Then there was an accident on the motorway so I got stuck there for over an hour. I've had a damn nightmare day. It's always like that when you want to get somewhere."

Time trials? "You were driving today?" I asked. He smiled and nodded, pulling me down onto his lap. "In Dorset?" I probed. He nodded again. My brain tried to make sense of what he was saying. "So, you drove from Dorset to London, then you're leaving just after midnight to go back to Dorset again? Why are you making a five-hour round trip?"

Has this boy gone crazy?

He laughed and pushed me off his lap. "Go get me a drink, Em. I'll have a Pepsi."

Still confused, I gave him a curtsey. "Yes, Mr Matthews," I said sarcastically. As I headed over to the bar, my mind was still trying to work out why he would do that. Driving all that way for an hour, it just seemed like such a waste of time.

The night was busy. I barely got to spend time with Carson because all my tables were full, so I was flitting about here, there and everywhere. When I finally did get a few minutes free, I headed over to him straightaway. Setting another Pepsi down in front of him, I looked at him apologetically. "Sorry, baby. It's manic tonight." I motioned around a little helplessly at my busy tables, which all seemed momentarily satisfied.

He took my hand, pulling me down onto the little velvet seat next to him. When he looked at his watch, his smile grew more pronounced. "Happy birthday, Emma."

Happy birthday? I glanced at his watch to see it was ten past twelve. Technically, it was now my birthday; he was right. I laughed, a little taken aback. *How does he always remember my birthday? Every freaking year he remembers!* "Thanks."

He stood and shoved his hand in his pocket before sitting back down and holding his hand out to me. "It's after midnight, so it's officially your birthday. Therefore, you're allowed to have this."

In his hand sat a little box about the size of his palm. It was a black leather box – obviously jewellery. My heart sped at the adorability of him. He remembered my birthday every year and always got me something. His blue eyes were burning into mine as he moved his hand closer to me, signalling for me to take the gift… but I couldn't move. I was overcome with emotions all because the love of my life had remembered something I told him only once, three years ago.

"You don't want your present?"

I bit my lip and nodded. Of course, I wanted it, it was from him! "You didn't need to get me anything," I whispered, not really trusting my voice to speak properly.

He laughed and rolled his eyes. "Just open it." He took my wrist, turning it over and setting the little box into my hand.

I gulped and raised the lid, and when I did my chest constricted. Nestled into the black silk was the most beautiful necklace I had ever seen in my life. There was a charm on it, a delicate-looking white-gold butterfly. Set into the wings in symmetrical patterns were three stones – a blue one, a green one and a clear one. It was beautiful, about an inch in diameter, and attached to a thin white-gold chain.

It was perfect and so special I couldn't stop the tear which leaked from my eye. He had put so much thought into it. I had a thing for butterflies, always had, and this was one of the most beautiful ones I had ever seen. I stroked it lightly with one finger, feeling the cold, hard gems under my fingertip. Now I would be able to wear that and always have a little something of Carson's with me every day, even when Sasha wasn't with me.

Suddenly, the happy smile fell from my face as realisation dawned on me. "Those stones aren't real, are they?" I whispered, looking at them with wide eyes. They *had* to be fake. There's no way he would give me – a lap dancer – a piece of jewellery which had what looked like two diamonds, two emeralds and two sapphires in it.

Carson laughed, taking the box from my hand. "I'm not going to answer that question, Em." He pulled the little cushion out of the box and removed the necklace, unclasping it and looking at me expectantly.

I couldn't move. I felt like I was going to pass out. He wasn't answering the question because they were real. "Carson, those aren't real, are they?" I choked out, needing an answer.

He smiled weakly. "If I say no, will you let me put it on you?"

Holy shit, they really are!

I gasped and shook my head, pushing his hands back towards the box. I couldn't accept it, it was too much. "Carson, I can't take that. Thank you for buying it for me, but that's just too much! You need to take that back and get your money back. Damn it, that's *way* too much!" I cried, shaking my head in disbelief.

He groaned, his shoulders slumping. "You don't like it? I knew I should have gone for something more generic. I'm sorry, Emma."

Oh, my God, is he kidding me? It was beautiful! How could any girl – even one who didn't have a thing for butterflies – not think it was the most beautiful necklace she'd ever seen? "Carson, baby, it's beautiful, but it's just too much. Please, take it back and get your money back. I'd be happy with a cheap card; you don't need to spend your money on me."

He seemed to relax a little and smirked at me, raising one eyebrow, managing to look beautiful, sexy and cocky all rolled into one. "I can't take it back. It's a custom-made necklace, an original. I designed it myself. Well, kinda, I told the guy you liked butterflies and then I chose the stones to put in it…" he trailed off, laughing.

I closed my eyes and willed myself to not faint. *So much thought. He's put so much effort into my birthday. So. Damn. Sweet.*

"You did?" I asked, swiping at the tear, which trickled down my cheek.

He nodded and scooted closer to me on the little love seat. "Yep, I wanted something as beautiful as you but I couldn't even get it close, so I went for this instead."

My heart melted into a puddle. "Aww, Carson, that's adorable! That's such a sweet thing to say!" I gasped, awed.

He laughed wickedly. "I'm just trying to charm you into bed, Emma."

I giggled. "Well, it's definitely working, baby. I'm very grateful; you're in for a good night!"

He laughed and brushed my hair over my shoulder. "I need to leave in a couple of minutes. But I'll take that gratefulness for another night." He smirked at me and nodded to my neck. "Hold your hair up for me."

I looked at him pleadingly, begging him with my eyes to take it back. I hated the thought of him spending money on me. I didn't need his money. But another part of me wanted that necklace so very badly, just because it was from him. "Carsonnnnnn…" I whined.

"Emmaaaaaa…" he mocked, grinning.

I sighed in defeat; I could see on his face there was no way I was getting away with not accepting it. Looking back at the beautiful thing in his hands, my heart swelled. "Thank you so much. It's so beautiful. Thank you," I gushed. Taking hold of my hair, I lifted it and turned on the seat so he could put the necklace around my neck. Once it was on, his hands brushed against my shoulders, his touch causing my skin break out in goose bumps. He kissed the back of my neck and I traced my finger over the cold little charm which now rested against my chest.

"Happy birthday," he whispered, his hot breath blowing across my skin, making me shiver.

"Thanks. Are you sure you don't want to come to the backroom with me and I'll thank you properly?" I offered, turning in my seat to look at his face, praying he would say yes.

He looked a little pained as he shook his head. "I can't, Em. I need to get back so I can get a couple hours of sleep. I have a really long day tomorrow." He brushed his hand across my cheek lightly, wiping my last tear away with his fingertip.

I nodded and bit my lip, swallowing my disappointment. It had now been a month without any real form of sexual contact at all – the longest time it had been since I left the club when I was pregnant.

He sighed and stood up. "I really need to go. What are you doing tomorrow? Are you working? I can drive back tomorrow and see you if you're working," he offered.

I smiled weakly and shook my head. "I'm actually going out tomorrow. I'm going to dinner with one of the girls who works here. Then I'm going drinking with my Uni friends. I've got the night off for a change." Although I had actually been looking forward to going out on my birthday, now that I knew he would come here, I didn't want to go out. I would definitely rather spend my birthday with Carson.

He smiled, seeming pleased with my plans. "That's good; sounds like you'll have a nice night. I'm glad you're not working on your birthday." He straightened my necklace against my chest. "That definitely suits you." He dipped his head and kissed my forehead for a couple of seconds, making me grip the front of his shirt and close my eyes, savouring the feel of it.

"Thank you so much, Carson. I really love it," I said honestly.

He smiled and nodded. "Good. Right then, I'm back next week so I'll see you then. Have fun tomorrow." I gripped his hand as I walked him to the exit, stopping just inside the door as he kissed my forehead again. "You know, nineteen definitely suits you. You seem to get more beautiful the older you get," he teased, smirking at me. I giggled and he turned and walked out the door, leaving me standing there, biting my lip and holding the little butterfly around my neck.

I sighed dreamily and immediately skipped over to Lucie, showing her my necklace. She gasped as soon as she saw it, her eyes wide and shocked. "Holy shit, that's beautiful! He said he had that made for you?"

I nodded, grinning excitedly. "Yep. He's so incredible." I grinned and tried to ignore the vibrating of the music as 'Petal' started doing her routine on stage. Not even a half-naked stripper was going to bring me down from my Carson-high tonight.

"That must have cost him a fortune. For goodness' sake, don't lose it! Hey, maybe you should get it appraised or something, get it insured in case you do lose it," she suggested, nodding enthusiastically.

As soon as she mentioned losing it, I suddenly started to get worried. I gripped it protectively in my hand. Now I was scared to wear it in case it broke and dropped off or something. "I don't even want to think about how much it cost him. Probably like a grand or something." I winced at the thought of him spending all that money on me.

Lucie made a scoffing noise in her throat. "Trust me, that cost *a lot* more than a thousand pounds. Jeez, the diamonds are probably easily two carats each, and then there's the other stones. You're probably looking at more like fifty thou," she guessed, shrugging casually.

I gasped in horror. "No!" Now I *definitely* didn't want to wear it, but I wasn't sure if I could bring myself to take it off, either.

She waved her hand dismissively. "Of course it would cost a lot, he's a freaking millionaire. He's not just going to give you a cheap necklace from the market, is he?" She laughed, rolling her eyes.

I frowned. "But why would he give me something like this in the first place? It's crazy!"

"He *is* crazy. Maybe he's got no one else to spend his money on," she suggested. My mind flicked to the girls he'd been in magazines and the papers with for the last few weeks. He sure as hell *did* have other people to spend his money on, that's for sure. Lucie nodded behind me to one of my tables. "Looks like someone wants a drink or something."

I groaned and headed over to the table of middle-aged men in suits who were waving to get my attention. Plastering on my work smile, I forced myself to let go of my necklace. One of the guys regarded me curiously as I took their drink orders. "You know Carson Matthews?" he asked.

I smiled and nodded, my hand instinctively going to brush my necklace again. "Yep," I confirmed happily.

He motioned toward my necklace. "I saw him give you that. Special occasion?"

I grinned. "Yeah, it's my birthday tomorrow. Well, technically it's today seeing as it's after midnight."

"Oh, really? Well, happy birthday. Sorry, I forgot your name..." he trailed off, looking at me expectantly.

"Emma."

"Right, yeah, of course. So, how do you know Carson? Are you friends? You two looked pretty close."

I looked at him more closely; he actually seemed a little familiar but I didn't know where I knew him from. Maybe he'd been in the club before. "Er, he comes in a bit, so I know him from here. We're friends, I guess, yeah." I skirted around the question, not really wanting to classify my relationship with Carson as just a client. I hated the thought of him just being that, even though that's what he was.

The guy laughed. "Really, and he gave you that? You two must be pretty good... friends," he mused, smirking at me. "So, how long have you known him? Will he be coming back soon? I'd love to get an autograph or something with him."

"I don't know when he's back," I lied, frowning and feeling a little uncomfortable with all the questioning. "I'm gonna go get your drinks. I'll be right back." I turned and headed to the bar, glancing back over my shoulder to see the guy talking quietly with his two friends.

When I delivered the order a couple of minutes later, the same guy was questioning me again, but slightly different this time. He wanted to know more about me: how long I'd worked here, if I had to dance on stage, how many lap dances I did a week. I gave vague answers and then went to Lucie, pushing that table onto her instead. I really didn't like the guy prying into my life all the time; it was a little weird.

By the time the club closed, I was exhausted and definitely ready for bed. I changed into my outside clothes and made sure the little necklace was hidden from view as I made the fifteen-minute walk home.

After making sure we were all safe and comfortable in the flat, I fell into my bed, thinking about Carson before hugging my pillow, overcome by a wave of loneliness.

Chapter Six

I looked at myself in the mirror again, checking my make-up one final time before flicking my eyes behind me to Lucie as she sat on the bed, grinning at me. I sighed, knowing there wasn't much else I could do to make myself look any better, and did a little twirl. "Look okay?"

She laughed and nodded. "You look great, Emma. You're gonna be fighting them off tonight. Maybe you'll even get some; that'll put a smile back on that frustrated face of yours!" she teased, smirking at me knowingly.

I laughed and rolled my eyes. She knew I didn't go with anyone other than Carson, so that was a silly suggestion and we both knew it. "Yeah, okay. Well, I'm ready to go then," I confirmed, letting my gaze wander to the mirror again. I was wearing a dress for a change tonight – something Lucie and Rory had jointly bought me for my birthday. It was black, pretty, and a little figure hugging, cutting off at mid-thigh. She was right, though; it did suit me and made my small breasts appear bigger.

Sighing, I followed her out into the lounge, smiling at Rory who was sitting there watching TV. Sasha was already asleep; we'd worn her out all day today so she would want to go to bed early and would be easier on my little brother while he babysat. I never went out unless she was asleep. Not that I didn't trust my brother to be able to put her to bed, because I certainly did, but it wasn't fair to ask him to do that.

"Right then, I've got my mobile, so ring if you need me. Knock next door at Mrs Miller's if there are any immediate problems, okay?" I instructed, patting the top of his head teasingly.

"Yep, have a great night. And no coming home unless you're drunk!" he replied, laughing.

Lucie winked at Rory. "Don't worry, I'll definitely get her drunk for a change," she affirmed, linking her arm through mine. I smiled and rolled my eyes, checking in my handbag to see if I had my purse and phone. "Come on then. I'm starving."

Letting her drag me along, we went to start our night.

The dinner was nice, and so was the adult, normal, civilised conversation. Talk of kids was banned, as was work and uni, so we'd sat there gossiping and laughing about anything and everything. I hadn't had a girlie night since we went out for Lucie's birthday seven months ago. I'd forgotten how much fun it was to just be myself for a change.

After, we went to Lloyds bar where I was meeting a few friends from my university. As we walked in, the music was banging and vibrating off the walls. The place was packed considering it was Sunday night. We pushed our way to the bar, and I tried my best to ignore the guys brushing up against me on purpose as we wove through the crowd. After buying a pitcher of cocktails, we finally found my group of friends. With them, there were a couple of guys I didn't know. I smiled tentatively, exchanging greetings with the girls I was meeting. Lucie knew all my friends already, so nothing was awkward.

One of the guys leant forward, his hand outstretched to me, his eyes raking down my body slowly. I laughed at his obviousness and shook his hand. "Nice to meet you. I'm Joe," he purred.

I nodded in greeting, noticing he hadn't released my hand. "Emma."

"Happy birthday, Emma. I hope you don't mind us tagging along?" he asked, motioning toward the other guy who was knocking back shots with my friend, Angie.

I smiled and shrugged. "Sure, why not. More people to buy me birthday drinks," I joked, taking a sip of my cocktail, watching him over the rim of my glass.

He grinned and turned back to his friend, doing a shot with him. I laughed at how easy boys were; a little flirting and they were putty in a girl's hand. Not that I would ever do anything about it, of course, but it was nice to be appreciated, especially since I hadn't had much attention in the last few weeks from Carson.

Lucie elbowed me in the ribs gently to get my attention. "You are *so* in there tonight! He's hot. Maybe you should take him home for a little sheet time," she suggested, waggling her eyebrows.

I laughed at her absurdity and rolled my eyes. "You know my heart and body belong to someone else!" I scolded playfully.

She laughed. "Yeah, but he's not here, and obviously, Mr Celebrity Driver isn't doing it for you at the moment. You look like some kind of sex-starved, depressed woman!"

I stuck my tongue out at her and chinked my glass against hers. "Cheers. Here's to getting wasted." She smiled and we both downed our drinks before pouring another glass from the pitcher.

TWO HOURS LATER, I was more than wasted. The bar was getting more fun, the music louder, the conversation funnier, and even Joe was getting more interesting the more I spoke to him. When my phone vibrated in my bag, I pulled it out, squinting at it but unable to read the number on the caller ID because my eyes refused to focus properly.

"Helllllllo?" I sang as I answered it.

The guy on the line laughed. "Emma, it's Jason."

Jason? What on earth is he calling me for? "Jason? What do you want? You do know I'm off duty, right?" I asked, giggling.

He laughed. "Yeah, and very drunk by the sound of it," he replied. "Anyway, I have someone here at the club who wants to talk to you. He wanted your number but I'm not allowed to give that out, so I agreed I'd call you and he could talk to you."

I frowned and gripped the edge of the bar as someone bumped into me from behind, making me giggle as I almost fell over. "I don't want to talk to any freaking perverts from the club," I stated, throwing Lucie a *'what the fuck'* look. She was laughing and mouthing 'hang up' to me.

"Oh, okay. I'll tell Mr Matthews you don't want to speak to him then," Jason replied.

I gasped at the mention of his name. "No! Carson's there? What's he doing there? He's supposed to be in Dorset" I shouted excitedly.

"Well, he's obviously back. He wants to talk to you; shall I tell him you don't want to talk to any *'freaking perverts from the club'*?" Jason teased, laughing and doing a bad impression of my drunken voice.

"Don't you bloody dare!" I cried, gripping Lucie's arm and jumping up and down in excitement.

"Okay, I'll put him on," Jason agreed.

"What's going on?" Lucie asked, prying my fingers from her arm and wincing.

"Carson wants to talk to me. He's at the club!" I squealed, grinning like a mad woman, ignoring the rest of my friends who were looking at me like I was crazy.

I heard Jason talking away from the phone and then the most beautiful voice in the world came on the line, making my heart beat a little faster and the hair on the back of my neck stand up.

"Hey, Em."

"Hey, baby. What are you doing there? I thought you were in Devon today?" I asked, sighing dreamily and already planning my escape to the club so I could see him.

"I was. I finished early. So, you're obviously having a great birthday…"

I nodded, and then remembered he couldn't see me so I giggled at myself. "Yeah, it's good."

He chuckled. "You sound drunk."

"I'm not drunk!" I moved my arm, gesturing the fact I wasn't that wasted, and accidently slopped half my drink over Joe's shoe. I giggled and looked at him apologetically. "Okay, maybe I'm a little drunk," I admitted, mouthing sorry to Joe and handing him a napkin from the bar to dry it.

"Okay. Er… So, I'm out tonight and I was wondering if I could buy you a drink?" Carson asked, sounding a little uncomfortable.

My breath caught. He wanted to see me outside of work again? "Really?"

"Yeah. I don't want to intrude on your night out with the girls or anything. Maybe it's not a good idea; I just wanted to get you a drink for your birthday. You can say no if you want to," he said.

Say no, is he serious? "Hell yeah!" I cried excitedly.

He laughed, probably at my embarrassing enthusiasm. "Okay, great. Just tell me where you are then; I'll come meet you."

"We're at Lloyds. You know it?" I asked, trying to think of directions from the club in case I needed to tell him.

"Yeah, I know it."

I grinned. "Okay. Well, when you get in here, we're over on the right-hand side, near the bar," I said, biting my lip and trying not to squeal like a little girl on Christmas morning.

"Right. See you in a bit then." He disconnected the call and I turned back to Lucie, barely able to breathe through my excitement. I really didn't think I was seeing him again until next weekend, so this was the best birthday present ever.

"Holy shit. He's coming here to buy me a birthday drink!" I hissed. My stomach was fluttering, which actually didn't mix too well with the alcohol I'd consumed.

Lucie grinned. "Awesome! Now *that's* put a smile on your frustrated face," she teased, winking at me.

We barely had time to down two more shots before someone touched the small of my back. I turned excitedly, and there he was. The love of my life, father of my child, and the one who made my heart soar. I squealed and threw my arms around his neck, hugging him tightly, bouncing on the spot.

He laughed and hugged me back, kissing my shoulder softly. "Hey. Happy birthday," he breathed, pulling back but leaving his arms around my waist.

I giggled and nodded. "It is now!" I confirmed, making him smirk at me. I bit my lip and groaned. *Damn it, I shouldn't have said that!*

He looked over my shoulder and smiled at Lucie. "Hey, how's the night going? Looks like you're having a good time," he said to her, laughing and tracing his hand up my back.

Lucie laughed and nodded. "It's good. I promised her brother I'd get her good and drunk, so I've done my job."

Carson laughed and I leant on him heavily. Pressing my face into the side of his neck, I breathed in his smell I had missed so much since last night. My fingers tangled into the back of his hair. "Looks like you have," he confirmed.

I pulled away, grabbing his hand and introducing him to my friends who, coincidently, were all completely looking at him in awe and practically eye raping him. The guy who had been doing shots all night - I think his name was Logan, but I couldn't be sure - just stared at him with his mouth hanging open like a total moron. Joe, on the other hand, frowned and looked him over slowly. For some reason, he didn't seem to like Carson.

After a couple more drinks, Carson thought it would be a good idea to buy a round of flaming Sambucas. I looked at mine, eyeing the little fire which burnt on the top of it. I was actually a little scared to drink it, which seemed to amuse Carson. He wasn't even drinking tonight; he was driving apparently, so he stuck to Pepsi.

Lucie laughed and counted to three. On three, we all blew out the flames and downed the drink. I winced as it burnt my throat and I knew that one drink would be my downfall. I could already feel the after-effects of the alcohol I'd consumed. I wasn't used to drinking, so this was more than I had probably ever drunk. I was definitely going to throw up in the morning.

I clung to Carson, who was standing just behind me, laughing and making little jokes in my ear, flirting outrageously with me while one arm wrapped securely around my waist. "Oh, man, I shouldn't have drunk that. You're a bad influence on me, Mr

Matthews," I teased, tapping my finger on the tip of his nose. He smirked at me, shooting me that devilish little smile I loved so much, and I swooned internally.

Joe turned to me and grinned. "So, Emma, if there is one thing you could have for your birthday, what would it be?" he inquired.

I didn't need to think about it. "An orgasm."

Everyone burst out laughing and Joe raised one eyebrow. "Oh, really? Well, tonight's your lucky night, because that's exactly what I got you."

I rolled my eyes and opened my mouth to turn him down, when Carson put his hand on Joe's chest. "Back off, she's not interested!" he growled. His other arm tightened on my waist, moving me further away from Joe to his other side.

"And how do you know that? You a mind reader now, hot shot?" Joe asked, pushing Carson's hand off him angrily.

Carson laughed humourlessly. "Oh, come on, you've been hitting on her for the last hour. Has she even showed the slightest bit of interest in you? No. So get over it, and go hit on someone more in your league," Carson said, smirking at him confidently.

If Joe had been hitting on me for the last hour, either I was really drunk or he was just plain terrible at it because I hadn't even noticed.

Joe made some sort of reply, but I didn't hear it because at that moment Carson pressed his mouth to my ear. "Wanna dance with me?" he whispered. His hot breath tickled my skin, making me shiver lightly. I gulped and nodded, handing my glass to a grinning Lucie.

Carson smiled and took my hand, leading me off a little way to where people were grinding on each other. I slipped my arms around his neck and grinned happily. In all the years I'd known him, this was actually our first dance together. Sure, I'd danced *for* him a lot, but never proper dancing like this. It was nice.

He smiled and pulled me closer to him, his blue eyes locked on mine, and I almost forgot how to breathe. Everyone else disappeared and all that was left was him. I could barely even hear the music which was sure to be banging around us. His hand went to my neck, playing with the cheap necklace I was wearing tonight.

"Don't you like the one I bought you? I could get you something else, if you want," he offered, looking at me apologetically.

I smiled and gripped my hands into his hair. "I love the one you got me. I was just a little scared to wear it tonight in case I lost it," I admitted.

He laughed and shook his head as if I'd said something silly. "You don't need to worry about that. If you lose it, I'll just get you another one."

I sighed dreamily. Sometimes he was almost too sweet and adorable for my sanity. "You are so damn sweet, baby," I whispered as I pulled his mouth down to mine.

He kissed me back hungrily. His soft lips moving against mine made everything seem right in the world. It didn't matter that I had to work so hard to pay the rent, or that I was stuck in a job I hated, working my way through Uni on about four hours sleep a night. It didn't matter how hard my life was as a single mother. When Carson kissed me, I felt like I could do anything and be anyone.

My whole body was burning for more. I was so turned on it was almost painful. I felt like some desperate horny junkie who needed a fix. My body was on high alert, jittery and needy. His tongue traced along my bottom lip, asking for entrance, so I pulled away, putting my forehead to his.

"Carson, I want you to do something for me," I breathed, looking into his eyes, which reminded me so much of his daughter.

"Sure, what?" he asked, kissing me again. I kissed him back but when he nibbled on my bottom lip, I pulled away again, making him groan.

I smiled teasingly. "I want you to walk away from me," I stated, watching as shock crossed his face.

"What, why?"

I gripped the front of his shirt, rubbing my nose against his lightly, like he always did to me. "I want you to go away and then come back and pretend like you don't know me. I want you to hit on me with your best pick-up line ever. Then I'm going to drag you to the bathrooms and have hot, nasty, stranger sex with you," I said seductively. As I spoke, the shock was slowly fading from his face, to be replaced by lust and longing.

"Are you sure this isn't my birthday?" he growled, slipping his hand down to my bum, squeezing gently.

I giggled. "Oh, no, baby, it's definitely mine," I confirmed, tracing my finger along the edge of his collar, feeling his soft skin.

He smirked at me. "And this is a little fantasy of yours, is it? Picking up a stranger in a bar for hot, nasty, bathroom sex?" he asked, his voice husky and thick with lust.

I closed my eyes and nodded. It wasn't exactly the 'picking up a stranger' thing I wanted. It was meeting him for the first time as a normal girl, in normal clothes. I wanted to feel like one of the girls he picked up in the clubs. I wanted to feel special and wanted, even if it was just for one night. I wanted him, and for once he wouldn't feel the need to offer me money; he would just be with me because he wanted to be. I wanted the full Carson Matthews experience all those other girls got.

He laughed and kissed my lips softly before pulling away from me and disappearing through the crowd. I bit my lip, giggling and blushing like crazy as I headed back to where Lucie was still propping up the bar. Thankfully, Joe and Logan were gone, off dancing and flirting with a group of girls by the look of it.

Lucie glanced over my shoulder and frowned as I walked back on my own. "Where's lover boy?"

"We're playing a game," I replied, shrugging.

She laughed and rolled her eyes. "You must be pleased with his reaction to the Joe thing," she said, nodding enthusiastically.

"Huh?" I questioned, confused as to what she was going on about.

She sighed dramatically, flicking her long, raven hair over her shoulder. "Oh, come on, possessive much? He was so damn jealous it was almost embarrassing!" she explained. *Jealous? Carson? Why would he be jealous, though? He got what he wanted from me all the time, so why would he feel the need to get jealous?* I looked at Lucie like she was crazy and she just laughed. "For a smart girl, you really are an idiot sometimes."

I shook my head, still confused, but before I could say anything, someone tapped me on the shoulder. I turned around, wondering who it would be… and there stood Carson. A goofy grin slipped onto my face. I'd completely forgotten we were playing this little game.

I took in his whole form in a matter of seconds: the way the dim lights made his hair look a darker shade of brown than normal, how his light-blue shirt stretched across his broad shoulders, and how the smile tugged at the corners of his full lips, making them look inviting and luscious.

Without speaking he raised his hand, holding something out to me. I frowned, confused, and opened my hand, watching as he dropped a little silver screw into my palm. *What the hell? Where did he get that from?* I flicked my eyes up to his face in time to see him smirk at me.

"Wanna screw?" he asked, raising one eyebrow curiously. Lucie and I both burst out laughing as his prop suddenly clicked into place. Carson grinned and held out his other hand to me. "So, anyway, I just wanted to come and introduce myself. My name's Carson, and you are the hottest damn thing I've ever seen in my life. If I was to Google the definition of natural beauty, I'd see a picture of your face," he said, his eyes locked on mine.

My heart was racing, my stomach doing little flips as my whole body grew hotter. *Oh, yeah, I love this game!* I bit my lip and shook his hand. "Emma," I replied, trying not to giggle.

He pulled me closer to him. "Want to go somewhere quiet and have some hot, nasty, stranger sex, Emma?" he purred, causing my whole body to tremble with excitement.

I nodded eagerly and winked at Lucie before weaving through the crowd, dragging Carson along behind me, holding his hand tightly.

As we approached the ladies toilet you could easily see the queue, so Carson tugged me toward the gents' instead. I grinned and kissed him forcefully, pushing him against the door. It swung open and we both stumbled in, slamming against the wall, still not breaking the kiss. I giggled as he kissed down my neck, letting his hands roam my body. His hand slid under the bottom of my dress as my fingers went to his belt buckle. I was in no mood for going slow right now; all I could think about was his body and nothing else.

He pushed me against the wall, gripping his hands on my bum and lifting me off my feet easily. I wrapped my legs around his waist and practically ripped open his jeans, shoving my hand down there eagerly. My stomach fluttered when my fingers brushed against the hardness I could feel through the material of his boxer shorts. The anticipation was killing me slowly. As his tongue tangled with mine, I moaned into his mouth at the sheer luxury of having his undivided attention.

That was when someone cleared their throat dramatically. I squealed from shock and Carson swore quietly, pushing me tighter against the wall, obviously trying to shield me with his body as he tugged my dress down quickly to stop the guy who was washing his hands from getting an eyeful.

I cringed and buried my flaming face into the side of Carson's neck, giggling as he spoke to the guy. "Sorry, man. I didn't realise there was anyone in here," he laughed.

The guy laughed, too. "No worries. Maybe you should lock the door," he replied as he walked out of the toilets.

Carson chuckled and flicked the lock on the door before looking back to me with lust written clearly across his face. "Now then, Emma. Just how nasty are we talking here?" he asked, grinning mischievously.

I bit my lip and squeezed myself to him tighter. "Oh, as nasty as you want… sorry, I forgot your name," I teased.

He grinned and stepped to the side, sitting me on the counter next to the sinks and pressing his whole body to mine. I could actually feel his heartbeat against my chest; he was so close. "It's Carson. Now, don't forget again because I want you to scream it." He kissed me again, pushing my dress up around my waist as he gripped my thong with both hands. I heard a tearing sound and I gasped from shock as the material was literally ripped off my body.

Well, you did tell him nasty…

He grinned and started kissing down my body, guiding me to lie back on the little counter. It wasn't actually very comfortable, but the situation was so hot I just didn't want to move. He grabbed my calves roughly and pulled my body to the edge of the counter before he bent to bite the inside of my thigh. I gasped and wriggled, flicking my eyes around the bathroom until I spotted a full-length mirror on the opposite wall. I had the perfect view of Carson on his knees, me lying back on the counter, my feet resting on his shoulders while he kissed and bit around the inside of my thighs, heading higher with each kiss. My breathing was coming out in pants; all I wanted was to scream at him to hurry because I felt like I was close to bursting point.

Holy fuck, this is sizzling hot!

Just as his tongue got to where I needed it, a toilet flushed off to our left. My mouth popped open in shock as my head snapped in that direction just in time to see the door to the last stall open and a guy in his early twenties walk out. Carson jumped up, yanking my dress down and looking over his shoulder at the guy who had totally caught us in the act.

I squirmed on the spot, blushing furiously as I fingered the bottom of my dress, making sure I was covered. Neither Carson nor I spoke; we just watched him with open mouths. The guy was clearly unfazed by us getting it on while he was using the toilet. He smiled and washed his hands, taking his time as if this happened to him every day.

Suddenly, his eyes widened. "Holy shit! You're Carson Matthews!" he cried excitedly. "I'm your biggest fan. Oh, my God, I can't believe I'm meeting you! Wow, seriously, wow. You're a driving god. I swear, you're my idol!" he gushed, still not fazed by the fact Carson had his jeans undone and was standing between my legs. The newcomer didn't even seem bothered that my ripped thong was wrapped around Carson's hand he was in the process of trying to take hold of so he could shake it in greeting.

Could he have not noticed what we were doing?

Carson frowned and nodded, quickly moving my underwear to his other hand before shaking the intruder's offered one. "Yeah, thanks, dude... er..." He flicked his eyes to me, looking a little confused.

The guy gasped suddenly, his eyes popping open as if he'd only just noticed the situation. "Oh, shit. Sorry, I'm interrupting! Go ahead, get your freak on! Can I get your autograph though?" he asked hopefully.

Carson patted his pocket as he swallowed awkwardly. "Umm… I don't have a pen. You have one?" he asked, his voice amused as I giggled and pressed my face into his arm, trying to disappear.

The guy groaned. "No. I'll go get one, though," he replied as he ran toward the door. "I'll wait outside until you're done so I won't interrupt you again. Have fun and don't worry, I won't let anyone back in here. I'll stand guard on the door for you," he vowed, nodding enthusiastically. He flicked the lock on the door and practically ran out. I could hear him saying Carson's name excitedly to himself.

Carson laughed awkwardly. "Well, that ruined the moment."

I burst out laughing and pulled his mouth back to mine, kissing him softly. It was a nice idea, but maybe I wasn't supposed to get sex for my birthday; maybe I was being punished or something. He kissed me back passionately, but both of us knew it wasn't going any further. Carson was right, that guy was a total passion-killer.

He pulled away and brushed one finger down the side of my face, rubbing his nose on the side of mine. "I'll do this little fantasy of yours another time, I promise," he whispered.

I smiled and gripped my hand in his hair. "I'll hold you to that, baby."

Taking hold of my hips, he gently set me on the floor again. Raising his hand, he showed me my ripped underwear and winced apologetically. "Sorry, I got a little carried away."

I giggled and went up on tiptoes, pressing my lips to his softly. "I hope it's not windy when I leave tonight," I teased.

He chuckled and took my hand, tossing my underwear into the bin before we walked out of the bathrooms together. As promised, the guy was standing outside the door, his arms folded across his chest, stopping a line of guys who were obviously waiting to use the bathroom. They all cheered and whistled as we walked out. My already-burning cheeks blazed harder as I pressed my face between Carson's shoulder blades.

The waiting crowd recognised him and all immediately surged around him, asking for autographs and photos. While he was busy, I snuck off back to Lucie, leaving him with the quickly growing crowd.

Lucie looked at me with an *'I know what you were doing'* expression, and I couldn't help but giggle guiltily. "That was seriously fast. Maybe he's not as good as you say he is," she teased.

I bit my lip and shook my head. "Some guy walked out of the toilet and caught him going down on me on the counter. Man, it was so freaking embarrassing!" I muttered, picking up my drink from the bar and topping it up with the last of the cocktail from the pitcher.

Lucie laughed and held up her glass, knocking it against mine. "Well, here's to not being interrupted next time," she toasted, smiling over my shoulder.

An arm wrapped around my waist, pulling me back into a hard chest. I squealed, giggling because I already knew it was Carson. "You're not supposed to run off and leave me, you know. You should have made some excuse for me and dragged me off, saving me from the crowd," he whispered in my ear, nibbling on my earlobe gently.

I smiled and sighed contentedly. Why did it always feel so right being in his arms? Why couldn't I just get over him already so I wouldn't feel the heartache when I remembered he wasn't actually mine to keep? "Sorry, baby," I said, leaning my head back against his shoulder and closing my eyes.

"Just remember that for next time, huh?" He stroked the side of my head. "Are you tired? I can drive you both home if you want," he offered, looking from me to Lucie.

I pulled back to look at him as horror built in my chest. "There is no way I'm getting on that bloody bike with you again," I stated, shaking my head fiercely.

He laughed and rolled his eyes. "I do own a car, you know. Why would I offer two drunks a lift home on a bike?" he teased, rubbing his nose against mine lightly.

Oh, yeah, I didn't think about that.

Lucie cleared her throat. "I'm actually gonna stay out a little longer with the girls. But you take Emma home," she insisted.

"I'm not leaving you here on your own," I rejected.

Kirsty Moseley

Angie wrapped her arm around Lucie's shoulder. "She's not on her own, silly. We'll all share a taxi. Don't worry, we know about safety in numbers, Emma," she scolded playfully.

I looked at Lucie to make sure she was okay with this and wasn't just doing it because she thought I wanted alone time with Carson. Jenny turned around and passed her a fresh drink she'd just bought.

"You're really staying?" I asked Lucie. She nodded and sipped her drink. "Okay, well you all stay together. No wandering off and I'll talk to you all tomorrow. Thanks for a great night, girls," I said, hugging them all one by one.

Once I'd said my goodbyes to everyone, Carson took my hand and led us through the crowd to the front door of the bar. As we stepped out, I was almost blinded by the flash of a camera. The light was so bright I had to put my hand up to shield my eyes. Beside me, Carson groaned loudly and then his arm wound around my waist protectively. The click and flash of a camera continued to go off furiously in front of me.

"Emma, where's your necklace Carson bought you?" someone shouted.

I squinted and looked around, confused, until I saw someone I recognised. The guy from the club last night, the one who was asking me loads of questions about Carson. He was holding out a little black rectangle thing towards me as the photographer he was with continued to snap shot after shot.

"I didn't want to wear it in case it got lost," I said weakly, not really understanding what was going on.

"Did you have a nice night?" the guy asked.

I looked at Carson, unsure as to what I should do. Was I allowed to answer his questions? What was the protocol for being papped outside a bar, whilst drunk? I didn't want to say anything and cause him any more trouble.

Carson smiled and nodded, leading me off in the other direction. "We had a great night," he confirmed.

I kept pace with him, clinging to him tightly as they walked in front of us, still taking pictures while walking backward, holding the little black thing out to me again.

84

What the heck is that? I studied it, suddenly realising it was a little tape recorder.

"So, you two met at a strip club?" the guy asked.

I gulped at that question. This was going to look really bad for Carson.

"Guys, seriously, come on, don't ruin the night for her. It's her birthday. Can't you give me a break for one night?" Carson said dejectedly.

The guy ignored him. "What does your management think about you dating a stripper, Carson? Your family? What about your friends?"

Carson frowned. "She's not a stripper!" he snapped.

"She works part-time in a strip club, lap dances a couple of times a week," the guy replied, smirking.

I groaned. I shouldn't have let Carson drive me home. I should have stayed inside with Lucie. Now he was going to be getting negative press and they were going to be talking rubbish about me in the papers. I could see it now: *'Carson's bit of rough'*, *'Scraping the barrel with a stripper'*. Rory was going to go crazy when he read that. He didn't know what my job entailed; I didn't ever want him to know.

"Just back off!" Carson ordered while putting his hand over the camera lens, his other arm tightening on me. Tears welled in my eyes; I felt dirty, cheap and nasty all over again. Carson grabbed his keys from his pocket. A car beeped and unlocked two cars away, and I didn't even have time to see what type or colour it was before he opened the door and pushed me in, slamming the door behind me.

My heart sank. Would he stop coming to the club now? Once he was slaughtered in the papers for going to strip clubs and fraternising with lap dancers, would I ever see him again? His management would probably make him stay away for his 'image'. I would be lost without him. He climbed in the other side of the car, starting the engine as they took more pictures of us in the car together, banging on the windows, and still shouting their questions.

Chapter Seven

"Don't cry, Em. What's wrong?" Carson whispered as we sped down the road. He took my hand, glancing at me worriedly.

I sniffed and wiped my face, turning away from him, watching the buildings whizz past. "Nothing. That was just weird." My voice broke around my lie.

He sighed. "Yeah, I know. I get used to this kind of thing happening. I'm sorry I dragged you into it, too," he said, rubbing the back of my hand lightly with his thumb.

I laughed humourlessly. *He* was sorry? *I* was the one with the dirty, nasty job, and yet he was apologising to me? "You don't need to be sorry. That was my fault. I'm the one who's gonna make you look like some kind of dirty pervert that takes lap dancers home for the night," I muttered, chewing on my lip, fighting the tears threatening to pour down my cheeks.

"Emma, just ignore them. They were just trying to get a story; it happens all the time. Everything's fine," he insisted, tugging on my hand, trying to get me to look at him. I looked over at him apologetically. He was watching the road but kept glancing at me quickly, smiling reassuringly. He squeezed my hand. "Everything's fine. I don't care where you work. What does it matter where you work? You're Emma Bancroft to me and nothing else. You could sell fried chicken for a living, and I'd still come eat at your restaurant every weekend," he teased.

I giggled and rolled my eyes at his little joke about chicken. "Again with the fried chicken?"

He laughed and raised my hand to his mouth, kissing my knuckles softly. We lapsed into silence. I didn't know what to say, but to be honest it wasn't an uncomfortable silence, so that was one thing to be thankful for.

When we pulled up outside my flat, I turned in my seat and smiled at him. "Thanks for the lift. I had a really nice time tonight. Thanks for coming to meet me," I said, my eyes flicking down to his luscious lips. I silently debated as to whether I could just ask him to screw me in the car. It had already been four weeks, and I needed him more than ever in case he never came to the club again. I needed one last time with him before his management forced him to stay away from me for his own good.

He smiled. "I'll walk you up." He pushed open his door and headed around to my side before I even had the chance to protest.

As he opened the door for me, I climbed out of his car and looked down at it for the first time. It was silver and small, and extremely expensive-looking: smart, sleek and beautiful. This car was Carson all over. I gasped and shook my head. "You cannot leave this thing out here! Wow, the bike was bad, but this…" I trailed off, laughing nervously. I knew nothing about cars but, damn, if I had to choose one, it would definitely look something like this. "What is it?" I asked, nodding at it.

He smiled and lovingly ran his hand over the bonnet. "An Aston Martin Vanquish," he replied, shrugging casually as if I should know what that meant.

"Oh, yeah, of course it is," I replied, pretending to know what he was talking about.

He laughed and took my hand, weaving his fingers through mine. "Come on, let's get you out of the cold before you sober up too much and don't ask me in for coffee," he suggested, giving me a little tug toward the entrance of my flats.

I led him upstairs and glanced at my watch as we walked in quietly. It was after one in the morning. Thankfully, Rory was in bed; he had school tomorrow. Carson leant on the counter next to me while I made coffee and like before, we took them into the lounge. He pulled my legs onto his lap again, turning in his seat to look at me as he traced his fingertips over my shins lightly, making my breathing shallow.

"I really am sorry about the photographers. I don't know how they knew so much about you," he said, looking a little confused.

I blew the top of my coffee before taking a sip. "That guy was at the club last night. He saw you give me the necklace. He was asking all kinds of questions about you, but I didn't know who he was so I didn't think anything of it. I didn't realise he was a reporter," I admitted, wincing as I pushed my mug onto the side table. Now that I thought about it, though, I had no idea how I missed it; he was asking so many questions about Carson. But I guess I wasn't expecting a reporter, so I wouldn't naturally jump to that conclusion.

"He was at the club? Wow, okay. You don't know who that was?" he asked, sipping his coffee, too. I shook my head in answer. Carson smiled sadly. "That's Rodger Harris. He's the most successful reporter for The Peoples' Post."

I frowned. The Peoples' Post was one of the most popular newspapers in England. They thrived on celebrities, dishing dirt, hounding them, and outing them of their wrongdoings. "Oh," I mumbled.

Carson smiled and gripped his hand around the back of my knee, his thumb rubbing the inside of my leg. "Like I said, don't worry about it. That guy has a hard-on for me. He's always got a photographer following me, trying to catch me doing something I shouldn't be doing." He shrugged dismissively.

"You don't think they'll print that I'm a stripper, do you? I don't want Rory thinking that's what I do. I don't want his friends giving him a hard time about it at school or anything." I cringed at the thought.

Carson shrugged, looking at me apologetically. "I'm sorry, Emma. I guess I've kind of landed you in the shit now, huh?"

I smiled and scooted closer to him on the seat, pressing my lips to his softly for a second before pulling away. "It's fine. It's my job, not yours. It's not like whatever they print will be a lie," I said honestly.

He stroked the side of my face lightly. "They may not even print anything. They might not have gotten any good pictures; we didn't give them anything to print. We'll see, okay? If it gets too bad then I'll speak to my press agent and see if we can calm it down, all right?" he offered, smiling reassuringly. "So, did you get anything nice for your birthday?" he asked, obviously wanting to change the subject.

I smiled. "I got a beautiful necklace from this eccentric millionaire I know," I joked. "And Rory and Lucie bought me this dress," I continued, gesturing to it.

His eyes dropped to my dress. "It's really pretty; it suits you," he mused, rubbing the material of the skirt between his finger and thumb. "What about from your parents?"

I frowned. "Er… I don't speak to my parents. We had a big falling out."

"Really? Right, yeah, I guess that makes sense what with you living on your own, looking after your little brother." He frowned and nodded. "You think you'll make up with them one day?"

I laughed incredulously and shook my head. "No. They don't approve of me and my lifestyle. I left when I was sixteen, and they burnt the bridge straight after I walked across it," I replied, trying to make light of the situation.

A sad smile graced his lips. "I feel sorry for them."

For them? Why would he feel sorry for them? Shouldn't he be on my side and feel sorry for me? "Why?" I asked, confused as to where he was going with this.

"They lost someone incredible from their lives. I feel sorry for anyone that doesn't know you."

Holy shit, that's the best line I've ever heard in my life! "Damn, Carson, that was flipping adorable," I congratulated, awestruck.

He laughed, and his hand travelled a little higher up my leg. "I'm just trying to charm you into bed, Emma," he joked, using his words from last night.

I laughed. "Well, it's definitely working, baby," I whispered, pulling his mouth to mine and kissing him hungrily. He smiled

89

against my lips, his hand heading even higher, brushing against my sex lightly. I gasped when I felt his fingers touch my flesh; I'd completely forgotten I wasn't wearing underwear after he ripped it off in the gents' bathroom.

He laughed and moved his hand away, running his nose up the side of my jaw, his lips pressing to my ear. "How about I give you that birthday orgasm now?" he whispered seductively.

I whimpered with need and bit my lip, nodding. I lay down, pulling him on top of me. His weight pressed me down into the softness of the sofa as his hard body pressed against mine. He kissed me deeply. I moaned into his mouth, unbuttoning his shirt and pushing it off his shoulders, trailing my fingers across his skin.

"Should we go to the bedroom, in case your brother comes in? I don't want any more interruptions," he growled huskily. He was already on his feet, pulling me up too before I realised what he'd said. I couldn't go to the bedroom with him, Sasha was in there! I opened and closed my mouth, unable to think of a single excuse as to why I could say no. "You don't want to?"

I gulped. "Let's stay in here. My bedroom's right next to Rory's, and I don't want him to hear anything," I lied, praying he would go for it.

He smiled and shrugged, stepping back to me again, wrapping his arm around me and guiding me back down onto the sofa as his mouth found mine. We launched into the most passionate make-out session we'd ever had. It felt different because we weren't in the club, and *we* were different this time. I prayed he felt the same. The kissing was getting so hot and passionate I was almost losing myself in it. Hours, minutes, or merely seconds could have passed but I had no idea, because all I could focus on was him.

By the time he pulled away to kiss down the side of my neck, I was gasping for breath. My head was spinning, and my whole body felt hot. I rolled him onto his back, forgetting we were on the sofa, so we tumbled off the side, crashing to the floor. The split-second falling sensation made my stomach lurch. The alcohol I'd consumed was coming back to haunt me. Carson merely laughed and carried on where we left off, nibbling on my neck. I tried to ignore the way the room was spinning but, when I closed my eyes, I felt dizzy. When my stomach squeezed uncomfortably, I knew.

Oh, God, I'm going to throw up!

I pushed myself up quickly, straddling his hips and grabbing the bin, just about managing to get it to my face before I emptied my stomach into it. Carson gasped and also heaved before I pushed myself off him and threw up again. It was like a floodgate had been opened.

"Oh, shit. Emma, I'm not good with sick!" Carson moaned, dry-heaving next to me whilst trying to rub my back at the same time.

I laughed into the bin and pushed him away from me, blushing furiously as I ran to the bathroom. I could still hear him gagging and I just couldn't stop laughing. Secretly, I prayed I was still drunk enough to blank this out in the morning, pretend like it never happened.

A couple of minutes later, there was a knock at the door. "Emma, you okay? I have water here if you want it," Carson said softly from the other side.

I flushed the toilet and rinsed my mouth out with mouthwash before unlocking the door. He stood there looking at me sympathetically, holding out a glass of water. I bit my lip and smiled apologetically. "I'm so sorry," I croaked, my voice husky from vomiting.

He winced. "Don't worry about it. I'm sorry, too; I'm useless with sick. Man, I'm really sorry, I didn't help at all."

I burst out laughing as I remembered him heaving next to me. The laughing made my stomach lurch again; I shoved the glass back toward him and ran back to the toilet. Behind me, the bathroom door closed and I could hear Carson heaving on the other side of it. I couldn't help but laugh again before expelling yet more alcohol from my system.

Well, if the papers printing horrible things about him doesn't scare him away, then this will!

A couple of minutes later, muffled talking started outside the door. I flushed the toilet again, slumping down next to it and trying to catch my breath. I looked up just as the door opened, seeing Rory step in. A huge smirk covered his face as he folded his arms across his chest.

"You're setting such a good example for me right now," he teased. I burst out laughing, holding my hand out to him. He gripped it and pulled me to my feet. "When I finally come home drunk and throwing up at two in the morning, you remember this night and no giving me hell about it," he stated rather smugly.

"Shut up, you!" I scolded playfully as he helped me over to the sink so I could rinse my mouth again. "Has Carson gone?" I asked, wincing because of how embarrassing the situation was.

Rory chuckled wickedly and shook his head. "No. He's in the kitchen looking a little green. I heard you throwing up and when I came out, he was gagging outside the door. It was hilarious. He's too funny." He laughed and I couldn't help but giggle quietly, too. I'd never seen anyone have such a bad reaction to sick before; Carson clearly had a weak stomach.

"Sasha didn't hear me, did she?" I whispered, grabbing my toothbrush from the glass on the side and squeezing on some toothpaste.

"Nah, she sleeps through anything, you know that." He smiled reassuringly. "I'm gonna go make you some coffee so you can sober up."

I shook my head, spitting out the minty froth and turning the tap on to rinse it. "Don't bother, I'm sober now anyway. It wasn't the drink so much, it was the falling off the sofa," I admitted.

Rory raised one eyebrow. "Oh, I'm *so* adding that onto my list of things I can do when I'm older!"

I scoffed and dropped my toothbrush back into the glass, wiping my mouth on a towel. "Don't you dare! This is not an example; this is a rare birthday occurrence you are only allowed to do when you're nineteen!" I teased, following him out of the room. "Go back to bed. You have school tomorrow. Sorry I woke you up, but thanks for coming to help me."

He smiled and kissed the top of my head. "No worries. I couldn't resist seeing my big sister hurl and hug the toilet bowl." He walked off laughing to himself.

Steeling myself against the embarrassment, I took a deep breath and walked into the kitchen. Carson was sitting at the table, playing with his mobile phone, avidly texting someone.

He jumped up when he saw me, looking both concerned and embarrassed at the same time. "Hey, you okay?"

I nodded, wishing the ground would just open up and swallow me. "Yeah. Are you okay now?" I asked, trying not to burst into a fit of giggles again.

He blew out a big breath and ran his hand through his hair. "I'm so sorry. I have a really shit gag reflex. I was totally useless, sorry." He winced, shaking his head disapprovingly.

I chewed on my lip and looked at him in awe. He didn't seem to care that I had just thrown up in the middle of a make-out session, more that he didn't help me. He really was just too incredible for words. "That was so embarrassing. I'm so sorry I did that."

He stepped closer to me and stroked my arm, smiling. "It was the Sambuca. You said you shouldn't have drunk it," he said, smirking at me slightly.

I shrugged. "Maybe it was the kissing," I suggested, raising one eyebrow playfully.

He grinned and inched his face closer, rubbing his nose against mine, giving me a little Eskimo kiss like he always did. "I've never seen that reaction in you before from my kissing. Moaning, yes. Panting, yes. Sweating, yes. Heck, even swearing, but never throwing up." He moved one hand to my neck, cupping it gently, his thumb tracing across my cheek. I laughed quietly, not meeting his eyes. Of all the people that could have happened in front of, it had to be him.

"Sorry."

He kissed my forehead softly. I closed my eyes and savoured the feel of his hot, full lips on my overheated skin. "Don't be sorry. I guess I should let you get some sleep, though. I'm glad you had a nice birthday, you deserve to," he whispered.

I smiled and gripped a fistful of his shirt, pressing my whole body to his. Was this the last time I was going to see him? Had I completely and utterly blown whatever small thing we had going on? "Thanks, baby."

He kissed my forehead again, then he held out a scrap of paper with a phone number on it. "This is my press agent's phone number. I've just texted him and told him about Rodger Harris, so if you get any problems then you call him and he'll help you. It's too late to stop a story being printed tonight, but if they harass you or anything then you just call him and he'll put a stop to it. Any fall back at all from this, then you call him, okay?" he instructed, looking at me sternly.

I smiled gratefully and nodded, reaching out and sticking the number on the fridge, using a magnet to hold it up. "Thanks, Carson."

"No worries." He took my hand and walked to the front door, opening it before turning back to me and planting a little kiss on my lips. "I'll see you next weekend at the club," he said softly.

My whole body relaxed at his words. He wasn't running away from me; I hadn't scared him away just yet. I nodded and couldn't keep the happy grin off my face. "Okay, baby, see you then. And drive safe," I instructed.

He winked at me, stepping out the door. "I'm always safe."

I watched him walk off down the hall, heading down the stairs until he was out of view. I sighed at the irony. Once again, he was walking out of my life and all I could do was watch and wait until he would grace me with his presence again.

Chapter Eight

I barely slept that night; instead, I'd lain awake, staring at the ceiling and worrying what they might print about me in the newspapers. What Rory was going to say, the fall-out on our lives, and his friends teasing him about his stripper sister. I finally fell asleep at around five, only to get up just after six with Sasha.

I sat helplessly in the lounge, having no clue what was going on in the outside world. There was nothing on the news as I flicked through the channels before settling on something Sasha would like. It was times like this I wished we could afford a computer or smart phone or something so I could go on the internet and search to see if there was anything written about me.

When Rory got up just after seven, I made some excuse about wanting to get some milk before he left for school. I left him watching Sasha while I practically ran to the nearest shop, scanning every single page of The Peoples' Post to see if there was a picture of me and Carson leaving the club, but there was nothing.

As I got to the last page, the tension seemed to leave my body in one big gust of breath. I closed my eyes, and smiled as I leant against the wall outside the newsagents. Maybe they hadn't managed to get any good photos of us together last night. When the flashes had started, I'd immediately put my hand up to shield my eyes from the light, so maybe I was covering my face or something. Then another thought hit me – maybe it was too late for them to be able to get the article in today's paper. Maybe they missed the deadline to send it to print; maybe it would be in tomorrow's instead. I groaned in frustration. I hated not knowing. No doubt this would cause me another night of missed sleep.

Swearing under my breath, I headed back to my flat.

Rory looked at me curiously when I walked in. "Well?" he asked, looking puzzled.

"Huh?" *Oh, crap, he doesn't know anything, does he? Was it on the TV instead?*

"The milk, Emma!" He laughed, looking at me like I had lost my mind. "You went out to get milk?"

I glanced down at my empty hands and silently cursed myself for not buying a pint to tie in with my lies. "They were sold out?" I suggested weakly, but it sounded more like a question.

He laughed and rolled his eyes. "Right, I'm leaving for school. Remember, I'm going to the library to finish my project after school so I'll be late home," he said, kissing Sasha on top of her head.

"Okay. I'll leave your dinner on the side if you're not back," I said absentmindedly, already starting to think about Carson and the papers again. Rory smiled and headed out the door just as Sasha threw her beaker onto the floor to get my attention. I smiled and looked back at my beautiful baby girl. "What shall we do today? It's just you and me; Mummy's got no classes today. We could go to the park?" I suggested.

She immediately held her arms up to me. "Pak!" she screamed excitedly.

THE REST OF THE WEEK passed much the same. Every day I would run down to the shop after giving Rory a stupid excuse and I would scan the paper, only to find nothing in there at all. With every passing day, I felt a little less scared about it. If they were going to print something they would have done it by now; they obviously thought this wasn't a very good story to run with.

On Friday night, I did my hair as usual, pulled on a pair of grey tracksuit bottoms and a black hoodie of Rory's and then made the fifteen-minute walk to work. As I was walking down the road, I noticed two people leaning against a car outside the club. Frowning, I put my head down as usual so as not to attract unwanted attention. My hand instinctively tightened around my can of pepper spray in my pocket. Sometimes, clients like to wait outside the club for opening time. I'd been grabbed once outside. Luckily, one of the bouncers had arrived at the same time as me and had pushed him off me, but it always made me a little more wary of people hanging around outside there.

I gulped and stole a glance at them, quickening my approach so I could get inside before anything happened. When I was about fifteen-feet from the entrance, both men sprang away from the car. I fought back the urge to scream as I almost jumped out of my skin. Instead of grabbing me, like I was expecting, a light started flashing as someone called my name over and over, trying to get my attention.

Oh, God, the reporters are at the club?

"Emma! Is Carson coming to the club tonight? How long have you been together? What do your parents think of you dating a celebrity? Are you in love with him? What do you think about him seeing other girls?" The questioning was relentless as I sprinted the distance to the club, with them keeping pace alongside me.

I burst through the doors and leant against the wall, panting for breath. They didn't follow me in. In a way, I wish they would have because then I could ask Jerry, one of the bouncers, to escort them away from the club with a not-so-friendly warning. After finally calming my heart rate, I pushed away from the wall and headed upstairs to see Jason. I needed to get hold of Carson and tell him not to come here tonight. If they waited outside on the off-chance of him coming then they would get pictures of him entering the club, and that wouldn't exactly look too good for him.

I spotted Jason and immediately went to him. He smiled as I walked in, obviously completely unaware to the little scene outside. "Jason, do you have Carson's number?"

He frowned and shook his head. "No. Why would I?"

"Don't you have to fill in paperwork to be a member?" I asked, looking at him hopefully. But I already knew the answer to that from when I was doing paperwork at the other club – clients didn't have to give personal details to have a membership, as long as they paid their annual fee.

"We don't hold that kind of information, Emma. You know that. Why, what's up?"

I groaned and put my head down on the bar. "I need to speak to him! There are reporters outside. I think they're going to wait there for him or something."

He touched my arm to get my attention. "Why would they do that?"

I groaned and told him everything that happened the weekend before: how Rodger Harris came to the club and asked a load of questions, how I didn't know he was a reporter, how Carson and I had our photo taken outside Lloyds. He just listened with a thoughtful expression on his face the whole time.

"Okay, so we have no way of contacting Mr Matthews to tell him not to come. He never gave you an emergency number? He's never texted you or anything?" he asked.

The number on my fridge! "I have a number!" I cried excitedly. Grabbing my phone, I called Rory, ignoring the little woman who was telling me I was running low on calling credit and how I needed to top up. Rory answered almost immediately. "Rory, I need the phone number from the fridge," I said quickly.

"Huh? What's up, Emma?"

"Just go to the kitchen and get me the number quickly! It's important. Go now, please," I begged desperately. I heard him walking through the flat and then he reeled off the number. I scribbled it onto a napkin and looked back to Jason, praying this would work. I could call this press agent guy and ask him to pass Carson a message telling him not to come to the club.

THE MAN ON THE PHONE was very polite and understanding. He told me not to worry about a thing, that he would contact Rodger Harris directly and get him to leave the club before my shift finished tonight. He requested I stay inside until he called me back to tell me the coast was clear, so they wouldn't harass me again. I thanked him, grateful, and Jason set a coffee on the bar in front of me.

"How about you work the bar with me tonight, instead of waiting tables?" he offered, smiling sympathetically.

"Thanks, Jason. I'd like that," I admitted. I couldn't face putting on a big, fake smile and having men leer at me all night. All I wanted to do was curl in bed and have Carson wrap his arms around me. This was going to scare him away from me now, for sure. He would see this as just another negative thing, another reason not to come here anymore, and I wouldn't even get a chance to say goodbye. My heart sank with each passing second.

Within half an hour, the club phone rang. Jason was busy serving so I answered it. "Angels Gentlemen's Club," I stated, trying not to let my building depression leak into my voice.

"Hi, can I speak to Emma Bancroft please?"

My breath caught. *Is that... it can't be, can it?* "Carson?"

"Emma? Is that you?" He sounded a little relieved.

My hand tightened around the phone as I pressed it harder to my ear. My eyes filled with tears. "Yeah," I croaked.

"Are you okay? I just had a call from Mason telling me to stay away from the club. He said Rodger Harris was there hounding you again tonight." He actually sounded angry about it.

My eyes widened. Was he angry with me? Was he blaming me for all this, for causing him all this trouble? "Yeah, sorry. I didn't have your number to call you; I only had your press agent's number. I hope you don't mind me calling him," I said, wincing and waiting for him to bitch me out about it.

Carson sighed. "Take my number now," he instructed. I grabbed my phone from my pocket and tapped it in as he told me it. "Emma, are you okay? I could come and get you... take you home?" he suggested.

"You can't come here, baby. Mason told me to stay in here until he called me to say it was clear outside. Do you think they'll leave,

99

or wait until closing?" I nervously glanced out the window. I couldn't see anything because it was too dark, but I still couldn't help but scan the pavement trying to see a figure lingering there.

"They'll leave, don't worry. Mason's going to offer them an exclusive interview with me after my next race, including photos; in exchange, they'll leave you alone. Everything will be fine, Em."

My eyes fluttered closed. I was so much trouble for him. He was having to put himself out, just to get them to leave the club? I hated how this celebrity thing worked. This was my only brush with it, and it made me feel so stressed my stomach hurt. I had no idea how Carson put up with this all the time. It was painful.

"Thanks. I'm so sorry," I mumbled guiltily.

He laughed. "Don't be sorry. I'm just sorry I won't get to see you tonight. You're working tomorrow, though, right? I'll be there tomorrow and see you then instead," he replied, his voice soft and caring.

Smiling at the thought, I pressed my forehead against the wall, letting the cold try to alleviate some of the tension headache building up. "Okay. You think maybe I could get a really big hug tomorrow or something?"

"Emma, if you need me to come there now, I will," he stated, his voice fierce. I knew he would, too. If I asked him to, he would get in his car and drive to the club, to Hell with the reporters. I loved him even more for that. He was so adorable and selfless sometimes, and sometimes it was hard to remember he was just a client of mine and nothing more.

I shook my head sadly, silently wishing I could just say, *yeah, come on over and hold me while I cry onto your shoulder.* "I'm fine. I'll see you tomorrow. I'd better go. I'm working the bar tonight, so I guess I should actually do some work before I get sacked," I teased, trying to lighten my mood. Even the sound of Carson's voice couldn't pull me out of the worried slump I was in.

"Okay. I'll call Mason now and see how he's getting on." He disconnected the call and I just stared at the phone for a minute, wondering just how my life became this complicated.

After another hour, Mason called me back. He'd sorted everything; the reporters had agreed to leave so I was free to go home. He asked to speak to Jason after, so I passed the phone over, watching and trying to work out what was going on. There was just a lot of agreeing and nodding in understanding from Jason's end, so I couldn't gauge anything from him.

When he hung up the phone, he smiled. "Okay, so you can go home now. One of the bouncers will be driving you and walking you to your flat, as per Mr Matthews' orders," he said, shrugging casually.

I gasped. Carson had insisted someone drive me home? No doubt he'd arranged for some sort of payment for this to happen, too. "Carson paid to let me finish my shift early, right?" I rolled my eyes in exasperation.

Jason's smirk told me I'd hit the nail on the head. "I'll go speak to Jerry, get him to pull the car up out front and check to make sure they're definitely gone from outside." He disappeared for a few minutes, sorting everything out, and I smiled sadly.

Hopefully with Carson doing this exclusive interview for them, then this would be the end of it. I prayed it was anyway because this was extremely stressful.

I WOKE THE NEXT MORNING to the sound of urgent knocking on the front door. Groaning, I pushed myself out of bed, glancing at the clock. It was barely seven. The knocking continued – and woke Sasha, too. She looked at me a little grumpily as I headed out of the bedroom, making my way to the door, rubbing my tired eyes.

After checking the chain was on the door, I pulled it open, wondering who on Earth would be knocking on my front door at stupid o'clock in the morning. As soon as the door opened a few inches, I could hear the clicking of cameras. Someone shoved their hand in through the gap, thrusting a tape recorder in my face.

I gasped and immediately tried to shut the door, but the group of people standing there were holding it open. "Emma, is it true what

The Peoples' Post are claiming this morning? Does Carson really have no idea? Why has it all been kept secret?"

I gasped and barged the door again, trying to shut it. "Just go away! What are you all doing here?" I cried angrily. How on Earth would they know where I lived? How could they just turn up at my door like this unannounced – wasn't this harassment?

Their relentless questions and clicking of cameras continued as I pushed the guy's hand back out of my door, finally managing to get it slammed shut. Slumping against the door, I burst into tears. A feeling of violation washed over me because of the group of people just turning up outside my flat, banging on the door at this time of the morning.

My mind flicked to Rory. How was I even going to begin to explain this to him? Something had to have been printed in the paper today, because the reporters were asking if it was true.

They were still pounding on the door and shouting questions when suddenly, the phone started to ring. Rory walked out of his bedroom, his eyes still half-closed. He stopped short when he saw me sitting on the floor, my back against the door, crying while people banged outside and shouted for my attention.

"Emma, what the hell?" he cried, running to my side and wrapping his arm around me. "What's going on? Who's at the door?"

I gulped and wiped my face. "Reporters. Don't open the door, okay? I'll get the phone." I pushed myself up weakly and headed to the phone. Sasha was crying in my bedroom, obviously not liking the fact I'd left her in her cot.

As soon as I answered the phone, I wished I hadn't. "Emma, do you have any comments on the article in The Peoples' Post today?"

They knew my number, too? "No! Just leave me alone. Please?" I begged. I really couldn't cope with any more stress in my life. My life was hard enough without people branding me a stripper in the papers. I hung up the phone and it immediately started ringing again.

"What's going on, Emma?" Rory demanded.

I closed my eyes as I spoke. "There have been a few reporters asking some things about me and Carson. They took some photos last week of him and me together for my birthday, then last night they were at the club, too. Apparently, they've printed something about me in The Peoples' Post this morning, and they're all asking for comments about it."

He frowned and snatched the ringing phone from my hand, an angry expression on his face. "Who is this?" he demanded down the line. I didn't hear the answer, but Rory looked even more pissed off. "No, she doesn't have any comment! Stop calling here!"

As soon as he disconnected the call, the phone started ringing again. *Oh, God, surely the fact that Carson is friends with a stripper isn't this big a story!* If they were hoping I was going to sell him out or do some sort of kiss-and-tell story on him then they were very much mistaken!

I walked over to the phone socket and ripped the lead from the wall, instantly silencing the phone. Everything was deathly silent for a few seconds – until Sasha cried louder, the banging resumed on the door and, thirty seconds later, my mobile started to ring.

I felt trapped; I couldn't even leave the flat because there were reporters outside waiting. It was actually kind of scary; the feeling of being penned in made me feel a little queasy. I debated calling Carson; after all, he did give me his number the night before. I quickly decided against it, though, because if I called him he would probably race over here and then it would just add more fuel to whatever story had been printed about us. Instead, I decided to call Mason; technically this was his job.

I ran to my bedroom, picking Sasha up from her cot and giving her a quick cuddle as I rejected the call from the unknown number coming into my mobile. "Can you just keep her quiet in the lounge for a couple of minutes while I call someone to try and get them away from the front door?" I asked, passing Sasha to Rory.

He nodded and immediately headed out of the room. I didn't have any credit on my mobile, so I quickly plugged the landline back in and dialled Mason's number. He answered almost immediately, yawning and sounding like I'd woken him. "Mason, it's Emma Bancroft. I'm sorry to call you so early," I started.

"No problem, Emma. What can I do for you?" he asked, his voice husky and thick with sleep.

"There are reporters banging on my front door and calling my phone right now. They're asking questions about Carson again. They said something about an article in The Peoples' Post this morning, but I don't know what it's about," I said weakly, swiping at the tears which just wouldn't stop flowing down my face.

"You have people there right now?"

"Yeah. There are about four or five guys banging on my front door as we speak." I looked down the hallway and saw my letterbox move. I frowned until I saw a pair of eyes peeking through; the shouting of my name got a little louder as he spotted me. I jerked back into the kitchen quickly. "And now they're looking through my letterbox," I added, sniffing loudly.

"Okay, don't panic; I'll sort everything. I'll have police officers there in a few minutes to move them away from your door. There are rules, and they're not allowed to harass you. I'll have them moved to outside your building while I try to sort this out." His calmness was very reassuring and made my worry fade marginally. "What was printed? Do you have a copy?"

I sighed. "No. I have no idea. Sorry."

"It's no problem. Damn Rodger Harris, he agreed last night not to print anything about you two." He sighed heavily. "Can I call you back on this number?"

I frowned. "Umm… They keep calling this number and my mobile number, so I was going to turn them both off," I admitted.

"Okay, yeah, that's a good idea. Disconnect your phone, don't speak to anyone. If there are any problems, you call me immediately. Call me in an hour for an update, okay? And, Emma…stay inside until I tell you, all right?"

"Absolutely. Thanks. I'll call you in an hour then."

As soon as I hung up the phone, I disconnected it and turned off my mobile, too.

Within ten minutes, the shouting stopped outside my door and a polite knocking sounded. "Miss Bancroft, please open the door. It's the police," someone called. I gulped and looked through my eyepiece to see two police officers standing there. Sighing with relief, I opened the door. They smiled kindly. "Miss Bancroft?"

I nodded. "Yeah."

"We've moved them downstairs, outside the main entrance because there are distance limits for reporters. The banging on your door will stop now. We'll wait downstairs until they disperse. You have Mason Bossley on the case, so hopefully it'll be within the next couple of hours. If you could just tell us if you plan on leaving your flat so we're aware," one of them said, looking me over a little curiously. Maybe he was wondering what all the fuss was about, and how a petite lap dancer in a pair of worn-out pyjamas could cause so much trouble.

I winced. I wasn't planning on going anywhere, but I didn't want to trap Rory and Sasha inside with me all day. *Maybe I should ask Lucie if they can go to hers for the day, and possibly the night, too.*

"Umm...I have a daughter. I was thinking maybe I should get her to my friend's house or something?" I suggested, looking at them for their opinions. They would have more idea of how to deal with this situation than me so I was open to their advice.

"Yes, we're aware of your daughter. Maybe it's a good idea to have her go to a trusted friend until this all blows over. I don't recommend you take her, though. Do you have someone who could take her out of the building and to your friend's? A neighbour, perhaps? Someone who could slip out unnoticed with your daughter," the policeman suggested.

I gulped. That made sense. I looked to the door next to mine. "Mrs Miller? She lives right next door. She could take her with my brother, too. My friend lives about a ten minute walk away," I agreed, nodding enthusiastically.

I left it to them to sort out with Mrs Miller, and I called Lucie who, of course, agreed quickly. She really was the best friend a girl could ask for. After half an hour, Rory, Mrs Miller and Sasha left to go to Lucie's. Rory went first and was to wait around the corner so they didn't all leave together. The police informed me that Mrs Miller and Sasha had apparently strutted out of the building without the reporters even batting an eyelid at them; obviously they just saw a woman carrying a child and thought nothing of it because she wasn't me. I sank to the sofa with relief. As soon as I got the call from Lucie saying they had all arrived safely, I disconnected my phone again, sat on the sofa and cried.

After another hour, there came another urgent banging on the door. I groaned and pushed myself up, opening the door, expecting to see the police who I knew were still here. But instead I saw Carson. He looked murderously angry, his eyes tight and stressed, his hair messy like he'd been pulling on it or something.

"Hi." I sighed with relief that he was here. I really, really needed a hug from him.

He didn't smile, his jaw clenched as he shoved a newspaper into my chest. "What the fuck is this?" he growled, his words coming out slowly and full of acid.

I frowned and looked down at the paper he'd thrust at me. Splashed across the front was a picture of Carson and me coming out of Lloyds last weekend, and another smaller picture in the corner of Sasha at the park, me pushing her on the swings. The title on the paper made my heart stop and my blood run cold. Now I understood why he looked so furious.

Chapter Nine

"Oh, God," I mumbled. I couldn't breathe. How did they know? How had they known she was Carson's? Why hadn't they just assumed I had a baby with someone else? How did they piece it together that she was his? And how the heck had they gotten these pictures of us at the park? That was Monday. I hadn't seen anyone following us around on Monday taking pictures!

"Tell me that's bullshit," Carson growled, stabbing his finger into the paper angrily. "Tell me that's your little sister or something."

I gulped and shook my head. I couldn't meet his eyes. I had hoped this moment would never come. I'd always tried to keep this away from him for his own good, so he could live his dream instead of being trapped with a waster like me. How was I going to explain this to him?

"That's not my sister," I whispered.

He let out a load groan. "That's your daughter?" he asked, his voice still tight with anger. I could tell he was trying hard to keep it together and not scream at me, and I was extremely grateful because I wasn't sure I could cope with that on top of everything else.

"Yeah." I nodded, looking at his feet, wishing the ground would open up and swallow me. Or maybe I could somehow magically jump back in time and call in sick the night Rodger Harris came to the club and saw Carson there.

"Is she…" he shifted on his feet uncomfortably, "… mine?" he whispered.

Could I lie and say no? Could I really lie right to his face and save us both the pain of going through this, to save him the burden of having a daughter with someone he didn't love? Deep down, I knew I had to tell the truth now, but I had no idea how he'd react. Maybe he'd want to see her and be in her life, or maybe he'd run a mile and all I'd see of him would be the dust cloud where he left so quickly.

"Carson," I started but stopped, unsure as to what I should say. I couldn't lie to him and say no, but I didn't want him to feel obligated or anything to us.

He snatched the paper from my hands, flicking from the first page, going a few pages in. He held up the double-page spread in front of my face. "You put on her birth certificate that I was the father."

Birth certificate? How would he know that? I glanced at the paper he was waving in front of my face to see Sasha's birth certificate printed there. They had blocked out my address, but everything else was clearly visible: her full name, date and place of birth, my name, where I was born. They had circled the father's name and occupation in red. 'Carson Gerard Matthews, Racing Driver' was printed there clear as day, with my signature at the bottom as the person who gave the information.

"How did they even get that? Why would they put that there?" I asked, shaking my head in disbelief.

He laughed humourlessly. "That's their job, Emma, to research things. They have people everywhere; they just slip someone a few quid in the records office and bam, easy. Now answer the fucking question!" he growled. "Is. She. Mine?"

His tone made the hair on the back of my neck stand up on end. I gulped and nodded.

"Jesus, Emma! For fucking hell's sake!" he shouted. He stepped into the hallway, grabbing my arm and making me step back as he slammed the door shut with so much force it sprang back open again. He smashed his hand on it, slamming it again. I whimpered; I'd never seen Carson angry, and he was actually scaring me a little. "How could you not tell me something like this? How? WHY?" he ranted. His face turned slightly red from anger.

I flinched and bumped into the wall as he stepped forward again. "I'm sorry. I thought I was doing the right thing," I whispered. He stepped forward again, his hand slamming into the wall by the side of my head. He was glaring at me with so much hate I actually felt scared of him, but at the same time he looked so hurt I just wanted to wrap my arms around him and hold him.

"You're sorry? I have a fucking daughter I didn't know about, and you're *sorry*?" he snapped, his face inches from mine.

"I didn't want to trap you," I whispered. Big, fat tears were silently rolling down my cheeks.

He pushed himself away from me and instantly I both missed his closeness and breathed a sigh of relief that he had given me some space to breathe. He turned his back on me and gripped his hands in his hair.

"She's two?" he asked, looking over his shoulder at me, his expression unreadable.

"Next month," I confirmed, nodding.

His body was still and tense. "How the hell could you keep something like this from me? Why didn't you tell me?" he spat, glaring at me.

I swiped at the tears falling uncontrollably. He was looking at me like he hated me, and it was breaking my heart. To see the man I loved look at me with such distaste and revulsion actually made my legs feel a little weak.

"I was thinking of you," I whispered.

He snorted and rounded on me again, trapping me against the wall, his angry face millimetres from mine. His breath was blowing across my cheek as he spoke. "You were thinking of me? Do you want me to thank you then?" he snapped sarcastically.

I whimpered and shook my head, silently wondering if he was actually going to hurt me. I'd never seen anyone so angry, and the way he was looking at me made me nervous. Deep down, I wondered if I deserved him to hurt me. Maybe I'd made the wrong choice, and I deserved to be punished like my parents had always told me. They had always reminded me every day of what a dirty little tramp I was, how I was a disappointment which wouldn't amount to anything and how I had the devil inside me. Maybe I really did and I'd just refused to see it until now.

"Thank you for keeping my daughter away from me, Emma. Thank you for keeping things like her first step or word away from me. Maybe I'm better off not knowing her. Is that what you mean by 'thinking of me'? Or maybe you thought I didn't deserve to share those things with you?" he ranted. His hands were on either side of my body, trapping me against the wall as his body pressed against mine heavily, pinning me there.

"Carson, I…"

"All this time, you've been seeing me every week, screwing me even, and you were keeping this from me?" he hissed, shoving himself away from me again and gripping his hands in his hair roughly, growling in frustration. "How could you not tell me? All this time!"

I slid down the wall, hugging my knees to my chest as I cried.

He laughed coldly. "Yeah, bring on the waterworks, Emma. That's gonna sort everything out!" he said sarcastically.

"I was thinking of you," I said again. My voice broke and hitched with sobs as I spoke. "When I found out I was pregnant, you were just starting to take off with your career. I didn't want to take your dreams away from you. I didn't want to trap you with a stupid little sixteen-year-old girl, because you deserved better than that. I wanted better for you than to be a teenage father," I admitted. I pressed my face into my knees, feeling my tears soaking into the material of my jeans.

He sighed heavily. "So, you went through that on your own. Instead of telling me and letting me help you, you did it on your own. This is why you work at the club, so you can afford a daughter and a little brother."

I nodded, and sniffed.

"You've kept this from me for two years. You've seen me make all this money, and the whole time you've been struggling to raise my daughter on your own," he said quietly. Movement sounded from beside me and something bumped my shoulder. I turned my head slightly to see he'd slid down the wall and was sitting next to me. His head was in his hands, his whole body language sad and defeated.

"I don't want your money." I closed my eyes and tried to think about anything other than the pounding in my head that was making me feel queasy.

We sat in silence for a little while; I didn't know what to say. I knew I needed to let him process this. I'd had two years and nine months to accept being a mum, but he'd had parenthood thrust on him this morning.

Finally, he spoke, his voice husky and deep where he hadn't said anything for a while. "Her name's Sasha?"

I smiled. "Sasha Eloise Bancroft," I confirmed.

He sniffed and wiped his face. "That's a nice name." I nodded; I loved her name. "What does she look like? In the papers, you can only see the back of her head." He turned to look at me. I gulped when I saw how red his eyes were. Had he been crying while we were sitting there? I desperately wanted to comfort him, but I couldn't even move my arms from my hugging position on my knees. It was like I was frozen there.

"She's beautiful. She looks like you." I smiled weakly as I looked at the bright-blue colour to his eyes. "She has the same colour hair and eyes as you, but her hair's curly like mine."

He smiled for a second before it faded again to be replaced by the heartbroken look. "Do you have a picture?"

I nodded and forced myself to move. Pushing myself off the floor and heading into the lounge, I picked up a photo frame from the side. I turned back just as Carson walked in and held it out to him. As he reached out to take it, I noticed his hands were shaking and his breathing was coming out a little shallower than usual. He looked at it silently, just staring at the picture with wide eyes and his lips parted. His face was so soft and tender I felt my heart melt into a puddle.

"She's beautiful," he whispered.

I chewed on my lip, unsure what I should say. I always thought I was doing the right thing by Carson, letting him off, giving him an out from my life. I never wanted him to have to live like I lived every day. I was always confident I'd done the right thing in letting him have his dream. But at this exact moment, looking at him as he looked at a picture of his daughter for the first time, I suddenly felt selfish. I felt like instead of giving him his dream, maybe I'd taken something away from him, taken *her* away from him. Sasha was the best thing that had ever happened to me, but it had never occurred to me that maybe it would be the same for him if I'd have told him.

"Where is she? The police told me she went to a friend's," he said quietly.

"She's at Lucie's because of the reporters. They were banging on the door; I thought it best to get her away from it until it calmed down. Rory's there, too; they're staying there tonight," I explained.

He nodded and ran his thumb over the picture lightly but didn't say anything.

My mouth was dry as his silence stretched on and on. I knew I needed to start this conversation myself. "Carson, you don't have to feel obligated to us or anything. We're doing fine. I don't want your money or anything, but if you want to see her, you can. You can see her as much as you want, or if you don't want anything to do with her, then I understand that, too. She was a mistake, and you don't have to pay for that for the rest of your life," I said, trying to let him know I wouldn't stop him from seeing her if he wanted to.

His head snapped up to look at me. "*If* I want to see her? Is that a fucking joke? Of course I want to see her, she's my daughter!" he retorted. His eyes turned angry again as his jaw clenched and unclenched.

I nodded and swallowed awkwardly. "Okay, well, you can come around here whenever you want."

He laughed coldly, shaking his head as if I were stupid. "I'm not leaving my daughter here to be brought up on a fucking part-time lap dancer's salary!" he hissed.

My back stiffened. 'Leaving her here.' I looked at him warningly. If he thought he was taking her away from me then he had another thing coming. "What's that supposed to mean exactly?" His eyes turned calculating as I spoke. "You can see her whenever you want; we'll arrange visits and stuff…" I trailed off, the hair on the nape of my neck standing up as panic gripped my stomach.

He snorted when I said the word 'visits'. "You think I'm leaving her in this shitty little flat with a mother who can barely afford to support her? You think that's fair on her, being raised like a fucking pauper?" He sneered at me distastefully.

Anger took over as the dominant emotion in my body, so I shoved his chest as hard as I could and glared at him. How dare he insinuate I wasn't giving her everything she needed! Sure, it was hard most of the time and we'd probably never have the money for laptops or iPods when she was older, but I loved her more than anything and I would give her everything she needed. Material things didn't matter as long as a child was loved, happy and healthy.

"You stupid prick! Don't you dare insinuate I'm not looking after my daughter properly!" I screamed, shoving on his chest again.

He snorted. "Emma, you can probably just about pay your rent each month and go to university. How can you give her everything she needs? What about when she needs a school trip or something and you don't have the money. Are you gonna pull extra nights at the club? What happens when you fall short on the rent one month? Gonna sell your body in the backroom? You think she'll thank you when she finds out her mother is a whore who sells herself?" he asked spitefully.

Before I could stop myself, I drew back my hand and slapped his face as hard as I could. His head whipped to the side and instantly my hand stung and burned. "Well, a whore who sells herself was good enough for her prick of a father!" I screamed. *How does this boy always manage to make me feel dirty, cheap and nasty?* He looked back at me, his eyes softening as if he knew he went too far. But it was too late. I wasn't going to let him make me feel dirty anymore; that was the last time. The way he'd said it just to hurt me, I never thought Carson would ever do that. "Get out," I growled through my teeth.

"I'm not going anywhere," he said sternly, his jaw clenching. I noticed with some small measure of satisfaction that his cheek was turning red where I'd struck him.

"Get the hell out before I call the police in here to remove you!" I ordered, defiantly crossing my arms over my chest.

He laughed and stepped closer to me, reaching out and stroking one finger across my cheek. "Oh, sweetheart, you really think the police are going to do something a lap dancer tells them to do, over me?" he asked, his voice teasing and mocking.

I swallowed loudly and looked at him with as much hate as I could muster. I tried not to look into his eyes because I knew my resolve would waiver as soon as I looked into those baby-blues I loved so much. "Get out," I repeated.

He leant in closer to me, gripping my chin and forcing me to meet his eyes. "Go pack a bag, we're leaving. No daughter of mine is going to live in a place like this. Pack your stuff, enough for a couple of days, and I'll get people to come and pack up the rest," he stated coldly. He released my chin and stepped back, crossing his arms over his chest, his face hard and determined.

My mouth popped open in shock. Did he honestly think I was going to let him take her from me? My mind started spinning through thoughts of how I could pick up Sasha from Lucie's and leave. There was no way I was letting him take her from me. My credit card would get us far away from here, and if I had to then I'd crawl to my parents for help. I couldn't lose the most important thing in my life. I couldn't let him take her; she was my everything.

"Carson, don't do this! I'll let you see her whenever you want, I promise, but I won't let you take her from me." I looked at him warningly. The only thing stopping me from having a full-blown panic attack was the fact he didn't know where Lucie lived. If I needed to, I could call Rory, tell him to take Sasha and get on a train and go as far away as he could, and then I could go and meet him.

His eyebrows pulled together in confusion. "What are you talking about? I'm not taking her away from you."

Now I was confused. "But you said pack a bag," I said weakly. The urge to run to collect my baby was making my legs twitch and my hands wring together anxiously.

Understanding suddenly crossed his face and he rolled his eyes, looking a little bored. "Stop being stupid. I meant both of you, and Rory, too. Go pack your stuff up. Now."

As his words sank in, the anger was back. He seriously thought he could just waltz in and order me around like some kind of prostitute he could buy with a few quid? I raised my chin confidently. I wasn't going anywhere with him, not after what he just said to me about being a whore.

"Screw you, Carson. I'm not going anywhere with you!"

He smirked at me and I fought hard against the urge to find that sexy. I hated that even after what he'd said and the way he looked at me so distastefully I still couldn't fight my attraction to him.

"Did I ever tell you my sorry-arse excuse for a father walked out on my mum when I was five? He left her to go be with some slut who was barely out of her teens. My mum struggled every day to bring up me and my two little sisters. I saw what that did to her and how it beat her down over the years, and I hated my father so much for it. Every time I saw my mum cry, every time I saw her look at something in a shop that she wanted but couldn't afford, every time I saw her put on a fake smile while she tried her best but fell short, it made me hate my father a little bit more. I refuse to have my daughter feel like that about me. So pack a sodding bag, Emma. I'm not letting my daughter grow up to be a bastard like I was. I don't give a shit what you want. You, Sasha and Rory are coming to live with me, and you and I... we're getting married."

My heart leapt into my throat. Married? Had he seriously just said that? My mouth dropped open in shock as I looked at his confident face. I actually didn't know whether to jump for joy because the man I loved had just suggested we get married, or punch him in his face because the one time I wanted to be proposed to and he just completely screwed it up and made it a demand instead of a question.

The anger won.

"Really? I don't think so, Mr Matthews. You see, there's this thing called free will and the last time I checked, you can't force someone to marry you because you don't want your daughter to hate you," I retorted acidly, shaking my head.

He gripped my wrist and yanked me to him so my chest crashed against his. "Oh, you're going to marry me, Emma," he countered, smirking at me.

I threw off his hold and stepped back to get some personal space. "You think so?"

He nodded and raised one eyebrow. "I know so." He stepped closer to me again, bending so we were at the same level, his eyes boring into mine. "Because if you don't go pack a bloody bag right now, I'm putting in a call to the best, most expensive lawyer in England. Then I'll take you to court and petition for full custody of our daughter. I'll tell the courts how you can't afford to live, and how you sell your body to clients at the club. My lawyers will rip you to shreds. By the time I've finished, they'll only let you see her for a week in the summer and every other Christmas for supervised visits. Don't you think I won't do it, because I will. And don't even think about running away with her somewhere, because wherever you go, I'll find you, and it'll just look even better for my case," he hissed in my ear.

I closed my eyes. This wasn't the Carson I fell in love with, was it? Had I really fallen for someone who would threaten to take away the most important thing to a mother, just to get what he wanted? Did I even know Carson Matthews at all? Maybe the Carson I knew was an act and this one was the real one, the hard, ruthless, heartless man standing in front of me.

"You wouldn't," I whispered, praying that was true. I don't know what hurt the most: the fact he was threatening this, or the fact I had just realised the love of my life wasn't the person I thought he was.

"Oh, I damn well would. You've already taken two years of her life away from me; I won't let you take anymore. Now, get in there, pack a bag for you, Sasha and Rory, and let's go," he ordered, taking my arm and giving me a little push in the direction of my bedroom.

I burst into a fresh round of tears. If he'd just asked me nicely, if he'd just suggested moving in with him and marrying him, then I would be the happiest girl in the world. I'd dreamt over and over of Carson proposing to me and us living in a cute little house with a garden. Never once had it happened like this. Never once had it been a demand or threat. Never once had it made me feel like a pile of dirt he'd just stepped in.

How could I marry a guy who I knew had no feelings for me? The only reason he wanted to get married was because his dad had left his family when he was younger and he didn't want Sasha to feel the same about him. He was breaking my heart because if someone had told me yesterday I would be getting engaged to Carson and moving in with him, I would have felt like I'd won the lotto. Instead, I felt like a dirty, used prostitute. Something for him to throw money at again – but instead of handing me cash this time, he was handing me house keys and his surname. But somehow, the fact that he didn't love me hurt me most of all. Sure, I would have his name, but he wouldn't love me. Was he seriously expecting me to stick around and play wife while he went out sleeping with anything that moved, like he did now?

I looked at him pleadingly. If he just told me he loved me, or at least liked me, he didn't even have to love me. I could live with the fact I would never be good enough for him. If he just took that hateful look off his face, if he just looked at me like he always did, his eyes soft and caring…

"You think raising a child in a loveless marriage is better than us just being friends and you seeing her when you want?" I asked, my voice breaking through emotion. The question would give him the perfect opportunity to tell me he felt something for me, a little something. I'd take anything, any small bone he would throw me.

He frowned. "I'm not into half-arsed jobs. We have a daughter together, therefore we'll *be* together. I'm not just gonna be one of those dads who turn up every other weekend to take their kids out. I want to be there for her."

My heart sank further. He hadn't said anything about me. It was all about Sasha. I was just part of the package that came with his daughter and nothing more, just the annoying lap dancer he liked to screw occasionally. The fact that I was nothing more to him almost killed me inside.

"I hate you," I lied, raising my chin and looking him right in the eyes, trying to get some sort of reaction out of him.

His eye twitched but other than that, he didn't even move. "Thanks. Now, go pack your fucking bags."

Chapter Ten

I headed to my bedroom, my heart broken. The love of my life was demanding we get married, so I should be happy; hell, I should be the happiest girl in the world. But I wasn't.

I looked back at him, and his hard, tight eyes stared straight back at me. The usual warmth and tenderness was entirely gone from them. He regarded me like I was an annoying, dirty little stripper he felt obligated to marry. He actually looked like he despised me.

Swallowing my sob, I grabbed a couple of sets of my clothes, putting them in the middle of my bed. I sorted Sasha's stuff next, bundling up nappies, wipes, clothes, sleepwear, and dummies. I pulled open the drawer containing her blankets and sheets, unsure if I needed this type of thing. I didn't want to talk to him again, but clearly I had to. I flicked my eyes over to him; he was leaning casually against my doorframe, watching my every move as if he thought I was going to bolt out the front door any second.

"Do I need bed sheets for Sasha?" I asked quietly.

He frowned at my question. "Er, I don't know. What does she usually have?" His eyes settled on the cot at the foot of my bed and his nose crinkled in distaste. "I'll buy a new cot," he stated, waving his hand at it dismissively. Obviously, the second-hand cot Lucie gave me wasn't good enough for him.

I closed my eyes and took a deep breath. He had a real talent for making me feel useless and dirty with just a few words. "Fine. What about sheets?" I asked, swiping at the tear which fell down my face.

He groaned, rubbing his temples in small circles. "I don't know... I'll buy all new stuff!"

I threw the sheets back into the drawer. "Have you even thought this through? Do you have any idea how hard it is to live with a two-year-old? It's not all fun and games, you know. This is my daughter's life we're talking about. Trust me, it's hard," I spat, looking at him knowingly. Maybe I could scare him into thinking about it again.

His eyes narrowed. "I'm not stupid, Emma. I know it's gonna be hard, but I'm not one to walk away from my responsibilities. I'm here now to make it easier for you, all of you. Please, just pack your shit, just enough for a couple of days. Everything else we'll get new or pick up another time."

I sighed, threw another armful of clothes onto the bed, and then headed to the bathroom, grabbing wash things and toothbrushes before heading to Rory's room. I tried not to go through his personal items too much as I grabbed his clothes. I had no idea what Rory was going to say about all this. How was he going to feel when he found out his big sister got knocked up by a client in the strip club she worked for? I hadn't told him. I'd lied and told him it was a guy I'd been seeing for a few weeks. I couldn't bear to see any disapproval from him at the time, so I'd hidden the truth.

I headed back to my room, setting Rory's clothes on my bed. I didn't bother with school books; he could have a couple of days off. Hopefully, I'd be able to talk some sense into Carson and then we could just go back to normal before this went too far. I looked at the huge pile of stuff on the middle of the bed wondering what I could put it in.

I bit my lip and Carson stepped up next to me. "You have a suitcase or something?" he asked, looking around my room.

I laughed humourlessly and shook my head. "No." Suitcases were for people that could afford to go on holiday. That certainly wasn't us.

He sighed. "A bag then? Anything?"

I sat on the edge of the bed and put my head in my hands. "Carson, please, I know you think you're doing the right thing, but you're not. Raising a child in a home where the parents don't love each other can be worse than being raised by a single parent. Let's just talk about this. You don't really want to marry me, and I don't want to marry you."

Only part of that statement was true. I would marry him in a heartbeat if he just told me he cared about me, even just the smallest bit. If he smiled at me and asked me to marry him, I would say yes immediately, and I would play the dutiful little wife for the rest of my days. The wife who did everything her husband wanted – the perfect little wife who had dinner on the table when he walked through the door and her sexiest underwear under her clothes just in case. I would do that for him in a heartbeat if he would just give me the smallest sign of affection.

I looked at him again, silently begging him for a smile, a touch, a kiss, anything.

"We're not talking about it, it's decided," he stated confidently.

I needed to try another tactic. "If you really don't like her living here, then set up some sort of trust fund for her. If this is about what I can afford, then help me. Please, don't force us all into something that's gonna make everyone miserable in the long run," I begged.

He didn't say anything, just walked out of the room, leaving me staring after his back with my heart in my throat. He was being so cold to me. Was it because I hadn't told him about Sasha? If I had told him when I was pregnant, would he have insisted the exact same thing he was insisting now? I gulped and rubbed my eyes. I just needed to go back to sleep and then wake up to find out this was just a horrible nightmare. That was what it felt like; the way Carson was looking at me with those hard hateful eyes felt like something from my worst nightmare.

He padded back into the room with a couple of black bin liners. Silently, I watched as he started picking up all the things I'd put on the bed, throwing them into the bags. "Is there anything else you want to take?" He didn't even look at me as he spoke.

I pushed myself up from the bed. He couldn't even be bothered to answer my questions or discuss it with me. It was my life, Sasha's and Rory's lives, and he was just making all the decisions. And we just had to go along with it?

"You're a fucking arsehole, Carson," I growled.

"Yeah, and you hate me, I know," he replied in his detached tone.

Anger fizzed inside me. Without thinking, I slapped his shoulder. He turned to glare at me so I slapped his chest, taking out all my frustration on him. When I raised my hand to hit him again, he grabbed my wrist tightly and shook his head. A second later, his other hand closed over my shoulder as he threw himself at me, slamming me against the wall and kissing me fiercely. He was kissing me so hard it was hurting my lips, but I kissed him back immediately.

It was raw passion. Anger-fuelled passion. He pinned me against the wall as both of us ravaged the other's mouth like animals. He let go of my wrist and his hands roamed desperately down my body as I wrapped my arms around his neck, pulling him impossibly closer to me, needing to feel his body against mine.

He pulled out of the kiss just as I was gasping for breath and started kissing down my neck. His hands went straight to the buttons of my jeans, pulling on them frantically. I could feel how turned on he was when he pressed his crotch against my hip, showing me just how much he wanted me physically.

I squeezed my eyes shut as a realisation hit me. This was all I was to him. A body, nothing more. Something for him to get his kicks with, just like he did with hundreds of other girls. He wasn't demanding we get married because he wanted to; he was doing it because he didn't want Sasha to hate him.

All this little thing was right now was him laying claim to me, him claiming his dominance over me and my body. But I wouldn't let him have it.

I gulped, trying to find my voice as he pushed my jeans down slightly, his hand groping my bum, one hand slipping down the front of my underwear. "Carson, stop." My voice was barely more than a whisper. His mouth came back to mine and one of his hands wove into my hair, halting my protests as he kissed me roughly. I whimpered into his mouth and pushed on his chest. "Carson, stop it!" I said louder, using my forearms to shove his body away from mine.

He stopped and looked at me, his eyes filled with both want and anger. "Why?" he asked, his voice husky and thick with lust.

I tried desperately to get my breathing under control. "Because I don't want this." Not like this, anyway. It would be easy to just give in to my body's urges because goodness knows I wanted him, but not like this, not just because he was demanding it.

He sneered at me, stepping closer to me again and pressing his hard body to mine. "Would it help if I offered to pay you? How much do you want? What's the going rate for your bedroom?" he shot out.

His spiteful words felt like a punch in the stomach. My eyes filled with devastated tears as my chin quivered. I felt so dirty and used. I'd never felt so low in my life. I couldn't speak. With that one little speech, he'd just showed me exactly how little he thought of me, and exactly how little he cared for me. With that one little speech, he'd ripped my heart out and had torn it into a million pieces.

Almost instantly he frowned, averting his eyes as if he wished he hadn't said it. "I didn't mean that. I shouldn't have…" He stepped back, gripping his hand into his hair as he scowled down at the cheap bedroom carpet. My shoulders slumped as the last of my self-confidence, self-worth and self-belief went out the window. I turned my face away from him as silent tears fell down my cheeks. "Look, I don't even know why I said that. I'm angry, it just slipped out."

I felt empty inside. Everything I'd fought hard for since I was sixteen, everything I'd been through, how hard I'd worked to make something of myself, going to university, being a mum – they were all nothing now, because I was a cheap, dirty whore. The man I loved had just made that clear to me.

I shrugged him off and headed over to the bed where my stuff was half-packed, buttoning up my jeans as I went. "Are you still making us move in with you?" I asked, trying not to display any emotion in my voice as I spoke.

"Yeah," he huffed.

I nodded and threw the remaining clothes and stuff into the bin bags and then picked them up, turning to walk out of the room. I kept my eyes firmly on the door; I refused to even look at him. As I got level with him, he took the bags from my hands.

"Emma?" he called, obviously trying to get my attention.

I just walked off; I couldn't even bring myself to talk to him. I tried to hate him for making me feel this way, but I couldn't. Instead, I hated myself, because everything I was feeling inside was my fault, not his. My parents were right about me all along; I *was* a cheap, dirty girl who had the devil inside her. Maybe I should have just joined that convent when they gave me the chance. Maybe then I'd have been able to save my soul.

I didn't speak to him as I picked up my keys and mobile phone from the side table.

"You're ignoring me now?" he asked incredulously as I stood silently by the front door. "One thing I say in the spur of the moment and I get the silent treatment?"

I gritted my teeth. "I'm not ignoring you; I just have nothing to say to you right now."

He groaned in frustration. "I'm the one who should be fucking angry! You're the one that's kept me in the dark about my daughter, yet you're angry with me?" He shook his head in exasperation. Clearly, he had no idea how much he'd wounded me with his nasty, spiteful comment about paying me for sex. "I'm sorry, all right? I didn't mean what I said. It just came out!"

I shrugged, trying to go for the unaffected approach. "Don't be sorry. You think I'm a dirty whore who sells herself for money, and you're right, I do." Technically, what he said was right; he paid me for sex all the time, so that made me a prostitute of sorts. It didn't matter that I never saw it that way, that I saw it as love-making, that I used the money as if it were a child support payment. Technically, I was a hooker, plain and simple.

His lips parted as his eyebrows rose in shock. "I don't think that."

I sighed sadly. "It doesn't matter if you really think that or not. You're making me move in with you and marry you, or you'll take my daughter away from me. It doesn't matter what you think of me.

123

All I need is for Sasha to be happy, and I need to be with her. So if that means living with someone who makes me feel cheap and used, then so be it." I pulled the door open and stomped down the concrete, graffiti-covered stairs without waiting for him. He was silent as he trudged along behind me, closing the door to my flat before following me down into the damp foyer.

As I reached for the handle of the main door leading outside, his hand closed over mine, stopping me. "Wait," he huffed. I didn't bother looking at him as he spoke. I didn't really care what he had to say because in that moment, I couldn't bring myself to care about anything. "The reporters are probably still outside. They're going to crowd us as soon as we walk out of the building. My car is over on the right-hand side, about four spaces in. Just get in the car and ignore anything they ask you," he instructed.

I nodded once in acknowledgement, keeping my eyes firmly fixed on the door, refusing to even glance in his direction. "Fine." I pulled my hand from his and caught the door handle, yanking it open and stepping out. As soon as I was out of the building, reporters swarmed around me, taking photographs and shouting questions. I raised my chin, put on a fake smile and stalked toward Carson's shiny silver car parked exactly where he said it would be. A second later, the door slammed closed behind me, and then the reporters were shouting questions at him, too. He answered 'no comment' to everything as he jogged to catch me up.

When his arm slipped around my waist, I didn't push him off in front of the cameras. If I had to act like the dutiful little wife so I could be in my daughter's life, then I would.

When we were level with his car, he opened the door for me, waiting until I was in before putting my two bin liners' worth of possessions in the boot and heading to the driver's side. As we peeled out of the car park, I slumped down in my seat and looked out the window, watching as he sped me away from the only place I had truly called home. Admittedly, it wasn't much, but it was home to me. The first and only place I had been happy.

Awkward silence filled the car as I ground my teeth, wallowing in my self-pity and self-hatred. I pulled out my mobile, turning it on and sending a text to Lucie to tell her I was with Carson and I'd call her later. Less than a minute later, she replied telling me Rory and Sasha could stay with her as long as I needed them to.

I relaxed marginally as I read her message, but then my thoughts drifted to Rory and what he would know now. He'd know I'd lied to him about who Sasha's dad was for the last couple of years. I'd have a lot of explaining to do. A lump formed in my throat as I wondered if my little brother would think I was some kind of dirty whore now, too. If he looked at me like Carson had, I wasn't sure how I was going to cope.

I didn't bother paying any attention to where we were going, just watched the streets whizz past without actually seeing them. When we slowed down, I looked out the windscreen to see a big white house, three stories, big windows and heavy-looking wrought iron gates outside. Those big, iron gates were currently swinging slowly open to allow the car inside. The place was incredible, beautiful even. It looked very, very expensive. This kind of property in London would easily set someone back a couple of million pounds. It was every little girl's dream house – but it looked more like a prison to me.

Chapter Eleven

A red light at the side of the garage flashed at the car and a couple of seconds later, the double garage doors automatically rolled open.

"Number plate recognition camera," Carson answered my unanswered question as I frowned at the light, wondering what it was. He pulled the car into the garage, cutting the engine before turning in his seat to look at me. I had nothing to say to him, though. It was like we were strangers now, because the Carson I had met three years ago was long gone, replaced by this mean, nasty person before me. I shoved my door open, climbing out, wanting to be as far away from him as possible.

As I stepped from the car, I couldn't help but gasp as I looked around. The garage I thought was just a double from the front was actually a large, expansive area, which must have stretched under the house itself. It housed five shiny, sleek cars and three motorbikes. It was perfectly clean and looked more like a showroom. I raised one eyebrow in understanding. I'd found what Carson liked to spend his money on.

Behind me, I could hear him getting my bags from the boot, but I didn't bother to offer help. He was the one who insisted on this ridiculous charade, so I figured he could struggle and suffer the consequences.

"This way," he muttered, stalking toward the door at the back of the garage.

I followed him quietly, watching as he punched a code into a little black box next to the door. When the door lock clicked, he pushed it open, stepped to the side and motioned for me to step through in a *'ladies first'* gesture. I resisted the urge to laugh. I'd gone from prostitute to lady in the space of half an hour; that was impressive.

After walking up a flight of stairs, I opened the door at the top and stepped into the hallway of his house. I stopped immediately; the damn hallway was bigger than my lounge, and it was exquisite. I gulped as I stared at the expensive-looking ornaments on the side. Glass doors led to, what I assumed was, the lounge because it had sofas and one whole wall was completely covered in a pull-down TV. The place screamed three words: money, show and bachelor.

I smiled wickedly to myself. *Sasha is going to have a field day smashing up all his expensive crap!*

Carson cleared his throat behind me, setting my bags down. "I'll give you a quick tour now, and I'll sort out keys and passwords and stuff for the doors later. Other than vehicle recognition, the main entrances are opened by keypad, so if you forget a key then you can still get in. Handy really, considering I've almost locked myself out tons of times," he joked, smiling weakly.

"Great," I mumbled, trying to fake interest.

He sighed and a frown creased his forehead, which I longed to smooth away with my fingertip. "You could at least smile or something. This place is infinitely better than the shithole you were living in. At least here you can step out the front door without the fear of being gang-raped or shot for sport."

I scoffed and shook my head incredulously. "Oh, I'm sorry, you were expecting me to fall at your feet and thank you for letting me live in your incredible house? Was I supposed to take one look at your stupid, elegant sweeping staircase and be all grateful you're making me marry you under threat of losing my daughter?" I retorted sarcastically. I made a show of patting my jeans' pockets before I shook my head. "Nope, sorry. Looks like I'm all out of fucks to give." If he was expecting me to be impressed by the fact he had a nice house and suddenly love the idea of being married against my will, even though he thought I was some kind of tramp, then he would be sorely disappointed. No one had ever hurt me as much as he had. It had been the look in his eyes. If it had been someone else that had said it then maybe I could have shaken it off, but seeing that look from the man I loved had crushed my soul a little. I'd never forget it.

His frown grew more pronounced as a muscle in his jaw twitched. His eyes told me he wanted to say something nasty back, but he was obviously choosing his words carefully. Instead, he said nothing and turned his back on me, stalking up the long, marble hallway toward the door at the end.

I chewed on my lip in anger. Maybe we needed to have a good argument, a good airing-out session before we could then talk about it and reason it out – but it appeared Carson wasn't the arguing type. After hesitating for a few seconds, I finally followed him, leaving a big gap between us. He stepped into the room at the end and held the door open for me, not looking at me. As I stepped through, I came face to face with the most beautiful kitchen I had ever seen. My stomach instantly growled at the thought of cooking in a place like this. The cupboards were white, sleek and shiny. There were no handles, so it was extremely sophisticated-looking. The built-in appliances were stainless steel, and the worktop was black granite. It looked like something out of a celebrity magazine.

"Obviously, this is the kitchen. You can use anything you want. There's not much food in at the moment, I don't think, but I'll fix that. You'll have to write me a list or something of stuff you three like and I can order it in." He pointed to the oven and frowned. "I don't know how that works. There are probably some instructions around somewhere."

I raised one eyebrow. "You don't cook then?"

He shook his head in answer. "No, I have a housekeeper. I pay her extra to cook for me."

"I guess this is how the other half lives," I muttered under my breath, touching the cold granite surface, still awed over how stunning it was.

"I'll show you the rest." He didn't wait for me as he stalked from the room and down the hallway. I followed behind him like a wounded puppy. After looking in the dining room, the games room, the conservatory, the study, the TV room, and then the formal lounge, I came to the conclusion that I would never, ever feel at home in this place. It was all too clinical, too white, no colour or personality. It was like Carson had a designer come in and set the house up just for show. He probably didn't even spend that much time in any of these rooms. With a two-year-old living here, it wouldn't stay this beautiful for long. Once sticky fingers touched the walls and juice cups were carelessly abandoned on the cream carpets, the place would certainly feel lived-in then.

Just as we were about to head upstairs, his phone rang. He looked at the caller ID and stopped walking. "I have to take this. It's Mason."

I nodded, folding my arms across my chest while he headed into the lounge. I tried not to listen to him talking to his press agent, but I couldn't exactly help it. His voice was getting louder as he spoke; they were talking about Sasha and me. He was telling Mason about how it was true and how we were moving in with him and getting married. The way he explained everything so calmly made it all sound so incredibly normal, and a little shiver ran through me. Mason obviously wasn't too sold on the idea, though, because Carson was getting angry. I could hear him telling Mason it wasn't a mistake, that he wasn't going to brush it under the carpet and he wasn't going to pay us off and deny everything to the press just to make his life easier.

Figuring the tour wasn't going to resume anytime soon, I sat on the bottom step and rested my head on the wall. Carson was getting even more passionate in there as he talked about wanting to get to know his daughter, and how he would take care of her – her *and* me. I couldn't help the little smile, which tugged at the corner of my mouth when he lumped me in with Sasha. Then they were down to planning, statements which needed to be drafted, and when we were going to pick up Sasha. Carson wanted something called a blanket order put on both Sasha and Rory. If I remembered correctly, that meant no one would be able to print a picture of their faces in the papers or magazines.

My eyes were getting heavy as I eavesdropped.

I SNUGGLED AGAINST THE WARM THING, pressing my face into it, breathing it in. It smelt delicious and made my heart race. Cracking my eyes open, I looked around. Confusion settled over me as I realised I wasn't at home. All I could see were white walls, splashed with the occasional canvas. I was laying on something soft; I turned my head and looked up to see Carson looking down at me.

What on Earth?

Then I remembered everything: the reporters, the arguing with Carson, the demands he was making. I gulped as my heart broke all over again, remembering the way he looked at me, the way those spiteful words sounded in his smooth voice.

It took me a couple of seconds to realise I was lying on my back on the sofa with my head in his lap. His arm was resting across my body, his thumb stroking my stomach lightly, making my skin break out in goose bumps at the feel of his skin on mine. I wanted to punch myself for reacting to his touch when I was supposed to hate him. Apparently, my stupid, traitorous body couldn't seem to remember the way he looked down his nose and sneered at me so distastefully.

I pushed myself up, sitting on the sofa, and blushed because I was so close to him. My body still reacted to his even though I didn't want it to. My mouth yearned to be on his, and my fingers itched to touch him and caress him. As I sat up, his hand dropped off my stomach and he looked at me with a small, sad smile on his face. I'd never felt awkward around Carson since the first moment I met him, but it was almost as if we didn't know how to act around each other anymore. As if we'd lost the connection we once had, the connection I treasured.

"Hey. You okay?" he asked, brushing my hair behind my ear, making the skin on my cheek tingle where his fingers touched. I gulped and nodded. The corner of his lips twitched with a smile. "You must be the only person I've ever met that can fall asleep sitting up with your head against a wall."

I laughed uncomfortably. "Yeah, it's one of my many talents."

Flicking my eyes around the room again, I spotted a clock on the wall. It was just after one. As if on cue, my stomach rumbled, signalling lunchtime. Carson smiled. "If you're hungry, I could make you something? My housekeeper doesn't work weekends, so it'll have to be sandwiches or something. Unless you want me to order in?" He raised one eyebrow in question.

"Sandwiches are fine," I muttered, pushing myself off the sofa.

He stood as well, his hand brushing against mine as he moved. I shied away from him, ignoring the flicker of disappointment in his eyes. I frowned, confused by the look. His disappointment and the caring way he'd obviously carried me into the lounge while I was sleeping didn't match the awful way he'd spoken to me or the threats of taking Sasha away from me. Him carrying me into the lounge and letting me sleep in his lap was something I could associate with the old Carson, the one I was starting to wonder actually existed or if I was too blinded by my feelings. Maybe I'd imagined him to be something he wasn't.

"Shall I make them?" I offered, trying to break the uneasy silence that had settled over the room. When he shrugged in answer, I stalked back to the kitchen, pulling open his fridge, just finding butter and a block of cheese.

As I put all the ingredients on the side, he was just watching me silently. The way his eyebrows were furrowed told me there was something he wanted to talk to me about, but he wasn't sure he should. I sighed deeply and turned to him. "Just spit it out, Carson."

He recoiled slightly before seeming to compose himself. "Okay, well, I've instructed someone from Selfridges to come over this afternoon and look around here. They'll put in an order for everything Sasha needs for her bedroom and the safety stuff like stair gates and things. If you could be on hand in case they have questions about what she likes, that'd be great. Obviously, I don't know what she needs." He scowled down at the worktop angrily. "The manager I spoke to while you were asleep said they can come and evaluate, you can choose which design you like and then they'll have everything delivered and installed tomorrow morning."

I gulped at the hard tone to his voice. Clearly, he was extremely angry with me because he didn't know what type of things his daughter needed. "Okay."

He nodded. "And I was also thinking we should talk about how it's going to work… with us, I mean."

Us. Wow, now there's an 'us'. I ignored the little thrill that went through me at the thought of there being an 'us'. I really needed to protect my heart because he was in serious danger of crushing me if I let myself buy into this little fantasy. I didn't say anything, so he continued.

"Because people are aware of Sasha now, there's going to be a statement put out about us being together and that we're getting married," he explained, massaging the back of his neck roughly. "It's going to say we've been secretly dating on and off for the last three years, and now we've decided to confirm our relationship seeing as The Peoples' Post forced our hand."

I averted my eyes. "Will I get a chance to tell Rory before this happens? I don't want him finding out through some newspaper." I stabbed the cheese, cutting it into rough slices as my anger escalated again.

"Yeah, you can talk to Rory. You want me to go pick him up or something? Bring him here?" His voice was soft and caring, just like it used to be.

I sighed in frustration. His kind voice made it hard to stay mad at him. "I'll call him and talk to him. I don't think I really want to see the look on his face right now." I winced at the thought of it.

"Everything will be fine, Emma. I'll take care of you all from now on. We'll sort everything out together. Rory will be fine, and if he's not, then I'll just buy him a car or something as bribery," he joked.

I laughed and rolled my eyes. "He's fifteen."

"Right, well, I'll buy him an iPad." He shrugged casually, winking at me playfully.

I wanted so very much to sink into our easy routine, but if I did that then I'd let myself believe in the lie. I'd let myself believe he wanted to marry me for *me*, and I couldn't do that because it simply wasn't true. Carson was only interested in being a good father to Sasha, and marrying me was just something he felt was morally right to do.

He sighed. "Look, I really want to make this work. I've missed two years of my daughter's life already, and I don't want to miss any more of it. You've been struggling on your own to cope with her and Rory, and now I'm here to take that all away. Why are you not happy about this? Seriously, most girls would love to have me propose to them and offer to give them everything in the world."

My eyes shot up to his. My heart was in my throat; burning rage simmered just below the surface. "You think that's what you did?" I growled.

He frowned and pulled the cutest little confused face I had ever seen, but my hand was itching to slap it off him. "Huh? What I did? What does that mean?" he asked. I closed my eyes and counted to ten, trying to rein in my anger before I took the blunt knife I was using to butter the bread and tried to butcher him with it. He touched my elbow, and I gritted my teeth to stop myself from spitting my words at him. "Emma?"

"You think that's what you did? You think you *proposed* to me?" I couldn't keep the bitchiness from leaking into my voice.

His body went ridged. "Yeah...?" he trailed off, suddenly looking a little unsure.

I couldn't even be bothered to explain that 'proposing' was when someone you loved suggested you spent your lives together. Proposing was getting down on one knee and smiling at someone with a ring, asking them to take your last name. Proposing was a good thing. He hadn't proposed; he'd demanded I marry him under threat of losing custody of my daughter.

I put down the knife and pushed the half-made food away from me. "I'm not hungry anymore." I turned to walk off, ignoring that he was practically on my heels as I marched back down the hallway, grabbing my handbag from the floor.

"Emma, what's wrong with you? Seriously, you're so bloody confusing! I can give you anything you want, anything in the world. You should be happy right now. Why are you being such a bitch?

I'm sorry for saying what I did about paying you for sex. I was angry! I didn't mean it. I don't think of you like that!" he said desperately, stopping at my side.

I blew out a big breath and shook my head. "Carson, it doesn't matter anymore. You want to be a good dad to your daughter, and I'm really grateful for that. She's going to love you, and I'm sure she'll be spoilt rotten and have everything a little girl could ever wish for. Just don't expect me to be happy that my life has suddenly started to be dictated. How would you like it if someone came along and demanded you move away from your home with someone who, quite frankly, looked at you like you were a piece of shit?" I glared at him challengingly, wanting him to shout at me, scream at me, something other than the confused and exasperated look on his face right now.

When he didn't bite, I shoved my way past him into the lounge and pulled out my phone. I needed to talk to Rory. As I dialled his number, the recorded voicemail message came on immediately, telling me I was out of credit and that I needed to top up before I could make a call. I shoved my phone back into my bag roughly.

Why is everything so fucking hard?

"What's wrong?" Carson asked quietly.

I gritted my teeth, pinching the bridge of my nose, wishing he'd just leave me alone and let me have some space for a few minutes so I could calm down. "Out of credit," I snapped harshly.

He sighed and dug into his pocket, producing his phone. "Use that. I'll arrange for a contract phone for you." He didn't wait for a response, just tossed it into my lap and turned, stalking out of the room.

It took me a while to figure out how to use it, but I finally managed to get it to dial Rory's number. When he answered, he sounded a little hesitant, probably because he wouldn't recognise the number on his screen.

Nausea rolled over me. I was actually frightened to tell him because I couldn't bear the thought of him thinking badly of me, too, or hating me for lying to him. "Hey, Rory. It's me," I said, trying not to let the sadness leak into my voice.

"Oh, hey! I've been worried about you. Is everything okay? Did the press guy sort everything?" he asked quickly.

I gulped. "Not really." I swiped at the tear that fell down my cheek. "Listen, I gotta tell you some stuff I should have told you a while ago. Please don't freak out on me because I really need my little brother right now, so please don't get angry with me. We're a team, right?"

"Sure, we're a team. What's up?"

I took a big breath. "You know I told you Sasha's dad was a guy I dated and that he didn't want anything to do with me and Sasha once we broke up?"

"Yeah..."

Oh, God, this is hard! "Well, that wasn't true. I lied to you when I said I was dating the guy. Sasha's dad is actually someone I met at the club. We slept together a few times. I never told him I was pregnant, so he didn't know about Sash until today when the paper printed it." I covered my eyes with my hand, waiting for him to shout at me for deceiving him.

He was quiet for a minute before he spoke. The silence was actually a little painful. "Okay, I get that you lied. But I'm still confused as to why all the reporters are suddenly all over our flat. Why would they even care about you and Sash?"

"Her dad is Carson Matthews."

"Holy shit! No fucking way!"

My mouth popped open in shock. I'd never heard Rory swear before. "Rory! Watch your language!" I chastised. "And you'd better not be anywhere near Sash speaking like that!"

"Oops, wait..." He went quiet for a couple of seconds, and I heard a door close. "No, she didn't hear me," he admitted sheepishly. "Carson Matthews, though? Seriously?"

I nodded even though he couldn't see me. "Yeah."

"Whoa, I didn't see that coming," he muttered. I swallowed the lump in my throat, grateful to Lucie for not spilling all and telling him what this was about. I needed to explain it to him personally. "He didn't even know about Sash?"

"No. I never told him. He found out this morning from the papers. He's really angry with me because I didn't tell him about her. We're trying to work some stuff out right now. He, er…" I frowned down at my lap. "He wants to be a dad to Sasha."

"That's good," Rory replied.

"Yeah, kinda good. But he wants something else, too." I had no idea how I could explain this to Rory. I decided just to put it out there and see how he reacted. "Carson refuses to let her live in our flat, so he's insisting the three of us move in with him. He wants us to get married." I winced, waiting for his reaction.

There was a sharp intake of breath down the line. "Married? Is this even what you want? How the hell is that going to work? You two aren't even dating, are you?"

"No, we've never dated, but Carson isn't seeing sense right now. He's being irrational, and he's not thinking clearly. He thinks this is a good idea for Sasha to have a parental unit. I don't get a say, apparently."

"Don't get a say? Of course you get a bloody say! If you don't want to move in with him and marry him then don't!" Rory ranted angrily.

"It's not that simple," I countered.

"Why isn't it that simple? Tell the twat you don't want to marry him and that's that. What can he do? Frogmarch you up the friggin' aisle and force you to say the words? No, he can't." His tone showed his fury.

I sighed. "Rory, I haven't got the energy for this right now, all right? I'm just going along with it for now, and I'll make him see sense before it gets that far. He's just angry and upset because I didn't tell him he had a daughter. He'll calm down, and then we can talk it all through."

"You should punch him in the face," he muttered angrily.

I smiled weakly. "I haven't got the energy for that, either," I admitted. Carson walked in then, setting a sandwich down on the table for me before heading over and pulling out a laptop, sitting on one of the other sofas. I looked at the sandwich. He must have taken over making it where I left off. That was actually quite sweet. I felt myself start to smile at him before I gritted my teeth and looked away. *No, I'm not going to forgive him because he made me a damn cheese sandwich!*

As calmly as possible, I explained everything to Rory: how Carson and I met, how we'd go to the backroom together, how he was now demanding we get married, how he would take me to court if I didn't, and how I'd already packed up a few days' clothes for the three of us. I deliberately left out the part about Carson's father leaving when he was a kid; it seemed like too much personal information to share with my brother. I told him about the statement going out in the papers that was going to say we were dating on and off for three years. The whole time I spoke, Carson just sat there, either not listening to me or pretending not to. I made sure to add a few digs in there about how I thought the idea was stupid and how I would rather just live at our place. I could have sworn I saw Carson's body twitch when I told Rory that two people who didn't love each other shouldn't get married, and that we were both going to be miserable in the long run. Carson's fingers drummed a little bit too hard on the keyboard as I spoke, so obviously he *was* listening to me.

Rory hadn't reacted as badly as I thought he would to the knowledge his big sister sold herself to a client at the club every weekend. In fact, he'd barely even acknowledged I'd said it. I had the distinct impression he didn't know how to deal with the information so he just chose not to address it at this point. No doubt his feelings on the subject would become apparent sooner or later, though. For now, he just sided with me and vowed to be there for us both regardless. He promised never to tell anyone about the real circumstances of our relationship, and that he'd let me deal with it as requested.

After I'd told Rory everything, I spoke to Lucie, explaining everything to her. Her reaction wasn't the doom and gloom or anger of Rory's; instead, she was actually a little excited about it. "You should just make the most of it, Emma! You're on easy street now. You're marrying a millionaire; you'll want for nothing!" she enthused.

I frowned. She sounded just like Carson with his 'I'll give you everything in the world' speech. "But I don't want his bloody money. If I'd wanted his money, I would have demanded it when

Sasha was born," I retorted, hearing the frustration leak into my voice.

"Well, there's not much you can do about it now, sweetie. Just suck it up and thank your lucky stars you get to live with the guy you've been in love with for the last three years," she said matter-of-factly.

I groaned. I *should* be happy, I really should, but I couldn't stop my anger about this whole situation. Since I'd moved out three years ago, I had been in total control over my life; I had the first and last say in everything. Right now, I felt trapped, like I wasn't in control of my life anymore. I silently wondered if this was what having an arranged marriage felt like.

"Whatever. Look, I'll call you tomorrow and tell you what time I'll come for Sash and Rory, okay? You sure you're okay having them for the night?" I asked.

She laughed. "Of course I am! We're all good, so stop stressing. You know what you should do?"

"What should I do?" I asked, running a hand through my hair.

"Go drag that fiancé of yours up to the bedroom and ravage his body. Everything looks better post-orgasm," she said, laughing to herself.

I snorted incredulously. "I don't want him anywhere near me again after what he said to me, so sex is off the cards, but thanks for the suggestion."

From the corner of my eye, I saw Carson's face crumble a little when I mentioned what he'd said. I knew he was probably sorry, but I couldn't let go of the hurt I felt inside. Carson really did think of me as a prostitute, and I would never be able to forget that.

"Shame. It might make you smile again," Lucie replied.

"I gotta go. Can you do me a favour and call Jason? I'm supposed to be working tonight. Can you tell him I won't be coming in because I need to get stuff sorted here?"

"Sure thing."

"Thanks. I'll call you tomorrow. Any problems with Sash and Rory then call me, okay?" I said, wishing I could just get a hug from my best friend or my brother. I disconnected the call and pushed Carson's phone onto the glass coffee table, already noting that

138

particular piece of furniture would have to go before Sasha could be let loose in here. Carson probably had no idea how one little almost-two-year-old could affect his life. It was going to be amusing watching his life change so rapidly.

"I'm ordering you a new contract phone. You have any preference which you get?" Carson asked, obviously choosing to pretend like he hadn't just listened to my whole conversation about him.

"I don't need a new phone, just credit."

"iPhone. Blackberry. Galaxy. What do you want?" he continued, ignoring my comment.

A tear escaped even though I was trying my hardest to keep them at bay. "I just want to go home, Carson," I whispered.

"You *are* home," he replied immediately. "I'll just get you an iPhone if you're not gonna choose."

For the next half an hour, we ignored each other while we ate and he tapped away on his laptop, ordering goodness knows what. When the ring of his phone cut through the deafening silence of the room, I watched as he looked down at the screen with wide eyes before answering it.

"Hi, Mum."

Mum. My back stiffened. I hadn't even had time to consider how his family were going to be feeling about the news.

"You're what? No, it's not a good time right now. Can't you just leave it until next week? I'll call you tomorrow or something." A frown lined his forehead. "Mum, but..." He groaned and shook his head, tossing the phone onto the seat next to him before looking up at me with tight eyes. "My mum's on her way over. I didn't get a chance to explain it to her; she's just flicked on the TV and seen us all over entertainment news. She'll be here in ten minutes."

Chapter Twelve

Dread settled in the pit of my stomach at the ominous sound of the doorbell. I looked to Carson for reassurance, which unfortunately didn't come because he looked just as nervous as I felt. For the last ten minutes, scenarios of how this meeting was going to go were running through my brain. In reality, I actually had no idea how his mother was going to react to me at all.

Carson set his laptop on the coffee table and stood. "Come on; let's get the awkward first meeting out of the way."

My mouth was dry when I tried to swallow. "Okay," I croaked, standing as well and following him into the hallway, deliberately hanging back and barely stepping out the lounge door.

Through the patterned, frosted-glass panel down the side of the door, I could see two figures standing there. As Carson opened the door, I held my breath and nervously wrung my hands.

Carson's mother looked the total opposite to what I thought she would. Carson was incredibly handsome - your typical heartthrob with his chiselled good looks and striking blue eyes - but his mother was plain in comparison to what I had envisioned. I had always figured she would look like a tall, leggy goddess, so I was a little shocked to see a shorter, dumpy brunette lady. She was dressed impeccably in a pencil skirt, high heels and white shirt combo. Behind her stood a girl about my age. Judging by the flawless complexion and light-brown hair, I immediately guessed this was one of Carson's little sisters. To my horror, it was then that I realised I didn't even know their names.

His mother barely stepped foot into the house before the inquisition started. "Carson, what's all this nonsense I'm seeing about you and a lap dancer this morning?"

I cringed, wishing the polished white marble floor would open up and swallow me.

"It's not nonsense," Carson answered, closing the door behind them. "I met Emma three years ago in the club she works at. We... hit it off immediately." He raised one eyebrow as he obviously left her to draw her own conclusions about what 'hit it off' meant.

"Hit it off? With a lap dancer? Carson Matthews, have I really brought you up to be this person? Someone who has sex with girls like that?"

'Girls like that.' Ouch. That stings. I stepped back into the doorway, half-hiding as my eyes filled with shameful tears.

Carson's forehead creased with a frown as his shoulders pulled back. "You brought me up to see the good in everyone, yes," he rebutted.

She made a distasteful sound in her throat and shook her head. "All you can ever see in a girl like that is what you can use her for."

Carson's sister's gaze flicked to me and her lips parted as her eyes widened. Carson's mother was clearly too busy glaring at her son to see me cowering in the doorway like a wounded puppy. I winced, squirming on my feet.

"It's not like that," Carson stated. "Emma's nice, you'll like her." Seeing Carson stand up to his mother on my behalf made me feel a little flicker of love inside. No matter what he thought of me and what he'd said to me earlier in my bedroom, he was standing there facing her and telling her he saw the good inside me. Even though he'd hurt me so damn much today, I couldn't help but feel proud he was willing to stand up to his mother for me.

"Like her? You're not seriously going to continue with this sordid little affair, are you? You need to think about your career and your sponsors. Have you even thought about the damage an association like this can do? You'll lose all sorts of advertising campaigns after this. People don't like to have their companies associated with scandal," she retorted angrily. "And what's all this bull poop about her having a child? For goodness' sake, they've even linked you to it! Have you spoken to Mason? What's he doing about all of this? They'll obviously have to print a retraction and apology. It's ridiculous."

They still hadn't moved far from the front door. His sister was just watching with wide eyes like I was. "Actually, it's *not* ridiculous," Carson answered. "Emma does have a child, a little girl called Sasha. She's mine." His voice was firm and confident as he spoke.

His mother's mouth popped open in shock as she recoiled. "Yours? Don't be obtuse!"

Carson sighed and raked a hand through his hair. "She's mine, Mum. Emma got pregnant not long after we met. I only found out about it today, too. I haven't even met her yet."

His mother's eyes closed as she massaged her temples in a small, circular motion. "But how can she be? Did you not use protection? Even with someone like that? Carson, for goodness' sake, she could have given you anything! Goodness knows what she's contracted through sleeping with other men or sharing needles!" Her eyes popped open. "Please, tell me she's not a drug addict."

"What the hell? No! She doesn't do drugs. Jesus. Judgemental much?" Carson snapped angrily. "It isn't like that. Emma isn't like that at all!"

"Well, she's a lap dancer!"

"Yeah, and she's also in her second year at university studying to become a social worker!" Carson rebutted.

"This has to be a dream. This can't be real," his mother muttered, shaking her head.

Behind her, Carson's sister stepped forward. "I'm going to go sit in the other room while you two shout this out," she stated, walking toward me and catching my elbow, pulling me into the lounge with her. Carson and his mother didn't even acknowledge her leaving as they glared at each other. "Hi. I'm Kimberly, Carson's sister," she said once we were safely away from the family feud happening in the hallway.

"Emma," I croaked.

She nodded. "I know who you are. Carson's told me about you before. He said you were really pretty and sweet-looking." She smiled kindly. "Please excuse my mother's behaviour. She gets extremely protective over her family. She'll calm down soon and see sense. She just goes off on a tangent and storms in without thinking everything through."

I nodded weakly. That was exactly what I'd thought earlier about Carson, too. Clearly he'd inherited a lot from his mother – just not her looks.

"He's told you about me?" I asked, watching the door to make sure they weren't going to follow us in here.

She threw herself down onto the sofa and pulled out a packet of chewing gum. "Yep. He said you two were friends."

"With benefits," I added, biting on my nails nervously.

She chuckled. "Yeah, with benefits."

Raised voices in the hall made the hair on the back of my neck stand on end. "And by working things out you mean that greedy little witch is putting in her claim for as much as she can! She'll bleed you dry. Just watch, she'll lay claim to everything you own. I bet you were an easy target for her. A young, impressionable boy with no clue how girls like that work. I bet her gold-digging eyes lit up when you first met!"

"I didn't have anything when we first met, actually," Carson shot back. "I hadn't even been signed to a team when I first met her. I was a nobody. Emma doesn't want my money."

"Of course she does!"

"If she wanted my money then why has she never demanded it all this time? Sasha is almost two, yet Emma has never asked me for a penny!"

I flopped down on the sofa next to Kimberly, and she patted my arm sympathetically. "This is a mess," I muttered, putting my head in my hands.

The shouting continued as I sat there with my heart in my throat, barely managing to keep my tears at bay. "That little girl isn't yours, Carson. Wake up! She's taking you for a fool and exploiting you! Have you asked for a paternity test?"

"I don't need a paternity test. Emma's word is good enough for me. She says Sasha is mine, and that's all I need to know."

I smiled weakly because I actually loved that Carson trusted me like that.

"If she really is yours then why did she never tell you about her?" Carson's mother shot back sarcastically.

Carson sighed heavily. "She said she was doing it for me because she wanted better for me than to be a teenage father."

"Sheer and utter bull poop!" his mother scoffed. "Another lie to lure you into her web!"

"Look, if Emma was after my money then she would be the one insisting we get married, not me. You've got her all wrong."

"Married?" his mother shrieked, clearly horrified.

"Married?" Kimberly whispered next to me.

I nodded and looked up at her shocked face. "Apparently," I confirmed noncommittally.

"You can't marry a stripper! Have you lost your mind?" his mother cried.

"Mum, seriously, you need to stop this judgemental act. That's the mother of my child you're disrespecting. You just need to get to know her. She's not like you're thinking she is!"

"What is she like then? Because I'm thinking she's approaching her thirties, boob job, slutty clothes, and crude tattoos covering her body."

Carson laughed incredulously. "She's just turned nineteen, definitely no boob job, she rocks a hoodie, and no tattoos at all," he answered before adding, "Not that there's anything wrong with tattoos, of course."

"And when do I get to meet the little gold-digger so I can make my own judgement on her?"

I sank into the seat further, wanting to disappear or run for the hills.

"She's right in there, hiding and probably listening to every nasty word you've said about her," Carson answered.

When two sets of footsteps sounded toward the room, I jumped to my feet and watched the door, horrified. His mother's eyes were hard as she stepped into the room. The blue to her eyes was the exact colour of Carson's and my daughter's. Without speaking, her gaze raked down me slowly as if sizing me up and seeing exactly what level of depravity she had to deal with. Carson walked into the room, bypassing his mother and coming to stand next to me. Unconsciously, I cringed into his side, wanting to hide from the judgemental, scathing look on his mother's face.

"Mum, this is Emma, my fiancée. Emma, this is my mum, Jillian Matthews." He placed his hand on the small of my back and the heat emanating from his skin was strangely calming.

"Nice to meet you, Mrs Matthews," I forced out, my voice small and intimidated. I knew right then and there I would never like this woman, and by the disgusted look on her face, the feeling was going to be mutual.

One of her perfectly-plucked eyebrows rose as her lips pressed into a thin line. She didn't answer as she swung her handbag from her shoulder and looked through it, coming out with a chequebook and pen. "So, how much will it take for you and my supposed grandchild to disappear?" She dropped her bag on the floor and flicked open the chequebook, looking at me inquisitively. "Ten thousand? Fifteen? Or have you set your sights higher than that?"

I almost choked on air. It looked like it wasn't only Carson who thought I was a nasty prostitute that needed money thrown at her. "I don't…" I shook my head firmly as Carson growled in frustration.

"Mum, what the hell? Just stop it!" he cried angrily.

She ground her teeth. "Well, someone has to sort this situation out! Her claiming you two have a daughter together will be disastrous for your career!"

That was when I saw red. "Claiming? I'm not claiming it, we *do* have a daughter," I growled. Clearly this woman thought I was after one thing and one thing only: money. Yes, I worked at a strip club and yes, we had a daughter together, but it wasn't like I was using the information to fund my own life. I had never wanted anything from Carson other than for him to love me – which would never happen. "But I've already told him he doesn't have to be involved. If he wants to brush this under the carpet, then he can. I'm not the one you should be waving your chequebook at! I'm not the one insisting we play happy families, he is!" I pointed at Carson angrily. Of course, I could understand I'd done wrong by her son in her eyes, but in my eyes I had always tried to shield him from this. It wasn't my fault the papers suddenly investigated it. If anything, it was Carson's fault for giving me that necklace when the reporter was sitting there watching.

Her hard gaze fell on Carson. "See, she's willing to let this all go away. Why can't you?" she asked harshly.

"And be like Dad?" he retorted. "You want me to be like him and watch my kid and her mum struggle while I just go on living my life? I wouldn't have thought you'd wish that on anyone seeing as you went through it once."

Her tough exterior faltered, her eyes twitched as her lips parted. "Of course not. I don't want anyone to struggle like we did, but you don't have to do this. You should do a paternity test. If the little girl really is yours, then you can see they're all right for money. This doesn't have to ruin your life," she said, her voice softer and calmer now.

I looked up at Carson, actually willing him to listen to her. He wouldn't listen to me when I said the same thing; maybe her being angry like this would actually make him see sense.

Carson's arm snaked around my waist and I was tugged closer to him, pressing against his side. "They're not ruining my life. Sasha is mine. Emma and I are getting married. Everyone else and their opinions can go fuck themselves for all I care."

Jillian threw her hands up in exasperation. "I can't believe this. Honestly, this is ludicrous. I refuse to stand by and watch you throw your life away for *that*!" she stated, jabbing an accusing finger at me on the word 'that'.

"Then don't watch," Carson answered calmly as he raised his chin confidently.

They scowled at each other for an agonising couple of seconds, locked in some kind of battle of the stares, before Jillian sighed and looked away. "Come on, Kimberly, we're leaving. Let's let your brother make his own mistakes," she stated, turning on her heel and marching out of the room.

Kimberly immediately stood and smiled sadly. "I'll call you later, Carson. It was nice to finally meet you, Emma."

I gasped and shook my head as she walked out the door, too. I didn't want to break up his family; I didn't want them to fall out over me. "Carson, go after her! Don't leave things like this, it's not right," I pleaded.

He ground his teeth, glaring at the door with rage-filled eyes. "I'm not going after her. If she wants to come back and apologise to you then she can. If not then screw her, too."

"That's your mother! She loves you and just wants the best for you, that's all," I persuaded.

"If she loves me then she'll support me and my choices."

I closed my eyes as an empty feeling settled in my heart. I had never wanted to hurt Carson or take things away from him, and now it appeared he was close to losing his family because of me. I hated myself for it.

"I'm not worth you losing your family for," I croaked as the emotion bubbled over and the tears finally fell.

He sighed deeply, pulling me against his chest and wrapping his arms around me tightly. I buried my face against his shoulder and cried silently for the hopelessness in this whole situation. "You're my family now, Emma. And I won't lose you, not because people are too narrow-minded and quick to judge before they've even gotten to know you. If she'd taken the time to talk to you, she'd see you're sweet and adorable, kind and caring. It's her loss if she chooses not to know you." While he spoke, his hand slid up my back, holding the back of my head, tangling his fingers into my hair.

"Sorry, I forgot my bag."

I jerked back quickly, seeing his mother standing in the doorway, watching us awkwardly. Through my blurry, tear-filled eyes I saw she was crying, too. Wordlessly, she marched over to us and stooped to pick up her handbag from the floor where she'd left it. I silently begged Carson to say something, to make this right, to fix his family before it was too late – but apparently he wasn't going to concede. His eyes were narrowed in anger, and every muscle in his body appeared to be taut with stress.

I cleared my throat, willing my voice to work. "Mrs Matthews, don't leave it like this, please? Can't you two just talk or something?"

She sighed and turned to me. "What difference does it make to you? Surely it's better for you if he cuts off from his family. It'll be easier for you to get your hands on his money then," she replied.

I pushed away from Carson, stepping closer to her, deciding to tell her the truth. "I fell out with my parents a few years ago. I lost any relationship I had with them. They look at me exactly how you do, and although I pretend like it doesn't, it actually hurts to think that I don't have that support there. I don't want Carson to go through that, especially not because of me. Please?" I begged.

Her eyes met mine, and I could see the indecision there as she pondered over what I'd said. When they left mine, they flicked to Carson and her chin trembled as cracks started to show in her hard exterior. "Maybe I was a little too quick to judge," she whispered. Her attention turned back to me. "Maybe I should get to know you before I make assumptions about your morals and your intentions."

I nodded in agreement, feeling the smile twitch at the corner of my mouth. I wasn't stupid enough to think I would ever get her approval, but that didn't matter, as long as Carson didn't lose his family over this.

Carson stepped forward, setting his hand on my shoulder. "Look, just leave it for now, all right? We've all had a shock and have a lot to take in. Call me tomorrow or something," he suggested uncomfortably. I could still hear the anger in his tone, but he was trying to disguise it.

Jillian sighed. "I didn't mean to be harsh; I'm just saying what everyone else is thinking." She shouldered her bag and stood tall, raising her chin, her hard exterior now back. "I'll speak to you tomorrow then."

I watched as she walked out for a second time. I didn't like her. She reminded me of the nasty Carson I'd met today, and I silently wondered if that was a sure sign I'd been deceived by an act all those years ago and that *this* was the real Carson Matthews. Maybe he'd just put on a front to 'charm me into bed' like he so often joked. It had certainly worked, but from now on I was putting my guard up so I wouldn't be hurt or fooled by him again.

Chapter Thirteen

O nce his mother and sister had left, Carson and I were thrust into awkward silence. I didn't know what to say. My body felt cold, and my insides squirmed with a mixture of anger and mortification. His mother's opinion of me hurt a lot more than I thought it would. Deep down, I had known the meeting wouldn't go well. In the ten minutes before she'd arrived, I'd prepared myself marginally for her disapproval, but I hadn't expected her to be that horrified at the thought of her son with someone like me. All I wanted to do was curl into my own bed, in my crappy little flat, and cry myself into oblivion.

"I want to go home," I whispered.

He sighed deeply. "Don't start that again. This is what's happening. People, including you, will just have to get used to it," he replied confidently. "Look, I'm sorry about her. She shouldn't have said any of that, and you shouldn't have had to listen to it."

I frowned and flopped down onto the sofa, keeping my eyes firmly fixed on the deep pile carpet. "It's no worse than what you said earlier. I don't know why you bothered defending me," I replied, swiping at my face and wiping the tears wetting my cheeks.

"I defended you because she was wrong. She just doesn't know you, that's all. She'll come around." He sat down next to me, so closely I could feel the heat emanating from his body to mine as he pressed against my side. "This wouldn't be such a bloody shock to everyone if you'd just told me two fucking years ago about Sasha." His tone was harsh and accusing again.

I closed my eyes, not having the words to explain this to him. I'd probably never be able to explain my actions to Carson. He'd probably never see I was trying to do the best thing for him, or that I thought he was better off without us. If I'd told him I was pregnant, his life probably wouldn't have gone down the route it was now. For all I knew, he might have given up racing to get a 'real job' so he could support Sasha, and then he wouldn't have the mansion he was currently trying to pretend was my 'home'.

Thankfully, a buzz of the doorbell deemed my reply unnecessary. "That'll probably be the personal shopper woman." Carson sighed and pushed himself to his feet, stalking into the hall to answer the door. I could hear him talking to someone through an intercom, and a couple of minutes later Carson and a lady dressed in a smart, blue business suit walked into the room. From her expression and the doe eyes she was shooting Carson, I already knew she had a thing for him and knew who he was. She smiled politely when Carson introduced us, telling me her name was Marian and she was here to order the furniture for Sasha.

It was weird watching Carson and her interact. She'd sat on the sofa between us, pointing out things and gushing about the way it was manufactured. Carson had seemed a little out of his depth the whole time and kept waiting for me to make the decisions, but when I didn't play along he'd had to take charge. I actually couldn't care less what type of wood Sasha's cot was made out of or if it turned into a toddler bed, or what was the 'most popular range' they had. We were happy at home with the cot Lucie had given me, but I didn't have the will to protest anymore.

By the time she got to the back of the catalogue, Carson seemed to have purchased one of everything in the most expensive range they had, regardless of whether it was a necessity or not. After she had a list almost down to the bottom of the page on her clipboard, they took a tour of the house while she noted down the safety equipment that needed to be ordered. I heard plug covers and stair gates mentioned, and when they went into the kitchen they were counting cupboards so they knew how many child locks to order. I didn't bother following them as they walked around the expansive house while Carson spent money as if it were water. I hadn't even been upstairs yet, but I didn't need to. I would bet my life it was just as breathtaking as the lower floor – either way, it still felt like a prison to me. I closed my eyes and sat back against the sofa, settling myself into the soft cushions and willing the dull aching in my head to subside.

The sales rep was in the house for a grand total of two hours, and in that time I had probably spoken less than ten words. Once they were finished, she assured Carson it would be delivered in the morning and her staff would assemble it and put it all in place for him. Clearly it didn't matter that it was Sunday tomorrow. No doubt there was no expense spared from Carson's direction to make that happen.

By the time she left, I was mentally exhausted and sat there listening to Carson making endless phone calls to the people he worked with: his press agent, removal companies which would pack up and transport all our possessions to his house, his family and his friends. The whole time, the depression was building and building inside me. Carson seemed determined to do anything other than speak to me.

AT TEN O'CLOCK, we'd barely exchanged more than a few sentences. I stifled a yawn and ignored him tapping away on the laptop ordering goodness knows what else he felt he needed to buy. "You want to go to bed?" Carson asked suddenly, catching me off-guard.

I nodded, blinking my heavy eyelids.

"I haven't even showed you upstairs yet, have I? Mason called while I was giving you the tour…" He frowned, turning off his laptop and standing.

I shrugged, pushing myself up to my feet, too. "It doesn't matter."

I followed behind him, watching as he checked the front door was locked before tapping in a code on the house alarm and signalling for me to go upstairs. When we got to the top, he stopped and pushed open a door. "I thought Rory might like this one. If not then there's another one down the hall he could have," he said, motioning for me to look in.

I gasped when I surveyed the room. The place was probably almost the same size as my whole flat. There was a little sofa area with an enormous flat-screen TV at one end and a bed at the other. Rory was definitely going to love it. It was plain, like the rest of the house; white walls, cream carpet.

"You don't go much for colour, huh?" I asked, still shocked at the size of the room.

"He can change it to whatever he wants. No one stays in there; I don't think I've ever used that room. It's probably a little boring for a teenager," he admitted. "Come on, I'll show you Sasha's room next." He took my hand and, before I could snatch it back, pulled me down the hallway.

He stopped outside another door and pushed it open, flicking on the light. The room was smaller than Rory's but, even so, was bigger than the lounge and kitchen in my flat. He followed me in and stopped behind me, his chest pressing against my back. "We'll decorate it and make it more girlie. What kind of thing is Sasha into?" he asked. He was standing so close to me I could feel his chest rumble against my back as he spoke. I gulped and willed my voice to come out normally.

Why does his body still affect me when I'm trying so hard not to forgive him?

"She likes anything really. The Fimbles and Charlie and Lola are her favourite things to watch on TV." I shrugged. She was too young to be into one thing, she just liked colourful cartoons at the moment.

"Not heard of either of those," he admitted sheepishly. "Maybe we could choose something together?" he offered hopefully.

I shrugged, forcing a smile. "Sure." I stepped away from him, wanting to get some personal space.

152

He smiled the dimpled smile that made my heart race. I put my hand to my mouth to stifle my yawn, and he smiled again. "Come on then, I'll show you where you'll be sleeping." I nodded and followed him out of the room. He pointed toward another set of stairs that led to a third floor. "There are another couple of rooms up there. I use it as a games room, then there's another bedroom. Rory could use that for studying if he wants, or maybe he'd prefer his own lounge or something up there for when his friends come over? If he wants that then I could order new sofas and stuff..." he trailed off, frowning thoughtfully.

I sighed, trying not to let how sweet he was being to my brother affect me. "I don't think he'll need his own lounge," I muttered, shaking my head in rejection. Carson was clearly trying to make me feel at home here, but it was never going to happen.

He smiled and walked to the room next to Sasha's. I breathed a little sigh of relief that her room was so close to mine. I'd been so used to her sleeping in the room with me that it was going to be a little hard to get used to being separated now. The expensive baby monitors Carson had just ordered would obviously come in handy.

I stepped into the room after him and felt the smile twitch at the corner of my mouth because there was actually a little colour in this room. One dark-red wall sat behind a gigantic, mahogany four-poster bed. There was an L-shaped brown leather sofa grouped around a fireplace, with a huge TV above it. Everything looked beautiful and expensive, like some sort of show home. The red duvet set matched the curtains. It was cute.

"Bathroom's there," he said, nodding to a door on the opposite wall.

"What's the other door?" I asked, pointing to the door next to the bathroom he'd pointed out.

"Walk-in wardrobe." He smiled casually and I nodded absentmindedly, already knowing my meagre clothes would look out of place in there.

"Okay. Well, I guess I'll see you in the morning." I nodded toward the door, signalling for him to leave so I could slope off to bed.

He smiled and rolled his eyes. "This is my room." He gripped the back of his shirt and tugged it over his head, tossing it on the chair by the side of the bed.

I gulped, and tried – unsuccessfully – to keep my eyes off his body. I needed to be strong. Sure, I still wanted him physically, but I just needed to remember what he'd said to me. What he was making me do, what he threatened to do to Sasha if I didn't marry him. Once I thought about that again I gritted my teeth angrily.

"So, where is my room?" I snapped, frustrated. I just needed to go to bed so I could sob myself to sleep like normal.

"This *is* your room," he replied, wrenching open the buttons of his jeans and sliding them down, kicking them onto the chair, too.

I frowned in confusion. "But you said this is your room."

He nodded. "It is. We're getting married, remember?" he replied sarcastically as he turned down the bed, ready to get in it.

Shock made me recoil. I glared at him with as much hate as I could muster. "If you think I'm sleeping in here with you, then you've got another thing coming!"

He laughed; he actually had the nerve to laugh at me. "You're so sexy when you're mad."

I didn't answer, I just pushed past him to go and find the spare bedroom he'd said was down the hall. I couldn't even look at him anymore. He obviously thought demanding we got married gave him 'husband's rights' over me. He obviously thought giving me his surname meant he got to use my body whenever he wanted. That feeling of being cheap and nasty washed over me again.

As I got halfway across the room, he grabbed my wrist, yanking me to a stop. "Where are you going?"

I ripped my arm from his grasp. "Away from you!"

"I thought we were going to bed?" He frowned, clearly confused by my change of attitude.

I snorted in disbelief. "I'm not sleeping in here with you! You think you can just order me to marry you? I'll fucking marry you if that means I get to stay with my daughter, but don't think I'm going to be performing like a wife just because you say so!" I spat, shoving on his bare chest as hard as I could.

He stumbled back a couple of steps and his face turned angry, too. "You're sleeping in here with me, Emma!" he argued, reaching for my hand again.

I whipped it out of the way quickly and turned for the door again. Before I got to the door, though, two arms wrapped around me and I was swept from my feet and into his arms. I gasped and struggled to get out of his grasp as he carried me over to the bed. I needed to get out of here quickly. I could feel the sadness creeping up and it wouldn't be long before I completely broke down in tears. I didn't want him near me when that happened.

He dropped me on the bed as I dug my nails into his shoulder. I immediately went to push myself up and run, but he gripped my hands, pinning me to the bed. The angry expression was back on his face, and I felt my blood turn cold as I wondered if Carson Matthews, man I had put on a pedestal for the last three years, was actually going to force himself on me.

"You're sleeping in here with me and that's final! I don't give a shit if I have to pin you to the sodding bed all night! We're getting married, so we'll behave like a normal married couple!" he shouted, his face tinted red with anger.

I struggled to fight him off again, thrashing my legs, screaming for him to get off me. Effortlessly, he shifted so he was on top of me, pinning my whole body down with his weight.

"Get off me! Let go!" I shouted. He gripped my wrists tighter, scowling at me. "GET THE FUCK OFF ME!" I screamed. I carried on trying to get free, but to no avail. In the end I just gave up, laying perfectly still underneath him as the sobs racked my body, making me gasp for breath. "I hate you," I choked out.

"I know."

"I hate you for making me do this, Carson," I croaked, squeezing my eyes shut and trying to stop crying.

"You said."

I turned my face away and just lay still under him, willing myself to stop crying. I couldn't fight him off; if he was going to use my body then it'd be against my will. I guess he thought us being engaged gave him that right now. "If you're going to rape me then just do it," I whispered, my chin trembling.

"Rape you?" he gasped. "What the fuck, Emma? I wouldn't… are you crazy?" He finally let go of me, pushing himself up so he was straddling me as he looked down at me in disbelief. "Seriously? You think I would do that?" he asked, clearly hurt by my assumptions.

I sniffed loudly, swiping at my tears as he moved off me, sitting on the bed next to me. "I don't even know you anymore, Carson. Maybe I never did. The Carson I knew wouldn't be making me do this. He wouldn't threaten to take my daughter away. He wouldn't make me feel like a dirty tart every time he looked at me." I looked up at him through blurry eyes as his face softened and he shook his head and settled down next to me, wrapping his arm over my stomach and pressing himself against my side.

"Don't cry," he whispered, stroking my hair softly. "You *do* know me. I'm sorry, but this is what needs to happen. You won't hate me forever. I can make you happy here if you just let me. I'll give you anything the three of you want. I'll be the best dad in the world."

And there it was again – the slap in the face that told me he was only doing this for Sasha and not me. If he just said he wanted me, that he liked me, that I made him laugh, anything…

I couldn't speak. I rolled over, facing away from him as I curled into a ball, hugging my knees to my chest as I sobbed harder. Behind me, he sighed deeply and climbed out of the bed. Seconds later, a soft blanket was placed over me as he tucked it under my chin before leaning in and planting a soft kiss on the side of my head. His touch was so much like the Carson I fell in love with that it broke my heart a little more.

"I'll go sleep somewhere else. You take this one," he muttered quietly before he stomped across the room and left, closing the door tightly behind him.

Chapter Fourteen

It took me an extraordinary amount of time to fall asleep. Everything was too quiet; there was no shouting going on outside in the middle of the night, no cars coming and going in the car park, no music playing in another apartment. Carson's house was utterly silent. I hated it.

I'd laid there awake for hours, going over everything that had happened, mulling over just how much my life had changed in the space of twenty-four hours. Thinking about being Carson's wife made me so confused I didn't even know what to think anymore. I wanted to be his wife more than anything in the world; I wanted the life he painted for us, the four of us together with him spoiling Rory and Sasha to the point of ruin. At the same time, I hated the thought of being his wife. He didn't love me; therefore, he would continue with his playboy act, humiliating both me and Sasha. I had no idea how I was supposed to cope with seeing pictures of him with other girls. Sasha would be old enough to understand at some point. No doubt she would end up resenting him more in the long run; his antics would tarnish the whole family name and end up embarrassing her, too.

I could almost see it; my life was going to be one long and painful, humiliating Hell. People would look down their noses at me everywhere I went. I would be the one who couldn't satisfy her celebrity husband and let him walk all over her with anything female. I wouldn't be able to do anything about it other than stand and watch for fear of losing my daughter. I would be a laughing stock, and the worst thing was part of me still wanted that because I loved him so much. I seriously was a worthless piece of shit.

Sadness ate me up to the point where I'd cried so much that my tears had dried up and I'd laid there a hiccupping, soggy mess. I thought I'd hit a depressing low when I was pregnant and alone, but this low, this was lower than I ever thought possible. I felt kind of dead inside, like my heart had been broken irrevocably and nothing would ever be able to fix it.

When I woke in the morning, my eyes stung with tiredness. The sounds of banging and drilling filled my ears, so I sat up, confused for a second where I was before I remembered the finer details of my predicament. My gaze settled on the alarm clock, and I was shocked to see it was past ten in the morning. I hadn't slept in this late since I'd given birth almost two years ago.

I sat in bed for a long time, just listening to people crashing around in the room next to mine, people talking and relaying instructions. When I couldn't stand not knowing what was going on any longer, I pushed myself out of bed and looked around for something I could get changed into. I'd fallen asleep in my clothes last night, so I was sure to look an absolute mess. I had no idea where Carson had put my bin bag full of possessions, though. After not finding my own bag, I ventured through the door Carson had said was the wardrobe. My eyes widened in shock. Rows and rows of expensive, designer clothes hung in colour-coordinated lines along both sides of the room. Although there were probably enough clothes for him to wear something and then discard it, there was still plenty of rack space so I'd be able to fit my small, limited wardrobe inside, too.

My hand reached out, touching the sleeve of a charcoal grey suit which hung there. My mind was already imagining what Carson would look like decked out in such finery; I'd never seen him in a suit before. His rack of jumpers caught my attention, so I walked over, choosing a black hoodie at random. Shrugging out of my crumpled T-shirt, I pulled his hoodie on before smoothing back my hair and attempting to tidy it.

The banging grew louder as I crept out of my room. I stopped in the doorway of Sasha's new bedroom, seeing Carson plus two workmen, all working to put her furniture together and make her room safe. I hadn't even heard them arrive.

They were already halfway through arranging her room with exquisite, white wood furniture. In the corner of the room sat the most beautiful chair I had ever seen in my life. It was an armchair, but the arms and back of it were made entirely from old-fashioned teddy bears. It was stunning, and my hand was itching to touch it and feel how soft it was.

My eyes suddenly settled on Carson. He was on his knees, hammer in hand, screws precariously placed between his lips as he frowned down at the instructions on how to assemble a changing table. Without my consent, a smile crept onto my lips because his cute little bewildered expression caught me off-guard and made my heart stutter.

"Excuse me, Miss."

I jumped as someone spoke behind me and sidestepped the doorway. "Sorry," I muttered, watching as two men carried in a seven-foot-tall toy giraffe. As they passed me, a little tag fluttered to the floor at my feet. I stooped quickly, picking it up. My eyes widened and a strangled choking sound came from the back of my throat when I saw the price of the giraffe was just under a thousand pounds.

Carson noticed me then. "Hey, sorry, did we wake you?"

I gulped, swallowing my shock and horror that he'd spent that much money on a stuffed toy. I looked up at him, fiddling with the tag absentmindedly. An extremely-uncomfortable sensation crept over me because I realised I was standing there in one of his jumpers after I'd cried in front of him last night and told him to get it over with and rape me if he was going to. I didn't know whether to mention it and apologise or not.

"No, I..." I smiled politely as one of the giraffe guys, now empty-handed, walked back out of the room picking up a bag full of plug socket covers. "I had to get up sooner or later," I finished. "You guys look busy," I muttered, eyeing the beautiful cot the two men were in the middle of assembling.

Carson nodded. "Hopefully won't be too much longer now." He set down his hammer and pushed himself to his feet. "If you're hungry, there's food downstairs," he offered, motioning toward the hallway and stairs.

Not wanting to stand there and watch while they worked, I nodded in agreement and headed downstairs towards where I remembered the kitchen being. On the way, I bypassed several other workers all fixing plug covers, stair gates, and screwing furniture to walls so it couldn't tip over if little people started climbing on it. It seemed as if everything had been thought of. There was even a storage van parked outside, and people were carrying out Carson's glass furniture, inappropriate ornaments and knickknacks to be stored. Clearly Carson had been busier on the laptop last night than what I'd thought because he'd managed to get everything under control. The house would be shipshape for a two-year-old in no time.

As I stepped into the kitchen, I came to an abrupt halt as my eyes landed on a petite, grey-haired lady busy taking cinnamon swirls out of the oven. My mouth instantly watered as the smell wafted up. Her eyes widened for a second before a lovely, warm smile graced her ruby-red painted lips.

"Emma?" she inquired, setting the tray of yumminess down on the side. I nodded, not having a clue who this woman was. Her smile grew larger. "Aww, it's lovely to finally meet you. I'm Gloria, Carson's housekeeper." She waved toward one of the stools that sat on the other side of the counter to where she was cooking up a storm. "Sit. Eat, before all those men traipse in and take all the good stuff," she encouraged, pushing an empty plate toward me and nodding at the array of things she had set on the side. I opened my mouth to speak, but she beat me to it. "So, Carson tells me this morning that you two have a child? A little girl, and she's coming to live here? I just love children! I can't wait to meet her. What kind of things does she like to eat? I'm going to make up a little tea for her so she can have all of her favourite things when she comes here. Obviously, it'll be a bit of a change for her. Where were you living before? Was it far?" She grinned at me expectantly.

I swallowed, blinking at the number of questions being fired at me in one go. If there was a contest for who could say the most words in the space of a minute, this woman would win, hands down. But I actually loved it. Her easy smile and kind eyes made me feel perfectly at ease as I picked up a freshly-baked croissant and set it on my plate.

"Um... well, she likes anything really, so don't go to any trouble. I mean, I can cook, so you don't need to." I chewed on my lip, not used to being waited on.

She made a scoffing noise in the back of her throat and waved a hand dismissively. "It's my pleasure. Plus, I get paid to cook, so if you take over then you'll be doing me out of a job," she chimed in, winking at me playfully. A nervous chuckle escaped my lips. I hadn't thought of it like that. "So, maybe I should bake a cake or something?" she continued.

I shrugged, picking at the edges of my croissant. "You really don't have to go to any trouble."

Before she could answer, I heard someone walk in behind me. Gloria smiled over my shoulder affectionately. "She's a sweetie pie all right," she stated to the newcomer.

I flicked my eyes over in time to see Carson walk in and nod at the statement. "Told you she wouldn't want any fuss," he replied, pulling out the stool next to mine and sitting down, snagging a plate and quickly filling it with one of everything from the counter. I squirmed in my seat. I had never expected to be sitting next to Carson having breakfast. It was strange, kind of a nice strange, but awkward at the same time because I knew he didn't truly want me here. I just came as an extra part to my daughter.

He looked up then and caught me staring at him. A sad smile twitched at the corner of his lips. "Don't go on Twitter today, all right?"

Confused by his words, I recoiled. "Why not?" I didn't even have a Twitter account, mainly because my cheap-as-they-come phone didn't even go on the internet.

A frown lined his forehead as he looked down at his plate. His shoulders hunched and a muscle in his jaw twitched before he answered. "The statement has gone out to the press now about us. There's some stuff on Twitter about... well, it's not nice stuff."

'Not nice stuff'. I had no idea what that would mean. I raised one eyebrow in prompt. "Not nice?"

He sighed and looked up to Gloria who nodded in encouragement. Finally, he turned to face me. "It seems the Twitter-world is under the same impression as my mother. They think you're after my money. There's a worldwide trend at the moment of Carson's gold-digger."

Anger built in my stomach. Not anger at the people who were trending – whatever that meant – about me being a gold-digger, but anger at Carson. This was *his* fault. People who had never even met me were now making assumptions about me because of *his* ridiculous demands. I pushed my plate away from me, no longer hungry.

"That's just perfect," I muttered, shaking my head. "I hate this. Seriously, this is your fault, Carson! Why the hell are you making me do this? It's stupid!"

"Look, this is what happens occasionally. I do something they don't like, and my Twitter feed blows up with shit and abuse. It's just part of this life. You'll get used to it," he reasoned. He sounded a little exasperated about it, as if maybe he was sick of having to deal with abuse, too. Maybe being a celebrity wasn't all champagne and roses.

"I won't get used to it," I countered.

He sighed and ran a hand through his hair. "Just don't look at it and don't respond. Rise above it. My stupid little fan-girls are just pissed because they now realise I'm off the market. They're annoyed at you for ruining their chances."

Even though I didn't want it to, a little thrill went through me at the words 'off the market'. That kind of insinuated he wasn't going to creep around behind my back with them, didn't it? A small part of me dared to hope.

"Well, they're welcome to you," I retorted, trying to appear aloof when my words had never been more dishonest. "Maybe I should go tell everyone I don't even want to be here and that you're forcing me to marry you because you're scared of your daughter not liking you! Maybe then they'll stop hating me for taking you off the market, huh?"

Gloria gasped at my outburst. "Carson, but... but... you said this was a mutual thing," she blurted.

I snorted, pushing myself up from the seat. "It is, if you call *mutual* blackmail into getting married, otherwise he'll take me to court and take my daughter away from me!" I ground my teeth, watching as her eyes latched onto Carson who didn't look so confident about his decision now.

Her mouth popped open. "Oh, Carson, you didn't!"

He frowned, ignoring her as he slammed his hand on the counter and shook his head, turning to me. "Stop making this hard, for fuck's sake. Get over it already and just be fucking grateful you now have everything people dream about." His steely glare bore into me as he spoke.

Words failed me. My mouth opened and closed, but nothing came out as I struggled to comprehend exactly how crazy he actually was. Apparently, he was expecting me to be grateful to him for forcing this life on me, disregarding what I wanted and taking away all my choices, free will and liberty.

He blew out a hefty breath, looking away from me as he gripped his hand into the back of his hair. "You hate me, I know," he muttered sarcastically.

I shook my head. The most pathetic thing about me at that moment was when I realised I would never be able to hate him because I loved him too damn much.

"I'm not hungry anymore. It was lovely to meet you, Gloria." I turned on my heel, needing to escape before the tears came. Behind me, I could hear his housekeeper laying into him on my behalf. I silently prayed she would drum some sense into him.

FOR THE NEXT TWO HOURS, I sat on the bed with my knees pulled up to my chest. My heart hurt. My tears had stopped over an hour ago. My emotions were now just resigned to the fact this wasn't going to change and I was trapped.

When a knock sounded at the door, I wiped my puffy face and went to answer it. As I pulled it open, Carson stood there, awkwardly kicking his toes against the expensive carpet. "Everything's done now. Maybe we should go and pick up Sasha and Rory?"

Not having the energy to argue anymore, I nodded, turning back and picking up my mobile phone and handbag from the side where I'd left them. The house was quiet as we walked through it. Lots had changed since I came in yesterday. Half of the furniture was now gone – stored somewhere, no doubt, because it was mostly sleek glass or expensive-looking china. Every socket was plugged with little plastic covers, and stair gates were fixed at the top and bottom of the sweeping staircase, ruining the beautiful effect of it.

Wordlessly, I followed him to the interior door and down the staircase, which led to his garage. Instead of going to one of the sleek sports cars, he pressed the key to a massive black off-roader. To me, it looked a little like a monster truck. When he opened the passenger door for me, I had to climb to get onto the brown-leather bucket seat. A child car seat was already placed in the back. He certainly had thought of everything, it seemed.

"So, where am I going?" he asked as he started the engine.

After giving him the address and some basic directions to Lucie's flat, I slumped down into my seat as he searched for her address on the satellite navigation system. When the garage door opened, my eyes widened as I spotted a few reporters camped outside the gates to his house. They all jumped up, snapping photos and shouting questions through the tinted-glass windows.

"They can't see in, don't worry," Carson assured me, turning carefully into the street as the reporters surrounded the car, still shouting their questions and asking for a quote.

"Why are they still hanging around here? Hasn't the story already broken? What more could they possibly want?" I asked incredulously.

He shrugged. "We're big news right now, Em. They have to make money somehow."

I huffed and folded my arms over my chest, knowing another outburst from me would do no good. Clearly Gloria the friendly housekeeper hadn't been able to make him change his mind, either. Silence weighed heavily on me as I stewed inside, wondering how long this attention surrounding us would last. I had work tonight – would they follow me there asking for an exclusive quote, too? I hoped not.

"What do I do if the reporters are at the club tonight? Do I call Mason?" I asked, chewing on my bottom lip.

Carson snorted and shook his head. "You're not going to the club."

I raised one eyebrow at the sternness in his tone. "I am. I have work tonight. I can't pull a sickie two nights in a row, Jason will be pissed." I didn't want to lose my job. Although I hated doing it, it was the only source of income I had.

"You don't work there anymore. I'll sort it out." He kept his eyes firmly fixed on the road as he spoke. "I can't let you do that anymore, I'm sorry."

I almost choked on air as I gaped at him. "What the hell are you talking about?"

He shrugged. "The press would crucify us if you carry on doing that. It's not exactly a respectable job, is it? Now that you're in the public eye, things will need to change."

"Not respectable enough for a celebrity's fiancée, you mean?" I spat. He shook his head but didn't look at me. "It was respectable enough for you to get your kicks with, though, huh? A lap dancer isn't exactly marriage material, though, is she? I guess you have to think of your image and what other people think of you." I ground my teeth in frustration at the disrespect. "What happened to the 'I don't care what you do, you're Emma Bancroft to me' shit you spouted last week?" I asked acidly. *Talk about double standards!* "My job was all right when you were just after a casual fuck, but now all of a sudden I'm not good enough?"

"I never said you weren't good enough!" he snapped, glaring at me before turning his attention to the road again. "I just can't have you do that job if we're getting married." He shook his head forcefully as he pulled into an empty space outside Lucie's block of flats. "I don't want to argue with you anymore. I'm done. You no longer work there. End of."

"'End of'? Are you shitting me?" I gasped, watching as he opened the door and climbed from the car, slamming it so hard the whole car shook. I laughed incredulously as he walked around to my side of the car and opened the door for me, silently motioning for me to get out. I held my ground, shaking my head in rejection. "I'm not done. No 'end of'," I stated firmly.

He sighed deeply, watching as a couple of cars pulled into the car park, screeching to a halt before the same reporters from his house sprang out and started running toward us. "I don't really want them to witness this domestic and have it spread all over the front page tomorrow. If you could just put on your happy face and smile, that'd be great." He smiled at me, but it was forced and didn't reach his eyes, which instead held a silent warning.

Knowing I had to play along, I forced a smile as well and took the hand he was holding out to me, letting him help me from the car. By the time I was on my feet, we were surrounded and the clicking of cameras filled my ears. Carson's shoulders seemed to loosen now that I was playing along. As he closed the car door, he bent forward and, before I could even guess what was about to happen, his soft lips covered mine. The kiss lasted no more than a second, and I didn't even have time to react and kiss him back before it was over. The excited buzz around me clearly signalled the one-second kiss was enough for the reporters, though. They would have the picture they wanted.

I gulped as Carson's hand tightened on mine, pulling me against his side as he turned to the reporters. "We're now going to pick up our daughter. If you print a picture of her, or Emma's brother, then I'm going to sue your arses for every penny you have. Just a friendly warning," he said sternly. The authority in his tone made the hair on the nape of my neck stand up. Without waiting for a response, he turned and stalked into the building, tugging me along behind him.

Once we were alone, I pulled my hand from his, ignoring how his face fell and his eyebrows knitted together. I didn't mind putting on an act for the cameras if we needed to, but there was no way I was belittling myself like that in private.

I stopped walking. "I'm not done talking about this. I need to work."

"Not there you don't," he answered forcefully.

I groaned in frustration, throwing my hands up in the air. "Well, what the hell am I supposed to do for money? I don't exactly have a line of people queuing up to offer me a job!" I snapped.

His hands fisted into his hair. "You don't need to worry about that anyway. I have more than enough. Over the next week, I'll sort out a bank account card and stuff for you. There's no need for you to work."

The air suddenly became thicker, feeling like it was choking me. Trapped. Now I was totally and utterly trapped because I'd never have the money for a way out if I didn't work. "So, I'm just supposed to be a good little housewife, relying on her husband like someone out of the forties? Times have changed, Carson. Women don't have to do that now; they can work if they want to!"

"You're in full-time education, Emma. You're a student. That and looking after Sasha is enough for a job, surely," he countered, eyeing me cautiously. "I'm not saying you can't ever have a job. Just finish your university course and then you can work wherever you want. You don't need to be working in that place anymore."

"Maybe I like working there. Did you ever think of that?" I countered, folding my arms over my chest and raising one eyebrow in question.

He scoffed and shook his head. "Do you?" he snapped. "You really like dancing for guys and having them leer at you while you parade around in hardly any clothes? You really like going into the backroom for sex?"

"Yes, actually!" I answered before I could even think it through. He recoiled, clearly shocked by my answer. It was then that I realised my answer only related to half his question. A frown lined my forehead as I backtracked. "No, I don't like dancing for guys, of course not. It's... There are parts of my job I hate, but others I actually lived for." I chewed on my lip. "The best part of my job was you." I hated to admit it, but it was the truth.

Silence filled the hallway as my face flamed with heat.

"Well, then you have no reason to go there anymore, do you? You have me full-time now," he answered. The hair on my arms prickled at his words. My heart swelled in my chest because that was the first kind-of-nice thing he'd said to me for the last two days. But then he had to carry on speaking and my hopes, which were only just starting to take flight, came crashing down to my feet again. "Besides, I'd much rather watch you dance in the bedroom anyway." A cocky little smirk crept onto his face as his eyes sparkled playfully. Maybe he was joking, I didn't know, but his words cut me deeply, reminding me that I would never escape this stigma. I would never forget what I was, because he saw that every time he looked at me.

"Screw you," I whispered. My chin wobbled as my stomach twisted in a knot. Needing to be away from him, I turned and marched up the stairs.

"Oh, for fuck's sake. I can't say anything right, can I?" he muttered dejectedly.

Lucie's flat was on the sixth floor, and her apartment block was slightly nicer than mine. The walls of the stairwell were painted an ugly grey, but at least they weren't covered in graffiti tags and crudely-scrawled notes about who had slept with whom and who needed to die, like mine were. I didn't speak to him again as I stomped up the stairs and stopped outside my best friend's door.

When the door swung open, Lucie smiled at me warmly before stepping forward and engulfing me in a much-needed hug. I sighed and closed my eyes, feeling my shoulders relax as she patted my back supportively. "Oh, baby doll, are you okay? Did you sleep? You look terrible!" she asked as she pulled back and regarded me with her motherly concern she used on her kids.

I forced a smile and shrugged. "I'm okay." That was a lie. I was far from it, but I didn't want to talk about it with Carson watching my every move. "Where's Sash and Rory?"

Lucie stepped back and waved me in, looking at Carson with tight eyes. I could tell he'd gone down a peg or two in her estimations after this. "They're in the living room."

As I looked toward the door, Rory stepped out, closing it firmly behind him. I sighed and relaxed a little more. It felt nice to be around familiar surroundings and people. He strutted toward me quickly and I smiled, opening my arms for a hug. Only, I noticed too late that he wasn't looking at me, and he certainly wasn't smiling.

He stalked forward, and before I could open my mouth and tell him not to do what I knew was coming, he raised his arm and threw his fist straight into Carson's face.

Chapter Fifteen

"Rory, what the heck are you doing? Stop it!" I cried as Carson slammed back into the wall behind him.

A livid-looking Rory turned back to me and pointed an accusing finger in Carson's direction as he clutched his bleeding nose. "You said you didn't have the energy to punch him in the face, so I figured I'd do it for you!" he barked.

An unwilling smile twitched at the corner of my mouth. Although I didn't approve of violence at all, the fact he was standing up to someone older than him on my behalf just served to remind me what a great little brother I had. I didn't know what to say. I didn't really want to reprimand him, but I knew I needed to.

Carson pushed himself upright, shaking his head. "You're fucking lucky you're underage," he grumbled, pinching the bridge of his nose.

One of Rory's eyebrows rose in challenge. "Oh, yeah, and why's that, dickwad?"

I shook my head quickly, stepping between them and holding my hands up in protest. "Rory, just don't," I pleaded.

"Tell me you're not seriously moving in with this bellend!" Rory snapped, narrowing his eyes over my shoulder. "I could just kick the snot out of him and throw him out."

"You could try!" Carson growled from behind me, stepping closer to me and gripping my hips as he attempted to push me out of the way so I wasn't between them. "Don't stand there, Emma. If your runt of a brother foams at the mouth again, you'll get hurt."

I shoved his hands off me and held my ground. "Just stop it, both of you. What are you, three? Grow up!"

"Runt of a brother?" Rory repeated, gritting his teeth. "Twat."

Twisting on the spot, I put one hand on each of their chests and pushed as hard as I could, separating them. "Stop it!" I shouted angrily.

"Mummy?" I heard from the living room. The four of us in the hallway fell silent and looked toward the living room door as the handle rattled where Sasha was obviously trying to get out because she'd heard me. "Muuuuuuummmmmmmmmyyyyyyyy!"

When I looked back to Carson, I saw his mouth was open as he stared at the door. He wasn't moving. The blood had stopped from his nose, but it covered his lips and chin and had dripped down onto the front of his shirt. He looked like something from a horror film.

"Your face," I muttered with wide eyes.

His hand shot up, cupping his nose and mouth. I didn't even see Lucie disappear, but she came running back from the kitchen with a tea towel in her hand which she threw at Carson just as the living room door opened.

Sasha's little face peeked out of the room, looking left before turning to the right. Her blue eyes lit up when she saw me, and a gigantic smile stretched across her face as she giggled and rushed out of the room, running toward me as her brown curls bounced with each step. "Mummy!"

I grinned and bent, catching her just as she jumped at me. "Hey, beautiful," I greeted, planting a big kiss on her lips. I stood and lifted her, hugging her tightly to me. "I missed you! Been good for Lucie?" I asked.

She nodded. "Play minoes. Falls down!" she replied excitedly, pointing back toward the door.

I looked at Lucie for help, not knowing what she was saying. "Dominoes," Lucie explained. "We're trying to make a domino trail, but it's not going well. Keeps falling down, right, Sash?"

I grinned and nodded. "Dominoes? Sounds like fun."

I turned to Carson. He was just staring at Sasha with wide, clearly-awed eyes. His mouth still hung open, the tea towel Lucie had given him long forgotten as he dragged his eyes over every inch of his daughter's face. His whole body was alert and on edge. The way he was looking at her so adoringly made my heart ache and my stomach clench. It was as if he were looking at the Eighth Wonder of the World. He wasn't even blinking, and he was barely breathing. I'd never seen love at first sight, but if I had to describe what it looked like it would be Carson looking at his daughter for the first time. Impossibly, my love for him seemed to double just because of the tender, adoring way he was looking at my little girl.

I looked back at Sasha as she played with my hair, wrapping it around her chubby fingers. "Sasha, there's someone here who wants to meet you," I said, swallowing the lump in my throat. Her big, blue eyes came up to meet mine. I motioned toward Carson with one hand, not really knowing how to make this introduction at all. "This is Carson. He's your daddy. Can you say hi, Daddy?"

When she looked up at him for the first time, he gulped.

"Hi, Daddy," she murmured in her singsong voice.

His breath seemed to leave his body in one large gust as his eyes glazed over. His eyebrows knitted together as a smile slowly spread across his face, his devotion and happiness clear. "Hi, Sasha," he croaked, seeming to be struggling to breathe.

"You gots a boo boo," Sasha informed him, pointing at his bloody nose.

Carson sniffed and nodded, putting his hand to his face. "Yeah, I ran into something stupid," he answered. I chuckled at that as Rory made a small scoffing noise in his throat. Carson grinned, putting the tea towel to his face and attempting to wipe the blood away but just succeeding in smearing it around so it looked even worse. His eyes were filled with tears as he looked over at me before looking back to Sasha again.

A little hand closed over my chin and forced my face toward Carson. "Mummy kiss boo boo," Sasha proclaimed rather proudly.

I chuckled awkwardly and took her hand. "I'm sure he's fine."

Carson laughed and let his eyes wander over her again. "She's so beautiful," he whispered. I nodded proudly, planting another kiss on Sasha's cheek. "She's amazing, I..." He shook his head, still clearly awestruck.

I smiled and set Sasha down on her feet, watching as she ran back to the living room, shouting about dominoes again. Lucie stepped forward. "Why don't you help Carson clean up his face while Rory and I pack up their overnight bags?" she suggested.

Rory answered before I could speak. "We're not packing. We're not going with him. All three of us are either staying here or going home." He turned to me and put his hand on my shoulder, bending to look me in the eyes because he was so much taller than me now. "You don't have to do this. Screw him. Let him try and take Sasha away. He won't win; a court won't side with a prick that's not been in her life for two years. You're her mother."

My mouth was dry. Rory didn't know the full story. If it went to court then of course I would lose. I worked in a lap dancing club, I danced on stage in barely any clothes, I let men push five pound notes into my thong, I took one of them in particular to the backroom for sex. They wouldn't view me the way Rory did.

I gulped and looked at Lucie for help. She smiled sadly back at me. Carson was watching me, waiting for my reaction and I knew what I needed to do. I couldn't take the risk of losing Sasha. I couldn't afford to go to court at all; I wouldn't even have the money to consult to a lawyer about it.

"I have to do this, Rory. Please, don't make it any harder, all right? Just... just go with this for now."

Rory shook his head adamantly. "I figured a way out of it. Kiss and tell," he stated proudly. "They'll pay you for a story, then you'll have money to fight him in court."

Carson's body jerked behind him. "The fuck? No! What are you smoking, kid? Whatever it is, it's messing up your brain. Kiss and tell? She'll make herself look like a slut!" he ranted.

I groaned and gripped my hands into my hair as Rory rounded on Carson again. "She's not a slut!" he growled.

"I never said she was," Carson spat back, stepping closer to him so their chests were practically touching. They stood the same height so they met toe to toe, eye to eye. "She'll make herself look like one if she does what you're suggesting. What's wrong with you two?

Why can't you see this is a good thing? The three of you will want for nothing, yet you're both acting like I'm forcing you to drink acid!"

Rory shoved on Carson's chest, pushing him back a step as he sneered at him. Anger was building inside me while they carried on arguing about me and what was best for me. Plus, they were both swearing in earshot of my daughter.

"You two need to stop this fighting and swearing, right now! If Sasha comes out here and sees this then I'm gonna go seven shades of crazy on your arses," I growled. I gripped Rory's arm and pulled with all my might, forcing him to step back. "Go pack up whatever you need to. We're going along with this for now, and that's final!" I motioned up the hallway with my chin, keeping my eyes locked on his so he knew I was serious. If he shot his mouth off to the reporters and I ended up losing my daughter because of this, I'd never forgive him. "Go pack. Seriously, I don't have the energy for all this. Just do as I ask. I don't ask much from you, do I? Just do this for me."

He sighed and his shoulders loosened as he bent forward, planting a little kiss on the side of my head. "Fine. But I'm never going to like the prick," he grumbled, pulling away from me and stomping off up the hallway.

"And this swearing stops immediately," I called after him, watching as he waved his hand over his shoulder in acknowledgement.

Lucie cleared her throat. "I'll go pack up Sasha's things, too." She stalked off quickly, leaving me and Carson alone in the hallway.

I gulped, not knowing what to say. "Sorry about that," I muttered, wincing as I looked at his blood-stained face and shirt.

He shrugged easily, his eyes sparkling with mirth. "It's fine. He doesn't hit too hard, so it's all good."

I fought a smile and nodded toward the kitchen. "We should probably get that cleaned up before Sasha thinks that's just your normal face." I turned and walked up the hallway, heading to the kitchen and picking up the kitchen roll from the side, running the tap and filling a bowl with warm water. "Sit there," I instructed, motioning toward the kitchen table. Carson sat obediently and looked up at me.

As I stepped between his legs and wet some of the kitchen roll, his eyes met mine. The beautiful colour of them startled me, as it did every time I looked into his eyes like this. His eyes were my favourite thing about him. They made my stomach flutter and my palms sweaty. His eyes were so much like the Carson I used to know, the one who would never threaten me or make these demands of me. My heart actually hurt, and I longed to turn back the time so he could always be the person I thought he was, instead of this person who felt like he was ripping my heart out.

For a few agonising seconds, I couldn't look away from him. My whole being longed to move closer, to settle myself on his lap and have his arms wrap around me. I wanted that closeness and intimacy which we only ever had after sex when we both caught our breaths. I wanted to press my lips against his and have his hands tangle into my hair. But I knew that intimate relationship we had was long gone.

"This might hurt a little," I mumbled, wiping the damp paper towel over his face, clearing the blood away.

"Sasha's beautiful." My hand faltered, and my lungs constricted at the emotion and feeling that went into those two words. "I can't believe I missed it all. She can talk and everything. You should have told me about her. This wasn't fair. I'll never be able to get that time back, Emma." His forehead creased with a frown as his jaw tightened, so I knew he was angry with me again.

I frowned as well and continued to wipe his face. He was probably right to be angry. Me keeping this secret, although what I thought was best for him at the time, had actually taken his beautiful little girl away from him for the last two years. He'd missed out on things I hadn't even thought he would be interested in.

"I don't want to argue with you anymore, Carson."

He blew out a big breath and looked away from me. "Me either." Suddenly, he sat forward, almost making me stick the wet tissue up his nose. A groan escaped his lips as he reached for the newspaper sitting on Lucie's table, pulling it to him before reading it aloud. *Poles Apart* – the headline jumped out at me before I saw the photo of me and Carson leaving my flat yesterday. "He's in pole position, she's a pole dancer. The two of them are poles apart." He made a scoffing noise in the back of his throat before he continued to read.

> Carson Matthews, MotoGP race driver and British heartthrob, is finally off the market. Petite blonde, Emma Bancroft, works at the lap dancing club Matthews frequents when he's in England. Emma, now nineteen, fell pregnant with the star's daughter when she was just sixteen, but the couple have been hiding it until now. The Peoples' Post suggested yesterday that the pair had an illicit relationship and Carson paid for Emma's services in the backroom of Angels Gentlemen's Club where she works part-time as a dancer and waitress. However, The Peoples' Post and Rodger Harris have printed a retraction this morning, apologising because they had made assumptions without facts. Carson's press team confirmed the couple have a rocky, on-off courtship and have been in and out of a relationship for the last three years. After the story broke yesterday, they appeared to be working things through as they left Emma's flat and then holed up at Carson's London home for the night. The statement from the Matthews camp also quashed rumours that Carson had no knowledge of his daughter until the story broke in the tabloids yesterday morning. The full statement can be seen on page five. The story continues to unfold, but young girls everywhere will be devastated that Carson now appears to be spoken for. If the social media site Twitter is anything to go by, the public reaction to Carson being engaged to a lap dancer hasn't gone down too well and has left a bitter taste in his female following's mouths.

He looked up at me then before shaking his head and pushing the paper away. "Pile of crap."

My body was kind of numb. Other than the newspaper Carson had shoved into my chest yesterday, I hadn't seen anything else that had been printed about us. Seeing it sitting there so casually on my best friend's dining table kind of brought it home to me a little more. Tears filled my eyes as I angrily tossed the wet tissue into the bin. I didn't know what to say, so I said nothing. Anger, shame and embarrassment swirled around in my stomach, making me feel a little nauseous. Everyone would now know what I did for a living: my university lecturers, my friends in my classes… my parents. The last thought actually hurt. It would just confirm everything they thought they knew about me. I *was* a dirty little tramp that brought shame on their family.

When arms slid around my waist and a hard chest pressed against my back, I jumped, startled by the sudden affection. I had no idea why he was doing it, or trying to comfort me after I'd lied to him all these years, but I welcomed the support. My eyes fluttered closed as I pressed back against Carson, letting his warmth surround and cloak me in an invisible layer of protection.

"Everything will be fine," he whispered. His breath blew down my neck as his arms tightened on me, crushing me against him. "You'll get used to this stuff. Just let it roll off you. Ignore it. Just get on with your life and don't look back. We'll make it."

'We'll make it'. The way I wanted that phrase to be intended – that we'd make it as a couple – wasn't how it was intended at all. I wanted it to mean we'd get through it together, that he would be part of the team Rory and I had formed over the last couple of years. But he didn't mean it that way at all. All that was meant by those three words were we'd get past this and people would forget about it soon enough and move on to the next freshly-broken story.

I gulped and swallowed my sadness. "I'm not so sure," I muttered, shaking my head and pushing myself from his arms. I had never been a person to wallow, so I needed to shake myself, dust myself off and carry on. Hopefully, in time, everything would get easier and this overwhelming sadness would stop creeping up on me unexpectedly.

Chapter Sixteen

To say the car ride with Rory and Carson had been awkward would be the understatement of my life. The air was practically crackling with waves of hatred coming from my little brother. Before we'd left Lucie's flat, I'd taken him aside and we'd had a long chat about how he needed to act, how he needed to go along with it for me so I could continue to work on Carson in my own terms and make him see this was not a good idea. I had every faith that my constant whining, Gloria's input, and the media attention would eventually wear him down and he would stop this ridiculous façade.

The media had again been waiting outside Lucie's flat for us to come out. As I'd carried my daughter from the building, Carson's arm was securely around my waist as he repeated his earlier words about them not being able to print a picture of Sasha or Rory because of the blanket order. Thankfully, as they were shouting their questions at us, Rory had kept his promise and kept his lips sealed.

Carson had been quiet the whole trip and kept sneaking glances at Sasha using his mirror. A little smile had twitched at the corner of his mouth the entire time. By the time we turned onto Carson's road, my head was aching from stress. The drive to his place had seemed to take forever as Rory sat there in the back, grumbling about not being able to walk to school or pop around to his friend's now that we lived in a different part of London.

"Jesus, how much money do you actually have?" Rory muttered as we pulled into the driveway of Carson's impressive house.

I rolled my eyes and, once in the garage, pushed myself out of the monster-like truck, jumping down because the seats were so high. As I pulled Sasha's door open, Carson had already run around the car and was standing close behind me, watching our every move as I plucked her from her car seat.

"Need a hand?" he offered.

I shook my head. "I've been managing perfectly fine for the last two years, thank you." I didn't mean it to sound as nasty as it came out; after all, it wasn't his fault he wasn't around and I'd been on my own.

Rory tossed a holdall bag full of clothes in Carson's direction. "Here, you can help me instead."

Carson's jaw tightened, but he didn't say anything in return as he waved his hand toward the interior door of the garage. I headed in that direction, watching as he typed in a passcode to get the door to open.

"You looking forward to seeing your new bedroom, Sasha?" Carson asked, smiling down at her.

She didn't answer, just turned her face into my neck. Sasha had been quiet for the last hour. She always could be a little shy around strangers. Like me, it took her a little time to fully trust someone, but once she did trust, she let them see every part of her. Carson just needed to keep working on her and she'd let him be part of her inner circle. He looked extremely disheartened by her not answering him, but he covered it with a sad smile.

"All right, Sash?" I whispered, kissing the side of her head. She nodded, gripping her hands into my hair and twisting it around her fist absentmindedly as she kept one eye on Carson. "Daddy bought you a beautiful new chair made out of teddy bears, want to go see?" I asked, trying to help him out a little because the sad look on Carson's face actually hurt me, too. She nodded against my neck, so I smiled over at Carson. "Maybe Daddy will show us the way?" I offered.

Carson's tense shoulders seemed to loosen as I included him. He smiled gratefully at me and placed his hand on the small of my back as we walked up the stairs to the house. "I can definitely do that," he said quietly.

Rory made a strangled choking sound as he stepped into the hallway behind us. "Damn. Big," he muttered, looking around with wide eyes.

Carson smiled over at him. "Go look around. My house is your house," he stated, waving his hand in invitation. "TV room is in there. Your bedroom is on the first floor, first door on the right."

Rory nodded, dropping his bag carelessly as he walked in the direction of the TV room. "You know, Emma, maybe this might work out after all. Live with him for a couple of years, then divorce his arse and take half of everything," he suggested, his voice serious, as if I should actually consider it.

I frowned at my brother for the mere suggestion. "I'm sure there will be a strict pre-nup agreement. Celebrities usually insist on those, especially if they're marrying someone like me," I muttered.

"I don't want a pre-nup," Carson chimed in, sliding his hand from the small of my back to my hip instead as he stepped closer to my side. "If you two girls want it, then take it. I don't care." He shrugged, looking down at Sasha.

I rolled my eyes and gritted my teeth. "How many times have I told you I'm not interested in your money?" I snapped.

He smiled warmly. "Plenty. And that's one reason why I don't need one."

I opened my mouth to answer, but Sasha tugged on my hair to get my attention. "Teddy chair," she whined in my ear, obviously impatient to get to her room.

Nodding, I looked at Carson. "Your little girl wants to see her room. Let's save this conversation for another time, huh?"

After following him up the stairs and into Sasha's bedroom, I immediately stalked over to the chair and sat down in it, settling Sasha on my lap. She didn't let go of me straight away as she looked around with wide eyes. "What do you think? See how cute this chair is? Mummy wants one of these for her room," I said, touching one of the bear's noses as I smiled. It was gorgeously designed.

"I'll get you one," Carson stated, walking into the room and watching me with a smile on his face.

I rolled my eyes. "It was just a turn of phrase. You don't need to buy everything I mention a fancy for, you know."

Ignoring my dig, he walked over to the tall, white-wood wardrobe and pulled open the door. On one side, there were two full racks of clothes in every single colour; on the other, shelves and shelves of teddy bears, dolls and toys. Sasha's little body jerked as she looked at the array of things inside.

"These are all yours," Carson stated, picking up a stuffed monkey from the top shelf and doing a monkey-type chatter impression.

Sasha giggled and looked up at me uncertainly. I smiled reassuringly and nodded. "They're all yours, Sash. Daddy bought them all for you. Go check them out," I instructed, helping her off my lap as she squirmed to get down.

She walked hesitantly over to Carson and took the offered monkey from his hand. "Sasha's?" she asked. When Carson nodded, she brought the monkey to her face and kissed its nose before smiling up at her dad. I didn't need to see inside his chest to know his heart melted at her smile – it was clear on his face.

Sasha immediately turned on her heel and marched over to me. "Mummy, up!" she ordered, taking my hand and tugging. "M'key chair!" she announced, setting the stuffed monkey in the space I'd just vacated.

I chuckled and sat on the floor instead, watching as she methodically made her way back and forth from the wardrobe, plucking out the toys one by one. She looked up at Carson each time as she asked, "Sasha's?" checking they were really hers before she marched over to the chair and arranged them all in one big pile.

By the time she was finished inspecting every inch of her room, the place looked like a bomb had exploded inside it. Carson was grinning from ear to ear, probably because Sasha had already been won over by his gifts and was now accepting of him and no longer shy. When my tummy rumbled, I looked at my watch to see it was after five.

"Do you mind if I make some dinner?" I asked nervously.

Carson frowned. "You don't need to ask my permission for stuff like that. This is your home now, Emma."

I sighed. "It's not home; it's just a place where I'm currently living because you told me I have to." As I pushed myself up from the floor, I looked down at Sasha as she emptied the contents of a 'match the card' game onto the floor. "Want to stay up here with Daddy, or come down and help me cook?" I asked.

"Cooks!" she answered, pushing herself up as well but not letting go of the 'tickle me Elmo' toy that she seemed to be favouring. Sasha loved to help me cook. Usually, she had just an empty bowl and spoon to bang around with while I cooked, but it was good enough for her.

As the three of us walked out of the room, Sasha's chubby little hand slipped into Carson's. He looked down at her hand in shock, and then the biggest, most spectacular grin stretched across his face. It appeared that Sasha had now accepted Carson into her inner circle, and he couldn't have been happier about it judging by the look on his face.

I WOKE TO THE SOUNDS of dramatic crying through the expensive baby monitors Carson had purchased. I groaned and pushed myself up, sleepily trudging from my room into Sasha's. My eyes stung and my head ached. I hadn't had much sleep last night. On top of the house and street being unusually quiet compared to my flat, I also didn't like being in a different room to my baby girl. It felt wrong and was something that was going to take me a long time to get used to.

From the sound of her cries alone, I already knew there was nothing wrong with her. You could hear the differences when she really meant it. This one was more a, I've-just-woken-up-and-am-already-fed-up-with-being-in-my-cot cry. I was used to this one early in the morning. Clearly Carson wasn't, though.

As I reached into the cot to pick up Sasha, he came pelting into the room in just a pair of navy, long-legged loungewear trousers which hung dangerously low on his hips. He still looked half-asleep as a worried frown creased his forehead. "What's happened? She okay? Why's she crying?" he asked, stepping to my side quickly and looking at her worriedly.

I smiled at the concern I could see on his face. "She's fine. She just woke up in a strange room, that's all," I said, elbowing him playfully in the ribs.

He blew out a big breath, raking his hand through his messy hair and causing it to stick up at the front. "Ugh, that's not a nice thing to wake up to," he muttered, shaking his head.

"You'll get used to it," I replied. As he stepped back and smiled at Sasha, picking up her dummy she'd dropped on the floor, I let my eyes wander over him. I bit back a groan of appreciation as the muscles rippled in his stomach and arms as he moved. My mouth watered with the strong urge to lean in and lick his chest while rubbing my scent over him like a cat. He looked damn fine in the morning. Better than I even dared imagine, actually.

He looked up then and caught me mid-inspection of his body. A sly grin crossed his face. "You can touch it if you want," he offered playfully.

The blush crept up on me unexpectedly. "I'll keep that in mind, thanks," I replied, shaking my head and fighting to control the girlie giggle trying to escape my lips. He grinned that boyish grin, causing the dimples that made my heart stutter. "You want some breakfast or something?"

He shook his head. "Nah, I think I'm gonna go grab a shower to wake me up."

The thought of a shower automatically made impure thoughts run through my head as I imagined the water trailing down his body, dripping off him. *The shower in my room is plenty big enough for two... maybe I need a shower, too...*

I shook my head to rid myself of the dirty thoughts and blinked a couple of times when I realised I was standing in the middle of Sasha's bedroom and not in a hot, steamy shower rubbing a soapy washcloth over Carson's body. The disappointment hit me hard.

AFTER BREAKFAST, I dressed Sasha and then left her playing in her cot with a couple of dolls, while I went for a quick shower and dressed myself for university today. Once ready, we both headed downstairs. Carson was sitting at the breakfast bar eating a cinnamon swirl left over from the day before. He was dressed in loose-fit jeans and a fitted white T-shirt, and his feet were bare. He grinned at us as we walked in.

"Daddy!" Sasha cried excitedly, suddenly squirming in my arms. I set her down, watching as she hurried to his side and held her arms up to him. He laughed and hooked his hands under her armpits, hoisting her onto his lap. Immediately, she twisted and took his cinnamon swirl from his plate, chewing on it messily.

Carson laughed incredulously. "And here was me thinking you were excited to see me, when all the time you were plotting to steal my breakfast!" he teased, poking her in the ribs and making her giggle.

I laughed at the adorable sight and headed to the fridge, pulling out butter and ham. "Okay if I make some packed lunch stuff for today?" I asked, turning back to Carson. He raised one eyebrow, and his jaw tightened. I sighed, already knowing what he was thinking. "Don't ask permission, Emma; this is your home now," I muttered, trying to do an impression of his deep, throaty voice.

"Exactly," he confirmed, taking a sip of his tea as he wrapped his free arm around Sasha, holding her securely on his lap as she ate his cake.

I nodded, getting to work making lunch. "Don't suppose you know the tube route to my uni, do you?" I asked absentmindedly. Today was my first day back there after all this blew up; I didn't really want to be late because I was lost on the tube.

"I can drive you," Carson answered. "If you tell me what time you finish, I'll pick you up after, too."

My stomach clenched at the kind gesture. "Are you not working today then?"

"No, I called and explained the situation. I have a few days off. I can't get out of the meetings I have scheduled this weekend, though, so I'll be going away on Thursday morning and not coming back until Sunday night."

He was going away? "Oh," was all I could think to say.

"I'm going to Italy," he continued.

"That's nice."

He cleared his throat. "You, er… want to come?"

Come? To Italy? Hell yeah, I do! But it wasn't possible. "I can't. Sasha and I don't have passports."

He frowned and nodded slowly. "Oh. Well, we'll have to rectify that, I guess. Won't get it sorted by Thursday, though." He pursed his lips in thought. "Maybe next time I go away?" he offered.

I shrugged noncommittally. Why would he even want us to go with him anyway? Surely he'd have more fun on his own living his single life than having his supposed-fiancée there and his two-year-old daughter?

"I'll get someone to rush you through some passports before my next abroad race. There should be enough time because I only race every other week, and next weekend is actually in England. I shouldn't need to leave the country again for another three weeks, so that should be plenty of time for someone to arrange some passports for you two," he mused. "Next weekend, I'm racing at Silverstone. It's my favourite track. Maybe you could come and watch? You've never been to one of my races before," he offered, seeming somewhat hopeful about it.

I gulped, not wanting to go because I hated that he had a dangerous job, but also knowing I needed to go so we could show a united front. It wouldn't look very good for him if I kept avoiding his races, and I didn't have a single reason why I couldn't go.

"Um… okay."

"Great." He seemed rather pleased with my answer.

"JUST IGNORE THE PAPS. Say 'no comment', and remind them they're not allowed to print pictures of Sasha," Carson instructed as he gripped the steering wheel tightly, glaring out the window at the group of photographers that had followed us to my school from his house.

"Okay," I agreed, picking up my bag of books and swinging it onto my shoulder. As I gripped the door handle and pushed the door open, Carson placed his hand on my leg.

"Emma?"

I turned back to him, noticing he looked kind of nervous. "Yeah?"

"Kiss me goodbye?" he requested, leaning over the middle of the seat toward me.

I gulped and my eyes immediately dropped to his lips. Not actually needing to be told twice, I closed the distance between us and crushed my lips against his roughly, kissing him fiercely. Deep down, I knew he only wanted this because the photographers were probably busy taking shots of us kissing in the car, but I actually couldn't have cared less. With Carson's lips against mine, nothing else mattered in the world. He moaned in the back of his throat and brought his hand up, gripping the back of my head and holding my mouth to his securely.

Of course, I wasn't the one to break the kiss because I never wanted it to end. Instead, he pulled back fractionally before kissing me again, softer this time. I smiled against his lips, loving the intimacy of the move. His nose brushed against mine in a little Eskimo kiss before he pressed his forehead to mine.

"Have a good day," he whispered.

I couldn't open my eyes. I was still lost within the bliss of his mouth on mine. When I traced my tongue along my bottom lip, I could taste him.

"Mummy?"

I gulped. Sasha's little voice brought me out of the little romantic haze I found myself trapped in. "Yeah, we're going, beautiful. Say bye to Daddy," I said, clearing my throat as I pulled back and smiled sheepishly at Carson.

"Bye, Daddy!" Sasha chirped, already pressing at the button on her car seat to release her seatbelt.

"I'll be here just after three then, all right?" Carson said before twisting in his seat and playfully tugging on Sasha's foot. "Be a good girl at nursery."

Carson had offered to have Sasha for the day today, but I had just felt it was a little too soon. Although she liked him, spending the whole day with her this soon would probably be a little awkward for them both. They needed time to adapt, and Sasha actually loved her crèche and her little friends who went there.

As I helped Sasha out of her car seat, I swung her onto my hip and pulled up her hood so it covered her face. The paparazzi immediately started asking me questions and walking alongside me. I just stayed quiet the whole time, keeping my gaze firmly focussed on the door of the building, counting the steps until it would be over. Carson had already assured me they wouldn't be allowed to set foot inside the building, some code of privacy or something schools and stuff had. They had to ask permission to set foot on campus grounds – and they wouldn't have that.

Once safely inside the building, I went to the next window and peeked out, seeing Carson drive off. I breathed a sigh of relief that it was over for a while. Hopefully by the time I came out of class at the end of the day, they would have lost interest and be gone.

The nursery Sasha went to was a little colourful wing of the building, which was especially for students who had children. There were only two nursery nurses who worked there, and an assistant. They only had about twelve children aged between zero and four. This place was a godsend for me and the sole reason I applied here in the first place.

As I stepped through the door, the two mothers I saw every other day – Katherine and Simone – both stopped talking midsentence and looked at me in disbelief. I forced a smile and set down Sasha, taking off her jacket and hanging it on her peg with her lunchbox before watching her run off to the kitchen/home play area to talk gobbledygook with her friend, Scarlet, just like every other day.

I cleared my throat and walked up to the pair who now had their heads together, whispering and trying not to look at me. "Hi. Good weekend?" I asked politely. "Did you get that assignment done you were worried about, Simone?"

Simone pressed her lips into a thin line and nodded. "Barely managed it." She shared a meaningful look with Katherine and then turned back to me. "We should really go. See you around," she stated, waving goodbye to the nursery nurse who had just stepped out of the bathrooms with one of the little boys from the crèche.

I nodded, hating that they looked at me with so much distaste and didn't even have the decency to try and disguise it. I had known both of these girls for over a year; Simone I knew for a year and a half. I saw them every day, laughed with them, chatted. They knew me. But yet they were now looking at me with distain and clearly couldn't get away from me quick enough. It actually hurt.

"Okay. Want to grab a coffee or something at lunch?" I asked, hoping I was wrong and they hadn't read the papers, that they weren't looking down their noses at me and I was just being paranoid.

Katherine's nose wrinkled unconsciously. "We're busy, sorry."

Nasty bitch! So much for the common bond we'd made over the last year that she'd been dropping her little boy off for! "Oh, with non-lap dancers I suppose," I muttered, nodding knowingly. She didn't answer; she just shrugged, clearly not even feeling guilty. I sighed and turned away, walking over to Sasha. I already knew people would react differently to me today, but I wasn't expecting it to come from people who actually knew me. I could hear them whispering behind me, but I didn't look back as they left the room, letting the door swing closed behind them.

As I got to Sasha's side, I bent and kissed her cheek, listening to her prattle on to her best baby friend in a language I had no hope of deciphering. "Mummy has to go to her lessons now. I'll see you later. I love you." She broke her chatter long enough to kiss me back, and then was frying up some fake eggs in the plastic kitchen.

When I got to the door of the nursery and twisted the safety lock to open it, the nursery assistant called my name. I stopped, turning and smiling at her. Hilda was a lovely, jolly, older lady who Sasha adored because she wasn't afraid to get down on her knees and be silly with the kids. "Hi, Hilda," I greeted.

She smiled awkwardly. "Hi, Emma. Umm… Cindy would like a word with you," she said, nodding over her shoulder. When I looked in that direction, I saw the two nursery nurses talking heatedly.

"What about? Is something wrong?" I asked, letting the door click closed behind me.

Hilda cleared her throat, looking down at the floor as she shrugged. "I don't know. She just asked me to ask you to speak to her if you came to drop Sasha off today. We weren't even sure you'd come after… you know…" she said.

'You know'. Yes, I knew exactly what this would be about. They'd seen the papers, and I was now about to be judged on it and my choice of profession. I suppressed my groan and nodded. "Sure, I have time quickly before class." I didn't actually have much time to spare, but I'd have to make time. I followed Hilda to the back of the room again, seeing Sasha still playing with her friend.

Cindy looked up as I approached. She didn't smile. Her eyes were tight, as were her lips which were pressed into a thin line. "Oh, Miss Bancroft, I'd like a word in the office," she stated, waving her hand towards her poky little cubicle in the corner that constituted an office just because it had a desk and a telephone.

The casual use of my title when she usually called me Emma alerted me to the fact this was going to be worse than I first thought.

Chapter Seventeen

As I stepped out of the nursery with a crying Sasha in my arms, I felt like giving up. Sasha was screaming and screaming that she didn't want to go and that she wanted to play with Scarlet.

Thankfully, my talk with Cindy, the stuck-up nursery manager, had lasted a fairly long time, so the paparazzi were gone by the time I made my exit with my wailing child. As Sasha was in full-blown tantrum mode at being unceremoniously booted out of her nursery, I winced as her flailing arm hit me in the face. Carrying a screaming, tantrum-throwing, almost-two-year-old was practically impossible, so I sat down on the nearest bench and pinned her on my lap, letting her get out all her frustrations.

I had no idea how to explain to her that she wasn't welcome at the nursery anymore because her mother was a dirty whore who danced for drunken men for money. Cindy had made out that Sasha no longer being welcome there was all to do with the photographers and reporters, and that it was a 'safety thing' and she needed to think of Sasha's welfare along with the other eleven children who attended. But deep down, I knew it was more a prejudice thing against me and my job. The way she'd looked down her nose at me, and frowned distastefully when I'd perched on the edge of her desk, made that perfectly clear.

"Sasha, please calm down and stop this," I whispered, smoothing her hair away from her face and trying to wipe her tears. "Come on, you can come back another day and play with Scarlet." Lie. That was a total lie. She wasn't welcome back at all, apparently. "Sasha, come on. Please don't make this any harder for me, please?" I begged, closing my eyes and pressing my face into her hair as I fought tears and a tantrum of my own.

"Scar..." Sasha sobbed.

A lump formed in my throat as she finally stopped struggling. "You can play with Scarlet another time." I'd have to find some way of keeping that promise. Maybe I could somehow find Scarlet's mother's number and invite her over for coffee or something – so long as she didn't think I was a dirty, gold-digging tramp, too. I kissed her forehead softly, wiping her tears from her face as she looked up at me with those big, blue eyes I loved to death. "How about we go to the park or something now for a little while?" I offered.

I wasn't ready to go home yet. I didn't want to talk about it to anyone. In fact, all I wanted to do was bury this whole day deep into my subconscious and block it out, pretending it never happened. The dirty, waste-of-space feeling washing over me was almost too much to bear. All I wanted to do was go to bed with a whole litre of ice cream and watch old movies while I wallowed in self-pity. But, being a mother, I wasn't afforded that luxury. Instead, I had to plaster on a happy face and pretend my heart wasn't breaking as I took my toddler to the park to ease her disappointment.

AFTER TWO HOURS IN THE PARK, I knew I couldn't put it off any longer because it was almost lunchtime. I needed to go home. The awkward thing about that was I wasn't exactly sure where Carson lived. I knew the street name and the area, so it was just a matter of working out which tube lines I needed to go on to get there. After help from the train ticket guy, we finally worked it out, and I broke into my last ten pound note to buy a travel card.

On the third train changeover, Sasha started yawning and her eyes started to droop. Fortunately, someone gave up their seat for us, so I hoisted her onto my lap and she was asleep before we even passed the next stop. That was good in one way, because I could stop pretending I was fine and wasn't ready to burst into tears at any second, but it was bad in another way because now I would have to carry her all the way home to Carson's place.

Luckily for me, Carson's house was easy to find on the beautiful and exclusive street. By the time I arrived outside the house and typed in the passcode for the gate he'd made me memorise, sweat was running down my back, and my arms ached from carrying the sleeping little girl for so long. I was gasping for a drink, a shower and a long sit down – but what I wanted the most was a huge, ginormous bar of chocolate to drown my sorrows in.

As I walked in the front door and closed it quietly behind me, Carson poked his head around the hallway. His eyes widened when he saw me, and he came strutting toward me with a worried expression on his face.

"Why are you back here so early?" Carson asked, frowning in confusion. "Is everything okay, what's happened?"

I sighed and walked into the lounge, carefully setting Sasha down onto the sofa so she could continue with her nap. "The university crèche won't take Sasha anymore. Apparently, there is too much attention surrounding her, and they don't want it to upset or unsettle her or the other children. They said that with the press following me and her around, they can't guarantee her safety or the safety of others, and it would be unethical to allow me to leave Sasha there with them for the foreseeable future. They've suggested I make alternative arrangements," I muttered, stalking into the kitchen and yanking open the fridge, looking for some comfort food.

"You're kidding," Carson gasped.

I shook my head. "Nope."

"Well, how are you supposed to go to your classes?" he asked angrily.

I shrugged. "Apparently, that's not their problem," I answered. Not finding anything good in the fridge, I slammed it shut and turned to face him. "You should have seen the way they looked at me. I felt disgusting. I hate this. I hate that everything has changed. I hate that I now can't go to class because I don't have anyone to watch Sash. Maybe I should just give up and drop out. Hell, I'll be surprised if I'm even allowed to attend anymore after this. If the crèche are binning me off, then the school will probably find an excuse to chuck me out, too."

Carson recoiled at my train of thought but shook his head adamantly. "You're not dropping out, and they're not binning you off, either. If they do then we'll take it to the board of governors and tell them we're suing them for discrimination. You love your course, and I won't let you give up on it," he replied. "If they don't want to care for Sasha while you're at uni, then we'll find someone else to."

I scowled down at the floor. "I don't know. It's going to be really hard for me in my classes anyway now that everyone knows." I kicked my toes against the marble tiles absentmindedly. "The other mums I talk to every day at nursery couldn't get away from me quick enough. It was like they thought I was going to infect them with something."

Carson sighed and stepped closer to me, hooking his finger under my chin, and tilting my head up so I had to meet his eyes. "You're not a quitter, Emma. If you gave up when life was a little hard, then you wouldn't be where you are today."

That was true. I usually never let anything beat me down, but right now I felt like I'd been kicked too many times and was finding it hard to get to my feet again. I shrugged, not having the words. What I longed for was to step forward, press my face into his chest, and let his warmth cover me like a cloak of protection.

Carson sighed deeply. "We'll just get one of those live-in nannies or something. You're not quitting your course," he said adamantly. "I'll make some calls and get the ball rolling and then once we have some suitable candidates, you can choose someone."

I scoffed at his idea. "I'm not having a live-in nanny look after Sash! No way."

"Why not? It won't be just a regular person. There must be some sort of service that other people in the public eye go to. I'll call around and see if anyone can recommend someone. You can do interviews, make sure the person is qualified and that you like them and trust them."

I shook my head in refusal. "No, it's not happening, Carson. I'm not letting you bully me into this one. We're *not* having a live-in nanny. I'm not having someone know her better than me. Sasha will be running to her when she's hurt herself, and she'll breastfeed her in the night and have Sash call her 'Mummy'. She'll make me look like I've lost my mind so she can sweep in and steal my family from me. No. No way."

Carson chuckled wickedly, looking at me as if I'd lost my mind. "Seriously?"

I placed my hands on my hips. "Yes! Have you not seen *The Hand That Rocks the Cradle*? The blonde woman in that was psycho. I'm not taking the chance."

He burst out laughing, shaking his head. "Emma, you're so awesomely funny. Who knew living with you would be so entertaining," he jibed.

I sighed and rolled my eyes. "I'm not having a live-in nanny." *He can make fun all he wants; it isn't happening.*

Carson stepped closer to me, so close I could feel his breath as it blew across my face. He'd been eating apple pie. My mouth watered as I longed to go up on tiptoes and press those soft lips against mine. I wanted to trace my tongue along his and see if he tasted like apple pie, too.

"Okay, fine, we don't get a nanny. How about we find Sasha a new private nursery then?" he offered, cocking his head to the side.

I smiled weakly and nodded, feeling some of the tension leave my body. "Yeah, I'd like that a lot better. Thank you."

When his hand rose and he brushed a loose curl of hair behind my ear, my whole body prickled with excitement. It had been so long since he'd touched me that my insides were melting and fizzing with apprehension. It was now five long weeks since I'd had any physical attention from him. That was seriously too long for my body to cope with.

I caught his hand, smiling weakly, knowing I needed to make my escape before I begged him to make love to me on the kitchen counter just so I could relieve some of this sexual frustration building inside me. A white blob on the tip of his finger caught my attention and I looked down at it, seeing that he had little speckles of white and silver flecking the back of his hand.

"You been decorating or something?" I asked, letting go of his hand and taking a step back.

"Yeah." He nodded, looking away from me.

"I thought you said you don't do decorating," I queried. Last night when we'd spoken about Sasha's room, he'd said he would get a professional painter in to decorate it. I frowned, not liking that he'd gone ahead and done it without me. He'd said we could choose the theme together.

"I don't, I just wanted to do this little thing." He shrugged, looking away from me before going to the fridge and rooting around inside.

I frowned at his back. "I'm going to take a quick shower. Can you listen out for Sash? She probably won't wake yet but..."

"Yeah, of course."

I turned on my heel and marched out, trudging up the stairs, wondering what the weird atmosphere was in the kitchen. As I walked past Sasha's room, I peeked in, not seeing anything different in there. The walls were still a plain, cream colour; I could see no traces of white or silver paint anywhere. I frowned, now thoroughly confused as I made my way to my bedroom. As I opened the door, something on the wall caught my eye. A glittering, shiny thing. I frowned, stepping in and closing the door behind me as I looked at it. My lungs constricted when I saw what it was. Now I knew the reason Carson had white and silver paint on his hands.

On the red wall behind my bed, there were now several white and silver spray-painted butterflies. He'd obviously used a stencil, as the pattern was very intricate but exactly the same, repeated in varying sizes. The little stencils floated up the wall and off to the side as if they were flying in a group. They were crude; one of them had a little chunk missing, and one was a lot darker than the others – probably his first attempt at it.

My heart melted into a puddle and my eyes glazed over with tears. Butterflies were my favourites – as well he knew. I put my hand up, tracing the line of one of them as my teeth sank into my bottom lip. He'd gone to so much effort, just for me. I loved it. "What a cutie-pie," I murmured, looking at the stencilled design in awe.

When I turned, something else caught my eye. On the middle of the bed sat a light-turquoise paper bag with the words Tiffany & Co printed on the side. I frowned, reaching for it and picking it up, curious. As I peeked inside, I saw a small square box of the same colour, with a white ribbon tied at the top. I glanced up, wondering if this was for me to open. Carson had clearly been in my room this morning painting, so if there was something on the bed then surely he'd put it there for me to find.

Curiously, I shoved my hand in the bag, picking up the little box as I chewed on my lip. Unable to stand not knowing what was inside, I sat on the edge of the bed and tossed the bag to the side, pulling the white ribbon from the box. As I lifted the lid, a smaller black box greeted me. My breath suddenly caught in my throat as I realised what this was. I had no idea how I'd not thought of it before.

Gulping, I lifted the lid, and there sat the most exquisite engagement ring I had ever seen. The diamond on it was huge and cut to perfection so the light glittered and shined off it. Smaller diamonds were set into the white gold band, making it look classy but not too overstated. It was perfection.

My hand shook as I reached out and touched it. Tears swam in my eyes as my finger touched the cool, hard band. "Oh, God," I breathed. My eyes drifted to the third finger of my left hand as I wondered what it would look like near my chewed and unpainted fingernails. It was so incredibly beautiful – too beautiful, in fact. I couldn't accept it. A ring from Tiffany's was just too much; it had probably cost him a fortune.

That was when the irrational anger started to creep up on me. The fact that he'd just left the ring on the bed for me to find actually bugged the shit out of me. Deep down, I knew why I was annoyed – I wanted him to get down on one knee and give me this ring. This was just another thing which showed how disconnected he was to me and this marriage he was insisting on. The ring, casually left on the bed, hurt me.

Pushing myself up from the bed, I grabbed all the wrappings and boxes and headed out of the room. As I walked into the kitchen, he looked up from the sandwich he was eating and smiled at me. His smile made my anger dissipate immediately, and I fought hard to hold on to it and remember why I was annoyed.

"I can't accept this," I stated, placing the bag and ring box down on the kitchen table and folding my arms across my chest defensively.

One of his eyebrows rose. "And why's that?"

"It's a ring from Tiffany's, Carson!" I replied.

He grinned, regarding me with playful eyes. "And you have a problem with Tiffany & Co?"

I sighed deeply. "Look, I don't need this, all right? The ring is beautiful, but I can't accept it." As I said the words, I realised how much I didn't like saying them. A conflict was raging inside me; part of me wanted that ring badly just because it was from him.

Carson shrugged and stood up, picking up his now-empty plate and walking to the sink. "Well, I can't get a refund now; I've lost the receipt."

I scowled at his back. "As if! You must have only bought it this morning!" I had been with him all weekend; this morning when I'd attempted to go to class was the only time we'd been apart.

He turned and a playful smile graced his lips, and all I could think about was flicking my tongue across his. He leant against the counter and shrugged. "You don't like the ring then? I can get store credit; you can choose something else if you don't like the design."

I picked up the ring box and popped open the lid, holding it out to him. I kept trying not to look at it because every time I saw it, my heart stuttered in my chest. "Look at it, how can anyone not like that? But it's too much, Carson. Seriously, this is just... no, I can't."

He didn't answer, just walked over to me and took the box from my hand. I watched as he plucked the ring from the box and carelessly tossed the wrapping to the side. "I happen to think this ring would look fucking incredible on you," he stated as he took my left hand. "So yes, you can accept it. And yes, you will wear it and show it off. And yes, you will love it." I gasped as he placed the ring on my third finger, slowly sliding it all the way down to my knuckle. "And yes, it *does* look fucking incredible on you." His eyes flicked up to meet mine. "Stop being difficult and thinking of the cost all the time. From now on, you don't need to worry about the price of anything."

I was lost in my own thoughts. I wanted to be angry at him for the situation we were in, I wanted to refuse to accept it because it was too expensive, and I wanted to shout at him for trapping me all the time and not considering my feelings or wants. But, in that moment, all that seemed to matter to me was that Carson Matthews had just pushed an engagement ring onto my finger. Everything else now faded into insignificance.

Before I could recover, he bent his head and pressed his lips to the corner of my mouth. I whimpered at the feel of it. The soft, intimate moment swirled around me; seconds seemed to drag on. Without my conscious permission, my hand gripped the side of his shirt.

As he pulled away, his eyes met mine, and I could see the desire there. Carson had always made me feel desired and wanted. His eyes were my downfall. I didn't let go of his shirt as the tip of his nose touched mine. His lips brushed mine ever so gently as he spoke. "Please take the ring. I saw it and knew it was the right one," he whispered, moving his hand to cup my neck as his thumb stroked the line of my jaw. My mouth watered as his breath blew across my lips. "Please?" he whispered again.

I gulped, swallowing the desire I was seemingly drowning in. "Okay." Embarrassingly, my voice cracked as I answered, but he didn't seem to notice.

A smile twitched at the corner of his lips as he stepped impossibly closer to me, pressing his body against mine. "See? A little compromise, that's all that was needed."

Compromise? "We didn't compromise. I conceded," I muttered, coming back to reality a little.

He grinned then and the intimate moment was over. "Different word, same conclusion," he observed as he stepped back and let his hand drop to his side. "Thank you for accepting it."

I looked down at the beautiful thing, which now resided on my finger. "Thank you for buying it for me," I replied breathlessly.

He chuckled and shrugged as if it were nothing. At that exact moment, Sasha came wandering into the kitchen, rubbing at her eyes. Her hair was sticking up everywhere, her eyes still half-closed as she yawned around her dummy. I smiled at the sight, a little grateful I would have a distraction and someone else in the room so Carson and I weren't alone anymore. I wasn't doing very well at holding my own against him at all.

Chapter Eighteen

Everyone was talking at once. There were too many voices, saying too many different things around me and my neck ached from turning back and forth so I could try to keep up with them. Magazines, colour swatches, sample napkins, fabric samples, lists of venues and flower brochures littered the table in front of me. The group pawed through them, gushing over them, all excited as they planned my wedding.

No one asked me what I thought.

I sat there, surrounded by people and noise, chatter, and champagne, yet I'd never felt more lonely in my life.

Margo, the haughty, snooty-looking wedding planner Carson had invited around, sat there gushing over one venue – some castle in Scotland – and tried to convince Carson it was the best place to host a wedding. She raved over a wedding she'd planned there just last year, saying it was the most spectacular thing she'd ever seen; though, of course, ours would be even better, according to her.

Margo had two assistants with her. The younger-looking girl, who certainly had her eyes on Carson, was more of a lackey. Every time Margo would say something, the younger girl would quickly dig through the pile of stuff they'd brought with them and hold up samples or photos, which matched the topic of conversation. The other assistant was busy scribbling notes down in a pad, firing off questions that Margo answered without consulting anyone else.

Carson seemed a little overwhelmed and was drinking his champagne too fast as he nodded along with stuff and spent goodness knows how much money – I wasn't even sure if he knew what he'd spent because I never once heard a price mentioned. It didn't really seem to matter; money was something of unimportance to Carson, it seemed.

Carson's sisters, Kimberly and Alice, were looking with wide eyes through the exquisite wedding cake design book, giggling to themselves and cooing over them.

The only one who didn't look very enthusiastic about it was Jillian, Carson's mother. She'd come around to sit in on the plans because Carson thought 'being a part of it all' would help me and her bond. It wasn't working. She was sipping champagne slowly; her face was a blank page and her eyes gave nothing away.

Thankfully, Sasha was in bed already. She was exhausted from her play in the park after we got unceremoniously kicked out of the nursery and the numerous games of hide and seek she and Carson played all afternoon. Rory, the lucky kid, also got to escape all this and was in his bedroom doing his homework. I envied him. Today had been one long, never-ending day, and all I wanted was to sit with my feet up and a cup of tea, watching *EastEnders* – not sipping champagne and planning a wedding I didn't even want to attend.

"So, if you'd just decide on a colour scheme we can move on to tablecloths and napkins," Margo suggested, holding out a colour wheel to Carson.

He cleared his throat, nodding in my direction. "Emma?"

Biting back my scoff and angry remark, I shrugged noncommittally. "I don't care. Whatever you want." Even to my own ears, my voice sounded depressed.

Carson's forehead creased with a frown as his lips pressed into a thin line. "You don't want to choose the colour that will run through the whole day?" he asked sarcastically.

Black. Black was dark, dank and depressing – that would suit my mood. But I didn't say that because I was supposed to be behaving in front of other people and pretending like this wedding was the best thing that ever happened to me.

I forced a smile, trying not to show how detached I was from it all, how emotionless I was inside about it. I couldn't even summon one ounce of excitement. The wedding planner and Carson had chosen a date just over five months away because it fit in with his racing season being over. That meant, in five months, I would be married to a person who barely even liked me. What exactly was there to be excited about in that? Nothing.

"I don't have a preference, baby; you just have what you want." *There, that answer should suffice and mean I don't have to talk for the next half hour!*

Carson sighed deeply, obviously seeing my unwillingness to be a part of this stupid day. He set down his champagne flute and scooted forward in his chair, taking the colour wheel from Margo's hand and tossing it onto the table. "Emma's favourite colour is red; dark red, like maroon. She likes butterflies, so maybe we could incorporate that somehow? I don't know, on the invites or place names or whatever. Book the Scotland castle then if it's a nice place. And as for the honeymoon," he shrugged, "go for somewhere ridiculously hot with a gorgeous beach and no paparazzi. Emma and Sasha will need to order passports as they don't have them."

My mind was reeling as he spoke. How on Earth did he even know my favourite colour? Had I told him, or was he some kind of mind reader?

Margo gasped. "Butterflies? We could definitely work that in!" she exclaimed excitedly. "We could have the napkins printed with a butterfly in the corner and your initials either side, or incorporated stylishly within in the wings. I'll get a designer on that and see what they can come up with. We could then have the same design throughout all the invites, thank you notes, place names, and table favours. I bet we could get some metal ones crafted and inserted into the bridal flowers. Oh, and I've just thought of the most beautiful idea for your hair instead of a tiara, Emma," she enthused, patting my knee excitedly. "Butterflies! Beautiful!" She even clapped her hands as she wriggled in her seat happily. The scratch of her assistant's pen filled my ears like a buzzing of a bee that I wanted to swat.

A butterfly theme. Had I not hated the whole idea of being forced into marriage, I would have swooned over the very thought of it. Instead, my wedding, which seemed as if it was going to be my perfect, dream wedding, was marred with thoughts that this wasn't what anyone truly wanted. It was just a marriage of convenience and nothing else.

"Great. Are we done now? I think I've had about as much wedding planning as I can take for today," Carson muttered, clenching and unclenching his hand on his knee as if it were painful.

I frowned, studying his hand to see if I could see anything wrong with it.

Margo cleared her throat and nodded toward all the books, magazines and other wedding planning essentials covering every inch of the brand new white wood table that Carson had bought yesterday. "Well, your part can be done for now if you want, Carson. Why don't we girls just spend a few minutes talking about wedding dresses?" she suggested, grinning wildly.

I groaned internally, willing Carson to tell them enough was enough and that we'd pick this up another time. Surely they had enough to be getting on with for now. He didn't jump in and save me, though; instead, he nodded and stood up, stalking from the room without another word.

Once he was gone, out came another book. Margo moved from her seat and sat opposite me. Her excitement was evident and burst from every pore. Clearly, this was her favourite part.

"I have some fantastic contacts, Emma, so if you have a designer in mind then let me know. But do you know who I think you should wear? Alexander McQueen!" she gushed.

Kimberly squealed, and the two assistants nodded in agreement, but I had no clue who they were talking about. Obviously he was some kind of famous designer, but I didn't much follow the fashion world.

"I personally know Sarah Burton, and although the timing is short, I'm sure she could come up with something stunning and elegant," Margo continued. "Something beautiful and form-fitting, something people will talk about and envy."

I cleared my throat. "Who's Sarah Burton?"

Margo raised one eyebrow before sharing a meaningful look with her assistants that clearly meant I was a level of stupid she wasn't used to dealing with on a daily basis. "Sarah is creative director at Alexander McQueen," she replied. When I still didn't get it, she laughed incredulously, but it was a mocking laugh that made me feel about three inches tall. "Sarah is the one who designed The Duchess of Cambridge's wedding dress."

I gulped and shrank in my seat. My mouth had gone dry. "Oh," I muttered before shaking my head. "I don't need a designer dress. What's wrong with me just going to a bridal dress shop and picking one out?" I didn't need a ridiculous amount of money spent on a dress that I would only ever wear the once.

Margo's nose wrinkled in disgust. "You don't want an off-the-rack dress. You want something original, something stunning, something that shines and glitters like a thousand diamonds are sewn into it. Something that will show off everything you have to perfection and make you look unforgettable. You want people to talk about you for months after, telling their designers they want to look like you on their wedding day. You want people gushing over your photos saying how jealous they are of you because you look so beautiful," she answered loftily, as if all of this should have been obvious to me.

Glittering like a thousand diamonds? Has this woman ingested a cliché romance novel? I wondered. I shook my head. "But I don't, actually."

Kimberly sat forward, reaching out a hand and placing it on my knee. "Alexander McQueen is incredible; I'd kill someone to get married in a one-off McQueen."

I felt bullied, trapped, forced upon. Taking a deep breath, I shrugged. "I don't know, can I think about it? Can't I just look around a few shops and see if there's something that I like? I mean, I don't want a big wedding dress anyway. I want something that's just simple and plain."

Margo's jaw tightened, but she nodded in agreement. Her forced smile didn't reach her eyes. "Of course. It's your wedding day; have what you want. We're here to help and organise, but every decision must come down to you," she answered before turning to her assistants. "Why don't we schedule a meeting with Sarah as soon as she's free, and she and Emma can talk? We can take it from there." She cleared her throat and stood, signalling for her assistants to start packing up. "In the meantime, I'll put in calls to designers for the butterflies, and I'll have some paper samples collated for the invites. I think it would look just lovely if we have them personally handwritten instead of printed, don't you?" She said it as a question, but it didn't really feel like one – she'd clearly already made up her mind on it. I nodded in agreement anyway. "Great. So next time I come, I'll also bring some samples of professional handwriting and you can choose."

Carson's mother stood, too. "If we're all done then Kimberly, Alice and I should be going. It's getting rather late," she said, eyeing the wall clock which said it was past nine already.

"Okay. Thank you for coming," I replied, forcing a smile even though all I wanted to do was curl into a ball in bed and pull the covers over my head.

Once everything was packed up, I saw them all out and waved goodbye at the door before closing it tightly and leaning against it. I closed my eyes and groaned in frustration. After listening to them all prattle on for the last hour and a half, the silence now filling my ears felt a little strange, almost as if I'd gone deaf.

Taking a few deep breaths, I headed back into the lounge, picking up all the empty glasses and stalking into the kitchen. Carson was sitting at the kitchen breakfast bar; he looked up as I entered.

"Hey, all done? Get a dress sorted?" he inquired.

I sighed in exasperation and set the glasses in the sink. "Sure, I'm wearing Alexander McQueen and it's going to glitter like a thousand diamonds are sewn into it," I answered sarcastically, eyeing the champagne bottle that was open in front of him. "There any of that left?" I asked hopefully.

He nodded and picked up the bottle. "Yeah, pass me a glass."

Instead of getting a nice crystal one out, I just grabbed a regular one which was sitting on the draining board and walked over to him, holding it out and watching as he poured me some. The silence between us stretched on as I leant against the counter, fuming on the inside about Margo and the stupid arrangements.

"So, why the attitude about the dress? You don't like this McQueen person?" Carson asked finally, pouring himself some more of the expensive fizz, too.

I shrugged, walking around the counter and taking the seat next to his. "Never heard of him, actually."

Carson laughed. "Me either. Some hotshot prick who designs women's clothes, obviously."

I chuckled wickedly. "Don't let Margo hear you say that. I thought she was going to stab me when I asked who Sarah Burton was. I dread to think what she'd do if she heard you utter the words 'hotshot prick'. Clearly, she has designer envy," I joked. Carson grinned boyishly, and his dimples appeared again. I stared at them, longing to reach out and touch them, to trace the line of one with my fingertip.

"She has a designer stick up her arse," Carson replied smartly. I giggled and nodded. "You, er, like the butterfly idea? If not then I'll tell her to scrap it."

An involuntary smile twitched at the corner of my mouth. I loved that he was being so sweet all of a sudden and that he'd suggested planning the entire day around something he thought would make me happy. "It's nice," I admitted.

The talk of butterflies suddenly reminded me that I never did get around to thanking him for decorating my bedroom this morning. By the time we'd finished arguing about the engagement ring, Sasha had woken so everything from then on revolved around her until the wedding planner arrived.

"I forgot to say earlier... thank you for painting my bedroom. I meant to say it before, but we started talking about other things and I forgot all about it until now," I admitted, looking down at the weighty ring on my finger.

He smiled, seeming a little embarrassed about it as he looked away. "No problem. I wanted you to feel at home here, so..." He shrugged. "It was my first attempt at doing something like that. They didn't turn out too great. I told you I was shit at decorating. I'll get someone to come in and fix them up and make them look nice for you."

I shook my head quickly. "I love them. They're perfect the way they are," I countered.

He looked up at me again then and a smile tugged at the corner of his mouth, his eyes soft and gentle. That expression reminded me of the Carson I fell in love with, and I felt heat spread through my whole body. No one spoke, but surprisingly, it wasn't an awkward silence as we both drank our drinks.

When he started clenching and unclenching his right hand again, I frowned. "Have you done something to your hand?"

He looked down at it and shrugged. "Nah, it's all right. I, er, hurt it the other day. It just aches now. Nothing serious."

"How did you hurt it?" I reached out, taking his hand and pulling it toward me as I turned it over, inspecting his knuckles and fingers for damage. His skin was blemish-free, though, so I traced my finger over his knuckles lightly, just marvelling over his warmth.

Carson sighed. "I punched a wall," he replied. I gasped, flicking my eyes up to his. He smiled sheepishly. "Your fault really. I was mad. It was the day I found out about Sasha."

Guilt settled over me, and I winced apologetically. Of course, he'd been mad. Who wouldn't be? Dropping my eyes away from the intense blue of his, I resumed stroking his knuckles.

"Maybe you should get an x-ray?" I whispered, unsure what else to say.

"Nah, it's all right, honestly. Don't fret." His hand twisted in my lap, capturing my hand and holding it tightly in his.

"I'm sorry I never told you," I croaked. I meant it. I *was* sorry. "I thought I was doing the right thing. I thought you'd be better off living your life without the burden of a daughter with someone like me. I didn't think of all the stuff you'd be missing out on. I should have told you. I'm sorry." I closed my eyes and let my head hang in shame. Now was going to be my punishment. Trying to make a life with him, living like strangers in a house while he went off and had affair after affair, was going to be my punishment for keeping him in the dark.

His hand tightened on mine. "I know you are, and I know you were thinking of me. I can't change the past now, so I think we just need to move on from it."

I sniffed and nodded in agreement.

"Though I do have some stuff I'd really like to ask you. I have a lot of blanks to fill in about Sasha," he said.

I looked up at him then and smiled weakly. "Like what?"

Carson reached out his spare hand and brushed away the tear that fell down my cheek. "Everything. About your pregnancy, your cravings, the birth, her first word, first step. Everything, I want to know absolutely everything. We could be here all night. I have *a lot* of questions."

I nodded toward my glass with the remaining inch of champagne in the bottom. "Pour me another drink then if we're in for the long haul," I joked.

Chapter Nineteen

s I started to wake, I realised I could hear both Carson's and
Sasha's voices. Forcing my eyes open, I looked around,
instantly confused when I didn't see them standing over me.
A flickering light on my bedside cabinet caught my eye and I
glanced over to see the baby monitor sitting on the side, was flashing
as he spoke. I smiled, realising he was in Sasha's room. They were
having some sort of conversation, though Sasha's side was more
gobbledygook than anything else.

A dull ache in my head registered as I sat up and stretched. Last
night, Carson and I had stayed up talking and polishing off the rest
of the large bottle of champagne until well after midnight. I was
feeling a little delicate because of that. It had been fun, though, and
Carson was right – he certainly did have *a lot* of questions.

I sat there for ages, just listening to them interact and laugh
through the baby monitor. I hadn't even heard her wake today, but
clearly Carson had if he'd gotten in there before me. "You know
what we should do today? We should spend some time together;
you, Mummy and me. Maybe we should ask Mummy if she wants to
go to the beach. Want to do that?" Carson asked Sasha.

"Beach!" Sasha chirped, clapping her hands, barely managing to
say the word.

I smiled. Sasha had never been to the beach before. She probably had no idea what one even was, yet she was excited about it by the sound of it.

"Well, let's leave Mummy sleeping for a little while longer. Mummy deserves a lie in, doesn't she? She works hard, your mum," Carson said. "And when she wakes up, we'll ask her if she wants to go. I have today and tomorrow that I can spend with you before I have to go away. Personally, I think it's great that you and Mummy aren't going to school this week. Means I get to hang out with you both."

"Hangs out! Beach!" Sasha practically screamed.

"Shh, you're gonna wake Mummy." Carson laughed. "Can you make me some more tea?"

Chuckling, I pushed myself out of bed and crept from the room. This I had to see for myself. As I peeked around the doorway, I spotted Carson sitting on the rug, cross-legged, wearing another pair of long-leg loungewear trousers and nothing else. In my eyes, he was perfection, made even more perfect by his surroundings.

Sasha's favourite teddy bears were all sitting in a semi-circle on the rug, too. They all had a little pink plate in front of them. While Sasha walked around pretending to refill everyone's cup, Carson raised the little pink plastic cup to his lips and faked a loud slurp.

"Eww, sugar! I need sugar!" he said with mock disgust, holding his cup out to her and pulling a funny face. Sasha chuckled and pretended to get something from her pocket and drop it in his cup. Carson grinned. "I would have preferred one from the sugar bowl instead of an old, pocket lint-covered sugar lump, but that'll do nicely. Stir, please," he instructed, holding his cup out to her again and laughing as she picked up a plastic spoon, swirling it in his cup.

My heart melted at the sight of them playing together. I never realised how much Sasha was missing out on. He'd known her less than a week, yet Carson was already a fantastic dad. It broke my heart that I'd denied them each other for almost two years.

Unable to watch anymore without speaking, I cleared my throat. "It takes a real man to drink from a pink cup at a toddler tea party," I teased.

Carson jumped, and his head snapped up. His mouth popped open before he laughed sheepishly, and a huge grin spread across his face. "Busted. I like tea parties, so sue me."

"Very cute," I teased, smirking at him. He shrugged, not even seeming bothered. "So, what's this I heard about going to the beach?" I asked, raising one eyebrow.

"Beeeeeeeeeeeeeach!" Sasha screamed at the top of her lungs, which made a dull thump come from Rory's room and then a groan of pain. Carson and I both burst out laughing because Sasha's screaming had obviously caused her uncle to fall out of his bed.

IT TOOK JUST UNDER TWO HOURS of driving before we arrived at Clacton-on-Sea. Thankfully, Sasha had fallen to sleep after an hour, so the drive was pretty peaceful in Carson's massive four-by-four with the plush leather seats. It was nice, and us talking so much the night before meant I didn't feel as awkward around him. We seemed to have made some peace last night and bonded over a bottle of champagne and a mutual dislike of designers. The drive time seemed to fly by in the blink of an eye.

After pulling in at the car park and buying an all-day ticket, the three of us set off to find the beach. On the way, Carson stopped and took Sasha into one of the little shops, buying buckets and spades, sand moulds and various other toys for her to play with. The ecstatic grin on his face as he helped her pick out what she wanted was enough to melt my heart. Clearly, spending money on her and giving her things was going to be one of life's pleasures for him.

When we stopped at the steps and looked down at the beach, Sasha's excited babble seemed to crank up a couple of notches as she pointed at the sea, her eyes wide. Smiling, I kicked off my shoes and rolled up my jeans before bending and doing the same to Sasha's.

"Shame it's not that warm. We'll have to come back in the summer or something so we can go in the sea," Carson mused, kicking off his trainers.

I frowned, shaking my head. "You can't go in the sea. There are fish in there, and crabs."

He chuckled, taking Sasha's hand and helping her down the concrete steps. "Don't tell me, you don't like fish or crabs?"

Crinkling my nose in distaste, I shook my head. "Not unless they're covered in batter and come with chips."

Carson chuckled. "Well, I'm taking Sasha crabbing later, and you're coming, so you're going to have to get over this little issue pretty quickly." He winked at me before smiling down at his daughter as she jumped the last step and landed onto the cool yellow sand, immediately wriggling her toes and giggling excitedly.

When she plopped down onto her bum and demanded one of the buckets, Carson swept her into his arms, juggling all the stuff he was carrying so he could hold her. "Let's go further up the beach, sweetness; we don't have to sit right on the steps. We'll pick out a nice quiet spot and set the blanket out, and then me and you, we're making the biggest, most-extravagant sandcastle Clacton-on-Sea has ever seen!" he joked.

I had to chuckle at his enthusiasm. It was like he'd opened his mouth and his inner child had tumbled out.

MY DAY WAS FULL OF LAUGHTER, smiles and sandcastle competitions. Carson seemed to go out of his way to ensure Sasha and I had a nice time. We paddled on the edge of the sea, running away from the waves, collected shells and pretty pebbles, built sandcastles and moats. We ate ice cream and hot doughnuts, and we'd even gone on the pier rides for a little while. It was lovely just to spend the day together and to do things I could never normally afford to do. Sasha and I even had our first go on a merry-go-round together while Carson stood at the side, taking photos and waving to Sasha each time she went past him.

After chips on the beach, Carson had made good on his promise of teaching Sasha how to go crabbing. That was my least enjoyable part of the day – especially when he'd caught a particularly large one and chased me around the pier with it while I howled with terrified laughter. All in all my day was amazing, and it was a shame to go home at the end of it.

Spending quality family time with Carson and watching him interact with his daughter had easily been the best part of the day for me. Every time they laughed together, every time she smashed down one of his castles while he was mid-build, every time he tickled her and made her smile just warmed my whole body from the inside out. I loved it all.

Carson and I had gotten along famously all day long, joking and talking and laughing. It was nice because while we were there, we had no pressure on us, no one watching us, no one judging us at all. There were no complications, no paparazzi, no ill feelings – just two people with a mutual love of the same child all spending the day together. I didn't want it to end.

The following day, we'd elected to stay in London, taking a picnic to Hyde Park. After eating, we'd visited some of the more tourist aspects of the city that I'd never really had the time nor the money for. Carson went above and beyond to make the two days spectacular. Sasha was now well and truly a daddy's girl – and the feeling was certainly reciprocated. Seeing him wrapped around her little finger was the most adorable sight I'd ever seen.

That night, he'd been a little deflated, though. As I'd helped him pack up a few things for him to take to Italy, he'd seemed a little sad. I'd kept him talking, asking about what he was going to get up to, who he was meeting with and what sort of things he would see in Italy. He'd promised to take me a few photos while he was there.

Finally, the dreaded Thursday came around. Watching Carson hug Sasha goodbye and try to explain he wouldn't see her for a few days was actually incredibly sad. As she took his hand and tried to lead him into the living room to watch TV with her, he actually looked like he didn't want to leave at all. He groaned, looking up at me for help, so I smiled at Sasha and shook my head.

"Daddy has to go to work for a couple of days. He can't watch The Fimbles," I told her. "Say bye, and you can see him again in a couple of days. Daddy has to go."

She frowned, clearly not understanding as she tugged on his hand and shook her head adamantly. "No go."

Rory stepped in then and picked up Sasha. "Right, we're going to go play in the garden. Want to ride that shiny new trike and see if we can get it all scratched up before Daddy comes back?" he asked, throwing a wicked grin in Carson's direction.

Carson rolled his eyes but didn't answer as Sasha finally let go of his hand and nodded in agreement with the trike idea. "Thanks, Rory," Carson said. "See you Sunday. Take care of the girls, huh?"

Rory smiled sarcastically. "I always have done." He carried Sasha back through the house and toward the garden. Carson waved at her, smiling moronically like a guy who was hopelessly in love.

"Ugh, I hope goodbyes aren't always gonna be this hard," he muttered under his breath before turning back to me and forcing a weak smile. "So, now you."

I kicked my toe on the floor and nodded. "Yep. Want me to hold your hand and beg you to come watch TV with me, too?" I joked, chewing on my lip uncomfortably.

He sighed and stepped closer to me as he shoved his hand into his pocket and produced his wallet. I frowned, confused, until he pulled out his credit card and a folded piece of paper. "I'm going to leave you my bank card. The pin number for it is written down. I'd hoped yours would be here before I had to leave, but it's not, so I'll leave you this just in case you see anything you want. Anything, Emma. If you see something, just buy it, there's no upper limit on the card."

I gulped, shaking my head. "I don't need your bank card. I have my own money," I protested.

"I'm not fighting with you about this," he stated, taking my hand and placing the card inside as he folded my fingers around it. "Take the card. You and I are getting married. What's mine is yours. End of story."

I sighed, knowing I shouldn't bother protesting because I knew I'd lose. I'd just agree, take the card for now, and just not spend on it. Simple. "Fine. Thank you." I nodded, pushing the card into the back pocket of my jeans.

A beautiful grin stretched across his face as he stepped closer to me and dipped his head so we were both almost level. "I'd better go before I miss my flight," he mused. "Kiss me goodbye."

I frowned, confused by his words. I looked around, seeing we were the only ones in the hallway; there was no one to put this act on for. "But there's no one around," I muttered.

"Exactly." His smile grew bigger as one of his arms wove around my waist, pulling my body flush against his, and his other hand slid up my back, tangling into my hair. I didn't even have time to work out what he meant by that before his mouth covered mine.

His soft lips felt so right against mine that I sagged against him and whimpered. When his lips parted and his tongue touched mine, deepening the kiss, my insides melted. Unconsciously, my arms rose and wrapped around his neck, pulling him closer to me as I crushed my body against his. Every nerve inside me seemed to come alive with excitement as he moaned in the back of his throat and pushed me against the wall, pressing his body against mine tightly.

My passion was spiking, rising through the roof as my hand fisted into his hair. The kiss was getting a little out of control. Well, 'getting' probably wasn't the right word because my control had slipped the second his lips touched mine. His hands slid down my body, caressing my buttocks before he gripped tightly and lifted me off my feet. My legs acted as if this were a well-practiced dance, wrapping around his narrow hips where they seemed to fit perfectly.

My clothes felt scratchy against my oversensitive skin as I moved, and I longed to peel them off, to feel his skin on mine, to have his body cover mine like a blanket. My loins burned as the intimate position made us rub together, the friction causing me to gasp and break the kiss. His lips didn't leave my body, though; instead, they travelled down my neck and his teeth sank into my shoulder gently, nipping me.

"Fuck, I don't want to go. I want to carry you upstairs and bite every fucking inch of you," he growled.

Don't go. Please, don't go. It was on the tip of my tongue.

"You always do this to me. It's not fair how much I want you," he murmured against the skin of my neck. "Ugh, I hate saying goodbye to you."

I guided his mouth back to mine again, kissing him roughly because I just had no words. My brain was a mess, my emotions were a mess, and his words were cutting me deeply because that was exactly how I always felt about saying goodbye to him.

A car horn blasted outside, but Carson didn't break the intense, steamy kiss. I was losing my breath; my body was writhing in need of relief as I kissed him like it was the last time I would ever be allowed to. When the car horn blasted again, longer this time, Carson groaned and pulled his mouth from mine. I gasped for breath, not opening my eyes as I tried to come down from the cloud I seemed to be floating on. My jittery body was like a live wire as he pressed his forehead to mine.

"You have to go," I whispered when he seemed to be making no move to set me on my feet.

"Yeah." He growled in frustration and traced his nose up the side of mine as his grip on me loosened, and I knew the moment was over. "Get a passport, okay? Let's not do this every other week when I have to go away," he muttered, holding me steady as I got to my feet.

"Margo's getting me one," I replied, smiling, silently wishing we actually *did* go through this every other week because making out with him like that was hot as sin.

"Good." He stooped and picked up his flight bag, turning and walking to the door. As he pulled it open, I waved to Bradley, Carson's friend who was taking him to the airport. I knew him from the club; he often came with Carson.

Carson turned and frowned, looking down at me with sad eyes. "I guess I'll see you Monday morning when you wake up."

I nodded, chewing on my lip. It seemed like an extremely long way away. "Have a safe trip."

He sighed deeply and stepped closer to me again, bending and capturing my lips in another kiss – this one soft, gentle and somewhat chaste compared to the one from moments before.

As I watched him drag his small suitcase and store it in the back of Bradley's car, my heart sank. Watching him walk out of my life for days on end was something I should be used to by now, but I wasn't.

It's just four days. Ninety-six hours. I can survive that, can't

Chapter Twenty

It was surprising how quickly you got used to someone being there. The house felt empty, cold, and a little lifeless. Of course, Sasha was still being her usual self, causing a ruckus wherever she went, but something was missing – and I knew exactly what it was. Carson Matthews. I always felt bad when I didn't see him on race weekends, but this was something more. I'd been used to seeing him around the house, sitting on the sofa, talking in that voice which made my insides tremble – or just in the kitchen, with his fine arse bent over as he looked into the fridge for something to snack on. It was the little things you got used to so quickly.

Sasha had been inconsolable. It seemed like once an hour she asked where Daddy was – Daddy dinner, Daddy play, Daddy bath, Daddy cuddle. It was cute, but heartrending at the same time. Maybe I wasn't the only one who was going to be counting down the hours until I next saw him from now on.

Luckily, on Friday I had something to keep my mind off him. As promised, he'd texted me a list of day nurseries that came highly recommended by people he knew. I busied myself calling around them and explaining the situation about who we were and asked if they had places available for Sasha. Two of them actually sounded nice, so I'd arranged appointments to go and visit the following week with Sasha so we could see if she fitted in to one of them. The phone calls wasted a significant proportion of my day.

By Saturday, though, I was just wallowing around. Lucie had come over to visit after lunch, bringing her kids around for a play date, which kept Sasha happy for the whole afternoon and well into dinnertime. Of course, a little gossip with my best friend perked me up to no end.

However, by the time she left and I'd bathed Sasha and got her settled into bed, I was back to not knowing what to do with myself in the large house. Rory was out with friends, so I just rattled around the place on my own. I actually missed my poky little flat which didn't echo when you walked or talked.

Not used to having my Saturday nights to myself because I would usually be working at the club, I didn't actually know how to keep myself entertained. Saturday night TV was an extreme let-down, so after an hour of channel-surfing, my boredom got the better of me and I ended up in bed by half past nine.

Sunday passed much the same, although I busied myself by cooking up a storm in Carson's luxurious kitchen, making a traditional roast dinner, followed by a homemade raspberry pavlova. That killed a few hours, and Sasha kept me busy for the rest of the day.

By the time she was in bed, though, I was counting down the hours until I would see his smile again. We'd exchanged a few texts over the weekend, but I hadn't had any real contact with him since Thursday morning. It was almost as if I was still working at the club and wouldn't have contact with him from one week to the next. I didn't realise how quickly I'd come to rely on seeing him every day.

Once Sasha was tucked in bed and Rory was off watching TV in his room, I decided a long soak in my incredible en-suite was in order. The large, claw-footed bath was practically calling my name.

Just as the tub finished filling and I had removed my last piece of clothing, my phone rang. I pulled it out of my trouser pocket, answering it without looking at the screen, thinking it would be Lucie because not very many people actually had my new number. When Carson's deep voice greeted me, I all but squealed and almost dropped my phone into the tub.

"Hey, are you busy?" he asked.

"Nope, not at all." I dipped my hand into the water, swirling it around to create a few more bubbles before I stepped in and sighed inwardly as the warm water caressed my skin.

"Ah, okay, good. I was just, er, well, I just wanted to check how you were and if everything was all right. Obviously it is, because you haven't called me to tell me otherwise, but, you know, just wanted to call and check." He seemed nervous as he spoke, and I instantly wondered why.

"Everything's fine. Is everything okay with you?" I asked curiously, sinking down into the warm, lavender-scented, bubbly water.

He sighed, not answering immediately, and my mind started to dream up things which could have possibly happened to make him call me and be all stuttery when he was usually so cool and collected. My mind jumped to one conclusion – he'd cheated and was now calling to ease whatever guilt he felt about it.

"Everything's all right," he answered.

My heart sank as I closed my eyes. The emotional pain was building like a storm in my chest, and soon it would burst from me in the form of hysterical sobs. I knew it would come at some point. I just prayed I could keep my sadness at bay until I got him off the phone.

"Actually, no, everything's not all right," he suddenly said. "I miss you. I'm lonely. The hotel room was too quiet all weekend. I'm just mooching around now waiting for the time when I can check out and go to the airport to come home. There's no little person running around, no Rory to backchat me, and no you to talk to or laugh with. I don't like going away. There, I said it. I miss you all, I miss home, and I just called to hear your voice. Make fun of me if you want."

My eyes flew open. "What?" I croaked. "What brought that on?"

He sighed deeply. "I'm just laying here on my bed and staring at the ceiling, thinking about how I'd much rather be home with you. I'm officially homesick."

I fought the smile trying to break free. He missed me. He would rather be here with me than in Italy surrounded by gorgeous models and dancers. My sadness was quashed immediately. "Well, would it help you to know that Sasha is asking for you *all* the time?" I asked. "Or that Rory said it was weird you not being at the dinner table to talk sports with?"

He laughed. "Runt's missing me, huh? I knew I'd grow on him," he joked. "Anyone else missing me?"

I smiled, laying back, letting the water lap around my shoulders. "I don't think so. Oh, Gloria said she missed your face," I joked.

"She did? Anyone else? No one you can think of who is remotely missing me and wishing I was there?" he prompted.

"Is there anyone else?" I teased.

"What about you?"

I smiled. "Me? I'm too busy in the bath to miss you, baby."

My answer was met by silence for a few seconds. "Bath? Like, right now?" he finally replied.

I grinned and purposefully let the water splash so he'd hear it. "Yep." I sank further into the hot water and closed my eyes.

"Naked?" he questioned.

"Obviously!" I chuckled.

He groaned loudly. "Now I'm even more homesick," he whined. "I have all sorts of things running through my mind right now."

I got his drift immediately. I gulped as the same thoughts started running through my head. I could just imagine him, lying on his back in bed, shirtless with those mouth-watering V lines. I could picture his tattoos and the warmth of his body and the glint to his eye, and those dimples in his cheeks…

"Emma, I should probably go before I start asking you to touch yourself. I'm getting dangerously close to that point right now, and if you do it then I'm gonna be even more desperate to come home so I can watch."

I giggled at his dirty words, clenching my thighs together tightly because my sex was starting to ache uncomfortably. "You're filthy," I scolded playfully.

He blew out a big breath. "Yeah, I know. Sorry. I'm gonna go. I have a monster hard-on now, and I need to get rid of it," he replied. "Don't suppose you want to send me a naked bath picture to help me along?"

I grinned, chewing on my lip as I thought about it. "Go get off the phone, you pervert," I joked.

"Okay, okay, I'm going," he grumbled. "I'll be leaving here in a couple of hours, and should be home just after two, so I guess I'll see you in the morning."

My heart leapt. My Carson-less weekend was almost over. He would be here by the time I woke up. I couldn't wait. "All right. Bye, baby. Safe trip home and I'll see you soon." I smiled, knowing I needed to give him a little something before I ended the call. "And, by the way, Carson, yes, I'm missing you, too. And yes, I'm going to touch myself tonight. And yes, I will be thinking of you when I do it."

He groaned. "Fuck, Emma, now I don't want to hang up!"

I giggled wickedly. "Goodbye, Carson." I disconnected the call without waiting for a reply and felt a blush creep up on my cheeks at my admission. I didn't feel bad about it, though. Knowing he was excited by my body made a little proud feeling bubble up inside me. Carson had always been attracted to my body; it was just a shame the rest of me didn't do anything for him.

As my hand touched my stomach, something sparked inside me. My eyes fluttered closed as I let my mind wander to Carson and what he would be doing right now. Memories of the kiss washed over me, how hot it had been and how my body had ached with need. As my mind wandered to his body, my hand wandered mine. Pretty soon, I was lost within the bliss of Carson, just minus the actual Carson.

After spending an hour in the bath, my fantasy and little party for one had only served to make me miss him more. I hadn't had that intimacy with him for weeks now, and my body was highly unsatisfied and needy even though I'd tried to alleviate that tension myself. It was only just after eight as I padded into my bedroom and looked through my drawer, trying to find some clean pyjamas to change into. Still only having limited clothes from what I packed the other day, though, I didn't see any. I frowned, wondering when Carson was going to arrange for the rest of my stuff to be shipped here, or if he was waiting for me to just buy new stuff like he'd instructed when he handed me his credit card on Thursday morning.

After roughly drying my hair, I dragged a comb through it and decided to let it dry naturally. *Tomorrow, I'll just tie it up if it looks like a bird's nest.* Wrapping my big, fluffy towel around my body securely, I stalked out of my room and into Carson's next door, hesitantly opening his drawers until I found what I was looking for – one of his T-shirts. I smiled, slipping it over my head and pulling it down over my body, silently wishing it was a dirty one so his scent would surround me. After pulling on a pair of his boxer shorts and folding them over at the waist so they'd stay up, I headed out of his room.

As I walked past Rory's room, I could hear the distinct sounds of the PlayStation so I didn't bother to interrupt. Once downstairs in the living room, I turned up the under-floor heating controls and snuggled onto the sofa, pulling my schoolbag onto my lap so I could finish off my assignments for university. If, by some miracle, they didn't kick me out after it being splashed all over the papers that I was a lap dancer, I would need to hand in my five thousand word essay on Friday. I sighed deeply, setting my head back and opening my textbook to the right place, preparing myself for some hard work and hand cramps.

"EMMA?"

I groaned, squeezing my eyes shut as a sleepy fog muffled my ears. My mouth was dry as I tried to lick my lips, not yet ready to wake.

"Come on, you. Let's get you to bed."

I swatted the hand away as it tried to take my books from my lap. "Rory, just leave me be. I'll just have five minutes," I muttered, turning my head and pressing my face into the back of the sofa.

My rejection was met with a throaty chuckle. Something solid slid under my thighs and around my back. I was jostled slightly, but my eyes stung when I tried to open them, so I just left them closed.

"Rory, leave me," I protested weakly as I was lifted effortlessly from the sofa and pulled against a warm, hard body.

"Emma, it's Carson."

Carson? I forced my eyes open, looking up into the face of the love of my life. An involuntary smile stretched across my lips as I reached out, cupping his cheek just to see if I was still dreaming. When my hand touched his cheek, the slight stubble gently scratched against my fingertips, and my stomach fluttered knowing he really was home.

"Hi," I whispered, grinning now as I slipped my other arm up and looped it around his neck, pressing myself tighter to him.

"Hi," he whispered back. The sound of his voice and the delicious smell of his skin made my whole body ache. "I thought I told you not to wait up for me," he scolded playfully.

I grinned tiredly, pressing my face into the side of his neck, as my muscles all seemed to relax as one in his arms. "I didn't. I was working on my assignment. Is it after two already?" I asked, yawning against his neck.

"Yeah, it's almost three. Come on, let's get you to bed." I smiled to myself, loving that Carson Matthews was carrying me to bed. This was another fantasy of mine I'd had over the years I never thought would come true. As he carried me effortlessly up the stairs and toward my bedroom, he chuckled. "How come you're wearing my T-shirt and pants?"

I was too tired to feel embarrassed at being caught, so I just shrugged. "I didn't have any clean pyjamas. I only brought two pairs," I answered sleepily.

"Well, usually, I would offer to buy you some, but in this case, I think I won't just because I actually like the idea of you sleeping in my clothes," he teased.

He fumbled with the door to my bedroom and after another few steps, bent and gently placed me on the soft bed. I tried to open my eyes but failed miserably as the deep sleep pulled at the edges of my subconscious. Carson groaned, pressing his lips against my cheek and brushing my hair away from my face.

"Don't suppose you've missed me enough that you want me to sleep in here with you tonight, have you?" he whispered, gently pulling the quilt cover up to my shoulders.

I smiled at the thought. *Carson in bed with me. Hell yeah, I want that!* "If you want," I muttered, turning to my side and snuggling under the cover, pulling it up so it covered my chin and my ear.

"Yeah? Seriously?"

"Mmm hmm."

Clearly not needing to be told twice, the bed dipped a moment later, and the cover raised as a warm body slid up close to me. A contented sigh left my lips as his chest pressed against my back and his legs tangled with mine. Being in the bed with him was something I'd fantasised about since I first met him. His body wrapped around mine and it was like some kind of magic wove over me, lulling me into a safe, contented, peaceful stupor. It almost felt like a dream. If I weren't as tired, I certainly would have instigated a little sexy time, but I couldn't even keep my eyes open so, unfortunately, that wasn't something that was going to happen.

"Oh, yeah, this is much better. I'm not going away on my own again; you're going to have to come with me from now on," he whispered, pressing a soft kiss against my temple as I drifted off to sleep in his arms.

Chapter Twenty-One

"**M**um! Mummy, Mummy, Mum, Mum, Mummmmmmmm!" Sasha's voice blasted through the baby monitor. "Mummy, up! Up! Sasha up!"

A loud groan came from behind me. "Jesus. She gets her loudness from you."

I jumped, squealing from the shock of someone else being in my bedroom, and twisted so fast it actually made me dizzy. Carson's sleepy smile greeted me as he rubbed at his eyes.

"Damn it. Shit!" I hissed, pushing on his bare chest, trying not to notice how magnificent his skin felt under my hand. "You frightened the life out of me! What are you doing here?"

He grinned that boyish smile and sat up. The covers fell down into his lap as he moved, exposing all of his brilliance. "You said I could sleep in here. I carried you to bed. You don't remember?" he asked, stretching. As he moved, the guardian angel tattoo seemed to dance along with his muscles. I resisted the urge to lean in and run my tongue over it.

Swallowing my wave of desire, I pushed myself up on my elbows. "Yeah, I remember now," I croaked. "I thought I was dreaming," I admitted.

He grinned over his shoulder at me and raised one eyebrow. "Oh, so you dream about me often?"

The blush crept over my face before I could stop it. '*All the time*' was the truthful answer, but I couldn't say that. "I'd better go see to Sash," I muttered, sidestepping his question because our daughter was still shouting at me to get her out of her cot.

He shook his head and grinned, running a hand through his messy hair. "I'll go. You sleep in. I need some catch-up time with my other girl anyway." Before I could process what he meant by that, he leant over and planted a kiss on my forehead. "I've never been happier to come home."

The blush crept up over my face before I could quash it. "Well, I know Sasha will be over the moon you're back." *I know I am,* I wanted to add, but didn't.

He grinned, swinging his legs over the side of the bed and picking up his jeans, sliding his legs into them before standing up and zipping his fly as he walked out of the room.

"Mummy!" Sasha called again. Through the monitor, I heard her door creak open and then a gasp of surprise. "Daddy? Dadddddddddddyyyyyyyy!"

"Hey, sweetness! You miss me? Oh, man, you have no idea how much I missed you."

EVEN RORY SEEMED HAPPY to have Carson back in the house, though he was trying exceptionally hard not to show it. When Carson suggested he kick my brother's arse on FIFA, Rory protested for a whole ten seconds before he agreed, and they both disappeared upstairs to play a game or two, or six based on how long they were up there and the jibing they were doing.

That afternoon, Jillian, Carson's mother called to ask if she could come over. She had yet to meet Sasha because when she'd come last time to sit in on the wedding plans, she'd already been in bed. Now, it seemed, Jillian wanted to meet her granddaughter.

Nervous didn't quite cover how I felt as I dressed Sasha in one of the beautiful dresses Carson had bought for her when we moved in. I also made a little effort this time, seeing as last time I met her I was in jeans and a hoodie. This time, I made sure to put on a nice, long shirt and some black leggings, tying my hair because it was still wild from me not styling it the night before.

Carson had just watched me running around, his eyes amused as he pursed his lips and teased me every now and again about me not having to impress her. By the time she arrived, I'd all but bitten my nails down to the quick. I didn't really care what she thought of me. I knew she'd never change her opinion of me, but I would hate it if she thought badly of my daughter because of me.

When the doorbell rang, I whimpered and looked at Carson. This time, he didn't look nervous. He'd spoken to his mother a few more times since she initially found out and had explained everything more fully. Apparently, Jillian felt terrible for the way she jumped to conclusions about me and wanted to get to know me better before she made judgement. Carson seemed very confident I could win her over.

As he pushed himself off the sofa, he bent over and kissed my cheek. "Deep breath, it'll all be fine," he whispered. I closed my eyes and nodded, praying he was right.

He disappeared into the hallway to answer the door, so I looked down at Sasha, trying to calm myself as I watched her play with her Elmo toy. When Carson walked into the room, flanked by Jillian, I bit my lip and waited.

But I needn't have worried. Of course, Sasha won over her nan with no problems. One little look at her baby-blues and Jillian was a goner. As she'd stepped over the threshold of the room, she'd burst into tears because apparently Sasha reminded her so much of Carson when he was a baby, though she couldn't get over her curly locks.

For the next hour, Jillian sat on the floor, playing with Sasha's dolls and braiding her granddaughter's hair while they sang nursery rhymes. It was nice to watch.

"So, when's the next race, Carson? It's next weekend, am I right?" Jillian asked.

Carson nodded. "Yep, Silverstone on Sunday. Emma's coming," he replied, smiling down at me as he rested his hand on my thigh. The heat from his hand was almost too distracting for me to think of anything else, but I tried my best to keep up with the conversation – well, parts of it anyway. Other parts, I was off in fantasy Carson-land where we had far fewer clothes on…

"Oh, that'll be nice. Have you ever been to a race before, Emma?" Jillian inquired.

I shook my head. "No, never been to anything like it."

She grinned. "Oh, you'll love it. You get to watch the whole thing from up in the family and friends lounge; you get such a fantastic view of it all."

I forced a smile. I didn't really want to explain that I didn't like to watch Carson race and I'd never made it through a full one before. But, I'd give it a go because Carson seemed extremely happy that I was going to watch.

As I sat there, pressed against Carson's side and watching his mother play with my daughter, I suddenly felt like everything was slotting into place again. Maybe this wouldn't be as bad as I first envisioned. Perhaps being forced to marry someone who didn't love me wasn't going to destroy my soul like I'd first thought.

Chapter Twenty-Two

I'd never seen so many people all in one place. Silverstone was enormous. The stand was filled with avid race fans. People shouted their favourite driver's name, waved flags and homemade banners, and they wore novelty hats and those silly foam hands. The atmosphere was electric, and I could feel the boom of the crowd in the pit of my stomach every time the Mexican wave went around the seating stands.

We'd been a little late to arrive because we had to swing by Lucie's to drop off Sasha for the day. We'd been here a little while now, though, sitting in the backroom while his team prepped him for the race and talked through strategies and plans. I chewed on my lip, watching everything with wide eyes, taking it all in and trying not to let the busyness of the place overwhelm me. They never really showed this part of it on television, so I had no idea of the volume of people who worked on Carson's team.

Carson was already kitted out in his team hat and all-in-one leather jumpsuit, and I must admit, seeing it close up did funny things to my insides. I had an awful feeling it showed on my face because a couple of times, Carson caught me looking at his butt and sent me a sexy little 'I know what you're thinking' smirk.

A small guy wearing a headset walked into the room and smiled at Carson. "You about ready to go down? Reporters are down near the paddock and want an interview," he said, clipping his walkie-talkie on his belt. "I'll take Emma up to the family area."

Carson stood but shook his head. "Not yet. I want to show Emma around a little. Let her sit on my bike and stuff," he answered.

The guy frowned, clearly not liking this idea at all. "There's less than thirty minutes left until the start, Carson. You'll have to do that another time."

Carson grinned and reached down, taking my hand and pulling me to my feet. "There's time. I just want to show her around. Five minutes, tops."

I opened my mouth to protest, but Carson squeezed my hand in warning so I immediately closed it. Clearly this was important to him if he was arguing against one of his team about it.

The guy looked at his watch as he shifted from one foot to the other. "Carson, I don't—"

"There's time," Carson interjected, pulling me close to his side as he stepped around the guy and headed towards the door. "I'll just be five minutes. Cover for me," he called over his shoulder.

Once we were outside the little room, which served as the office headquarters for his team, Carson grinned at me. I smiled weakly in return. "You're going to get in trouble. I don't need a tour," I said quietly.

"Well, maybe I want to give you one," was his smart-alecky answer.

For the next few minutes, Carson walked around, pointing out people and telling me who they were. We went into some sort of workshop where they stored all the spare parts for his bike. After, we stepped out into the area Carson referred to as 'the paddock'. The atmosphere was different out here; people were standing around and laughing, not serious and intense. A couple of TV camera people I recognised from watching the show were off to one side interviewing another driver. I smiled, pressing close to Carson, listening as he spoke so passionately while telling me about the track and why it was his favourite.

"Carson?"

We both turned at the sound of a high-pitched girlie voice. And, just like that, my happy mood sank. In front of me stood one of the

MotoGP paddock girls I often saw Carson with before the race. Her ruby-red painted lips curved into a smile, exposing a row of brilliantly whitened, straight teeth. My shoulders unconsciously pulled back as a feeling of inadequacy washed over me. Compared to this beautiful, tall, skinny yet somehow still curvy girl, I looked like a troll.

"Hi, Siena, how are you?" Carson asked, immediately dropping my hand for the first time in ten minutes. As he stepped away from me toward the big-breasted, barely-clothed, model-like girl, jealous waves crashed over my head. I tried my best not to scowl at his back.

"I'm good. I missed you; you've not been in Devon again all week," she replied, smiling at him and flashing him her come-to-bed eyes.

"Yeah, I've been busy. Next week I'll be back to normal." He winked at her and my jealousy suddenly turned to anger.

This was it; this was the first time I was about to witness him getting it on with another girl – and he had the gall to do it right in front of me. A lump formed in my throat, but I refused to cry. My teeth gnashed together so tightly my jaw ached. All week, I'd fooled myself into thinking we were building something, that something was blossoming between us, that I stood a chance of winning his heart, or at the very least, his respect. But with one of her beautiful smiles, this girl had ruined it all and he was going to throw all that progress away for a quick thrill.

I needed to leave. I wasn't going to just stand there and watch it. I couldn't.

Not even bothering to tell him I was leaving, I decided to find my own way back to the little office area and then ask someone to direct me to the family area. After the race, I would tell Carson I was never coming to another of these fucking races ever again.

As I spun on my heel and marched back in the direction I came from, I heard Carson call my name. Ignoring him, I stomped back into the building and walked along the edge of the workshop, immediately regretting not paying much attention to Carson's tour because I had no idea which door I had come through to get down here.

"Emma!" Carson called again behind me. "Where are you going?" he asked. "You're not allowed to just wander around down here. You shouldn't even be here really."

I scoffed and carried on walking down the little narrow walkway, looking for an exit door, which would lead me to outside or inside, or anywhere that was away from him. "I can't even stand to look at you right now," I retorted, shaking my head. Seeing it in person was ten times harder than seeing it in the newspaper.

"You can't even... what?" he repeated, jogging to catch up with me. "What are you talking about?"

I scowled in his direction, wishing I could somehow hurt him the way he seemed to be able to hurt me so effortlessly. "Just leave me alone!" I snapped.

He practically growled in frustration as his hand closed over my wrist. I was yanked to a stop and he shoved open a door at the back of the workshop, stepping in and dragging me inside with him. "What the hell have I done now? For fuck's sake, I don't get you sometimes, I really don't. One minute I'm showing you around, the next you're storming off and are mad at me! What the hell did I do? Clue me in; give me a little sodding hint to this one, huh?" he ranted.

"You and Miss Shorts-up-her-arse, tits-around-her-neck, blonde Barbie doll lookalike out there!" I practically screamed. "I'm not going to stand around and watch while you hook up with that girl right in front of me!" I shook off his hold on my arm.

His eyebrows shot up. "Hooking up with her? What the...?"

I groaned in frustration, wanting to grab the nearest thing and smash it – unfortunately, the nearest thing to me was him, and he was too big for me to pick up and throw. "Oh, don't play dumb, Carson. I've seen it all before! I'm not going to just stand there and pretend I'm okay with it while you shag her like you do all those other girls!"

"Other girls? What on Earth are you talking about, Emma?" he asked, looking at me like I was crazy.

I scowled. *Is he really going to deny all this? Does he think I'm stupid?* "The girls, Carson! The ones from the papers. The models, the singers, the dancers!" I spat sarcastically.

His brow furrowed as he shook his head slowly. His eyes bored into mine as he spoke. "I think you're confused about something." I opened my mouth to shout at him to stop lying to me for once in his life, but he cut me off by speaking first. "How many girls do you think I've been with in the last three years?"

I gulped as an acrid taste seemed to burn in the back of my throat. "I really don't want to play this game with you!" I huffed and tried to push past him so I could leave, but he grabbed my wrist and pulled me to a stop. He was glaring at me.

"This isn't a bloody game, Emma! This is our lives, and you're making this really ruddy difficult!" he shouted, making me flinch because of how loud his voice was and how close he was to me when he did it.

I growled in frustration and ripped my wrist from his grasp. If he really had to tell me how many girls he'd fucked in the last three years, if it was really that important I know, then I guess I had to play the game like a good little fiancée! "Two fucking hundred?" I retorted, clenching my jaw, waiting for his answer.

His mouth dropped open in shock. "Not even close," he muttered.

"Five hundred then?" I spat venomously.

He sighed and shook his head sadly. "Seriously? That's what you think I've been doing for the last three years? Screwing anything that moves?"

I closed my eyes and tried not to let his sadness get to me. He was trying to hurt me with this conversation. I knew that. There was no other reason except to rub into my face I was nothing more than one in a long line of girls he'd screwed – I just so happened to be the only one he got pregnant.

"Just tell me the number then if you have to." I tried to keep my voice emotionless, as my heart broke a little more. I silently wondered how one person could live through so much heartbreak but still survive it only to have it happen all over again the next day. There had to be a limit on how much pain one person could take before they just died from it. I must have been close to that limit now.

He took a deep breath before he answered. "Three."

I nodded, trying not to show a reaction. "Three hundred girls. That's awesome, Carson. Good for you," I said sarcastically, clapping my hands in fake applause as I stepped back to get some personal space but bumped into the wall behind me.

"Not three hundred! Three!" he shouted, slamming his hand on the wall next to my head.

My mind worked furiously to take in the word. I must have heard him wrong; he must have said something else. That just couldn't be right. Three? How could that be possible? He was Carson Matthews; he was rich and famous and was with pretty swimwear models all the time in the papers. How could that be true? I looked up at his angry face. His eyes were locked onto mine, his jaw clenched tight as he glared at me, daring me to challenge what he said.

I gulped. I needed to check I heard him right. "Three?" I whispered, not trusting my voice to speak.

He nodded stiffly, stepping back and running one hand through his hair. "Yeah," he confirmed. "And that includes you."

"But h-how? Three? But... but... the photos in the paper... the girls..." I shook my head, not sure I could make myself believe him.

A muscle in his jaw twitched as his eyes narrowed in anger. "You shouldn't believe everything you read. Most of those photos are friends, or friends of friends. I go to a party on the beach and the paps somehow manage to take a photo where it looks like it's just me with a load of girls. I talk to someone in a club or ask a girl for the time and immediately she's my date for the night. None of it is true, Emma. There have only been three girls since I met you."

The intensity with which he spoke the words was making me feel slightly sick. It was like this was building to something, but I just didn't know what. All this time, I had read things about him being a playboy and going with all these women, yet he actually wasn't? Could I believe him? Why should I believe him in the first place? Didn't they say a picture spoke a thousand words? And I had seen hundreds of pictures, which spoke volumes against what he was telling me right now.

But the way he was looking into my eyes right now was making me want to believe him, was making me wish this were possible.

"Really?" I asked, my voice breaking.

He moved closer to me and reached out, brushing his fingertip against my cheek lightly, wiping a tear away. Until he did that, I didn't even realise I was crying. I wanted his words to be true, but I couldn't get my hopes up only to have him crush me again.

"Really." He nodded. "I met you at the club on my eighteenth birthday and since that day, there have been only three girls I've had sex with. One is you. Both of the others were when you left the club, when you were having Sasha. I didn't know that was why you left. I thought you just up and left. I was hurting so much. I thought I'd lost you, so I slept with a girl. I can't even remember her name or what she looked like; she was just a one-off. I was trying to forget you because you hurt me by leaving and not even saying goodbye," he said, his voice soft and caring.

My stomach twisted in a knot. Was he telling me he had feelings for me? Was this some sort of revelation that he actually *did* like me? I couldn't breathe properly. I wanted to speak. I had no idea what I even wanted to say, but nothing was coming out of my open mouth as I stared at him dumbfounded.

"After about a month of you being gone, people told me to forget you and that I needed to move on and accept the fact you weren't coming back. They just kept going on and on about how I should stop pining for you because you obviously didn't care about me, that I was just one of the many guys you screwed for money, and if I'd been important to you at all then you wouldn't have left like you did. They convinced me that what I thought was a real connection was in fact just good sexual chemistry, and that you only wanted me because it was your job. I believed them." He frowned and shook his head dejectedly. "One night, I met a girl. She was nice and my friends were hounding me so much that, in the end, I asked her out just to get them off my back. We dated for about three weeks, but then I realised I just couldn't do it. I didn't want anyone else." He moved closer to me, cupping my face in his hands, just looking at me as if he was trying to choose his words carefully.

My mind was totally blank. I couldn't look away from his eyes as he looked back at me with such intensity it was almost too much to bear.

A smile tugged at the corners of his mouth as he carried on speaking. "Then, after another agonising couple of months, you walked back into my life again. Since then, it's only ever been you. I'm crazy about you, Emma. I love you, and I want to be with you. I want to be your husband. I want to take care of you and make you look at me like you used to, instead of this." He clenched his teeth as a pained expression crossed his face. "I hate myself for making you look at me like this. I hate this hard look in your eyes. It's painful and I can't take it anymore. I didn't mean to behave like this toward you. I know I'm hurting you by forcing you into things, but I just wanted to be there for you. I wanted to be there *with* you. You, me and Sasha, a proper family. Just like I've daydreamed about for so long."

My mouth was dry. He was killing me. His words were literally killing me with emotion. I was drowning in feelings. Things were hitting me so fast and so hard I just didn't know how to cope with it. Carson Matthews, the love of my life, was in love with me, too? He'd just declared his love for me. Me, a dirty little lap dancer. How was this possible?

I had no idea what to say. I felt a little numb, like someone had just thrown a bucket of cold water at me, and I was trapped in that split-second of shock where you just don't know what to do or what to feel. Except that split-second was stretching into almost a minute of painful silence. His face fell as he continued to look at me. I wanted more than anything to tell him I loved him back, but I could do nothing other than stand there like a statue.

"But I've gone about this completely the wrong way. I wish I could turn back time. I wish I could go back to that day I found out about Sash. If I could, I would do this all differently. But I can't, and now I've ruined the relationship we had, and I hate myself even more than you hate me," he whispered. "Is there anything I can do to make it up to you?"

I opened my mouth, praying something intelligent would come out. "Huh?" I groaned inwardly. *That wasn't intelligent at all! Stupid, stupid Emma!*

He smiled sadly and his hands dropped from my face as he stepped back. "You don't have to marry me. I'll have a lawyer sort out a trust fund for Sasha. I'll set the three of you up in a nice place and pay you whatever amount you want in child support each month. I'd really like to have open access to Sasha rather than scheduled times for visits, but if you don't want that then I understand. The way I've behaved the last couple of weeks doesn't really give me the right to make demands or anything." His shoulders slumped as he spoke. "I'm sorry. I should... I should go. I should be out in the paddock getting ready to start the race. My team are probably going mental looking for me."

He strode over to the door, his hand gripping the handle tightly as he turned back to me. His face was defeated and resigned, and the pain I could see etched across it made me feel sick. That one sad, devastated look on his face told me exactly how he felt about me, that look spoke volumes, and I didn't doubt his love for me anymore. Only someone who was in love and felt like their heart was breaking could look like that. You couldn't fake that look; there was no way.

"I love you," he whispered as he pulled the door open and stepped over the threshold.

I was stunned. Frozen. Completely and utterly immobile as I watched the door close behind him. I couldn't take it in. My mind was scrambled as I struggled to comprehend what he'd just told me. My heart slammed in my chest as it slowly sank in. *Carson Matthews loves me.* The realisation that I'd just let him walk away seemed to snap me out of my daze, and my muscles suddenly thawed. My stomach did a little flip as I started to believe it. *Carson Matthews actually loves me!* I shoved myself away from the wall and sprinted across the room as a huge smile stretched across my face.

My heart was in my throat as the ten steps it took me to streak across the room seemed to take forever. Finally, I got to the door and wrenched it open, throwing myself through with so much force I almost fell on my face and slammed into the wall opposite. My eyes flicked around, seeing Carson's back as he strode through the building toward the paddock behind.

"Carson?" I called. My voice was weak and slightly breathless from the panic I felt seeing him walk out the door. He didn't stop; I probably couldn't be heard over the racket his team were making in the workshop. "Carson!" I called louder.

When he stepped from the building and into the paddock where his team and all the MotoGP girls were standing, he was immediately swarmed with people and TV cameras. He was completely oblivious to my panic-stricken attempt to catch him.

My eyes widened and then I was on the move again, streaking across the workshop, dodging around piles of tyres, tools, and wires strewn everywhere.

"Hey! You can't go out there!" One of Carson's team stepped in front of me so quickly I actually slammed into him where I was running so fast. I let out a little yelp as we collided, and his arms wrapped around me stopping me from falling to the floor. "What are you doing in here? Public aren't allowed in here. It's a safety hazard." He frowned at me in reprimand as he let go of me.

I righted myself, looking over his shoulder to the last place I saw Carson, but he was lost in the swarm of people. "I need to speak to Carson. He's right there," I replied, pointing to the door and trying to step around him.

He shook his head adamantly. "Sorry, Miss, but no one goes out this way apart from the team. You'll have to go back to the spectator area. I'll have security escort you back to your seat." One of his hands closed over my elbow, and he gave me a little tug in the direction I had come from.

I frowned and pushed his hand off me. "No, no. I'll be quick. I just need to tell Carson something. I'm his fiancée." A smile twitched at the corner of my mouth when I said that. That was the only time I had ever said it and actually liked the word being associated with me.

The guy's eyes widened a little at my revelation, but then he shook his head. "Sorry, I didn't recognise you, Miss Bancroft. But I still can't let you through this way. You'll have to speak to Carson after the race. He'll be on his way to the starting line any second. He was cutting it pretty close already."

My heart sank as I shook my head. "Please? It's so important, please?" I stepped around him, meaning to head to the door anyway, but he sidestepped as well and shook his head firmly.

"Sorry. Rules are rules. I'd get in a bucket-load of trouble if they even saw you in here." He looked over my shoulder and waved his hand. "Bert will show you the way up to the lounge where family usually watch the race."

I groaned in frustration but knew there wasn't anything I could do about it. The race would start in a few minutes. I'd just have to wait until after.

Chapter Twenty-Three

I couldn't keep the smile from my face as I followed the guy named Bert back through the building and up the stairs. When I got to the top, a rather large, beefy guy in a black T-shirt raised one eyebrow at me before looking at Bert.

"This is Carson's fiancée," Bert announced, nodding back at me. "Miss Bancroft, this is Spence, our resident door ape who stops undesirables from entering the family VIP section."

Spence frowned and slapped Bert on the shoulder. "Resident ape? Sod off," he retorted, rolling his eyes. "Nice to meet you, though, Miss Bancroft," he greeted, smiling warmly.

Grinning, I shook my head. I'd never had so many people call me Miss Bancroft as I had today. It was a little unnerving. "Emma is fine. Nice to meet you, too."

He sidestepped and pulled open the heavy-looking, frosted-glass door and motioned for me to go inside. "Enjoy the race."

I nodded in acknowledgement, even though I knew I wouldn't. I hated to watch these things because my imagination ran rampant every time I saw Carson lean so dangerously close to the ground as he sped around the corner. "Thank you." I smiled politely and stepped hesitantly over the threshold.

The large room which stretched out before me was extremely expensive-looking. The right-hand side of the building was pure glass, which stretched across the whole wall. Little black leather stools and small tables with black leather armchairs were dotted along the edge of it so spectators could look out over the racetrack. Massive television screens were located in the centre of the room, showing the motorbikes as they lined up at the starting line. Cameras were panning across the drivers as they sat there. I couldn't hear any sound from there, though; it was as if they were muted. The people who stood around drinking champagne were all dressed impeccably in suits or designer dresses. The women had a full face of make-up, and not one hair was out of place. They were all a fair bit older than me.

I wrung my hands, wincing as I thought about what I must look like. I was wearing my smartest three-quarter jeans (which actually weren't that smart) and a simple, white shirt. My hair had just been pulled up last-minute into a bun, and I wore no make-up at all. I was so out of place it was actually comical in a pitiful way.

As I stepped into the room, a couple of people turned to look at me. Recognition crossed their faces before they turned back to their conversations, leaning in and whispering. My stomach squirmed. Clearly they read the tabloids and knew what my profession was. I frowned down at the floor. My happy mood was now gone. I didn't like this place. I didn't like these people who looked down their noses at me, figuring I was beneath them. Of course, I *was* beneath them, but they didn't even see fit to put on a polite act.

"Champagne?"

I jumped as a waiter held out a silver tray toward me, smiling politely. "Umm… no, thanks. Do you have a Pepsi or anything?" I asked, chewing on my lip nervously.

He raised one eyebrow before he nodded and disappeared without another word. I gulped, heading over to the wall of glass, looking down at the racetrack. The drivers on their bikes looked so far away from up here. They were all stopped on their respective marks on the ground, waiting for the race to begin. A smile twitched at the corner of my mouth when I saw Carson. He was in ninth position today following his time trials the day before. He'd told me it was due to a tactical move – something about the amount of fuel they carried at the start of the race. He wasn't worried about his starting position.

People from his team milled around him, talking to him, holding his bike still with some chunky metal thing on wheels. My eyes wandered over him slowly in his little blue outfit. The way he looked in it, even with his head covered with a helmet, made me shift from one foot to the other as my skin seemed to come alive with desire. When they pulled the chunky little metal thing from behind his back tyre, I frowned and started to gnaw on my lip. I knew the start was approaching. People in the stands waved their flags and their foam hands as the drivers prepared to race. The sound inside the family area was just general chitchat, though, so the walls had to have been made with some sort of sound-reducing glass.

Just as the team members with each driver started to make their way off the track and in through a little gate on the side, someone stepped up next to me. I turned, smiling gratefully, expecting it to be the waiter back with a drink for me. Instead, a smiling lady in her mid-thirties stood there. I gulped, suddenly nervous because I hadn't actually expected anyone to approach me.

"Hello, you must be Emma. I've heard so much about you from Carson," she greeted.

I recoiled, trying to keep one eye on the track but talk to her at the same time; I didn't want to miss the start. "Um, yeah, I am. Sorry, I don't..." I shook my head as a blush crept over my cheeks. I had no idea who she was.

She laughed a high, tinkering laugh and held her hand out to me. "I'm Stuart's wife, Katrina. We're co-team supporters, you and I. We head up the wives' club for our team," she joked, winking at me as I shook her hand politely. "It's nice to finally have someone here for Carson so I can have a girlie gossip while we watch the race. Usually, I'm alone at these things. Some of the other wives can be a little..." she turned her nose up distastefully, "snobby," she finished.

I chuckled awkwardly, hoping this wasn't some kind of test I was about to fail. "Yeah, I kind of guessed that," I admitted. "I'm kind of used to that reaction to me now, though; it happens a lot."

She rolled her eyes and perched herself on one of the stools, crossing one trousered leg over the other. "Who cares? We all have to make a living. Ignore them. They're all just jealous because their behinds don't look as cute as your tiny little booty does in those

243

jeans." She winked at me jokingly and patted the seat next to hers. "Sit down, I won't bite."

I slid onto the stool, chuckling awkwardly. The waiter came over then, setting a glass of Pepsi in front of me. I chewed on my lip, looking back down to Carson. Suddenly, the pre-race lap started, and all the bikes moved forward. Carson took a few seconds to go, though, seeming hesitant as the others all breezed past him. I'd seen the start of a few of these races, so I knew he never really pushed it hard on this lap, just travelled at a leisurely speed around the track. Within seconds, the bikes were all out of sight and I twisted in my seat, watching the TV screen instead so I could see them all find their groove around the track. This lap was just to warm up their bikes and tyres, so there was no real rush or competition.

"You ever been to a race before?" Katrina asked, picking up a set of headphones hooked on the rail near my knees.

I shook my head in response. "No. I'm not sure I'll like it," I admitted.

She chuckled and nodded, picking up another set of chunky black headphones and holding them out to me. "I never used to like watching, either. You get used to it as time goes by. Want to listen to the commentary?"

Hesitantly, I took the offered headgear, watching as she covered her ears with hers but left the overhead strap thing under her chin – probably so it wouldn't mess up her hair. I did the same, pressing mine to my ears, listening to the commentator who usually did the voice over on the races. He was talking about form and who needed what points today. He announced that if Carson won this race he'd be uncatchable on the leader board, meaning he would win the championship for the year. I smiled at that and silently crossed my fingers.

When the bikes had done a full lap, they came back into view again, all of them stopping on their respective marks on the ground. My chest was tight as I watched, and I could barely sit still. The race was twenty laps, which Carson said would be about forty minutes in duration. I couldn't wait for it to end. My nerves and excitement about telling him I loved him back was actually starting to overtake the worry which usually plagued me during race time.

Once all the racers were settled on their positions, the family members all crowded around the window, taking their seats and looking at their loved ones excitedly. My eyes were trained on Carson as I gripped the edge of the seat tightly, willing him to do well. When the green light flashed, the sound through the headphones was momentarily deafening as the bikes screeched off their lines in a cloud of smoke and exhaust fumes. No longer able to sit, I jumped up, looking down with wide eyes as Carson immediately blasted past two other racers, weaving in and out on his heavy-looking bike, taking the inside edge of the track and bumping up to seventh place in an instant. A couple of other people switched positions, too, but my eyes were firmly fixed on my fiancé.

"Go, baby! Kick some arse! You got this!" I shouted before I could stop myself.

Katrina chuckled next to me, but I noticed no one else was standing or shouting. Heat spread across my cheeks as the group of bikes rounded the corner and were out of sight again. The distasteful, disapproving look on some of their faces was enough to make me cringe back into my seat.

As the dust and smoke settled, it was clear that one of the drivers had incurred a problem during the start. He still sat in his starting position as his team ran out to him, taking his bike. The guy threw his hands up in exasperation, gesturing wildly at his bike before stomping out of the gate and off the racetrack.

"Well, Sinead won't be a happy bunny. Shame," Katrina said beside me, giggling and nudging me in the ribs, nodding toward one of the more haughty-looking women sitting in the row at the end. Sinead stood, scowling down from the window before she made a disapproving scoffing sound and stormed out of the room. Clearly, that was her husband or partner, and judging by the look on her face, she wasn't impressed that he hadn't even started.

I shared a conspiratorial smile with Katrina before turning my attention to the television screens, watching as the cameras followed the lead group around. In my ears, the commentator was busy analysing their form and bikes. When the camera cut to Carson as he went around the corner, I gasped and averted my eyes, not wanting to see how close his bike and body got to the ground as he leant in. I immediately doubted my ability to watch this race. My stomach was churning; my heart was in my throat, and my palms were slick with sweat. Internally, I was counting down the minutes, listening to the laps ticking by, thinking that each lap brought me one step closer to seeing him and saying those words I'd longed to say to him for three years.

Within ten minutes, Carson had crept up another three places and was now in fourth. I had barely watched any of it but was listening avidly to the commentary through my headphones. It appeared Carson wasn't having a good race today according to the experts. They'd already slammed him for an earlier move where he undershot a corner and lost time when he cut into the grass.

"Oh, what was that? He didn't even see that coming! Carson Matthews just conceded a place. Martin Bashing just took that easily!" the commentator yelled excitedly in my ear. I frowned. "It seems like something is wrong with Carson today. His mind seems to be elsewhere. On each of the last three laps, he's lost four tenths of a second. The distance time is growing between him and the leader. If he wants that first place, he's going to have to work for it."

"That's right, Simon. He doesn't look like the Carson we've come to expect."

I frowned, looking up at Katrina to see she was frowning, too. I flicked my eyes up to the television screens, seeing Carson there. He was heading toward a corner. As the others in front of him were braking, he wasn't. He caught up with them quickly, his brake light finally flickering as he slowed down for the corner. My eyes widened as he suddenly pulled to the right-hand side of the track, narrowly avoiding the back of the bike in front of him. He accelerated and leant into the corner, squeezing into an almost non-existent gap, forcing the other bike over so they didn't collide. The two hulking bikes were level now, but by squeezing into the gap, Carson now had the inside edge. As they straightened up, Carson was just ahead and gunned his engine, blasting down the straight and finally overtaking the other driver who immediately veered to the right. He was looking to overtake again but Carson veered to the right, too, thwarting his attempt.

I groaned and covered my mouth with my hand. I was pretty sure I would never get used to seeing him do this.

"Oh, that was a risky move. Matthews is lucky he didn't take them both out doing that. Bashing won't be happy with him at all," the commentator observed. "Carson certainly isn't himself today. That was a rookie, dangerous overtake, and I don't think I've ever seen the youngster put himself or others in danger like that. His mind really isn't on task today at all."

Suddenly, it hit me what this was about and why he was driving so differently today. Just before the race we'd had a huge argument, he'd told me he loved me, and I hadn't said it back. He wasn't concentrating properly on the race now because of me and what had transpired between us earlier.

I covered my mouth and shook my head, hating myself for not managing to say the words back before he left the room. He was driving badly today because of me. If he lost this race due to lack of concentration, it would be entirely my fault.

The television cameras left Carson and cut back to the three race leaders who were going around a particularly sharp-looking bend the commentators called The Loop. As I watched them, hating myself because Carson was obviously upset, shocked voices burst through my headphones.

"He's off! Carson Matthews has just crashed out of the race!"

The words made my heart stop as my mouth popped open in shock. Time seemed to stand still as their words washed over me like a bucket of cold water. I jumped to my feet, staring at the screen in disbelief.

"I can't see what's happened. Medics are on their way," the commentator said.

The cameras cut to pieces of Carson's bike strewn everywhere. Tyre tracks stained the road and trailed across the grass. People in white jumpsuits were running toward a sign, which had been smashed and lay in a pile along with Carson's bike. When I saw legs in that tangled mess, a loud whimper left my lips.

No. No. No. This can't be happening. Please, no.

"Let's get a replay of what happened." The camera changed, showing Carson's bike bypassing the pit lane, still cutting off every attempt the guy behind him made to overtake. When he approached the bend, the guy behind him slowed marginally and backed off, but Carson again left it later to brake. As he approached the corner, it looked like he was going too fast and as he leant into the turn, he lost control and the bike wobbled before clipping the ground. Carson was flicked over the top of it, smashing into the ground and bouncing like a rag doll, rolling a couple of times with his arms flailing everywhere before skidding along the road and hitting the barriers on the left-hand side of the track. Horrifyingly, his bike was skidding along behind him so as he hit the barrier, his bike smashed into him, too.

"No! Oh, God, No!" I shouted, covering my mouth with my hands.

Chapter Twenty-Four

"No, he can't have. That's not..." I shook my head, my eyes glued to the screen. My legs swayed, and I bumped into the stool behind me, sending it clattering to the ground. The whole room had gone quiet, and everyone was staring at me. The TV replayed it over and over, slowing it down; showing Carson flick over the handlebars of his bike, showing his body hit the ground. In slow motion, I saw his helmet hit the road before it bounced back up again. His shoulder smashed into the tarmac, and his arm twisted behind him before he started skidding along the track with pieces of his bike whizzing past him.

My lungs constricted as my heart squeezed in my chest. I couldn't take my eyes off the screen, watching it over and over. The voices in my headphones were talking, but I couldn't understand a single word they were saying. My head was muffled; my vision swam before me as my eyes filled my tears.

Carson's legs weren't moving. He wasn't moving at all. People were trying to dig him out, pulling pieces of the wooden sign off him, throwing them to the side carelessly. It took two of them to drag his bike off his body. I watched it all, knowing I'd caused this accident because of the argument we'd had and by me not admitting my feelings for him. And now it was too late. He had crashed and died, and he would never, ever know I loved him more than life itself, that I had always loved him and would give my life for his in a heartbeat. He would never know he was my whole world.

Suddenly, the cameras flicked back to the race. That was when I finally snapped back into reality. I pulled my headphones off, dropping them carelessly on the floor. "What do I do?" I cried, turning to Katrina and grabbing her elbow to steady myself as my legs almost buckled. "I need to go there. How do I get there?"

Her eyes were sympathetic as she looked over my shoulder. I glanced in that direction, seeing two men walking toward me, both wearing staff T-shirts. I gulped, swiping my tears as they started to stream down my face. My whole world was disappearing into nothingness around me as I realised I might never get to see his smile again, never get to look into his eyes or feel his skin under my fingertips.

"Miss Bancroft, there's been an accident. Carson's with the medics right now. Would you like us to take you to him?"

I nodded quickly, stumbling forward as my heart began to hammer in my chest. "Yes," I whimpered. "Is he okay? It looked so bad. He wasn't moving, please… is he going to be all right?" I gripped the man's sleeve as my chin wobbled. I needed an answer. I needed him to reassure me I wasn't going to have to tell my little girl that the daddy she'd only just met and fell in love with had left to go up to Heaven. I didn't want to have to say those words. I couldn't.

The guy smiled sadly and motioned toward the door with his spare hand. "I don't know any details, miss. They just told me to bring you down." His hand closed over my elbow as he started guiding me through the room. As we walked past people, I saw their sullen, sympathetic faces. The distaste was now gone from them; now I was one of them, and they felt empathy for me. In that moment, my past and my job didn't matter because they could feel my pain.

"He'll be okay. He'll be okay." Repeating it as we walked out of the building and out to a golf buggy didn't help at all. "Where is he? How long will it take to get to him?" I mumbled, wringing my hands.

Without answering my question, the guy helped me in and then slid beside me as someone else jumped into the front and pulled out.

The little road we were on ran alongside the track, and spectator stands stood to my left. People continued to shout and cheer. The other drivers whizzed past us on the other side of the fence, their engines making such a loud noise it made my ears ring. Everything was carrying on as normal, completely oblivious that my whole life was over and my world had stopped turning.

Suddenly, the guy holding my arm put his hand up to his ear before turning back to me. "He's alive. They're assessing him now, but he's conscious."

My heart leapt at his words and I closed my eyes, silently sending up thanks to whoever was watching over him. "He is?" My voice didn't even sound like mine as my whole body sagged with relief. "Is he all right? How long will it take to get there?"

I didn't need him to answer my question though because, in front of me, I could see two ambulances, a fire engine, a large crowd of people and security, and some of Carson's team all milling around. To my right, on the track, I could see the remains of Carson's bike and the rubble he'd caused when he'd smashed into the sign and the fence beyond. My mouth popped open, seeing the wreckage and carnage left in his wake. A whimper left my lips as the terrifying truth hit me head-on. I had no idea what I was going to see as the golf buggy skidded to a stop next to the ambulance.

I jumped out, stumbling and just managing to catch myself as panic took over. I needed to get there, I needed to see him. There was no time to lose because the wreckage I'd just seen was so severe he wouldn't survive. He couldn't survive that. I'd inadvertently killed him.

As I ran toward the large crowd of staff and emergency response teams, a security guard stepped in front of me, throwing his arm in front of me and stopping my panic-stricken attempt to get to Carson. "No public!" he barked, shaking his head adamantly.

I whimpered and struggled, trying to get out of his hold. "I need to see him, let go of me!" I cried, unashamedly aiming a kick into his shins. "Get off me!" I shouted. Anger was simmering in my veins. He was wasting valuable seconds.

"Phil, Phil, let her go!" someone called behind me.

I didn't stop to look who it was as the arms suddenly loosened around me. Instead, I pushed myself away from him and ran, weaving through the five-people-deep crowd. They all seemed to be looking in the same direction. I could hear them whispering. Terms like 'lucky' and 'close call' filled my ears. I didn't stop to try and digest them, though, just pushed my way through the crowd toward the ambulance parked with its doors open.

As I shoved myself past the last person, my eyes landed on him. Carson. He *was* alive, just like the guy had told me. He was lying on a gurney, a thick white brace covering his neck and holding his head in place. Black smudges marred his face, and his leather jumpsuit was scratched up and ripped in places. They'd taken it half off, leaving it loose around his waist. He had his eyes closed and was wincing in pain as the paramedic poked and prodded at him.

I choked on a sob, feeling relief and gratitude wash over me. He was alive. I hadn't lost him. And, surprisingly, he didn't look in terrible shape, either. My mind was whirling as I hesitantly stepped forward, my whole body shaking and my legs barely supporting my weight. The pain of losing him and thinking he was dead haunted me still, and I knew it would take me a long time to get over that feeling completely. It still sat in my stomach, churning, mixing with the relief I felt because he was alive and relatively unscathed.

As I stopped at his side, he opened his eyes, looking up at me. The blue of his eyes caught me off-guard, as it did every time I saw them. My breathing faltered, and my legs finally gave out. I sank to my knees in front of him and burst into tears, pressing my face into his stomach and sobbing uncontrollably.

One of his hands touched the back of my head as my body shook with sobs. "Em, shh… it's all right. I'm okay," he croaked somewhat breathlessly. "Don't cry, come on," he whispered.

I sniffed and pulled back, looking up at him as my chin trembled and my breathing hitched. "You're okay? That looked," I shook my head, not having the right words to describe the terrifying, soul-shattering accident I'd watched on repeat on the television, "awful," I finished.

He reached over and brushed the back of his fingers across my cheek before doing the same to the other, wiping my tears away. "I have a few knocks. Something funky has definitely happened to my arm, but I'm not too bad. I was lucky," he answered.

I swallowed around the lump in my throat. I had no words to tell him how much he'd frightened me, how terrified I was, how guilty I felt for being the cause of his lack of concentration. "It's lucky your guardian angel could keep up with you," I mumbled, echoing the words of the tattoo he had on his side.

A sad smile twitched at the corners of his lips. "My guardian angel is on her knees in front of me."

My heart stuttered in my chest as I closed my eyes and turned my face into his hand, relishing in the feel of his skin against my cheek. "In that case, your guardian angel desperately needs a change of underwear," I joked, pushing myself up to my feet so I could look down at him properly. He chuckled awkwardly, wincing at the small movement. "Carson, don't do that to me again. I thought you'd died; I thought you'd gone before I could tell you…" I took a deep breath and prepared myself to make a life-altering confession to him, but before I could finish speaking, the paramedic cleared his throat.

"Let's get this on you. It'll relieve some of the pressure from your shoulder and should make you more comfortable," he said, holding out a skin-coloured foam strip shaped like the figure eight. He unfastened one end and carefully looped it around Carson's neck before gingerly picking up Carson's arm and pushing his hand through the loop at the bottom. The groan of agony Carson made had the hair standing up on the back of my neck. Once he was done, the paramedic smiled sympathetically. "I'm fairly satisfied there's no head or neck injury, but we'll have to leave the collar on until they can do some proper tests. We're ready to move you to the hospital. They'll pop that back in when we get there. I think there may be some broken ribs, too."

I glanced up at him when he spoke. "Pop what in?" I questioned, confused. Carson scrunched his nose as another paramedic helped the first wheel the gurney toward the open doors of the ambulance.

"His shoulder. It's dislocated," the first paramedic answered.

A shudder washed over me, but I tried my best not to show any reaction. Carson saw it, though, and he chuckled quietly. "You can wait outside when they do it," he offered.

Bile rose in my throat. *Too bloody right I'm waiting outside. I cannot see that!* Ignoring his smug face, I looked at the paramedic. "I can get in the ambulance, too, right? I'm his fiancée." I sniffed, wiping my nose on the back of my hand discreetly, silently wishing I had a tissue because I was sure to look an absolute mess.

"Of course," the paramedic answered. As soon as they'd settled Carson's bed over on the right hand side, I climbed in. I sat opposite him and looked at him worriedly, wondering what I could do to help him. It was clear just by the stiff way he was lying and the paleness to his face that he was in a lot of pain.

Just before the doors closed, one of Carson's team stepped forward and placed Carson's helmet on his stomach. "Don't forget that, mate. Lucky helmet that," the guy grinned.

My eyes settled on the helmet and my stomach clenched, seeing just how much of a close call it really was. Carson's helmet was cracked all around one side, scratches covering almost every inch of it. The visor was gone, ripped off no doubt because the clip on the side was shattered. As I looked at the thing that had saved Carson's life, I burst into tears all over again.

Chapter Twenty-Five

It didn't take long to get to the hospital. I didn't get much chance to talk to Carson on the journey there because the paramedic was fussing over him the entire time. I *did* get to hold his hand, though. By the time we arrived, I was even more of a hysterical mess than I was minutes before. I had a feeling they were mostly tears of relief and 'what could have been' thoughts.

When the ambulance pulled up outside the hospital, I tried my best to stay out of the way as they wheeled him inside. Doctors fussed over him, checking his eyes and head thoroughly, whilst asking him simple questions like his name and what day of the week it was.

I pressed my back against the wall, watching it all with wide eyes, not knowing how I could help or what I should say. The guilt inside me was making me feel nauseous because this was entirely my fault.

After finally concluding he had no head trauma, they removed the neck brace. When a nurse wheeled in an ultrasound machine, the doctor checked over Carson's shoulder. "This is definitely dislocated. Your records show you've done it before," the doctor stated, eyeing the screen carefully as he moved the little plastic thing around Carson's shoulder.

"Yeah, a few years ago," Carson confirmed. He turned his head, looking over at me and a weak smile twitched at the corner of his lips. "Em, you can wait outside. You don't have to be in here for this."

I gulped, wondering if my voice would work if I tried to speak. "I don't want to leave you," I admitted, even though in that second, I would rather be anywhere but there. I hated hospitals at the best of times, but knowing they were going to pop Carson's shoulder back in was making my knees weak.

His smile grew, and his eyes showed his appreciation before he turned back to the doctor. "Is there muscle damage? I won't need surgery, will I?"

Surgery? My breath caught in my throat.

The doctor pursed his lips. "I've checked thoroughly for nerve damage and muscle tears, but it actually looks good. I can't see anything which would require surgery." He pulled the plastic wand-type thing away from Carson's shoulder and smiled. "I think we can get this back in using reduction."

Carson winced but nodded.

"What's reduction?" I asked, finally pushing myself away from the wall.

The doctor turned to me and smiled. "It's the term we use. I'll basically just manipulate the shoulder back into its socket manually, using massage and arm movements," he explained. A lump formed in my throat, and I silently wished I hadn't asked. He turned back to Carson. "Of course, we'll have to get some pain medication and a mild sedative inside you first," he added. "Let's send you for x-ray to make sure nothing's broken, and then we'll get to it."

Carson nodded, wincing as they eased his arm back into the sling. "Can I request a full-blown sedative rather than a mild one? I'm a bit of a pussy, and I scream like a girl," he joked.

The doctor chuckled and pulled off his gloves, tossing them into the bin. "I'll see what I can do." He nodded to the nurse. "Rush him through x-ray and call me when he's back."

"Emma, come here, will ya?" Carson asked, holding out his good hand to me.

I nodded and obediently trotted to his side, taking his hand and gripping it tightly. Worry was eating me up inside. I felt useless just standing around and waiting. "You okay?" I whispered, squeezing his fingers gently.

He nodded. "I'm all right. Listen, while I'm up in x-ray, can you call my mum and just tell her what's happening? She'll be going crazy, and the hospital probably won't tell her anything because I changed my next of kin to you."

I frowned. "You did? Why did you do that? When?"

He smiled, pulling my hand up and kissing the back of my knuckles softly. "I have to check over my medical forms and details before each race. I changed my next of kin to you a couple of weeks ago when you moved in with me."

I didn't know what to say. That was kind of a big responsibility. Before he made his 'I love you' confession, I hadn't even known he considered me to be his kin, let alone the most important one. "Oh."

He smiled weakly. "So, yeah, if you could possibly call my mum? Or if you don't want to speak to her, then maybe you could call one of my sisters? Just tell them I'm fine, that I don't need surgery and that I'll call them later," he asked.

I nodded in agreement. "Of course, I'll call her." I didn't really want to speak to his mother. We had barely exchanged more than a few polite words in the last few weeks, but I knew I needed to let it go for now. She may not like me, but I had no problem with her really, and she was still his mother, after all. If Sasha had been hurt and I didn't know how she was, I would be beside myself with worry, so I knew what she'd be going through.

"Thanks." He kissed the back of my knuckles again, just as the nurses and an orderly unclicked the wheels of his bed and started to push him toward the door. I whimpered, tightening my grip on his hand, not wanting to let go. As I started walking along by the side of his bed, meaning to go with him, he chuckled. "Emma, stop stressing. I'm fine." He eased his hand from mine and smiled at me reassuringly.

I stopped walking, feeling the lump in my throat swell as he was wheeled out of the room and down the corridor. As soon as he was out of sight, I slumped into the nearest chair and put my head in my hands.

The phone call to Carson's mother was an emotional one. As I suspected, she was beside herself and could hardly even speak to me on the phone. She was sobbing so hard I couldn't quite make out her words, but I'd just cooed soothing things down the line, telling her he was fine and he didn't want her to worry. She'd thanked me profusely for calling her and asked that I call again later to let her know when he was coming home and when she could come and visit. Lastly, she asked how Sasha was and if I needed her to go over and watch her while I was at the hospital. The gesture, although a relatively-small one, actually meant a lot to me. Sasha had certainly worked her magic and woven a spell over Jillian.

After fifteen minutes, Carson was wheeled back into the room and smiled at me. "X-rays are all done, just gotta wait for the results and then they'll pop my shoulder back in. I think you should probably go get a cup of tea or something while they do it," he recommended.

"Is it that bad?" I asked, pulling a chair up by the side of his bed.

"It's not exactly a walk in the park. I may swear a lot and even cry," he joked. I smiled and behind me, the doctor walked in, x-rays in hand. We both looked up, eagerly awaiting the results.

"Good news: no breaks in the shoulder. I was worried about the top of the humerus, but the x-ray shows no breaks. Also, the chest x-ray came back clear. No rib fractures either. You were extremely lucky."

Air rushed out of my lungs at the news and a smile crept onto my lips. No broken bones – that was certainly something to be thankful for.

"All we need to do now is get that shoulder back into place. I'll have a nurse come in and give you a sedative. Once that's started to work, I'll be back and we'll get you back to fighting fit," the doctor announced.

WATCHING THE DOCTOR ease Carson's arm back into place was one of the most horrifying things I'd ever seen in my life – probably second only to watching his accident earlier. Seeing him in that much pain while they moved his arm around in circles and massaged his shoulder was actually soul-shattering. I couldn't watch most of it. I'd squeezed my eyes shut and turned my head away, gritting my teeth while he squeezed the life out of my hand with his good one. It was awful.

After, they'd put his arm into a sling and performed another ultrasound to check again to make sure there was no damage to nerves and tissue. Thankfully, the doctor announced he had the all-clear and would just need to be referred to physiotherapy for aftercare.

Once we were finally alone in the room, I smiled down at him. My heart ached with love for him as our eyes met.

"Thanks for staying," he said quietly.

I nodded. "Of course. Although, I don't think I'll ever get the sound of that out of my head," I winced and shook my head at the memory of the groans of agony which came from Carson.

"Me either." He chuckled awkwardly before he winced at the moment and gritted his teeth.

I gulped, knowing I needed to broach the subject of the cause of this accident. I needed to apologise for it. "Carson, what happened? How did you lose control like that?"

He blew out a big breath and shook his head. "I don't know. I just wasn't thinking clearly, I guess. I was stupid. I should have known better; it was a rookie mistake."

Shifting on my feet, I perched on the edge of his bed and pulled his hand into my lap. "It was my fault. You weren't concentrating properly because we'd just argued. This is all my fault, all this pain you're in, I caused that." Tears overflowed in my eyes and trickled down my cheeks.

He smiled weakly. "Emma, this isn't your fault. It was mine. I was stupid and reckless today."

"Yeah, all because I didn't tell you I loved you back before the race," I countered, bending my head and pressing my face into the side of his neck. Feeling his soft skin against mine and having his breath blow across my damp cheek made my stomach flutter.

His one good hand left mine and moved to cup the back of my head. "You shouldn't have to lie to me just so I won't drive like a dickhead."

I sniffed in an extremely unladylike fashion. "It wouldn't have been a lie, Carson," I mumbled against his neck.

His whole body seemed to stiffen against me. "What? It... huh?"

I smiled, finally pulling back and looked down at him. "You ran out of that room before I could compose myself. I was still in shock from hearing you say it to me. Your confession was so unexpected it just stumped me, and I couldn't quite process it. And before I had the chance to accept what you said and say it back, you jumped to your own conclusions and ran from the room," I explained, watching his eyes widen and his lips part.

I gulped and tried to quash the ridiculous happiness trying to take over my body. Carson looked like he was barely breathing as his eyes scanned my face. Hope danced in his eyes as his hand tightened in my hair. "Emma, what?" he whispered. "You... you..."

I smiled, reaching out to touch the confused frown lines on his forehead. "Why don't you say it again? Now that you can't run from the room, maybe I'll get the chance to say my piece, too," I suggested, grinning. I pressed myself closer to him, leaving barely an inch between our mouths. The heat from his body seeped into mine, making my skin tingle all over.

Without missing a beat, he said the words I had longed to hear come out of his mouth for the last three years. "I love you, Emma."

My eyes fluttered closed, and I immediately pressed my mouth to his, kissing him as if it was the last thing I would ever get to do. Everything finally clicked back into place. The hurt and sadness I'd been feeling for the last few weeks just disappeared with that one kiss. When Carson's lips were against mine, it felt right and whole and perfect – just like it always had done. He moaned in the back of his throat and kissed me back immediately. His arm wrapped around me tightly, as if he was afraid to let go.

Not really wanting to, but knowing I had to, I broke the kiss. I needed to say it back this time; he needed to know he was my whole world and everything good in it. But clearly he wasn't ready for the kiss to end yet because he guided my mouth back to his again. I smiled against his soft lips and broke the kiss for a second time, pressing my forehead to his. As I spoke the words, I looked deeply into his blue eyes that had me hooked from the first time I looked into them.

"I love you, too."

He closed his eyes and his whole body relaxed as he seemed to breathe a sigh of relief. A beautiful smile stretched across his face that I couldn't help but mirror. "That sounded even better than I imagined it would," he said, laughing quietly. His hand guided my face to his, and he leant up, brushing his nose across mine in a little Eskimo kiss. That one small, familiar gesture warmed my heart and seemed to set my body on fire as my hormones started to rage. "Move back. I have something I need to do," he muttered, tilting his head and kissing my lips gently for a second.

"What?" I asked, confused as I moved and stood up, looking down at him in question. But he didn't answer, just pulled back the sheets on the bed, and used his elbow to push himself up to sitting. I gasped, putting my hand on his good shoulder, trying to thwart his attempt to get up. "Carson, what are you doing? You need to stay still," I protested, shaking my head in disbelief. "I'll do whatever it is. What do you need? A drink, the bathroom, what?" I asked desperately.

He grinned, his eyes twinkling with mischief as he moved his legs, swinging them off the side of the bed. "I just need to do something and then I'll get back in bed. I promise."

I groaned in frustration, taking his arm and helping him stand when he wobbled. "Carson, you're going to hurt yourself! You should be resting!" I scolded.

Without answering, he reached out and used the bed to brace himself as he bent his leg and got down on one knee, wincing and groaning in pain as he did it.

"Carson, what are you doing?" I cried in exasperation, scowling at him. He was going to hurt himself, or cause more damage to his body. The doctors had said he was to rest for a couple of days; he shouldn't be out of bed at all.

Finally, he looked up at me. The smile that stretched across his face was beautiful and made the hair on the nape of my neck prickle. "I'm doing what I should have done weeks ago. I'm proposing," he answered.

My mouth popped open in shock at his words. Proposing. He was on his knees in front of me. He loved me. He wanted to marry me for real, and not because he didn't want Sasha to grow up in a one-parent household.

"But you already proposed," I whimpered, watching him through teary eyes.

He shook his head and frowned, seeming annoyed.

"No, I didn't. I didn't ask the question. I didn't ask you to be my wife. I told you instead."

My teeth sank into my bottom lip as happiness washed over me. When he shifted on his knee and sucked in a breath through his teeth, I could see how much pain he was in, but he made no moves to get up as he reached for my left hand.

I whimpered, looking down at the love of my life. His eyes met mine as he spoke. "Emma, I'm sorry I didn't do this properly before, really I am, and I hope you can forgive me for being such a wanker for the last few weeks. I'll make it up to you, I swear." He gulped, and I could see the sincerity on his face as his thumb brushed over the back of my hand. "I want to take care of you. I want to be there for you, always. I love you *so* much. Will you marry me? Not because you have to, but because you want to? Will you be my wife and let me love you forever?" he pleaded.

My tears were back in force now at his words. His proposal, although done in a hospital surrounded by the busy goings-on and people rushing around in the corridor outside, was the most perfect thing ever. The only sound I'd ever heard which topped Carson's proposal was hearing my daughter say her first word.

"Yes," I whispered, nodding excitely. "I'd love to marry you." That was the truth. I'd always wanted to be his wife, but just not under the circumstances he had demanded last time.

The dazzling grin that crossed his face made my knees weak. He pushed himself up, using the bed for leverage, and stepped closer to me. His eyes were burning into mine and showed a passion which took my breath away. "I love you so fucking much, Emma," he growled.

Before I could answer, his lips pressed against mine, kissing me possessively. I smiled against his mouth and wrapped my arms around his neck, pressing my body against his carefully. As the kiss deepened and his tongue touched mine, and with his hard body against mine again, I couldn't help but want him. It had been so long since we'd been together physically that the passion and lust building inside me was a little overwhelming. I whimpered into his mouth and gripped my hands into his hair as the kiss grew in intensity until it was almost a raging inferno.

When he pulled back, I gasped for breath, feeling my heart crash against my ribs. "Let's do it soon. Like, as soon as possible," he rasped. "I don't want to wait five months to make you my wife."

I nodded in agreement. Now that it was official, I could hardly wait to get that second ring on my finger and take his surname. "The sooner the better. I don't need a big, fancy wedding. Why don't we just go to Vegas?" I suggested.

He nodded eagerly. "Vegas it is then," he agreed, claiming my mouth in a kiss which set the very essence of my soul on fire.

I grinned against his lips. "Margo's going to be pissed," I chuckled, thinking of the wedding planner who had already made so many arrangements for us to get married in five months' time.

"Margo can go take a long walk off a short pier," Carson answered. "All that matters is that I get my ring on your finger before you change your mind and realise you can do better than a dumb-arse race driver who can't do anything other than handle a motorbike."

I shook my head at his absurdity. "I'm not changing my mind. There is no one better than you," I whispered, going up on tiptoes and gently brushing my nose against his.

Epilogue

"Vegas!" Lucie squealed, leaning on the handrail and looking out over the spectacular view of The Strip. "I still can't believe we're in Vegas!"

I grinned and nodded, moving up next to her and casting my eyes over the beautiful, twinkling lights of the Las Vegas Strip below. Although I had suggested we get married here, Carson had chosen the actual venue, and I couldn't have been happier with his choice. We were currently in the 'Chapel in the Clouds' – i.e., the tower part of the Stratosphere Hotel, Casino and Tower. Being 112 floors up, the view was uninterrupted and majestic. You couldn't get better.

"I know, it's so incredible!" I gushed, shaking my head in awe at the view before me. We'd arrived yesterday, but by the time we'd settled into our hotel rooms and then gone for a couple of drinks last night, it was time for bed. Today, being my wedding day, had been filled with giggling, champagne breakfasts, and hair and make-up appointments. We hadn't had the opportunity to explore The Strip yet.

It was exactly three weeks today since Carson's accident. As soon as he was out of hospital, he'd put in a call and booked the first available wedding slot he could. He'd been a little disappointed it had taken three weeks before we could do this, but we had to abide by his racing schedule because he couldn't take time off during the season.

Lucie sighed dreamily and turned back to look at me, gripping my upper arms as she grinned at me. "Look at you, about to get married to the man of your dreams," she gushed. "Oh, Emma, you look beautiful. Although I really wish we'd gone for a dress that sparkled like a thousand diamonds were sewn into it," she joked, winking at me while jibing Margo's description of the perfect wedding dress. Lucie had found it highly amusing when I'd told her about it.

"I know. Diamonds are a girl's best friend, after all," I replied, trying to mimic Margo's posh accent. "After you, of course," I added, linking my arm through hers.

"Of course!" she agreed, grinning wildly.

I looked down at myself, brushing my hand over the simple, yet elegant, silk dress which was off the rack at a cute little boutique I had found once. Not designer. Just purely me. I loved it but was actually secretly worried if Carson would, knowing his penchant for flashing the cash.

"Mummy pwincess!" Sasha gushed as she stepped into the room holding Jillian's hand.

I smiled at my baby girl, sighing at how beautiful she looked in her little maroon-coloured princess dress with the meringue-netted skirt. Sasha and Lucie were both my bridesmaids today, but Lucie's dress was decidedly more elegant.

"Aww, don't you look beautiful!" I complimented, seeing her for the first time in three hours. Jillian had taken Sasha for me while Lucie and I had our hair and nails done.

Sasha grinned and nodded. "Sasha pwincess!"

I nodded in agreement. "Daddy's gonna think you look so lovely," I predicted. *I just hope he thinks the same about me!* On that, I wasn't as confident.

I looked up at Jillian and smiled. She had actually asked to come to the wedding today. Carson had told her about us jetting off to Vegas, and he hadn't expected her to care that much, but she'd insisted she wanted to come along to support us. In the three weeks since Carson's accident, Jillian and I had been making a real effort to get along. Our relationship wasn't perfect by any means, and we would never be close, but we could be polite and accepting – that was all I needed actually.

"Has she been well-behaved?" I asked, raising one eyebrow at Sasha, looking for a tell-tale sign that she'd been naughty.

Jillian grinned. "Oh, she's been as good as gold."

A clearing of the throat from the doorway made me look up. Rory stood there in a suit Carson had taken him out to buy and a maroon tie, which matched the girl's dresses. He looked rather handsome. "The guests are getting bored. Gonna get this show on the road yet?" he asked.

I smiled and nodded, bending and planting a soft kiss on Sasha's cheek. "Yep, let's make this official."

Lucie took Sasha's hand, and Jillian disappeared from the room, probably to take her seat on the balcony where the ceremony was being conducted. "Ready?" Lucie asked.

I nodded and opened my mouth to say yes, but Rory shook his head quickly. "I just need a word with my sister before we do this," he said confidently.

Lucie groaned and shook her head. "You're wasting your time, I told you this already."

Rory waved his hand toward the door, a clear indication he wanted her to leave. "I have to check," he replied. I watched, confused, as Lucie led Sasha from the room, leaving me alone with my brother.

"Check what?" I asked, fussing with my dress with one hand and picking up my small bouquet of flowers with the other.

Rory sighed and stalked to my side, stopping in front of me and looking at me intently. "I need to check you're doing this for the right reasons."

I tilted my head and met his eyes as I answered his question. I knew he was worried about me; it was because he was such an awesome little brother. Clearly, he wanted confirmation that my change of heart toward the wedding was something I genuinely wanted and not something Carson was forcing me into.

"I love him, Rory, and he loves me. We're getting married because I want to get married; no other reason, I promise," I confirmed, reaching out and taking his hand. "And I love you for worrying about me and for always having my back and for looking out for me and Sasha all the time, but you don't need to protect me from Carson. I promise that, too."

He pursed his lips, seeming to consider my words for a while before he nodded. "Okay, good. I guess he's an all right bloke. You know, as dickheads go."

I giggled and squeezed his hand. "I'll tell him you said so." When the violin music began from the other room, my whole body stiffened. It was time. "Oh, God, I'm about ready to shit a brick," I admitted.

Rory chuckled. "Does Carson know he's marrying a potty mouth?"

I gasped and pinched his side in reprimand but before I could scold him or anything, he bent forward and planted a kiss on the side of my head and then held his arm up in offer for me to take.

As my arm slipped through my little brother's, my body was a jangled mess. So many emotions were running through me I didn't know which to feel first. When Rory led me out through the hotel function room and toward the balcony beyond that was cloaked by red curtains, my stomach was churning. I watched, silently chewing on the inside of my mouth as Lucie proudly led Sasha through the curtain and disappeared.

And then it was my turn.

As one of the hotel staff pulled back the curtain so we could pass, I was excited, nervous, thrilled, happy and scared all rolled into one jittery package. I had no idea how my legs were even managing to support me. But none of that mattered as soon as I stepped out onto the balcony, for as soon as I laid eyes on him, everything else faded into insignificance.

The gentle, Nevada breeze blew his light-brown hair, ruffling it in the way that made my stomach twist into a knot. He turned, facing me, watching me walk to his side. The smile on his full, pink lips made my palms sweat. His eyes consumed me, drawing me in, leading me to him up the little white carpet they'd laid out. I tried to walk to the beat of the music, but it was almost impossible to hear over the squeeze of my heart.

After what seemed like a lifetime, I stopped at his side and Rory stepped back, grinning and slapping Carson on the arm affectionately. My mouth was dry as I stared up at him. His eyes didn't leave mine as he stepped closer to me and shook his head. "You look incredible," he whispered, reaching out and catching a curl of my hair that had escaped the elegant twist I had at the back of my head. His tongue darted out, wetting his lips as he looked at me through sultry, heavily lidded eyes. "You ready to become Mrs Matthews?" he asked.

I nodded slowly. "I've been ready for three years," I admitted.

His resulting grin was dazzling as his hand slipped down to mine and he tugged me a little closer to him as the pastor stepped forward and grinned. As the ceremony began, I made sure to memorise every single second of it, every single one of Carson's smiles and the twinkles in his eyes. I wanted to be able to remember this moment with crystal clarity when I looked back on it on our sixtieth anniversary. After being given the gift of my baby girl's birth, this was the second most special thing that had ever happened to me.

"ARE YOU TWO GONNA come on the roof rides? They're supposed to be amazing!" Rory asked after the ceremony and photographs.

I grinned and shook my head, fighting the blush trying to colour my cheeks. I had much more exciting things in mind for now, and it didn't involve anything else other than my new husband and a king-size bed.

"No, er, I'm pretty tired actually," I lied, losing the battle against my blush. "I think I'll just go to bed."

Carson's fingers dug into my waist as his arm tightened on me. His whole body seemed to stiffen. "Oh, hell yeah, I'm tired too," he chimed in, grinning down at me knowingly. My girlie giggle made Rory scoff and shake his head, now understanding.

Lucie chuckled, raising one eyebrow. "Yeah, the newlyweds will be riding their own Vegas thrill ride tonight," she teased, winking at me.

"Eww, Christ, TMI!" Rory stated, fake gagging dramatically.

I chuckled and pressed against Carson's side, grinning up at him happily.

Lucie grinned wickedly at Rory's uncomfortable face. "Oh, come on, how do you think Sasha was made? Immaculate conception?" she joked. "Just accept it. Your sister is madly in love with a hottie, so she's gonna want to jump his bones from time to time."

Rory closed his eyes and wrinkled his nose in disgust. "I don't ever want to hear the phrase 'jump his bones' and my sister mentioned in the same sentence again." He shuddered.

Everyone laughed, even Carson's mum who had been fairly quiet through the whole ceremony and flight over here. I smiled awkwardly at her, and she smiled nicely in return.

Lucie grinned. "Go on, you two. Go have your fun. I'll look after Rory and Sash," she said, winking at us.

I chuckled and nodded, slipping my hand into Carson's back pocket and giving his bum a little appreciative squeeze. "Okay, you sure you're all right with Sash? You won't get to go on the rides tonight," I countered worriedly.

She rolled her eyes and waved a hand dismissively. "Just get out of here."

Jillian stepped forward then and smiled. "I'll help you watch Sasha. If you want to go on the rides for a bit, we'll wait down the bottom and watch, won't we, sweetheart?" Jillian asked, holding out her hand to her granddaughter.

Lucie's smile widened. "Yeah? Thanks! I'd love to go on the mechanical arm thing that hangs you upside down over the side of the building!" she chirped, clapping her hands together excitedly.

I winced, secretly glad I had an excuse to get out of that ride. "Okay. Well, I'll call you in the morning and arrange picking Sasha up," I suggested.

"Whatever, though I can't imagine he'll let you come up for air before dinnertime," she replied, nodding toward Carson.

My insides squirmed at the thought alone, and I actually hoped she was right.

"All right, see you guys tomorrow. Be safe and have fun," I said. Sasha was sitting on Jillian's lap, playing with the fake flower in her hat. "Goodnight, beautiful. See you tomorrow. Be good for Auntie Lucie. I love you." I bent and planted a kiss on her cheek.

"Bye, Mummy!" she chirped, not even the least bit tired even though it was nine o'clock at night.

After Carson had bid his farewells, we both climbed into the lift, and he swiped his card, which would take us to the honeymoon suite where we were staying for the next week.

The air in the lift seemed to thicken as the doors closed and we were finally alone. Wordlessly, his hand closed over mine and he gave me a little tug toward him. His hand cupped the side of my face as he dipped his head, looking directly into my eyes. "I love you, Mrs Matthews."

The thrill the new name gave me actually made me squeal with delight as I grinned and pressed myself to him tightly. "I love you, too."

The lift ride was taking too long in my opinion. The passion was spiking to dangerous levels inside me with each passing second. He stepped forward, pressing me back against the wall as I bit my lip and looked up at him through my eyelashes. His resulting smile set my heart racing and made my scalp prickle. When he finally pressed his lips against mine, I seemed to lose all control of myself. The passion took over as I threw my arms around his neck and kissed him as if I could devour his soul. Grunting, he pushed me tighter against the wall, crushing his body to mine before his hand slid down to my bum.

My hormones were raging. This was the part of our relationship Carson and I were the best at – the physical stuff always seemed to happen perfectly naturally between us. My teeth unconsciously sank into his bottom lip when he tried to pull his mouth from mine. He gasped and effortlessly lifted me off my feet as the lift door pinged, signalling our floor. I whimpered into his mouth as I awkwardly wrapped my legs around his waist, clamping myself to him as best I could in my dress.

After way too long, the door creaked open. It opened up directly into our suite so in a few quick strides, we were on the bed. I didn't even take my eyes off him long enough to look around the suite which was sure to be as spectacular as the brochure promised.

Carson's hands traced down my body over my dress, skimming my sides and down my thighs as his hand slipped under the silky material and onto my bare leg. As he pushed his hand higher, following the line of my thigh, he hitched my dress up around my waist. I let out a moan at the feel of his hands on my skin. When he looked down, lust and passion were clear in his eyes, but more importantly, I saw the love there which made my heart ache.

My breathing was so heavy I should have been ashamed, but I was too caught up in the moment to care as he slowly peeled my wedding dress from my body while I rid him of his suit jacket and shirt. I traced my hands down his back, drawing my fingernails across his shoulders, just picturing the guardian angel tattoo on his back as I did it. I was so turned on I couldn't stop squirming and wriggling underneath him, trying to get closer to him and feel him on every inch of me. My whole body yearned for his.

Carson kissed me deeply as I worshipped every inch of his chest and back with my fingertips, just marvelling over the perfection I was touching. My love for him was overwhelming, and I could feel from his kissing he felt the same as me, which made this ten times better than anything I had ever experienced before.

"You really do give me wings, you know," he murmured against my neck. His voice was so husky and sexy I actually shivered under him, which in turn caused him to let out a breathy moan.

His words hit me hard. I'd heard that before. Well, not *heard* exactly... read. His tattoo. The beautiful butterfly one he had just below his navel, the words which made up the outline of the wings... *You give me wings and make me fly.*

I gulped, unsure what to say. "Your tattoo," I whispered, sliding my hand down his chest and feeling the soft skin below his navel.

He pulled back, grinning down at me as he nodded. "I had that done for you. It's yours, a little symbol that reminds me of you."

My heart seemed to stop as I flicked my eyes up to his face to see if he was joking or teasing me. His expression was deadly serious, though. Impossibly, my love for him seemed to grow and flourish even more. Carson had that butterfly inked onto his body not long after I'd given birth to his daughter – probably only a couple of months after I'd returned to work at the club. I remembered him having it, and how excited he'd been to show it to me. At the time, we were just 'lap dancer and client' – maybe we were never really just that to him after all.

He smiled at my stunned expression and lay down at my side. "You're the only girl who has ever seen it. I had it done down there because I knew no one would see it unless I was naked. You're the only person I ever want to see my naked body, so it only seems right that I should have a symbol for you there. Like a little stamp for something that's yours. Kinda like an ownership branding," he joked, smirking at me.

I burst out laughing and shook my head at how silly he could be sometimes. "Like a tramp stamp?" I joked. He nodded, leaning half over me and blanketing my body with his. My hand trailed up, tangling into the back of his hair. "So, do I have to get a symbol for you tattooed on me now?"

I giggled as he nodded sternly. "Yeah, you do. A motorbike helmet. I can't decide if I want it here," he whispered, touching the inside of my thigh, making my heart thump in my chest because of how close his hands were to my centre. "Or here," he finished, his hand moving round to grip my bum.

I laughed and wrapped my arms around his neck, pulling him on top of me fully as my legs wrapped around his waist. It had been way too long since I had his undivided attention. I needed him now, so talking was going to have to take a back seat for an hour or two.

"No more talking. We have forever to talk, baby. I want to see some action," I purred suggestively.

His eyes sparkled with excitement at my words. "Pervert," he teased breathlessly, brushing my hair from my face.

"Says the guy who's pinning the ex-lap dancer to the bed," I answered smartly, smirking at him.

He shook his head in disagreement. "No, I'm the guy who's pinning the love of his life to the bed."

His lips pressed against mine again, but this time it wasn't quite as soft or gentle as before. Instead, it was more of a possessive kiss, as if he was laying down his claim. I submitted to him, melting at his touch. I loved how this one kiss made me feel like I belonged, like I was wanted and needed. That one kiss showed me everything he felt for me. I secretly hoped he kissed me like this for the rest of our lives.